A BAD DAY GROWS WORSE

"Listen, Ho, we can't be too careful. We've got enough trouble as it is," Alacrity whispered as they peered carefully around the pilaster.

"Trouble?" said a voice behind them. "Yes, you most definitely have that."

They leaped into the air, Alacrity clawing automatically for his sidearm. Dincrist, father of the woman Alacrity had loved well—but none too wisely—stood watching them. "You'll have all the trouble you can handle, and far, far more."

He pointed a finger at them. "Alacrity Fitzhugh and Hobart Floyt, I, Captain Softcoyne Dincrist, declare myself to be your sworn enemy and you both to be mine. By the Bans and the Pandect, by word and by deed, I swear to harm and to hinder you, to break and to kill you. I call down upon you misfortune, reversal, calamity, and affliction."

They were so awed by his tone that it took them a moment to realize he had finished. Finally, Alacrity jumped into the gap. "Oh—oh, yeah! Well don't count on it!"

JINX
on a
TERRAN
INHERITANCE

Brian Daley

A Del Rey Book

BALLANTINE BOOKS • NEW YORK

This one's for the house-apes:
Eileen, Kevin, Danny and Mike, and Erin and Nicholas

CONTENTS

CHAPTER 1

PARDON US

"HOLD IT!" ALACRITY YELLED, GRABBING FOR THE CONTROLS. "That's her!" He yanked the corridor tram out of autoguide and changed course so fast that Hobart Floyt had to clutch frantically to keep their scant luggage from flying down the corridor. The tram came to an abrupt stop behind a huge pilaster—the stronghold Frostpile was built on the grand scale in every way—nearly throwing them both off.

The robes they'd worn to the funeral of Cazpahr Weir, and in which they'd nearly been killed an hour earlier, hung limply, bedraggled and ridiculous. Floyt bruised his hip against his Inheritor's belt, a waistband of heavy reddish alloy plaques.

"Who'd you see?" Floyt demanded in a whisper. "What's going on? We should've demanded that Governor Redlock give us back our guns, that's what!" Until a few weeks earlier, Floyt, native of preterist, isolationist Terra, had refused to so much as touch a firearm. But then again, he'd been through a lot recently. "Hey, watch where you're stepping," he added as Alacrity clambered over him.

Alacrity winced at the pain from the rib he'd cracked that morning in an airbike crash. He peered cautiously around the pilaster, motioning Floyt to silence. Alacrity's big, oblique eyes, their great irises a radiant yellow streaked with red and black, were wider than ever.

1

His baggy robe had slid back off his shoulders, revealing a mane of slate-gray hair, shot through with strands of silver, growing in a sharp V down the muscular channel of his back. He was a lean 197 centimeters tall.

Floyt left the tram, padding up behind in soft tabi. More than twenty centimeters shorter than Alacrity, he had close-trimmed brown hair and a beard going to gray. Recent events had left him less stocky than formerly. "Who is it? Did you see Heart?"

"Heart? Why would I be hiding from Heart? I'm in love with her! No, I thought I saw Sintilla."

Floyt snorted exasperatedly. "Sintilla went to one of the lesser wakes before Weir's last rites, remember? She'll be gone for hours. Now, stop being such a worrywart and let's—"

"A what? *Wari*-what?" Alacrity babbled.

"Hah? Not *wari*, '*wari*-wart!' I mean, *wari*-what! Goddammit, worry*wart*, *wart*!" Floyt gibbered.

"Keep it down, Ho! That's all we need, for Tilla to spot us now! Or d'you *want* her tagging along all the way to Blackguard?"

Floyt drew a slow breath between clenched teeth. A patient and reasonable man, he was near his limits. He eased around the pilaster just below his friend, whispering, "Even if it is her, she won't be looking for us yet. And by the time she finds out that we've—"

He straightened up suddenly and shouldered past the rangy Alacrity. "That woman's a food technician! Couldn't you tell from the Suit of Lights, or whatever that outfit's called? She's twice Sintilla's size, besides! Now, will you come on, before the *Blue Pearl* leaves without us?"

"Looked like her at first; same hair. Listen, Ho, we can't be too careful. We've got enough trouble as it is."

"No argument there," Floyt conceded. Their Earthservice behavorial conditioning was eating at them—they *had* to take this mysterious bequest from Weir, a starship called the *Astraea Imprimatur*, back for the enrichment of the Earthservice Resources Bureau.

That meant going to a planet called Blackguard—about

which they knew slightly more than nothing—to claim her. Provided they could get out of Frostpile alive.

"Trouble?" said a voice behind them.

The two leapt up into the air, colliding with each other, Alacrity clawing for a sidearm he was not carrying. Dincrist, Heart's father, stood watching them.

He'd already changed from funeral robes to the heavily decorated uniform of a commercial starship captain. He didn't seem to be armed. *But if looks really* could *kill* . . . Alacrity thought.

"You have all the trouble you can handle, and far, far more." Dincrist was the picture of a patrician-sportsman, even taller than Alacrity and very fit, white-haired and deeply tanned.

Alacrity, at twenty-two a working spacer—a breakabout— for many years, held himself ready. He and Dincrist had already mixed it up twice, more or less to a draw, but Dincrist hadn't been through any airbike disasters or murder attempts yet that day, and was in excellent condition.

Still, Alacrity bristled. "What, *you* again? Shouldn't you be off flogging a *real* breakabout someplace?"

Dincrist flushed slightly. The head of a powerful shipping and shipbuilding empire, he'd had only a minimum of actual experience in starship service—had only the technical right to be wearing his magnificent uniform.

"I heard about Endwraithe's trying to kill you," he said, tight-lipped. "I'm very glad that he failed; I mean to see to you myself, Fitzhugh."

"See how *good* the guy is at that kind of talk, Ho?" Alacrity said out of the corner of his mouth.

"Very effective facial expressions, too," Floyt replied lightly. Inside, though, he was fighting dread and despair. Dincrist was a man to be feared.

"I've no time to waste on nitwits." Dincrist took a half step toward them, and Alacrity braced for a dustup.

Instead, Heart's father pointed a finger at them and proclaimed, "Alacrity Fitzhugh and Hobart Floyt, I, Captain Soft-coygne Dincrist, declare myself to be your sworn enemy and you both to be mine. By the Bans and the Pandect, by word and by deed, I swear to harm and to hinder you, to break and to kill you. I call down upon you misfortune, reversal, calamity, and affliction."

The rolling cadence of the avowal was so hypnotic, Dincrist's tone so orotund, it took them a moment to realize that he'd finished.

"Oh, oh yeah?" Alacrity parried weakly. "Well, don't count on it."

"Right!" Floyt jumped in, surprisingly ferocious. "If you give us any trouble, we'll spin your head around like a *weathervane*!"

Alacrity took heart. "That's right; we'll stomp you flatter than a month-old road-kill!"

"Kill you faster than anything in the pharmacy!"

"Polish our shoes on your balls!"

Their uncouth counterspell took Dincrist by surprise. Too furious to retaliate in kind, he turned and strode away quickly. They called parting incantations after him.

"Dog your dong in a hatch!"

"Do the Dance of Death on your face!" Alacrity lowered his voice. "Did you hear that, Ho? He, he *jinxed* us!"

"The way things have been going, how will we know if it takes?"

"We'd better get moving."

They reboarded the tram and resumed the trip to the tower roof. From there, Governor Redlock's opulent shuttle, the *Blue Pearl*, was to depart. The governor had a lot of things on his mind, including the death of his father-in-law, First Councillor Inst, who'd attacked Alacrity and Floyt during the airbike race, and the discovery that his wife, Queen Dorraine, wasn't quite who he'd always thought she was.

The two companions-in-adversity doubted Redlock's willingness to delay lift-off just for them, so they put on all speed.

Then, too, there was Sintilla, the lively, determined little free-lance journalist who'd become something of an ally to them at Frostpile—in part for her own gain. They'd discovered, only minutes earlier, that she planned to write a series of lurid and completely fictionalized adventure books about them.

Anonymity and a certain freedom of movement were just about the only things they had going for them, but Sintilla meant to bandy their names around in purple-prose penny dreadfuls with the most sensationally absurd titles Floyt had ever heard.

"Hobart Floyt and Alacrity Fitzhugh Challenge the Amazon Slave Women of the Supernova." Floyt groaned to himself.

Alacrity shook his head dejectedly. "I know, I know. But don't let yourself think about that now, Ho. Just stay alert. Endwraithe might've had some backup. Or Dincrist could try something, High Truce or not. Scheisse, I wish Redlock had given us back our persuaders."

They cruised past security checkpoints manned by Invincibles, elite troops of the Weir forces in dress uniforms of crimson and gold. The Invincibles had been ordered to insure that no weapons were smuggled into Frostpile during the High Truce. Their searches were quite thorough. Yet they'd somehow missed Endwraithe's. Why a top officer of the powerful Bank of Spica should want to quiz Floyt about his inheritance, then try to shoot him and Alacrity, was still a puzzle.

Floyt delicately felt at his nose, broken—in the same crash that had cracked Alacrity's rib—and still smarting despite medical treatment. His tongue probed at the gap where Alacrity had knocked out two of his teeth.

"What's the point of watching out for assassins?" Floyt grouched. "The underhanded bastards are always sneaking up on us anyhow."

With the Willreading and other ceremonies over and the High Truce near its end, a good deal of traffic, mostly departing guests, was traveling the cyclopean corridors of Frostpile. Floyt, who'd only met a small fraction of them, stared at the dignitaries who'd converged on Epiphany, Weir's seat of power, from dozens of worlds. Weir had been a major power in that region of space; reapportionment of his domain was an important event. He doubted that his family and friends back on Earth would be able to believe him when—if—he got back to describe the hodgepodge of racial subtypes, costumes and finery, and babel of tongues.

Alacrity raised his arm to see how much time remained before the *Pearl* was due to lift and realized that his wrist was bare.

"*Damn!* Ho, our proteuses! We left them with Tilla!" Alacrity was racked by indecision but leaning toward writing off the proteuses. The two had little money, and *Blue Pearl* was their only ticket offplanet.

With a magician's flourish, Floyt drew the two instruments from the pocket of his robe. "I spotted them while we were, um, visiting Tilla's rooms."

"Searching" was more the word. But Alacrity took his proteus gratefully; he had very few possessions, but it was just about his most treasured, a commo device, databank, systems accessor and more, in a wrist torc of overlapping, chitinous black metal plates tinged with verdigris. He ran a quick check. "It's okay; she didn't tap into the protected stuff. I guess Tilla didn't mess with it."

"Same here." Floyt's was a very cheap, simple model provided for his offworld mission by the Earthservice. Alacrity hid a grin. There was little enough anyone could learn from Floyt's proteus, but some of the secrets stashed in Alacrity's could command serious amounts of money and bring down upon him enemies prepared to do a lot more than jinx him.

Just then the tram floated out onto the tower roof under the night sky of Epiphany. Frostpile lit the sky, a shining faerie city. It was too bright to see many stars, but Epiphany's two moons, Guileless Giles and the Thieving Magpie, were visible.

They were on the same roof where they'd disembarked from the *Blue Pearl* only four and one half days before. The acreage of formal carpet was still in place, lustrous black, worked in thread-of-gold with Weir insignia and symbols, the broken slave collar most prominent among them. The *Pearl* was nowhere to be seen.

"Do you think they left without us, Alacrity? Redlock and Dorraine invited us along, after all. I mean, even if Inst did get killed when we crashed the airbike, I thought—"

"They're still here, Ho." Alacrity pointed to where the shuttle was poised on the tip of a spiral resembling a unicorn's horn, at the far side of Frostpile. It might have been the tower where Endwraithe had cornered them before Alacrity shot the banker with one of Floyt's teeth.

Redlock's shuttle deserved her name. She was a glassy-blue

sphere with a nacreous sheen, forty meters in diameter. She was lit from within; inside, shadows moved about.

"You two going with the gov'nor?" a ground crewman called from a low service dome.

"Yeah, what's the holdup?" Alacrity shot back.

The man trotted over to them. "The *Pearl*'s waiting for the Severeemish, Queen Dorraine, and one or two others. Then they'll light here for you two. You're that Earther groundling and the other one, right?"

"I'm the Earther; so what?" Alacrity frowned, knobby fists clenched. He was lean but surprisingly broad through the shoulders; for all the gangliness, there was a lot of muscle to him. He didn't like people giving his friends a hard time.

"I'm the other one." Floyt went along with it.

"Just checking, just checking. No offense meant. You can wait out here or inside, as you like." The ground crewman seemed to recall something urgent, and left.

The two looked up to where the incandescence of Frostpile met the night of Epiphany. Air cabriolets and sky gondolas, hover pavilions and skimmer pods, glided and drifted overhead, elegant and graceful.

"I'm going to miss this place," Floyt found himself saying. For him, at the very optimum, there would be the claiming of *Astraea Imprimatur* and the irrevocable return to Earth, where he would live out his life.

"Me too," Alacrity agreed, throat taut and almost vertical as he watched the gorgeous fliers. "Oh, me too." His gaze strayed to where Weir's catafalque had been and where the late Director's remains had been projected out into the Infinite a few hours earlier.

Floyt said something Alacrity didn't pay attention to right away. Then it sank through. "What data station? Hey!"

Long-legged and hurrying, he caught up with the Terran as Floyt entered the dome. No one was around. They confronted the data station.

"I know Dame Tiajo said she didn't have any information on the *Astraea Imprimatur*," Floyt said, "but I thought I'd check—in case she, ah, overlooked something."

"Um. Good idea, Ho."

Floyt went to work, shooting back his floppy sleeves. A
trained Earthservice info accessor, he'd quickly made himself
familiar with Frostpile's system. He slipped off his proteus and
seated it in a peripheral.

But there was nothing to record.

"No registration for a ship by that name," Floyt reported.

"What's it mean, Ho? *Astraea Imprimatur*?"

Floyt worked for a moment. "Latin, of course. 'Imprimatur'
is permission to publish, or make known. 'Astraea,' uh..."
He scanned some more. "Has to do with the Roman goddess
of justice and innocence. Also refers to the stars, naturally. It
could mean 'let it be sanctioned by Astraea,' I guess."

"Let it be... huh." Alacrity shook his head. "But nothing
about a ship?"

"Tiajo said Weir kept everything about it in his head, remember? I guess she was right. At least, there's nothing unclassified
about it."

"How about Blackguard?"

"Just a tick." The displays flashed. "Not much. Allusions
to illegal activities. Someone calls it a 'kleptocracy' here, just
like Tiajo did."

"Big help. Let's get back outside."

"Wait a second." Floyt transferred the meager data, just in
case, then reached for the proteus, but hesitated.

"What's the holdup?" Alacrity said.

"I dunno; some glitch. What's your hurry?"

"Unless you'd care to stick around here, *that's* my hurry,
there."

Floyt looked up. The *Blue Pearl* was drifting in their direction, light as a soap bubble, smaller craft making way for her,
an arresting sight even in the aggregate glory of Frostpile's
nighttime.

"Okay; whatever it was, it's all set now." Floyt clamped the
proteus back onto his wrist.

They hoisted their bags as the *Blue Pearl* settled onto the
roof without a jar or a whisper. Nothing happened for a moment,
then a circular hatch appeared in her lower hemisphere and a
gangplank extended itself as music, laughter, conversation, and
the clink of drinking vessels drifted out into the night air.

They jogged toward the shuttle, slowing a bit as they crossed onto the grand black and gold carpet.

"Hobart!" It came from afar. "Alacrity!"

Floyt paused. "Alacrity, did you hear what I—"

Sintilla, afoot, was just emerging onto the roof through a distant door. She had a small travel bag over her shoulder.

"*Trois fois merde!*" Alacrity spat. "Run for it!"

They pounded across the last meters of carpet to the *Pearl*, bags tugging and slapping, robes fluttering like disheveled banners. Floyt, almost twice Alacrity's age, stayed neck and neck. They galloped up the plush gangway.

At the hatch a Celestial waited in dress uniform. As they charged inboard, Alacrity yammered, "Present-and-accounted-for. Let's-get-this-crate-moving!"

The interior of the shuttle was a striking salon of terraced gardens, furnished alcoves, split-level dance floors, and assorted mingling spots, under a translucent three-quarter sphere. Servants circulated quietly with trays of delicacies, beverages, and other treats.

Passengers paused in their conversations to stare curiously at the two harried-looking late arrivals. The Celestial—like all the others they had seen, a big, tough specimen—gave them a dubious glance, then signaled the *Pearl*'s bridge, which was concealed in her base.

The gangway retracted and the hatch swung back into place. The ship lifted away smoothly, without a sound. The chitchat of the passengers resumed.

Out on the roof, halfway across the carpet, Sintilla slowed to a disappointed trot, then stopped.

She was a small woman, barely 150 centimeters, who at times seemed a lot like an energetic adolescent. She had a dimpled, winsome face and a mop of ginger-brown hair worn in kinked curls. She was dressed in dazzling, metallic cinnabar rompers.

"You *bums*!" she yelled up at the departing Alacrity and Floyt. "Just you wait!"

She glowered at the *Blue Pearl* as it drifted grandly over Frostpile, allowing the passengers a final look. Sintilla pondered whom among the stronghold's personnel she might buttonhole to find out what had happened to the breakabout and the Earther just after the Willreading. All sorts of delightful rumors were bouncing around the scuttlebutt circuit. She also wanted badly to know where they were bound.

Then she spied the ground crewman, lounging against the door of the service dome. Through the door she saw the data station. Putting on a cheery smile, she headed that way in her resilient, peppy stride.

Floyt and Alacrity, meanwhile, set down their bags as several servitors closed in on them with trays of goodies and others took their luggage. Selecting a long-stemmed goblet of greenish wine and a stylish little Perkup nasal inhaler, Alacrity sighed. "Now maybe we can take a few minutes out for a nice, relaxing attack of the shakes."

Floyt, munching a marvelous little hors d'oeuvre, a red ceramic mug of lager in his right hand, nodded. "I endorse that plan." He gazed around.

The shuttle was a splendidly airy place, with sculpture and foliage, flowers and small trees in abundance, the plants buoying the air with their fragrance. The lighting was pleasantly subtle, the carpets were handwoven masterworks.

There weren't many other passengers. Queen Dorraine was standing alone in a small, lecternlike structure high and off to one side in the dome, staring out into the night, lost in thought. Her father—first Councilor Inst—had died only that morning.

The Severeemish envoys, Minister Seven Wars and Theater General Sortie-Wolf, father and son, stood with their two bodyguards. The four hulking males of a genetically engineered and selectively bred race, they dwarfed everyone else inboard.

In Floyt's opinion, they couldn't really be called human at all. They had long, bony, top-heavy skulls, putty-gray skin, nails like metal talons, and hair resembling white steel wool. They were on their way home, taking along Redlock and Dorraine in order to work out an urgently needed alliance.

In the middle of the *Pearl*'s central dance floor, which was empty, a small pedestal of ornate Epiphanian wheywood supported a small, smooth, white porcelain box. Floyt wondered if it were some sort of goodwill offering.

No longer the center of attention, the two made their way

to an observation point—the shuttle being mostly observation points—for a last look at breathtaking, ethereal Frostpile.

"There's Weir's suite," Floyt said. "You can tell it from the whatsit on the terrace."

"Causality harp," Alacrity supplied, his eyes locked to it. "That's what old Dame Tiajo called it." The causality harp was a shifting, glowing nebula five meters high, hanging stationary, filled with mists of light, shimmering phase-portraits, and hazy half images. Floyt could almost hear its eerie tonalities and deep, nearly subsonic hum. Tiajo had said it was comparable to wind chimes.

"Was she serious, d'you suppose? Alacrity?"

Alacrity shook his head slowly, not to signify no, but to show that he didn't know.

The *Blue Pearl* put Frostpile behind her. They realized someone was coming their way.

Governor Redlock was only a bit taller than Floyt, but broad as a door and powerful-looking. He had battered, canny features and a lumpy pug nose; the topknot that gave him his name was going gray. He wore the black dress uniform of his Celestials and a crescent gorget with nine assorted sunburst insignia picked out in glittering gemstones against black enamel, to represent the star-systems under his governance. He also wore an Inheritor's belt.

"You needn't have run, gentlemen," he said with a half smile.

"We, ah, needed the exercise," Alacrity explained lamely.

The governor looked from one to the other. "But, of course; that's understandable enough. After all, you two haven't been in any trouble for—what is it now? Nearly an hour?"

While Alacrity stammered, determined not to mention Sintilla, Floyt filled in. "At any rate, we're very, very grateful to you and Queen Dorraine. If you hadn't offered us a ride, we'd have been in an awfully bad fix."

He didn't need to add that they were destitute and desperate for the reason that Dame Tiajo, Redlock's sovereign, had denied them any funds for travel to Blackguard. Like her late brother, she disliked Earthservice; she therefore detested Floyt's aim to take the starship back home for the profit of the bureaucracy.

She was unaware of the conditioning that compelled Alacrity and Floyt to carry out their mission, and they were prevented by that conditioning from mentioning it.

"Quite all right. Dropping you at the spaceport's no inconvenience. I wish we could do more, but—" Redlock waved one thick hand to indicate that that was the way things went. But they already knew the way things went, and one of the ways things *didn't* go was for even a strong and independent governor like Redlock to defy a hard-nosed old bat like Tiajo once her mind was set on something. Especially for some inconsequential interstellar spindrift the likes of Hobart Floyt and Alacrity Fitzhugh.

"At any rate," Redlock continued, "there were one or two things I thought I should bring up, the first being how you will prove your claim to your inheritance."

"I'd wondered about that," Floyt admitted, "but we never got a chance to ask anybody, so I was hoping you'd tell me. Don't I need documentation, or authorization from Tiajo? Or *something*?"

"Your proof is right there," Redlock explained, waving at Floyt's belt. "Provisions were made by Director Weir—and don't bother asking me what they were in your case, because I don't know. But I do know that the belt is all the identification you'll need."

While Floyt was expressing his thanks, musical instruments began tuning up over by the main dance floor. Four young women—the same ones who'd played as a string quartet during the *Pearl*'s voyage to Epiphany—struck up "frisking music" in the lively style originated on Murphy's Law. They played jingle sticks, sonic withes, ocarina, and fingerdrums. They looked the part of a traditional Daubin' Band too, dressed in one-shoulder shimmerskins with mitered vertical black-and-white stripes, pageboy hairstyles, and whiteface makeup.

The music sounded so jaunty that Alacrity and Floyt both looked up at Queen Dorraine, who was still silent and distracted in the lectern. But she didn't seem to hear, and Redlock didn't appear inclined to halt it. Clearly Dorraine's mourning rituals didn't require that everyone else take part.

"By the way, since you're here, Governor"—Alacrity seized

the moment—"there's something else. Our guns, I mean. There're still in *King's Ransom*, I guess?"

"The fact of the matter is, Alacrity, I had them transferred; they've been inboard the *Blue Pearl* all along. You may have them back when you disembark."

Now it was Alacrity who said thanks, and even the peaceable Floyt was glad he wouldn't have to face the glaxay without an equalizer.

In the meantime, another passenger padded up behind Redlock soundlessly. Alacrity focused in on her right away.

Typical, Floyt thought, looking at his friend. *I know he really loves Heart, and I believe him when he says he's going to find her no matter what, but his libido's always set on SCAN.*

Exquisite was the word that came to mind first. She wasn't much taller than Sintilla, which made her all the more unusual to Floyt, what with most offworlders ranging from gangling to behemoth. She had golden skin, long, straight black hair that fell to the level of her hips, and dark almond eyes with a slight epicanthic fold. The delicate perfection of her face started Floyt's own pulse quickening.

"I don't believe you two have been introduced to Yumi," Redlock said. "She's part of the Daimyo's entourage."

The Daimyo of the planet Shurutzu had been a minor sensation at Frostpile owing to some fairly zany misadventures.

"Oh, right," Alacrity said, smiling, heavy-lidded, at her. "Didn't recognize you with your hair down and without the kimono."

She was wearing a feathery white neck frill, crossed bandeau top of wetsheen, fringed hip-yoke, and high-heeled sandals. Around her upper right arm, her proteus was disguised as a serpentine of rubies, moonpures and kaleidobursts. Her presence brought a subtle odor of jasmine to the air.

"Stop drooling, before your robe gets soggy, Alacrity." Alacrity looked at Floyt, but just grinned wider, anticipating.

However, once Redlock had finished the introductions, Yumi began in a strangely accented sing song: "Citizen Floyt, my master the Daimyo bids me come before you with an earnest request, which I entreat you to hear."

"Uh? Ah, oh . . ." was all Floyt could get out for the moment.

Alacrity, at least as astounded and feeling put upon, broke in, "Request? For what? I'm the bodyguard here, so I guess I should be the one to talk to you about it before you—"

"Oh, no; that's quite all right, Alacrity," Floyt headed him off. Redlock looked on expectantly, enjoying the show.

Yumi smiled, and their little region of the *Pearl* brightened. "Citizen Floyt, what the Daimyo asks, in fine, is whether you might deign to consider parting with one half liter of your very esteemed and illustrious Terran blood."

"My blood?"

"Not a chance," Alacrity decreed, from conditioning and from habit, apprehensive *and* disappointed.

"You will pardon my speaking bluntly, since time is limited. The Daimyo would place great value on such a gift, Citizen Floyt. Your blood, produced in the hallowed biosphere and magnetic fields of Earth, containing vital potencies and unique essences available nowhere else in the universe—it is the true elixir of Manhome."

"You can tell that superstitious, priapic old vampire for us, that—" Alacrity began.

"My master the Daimyo would of course wish to make a gift in return," Yumi interjected. "Three thousand ovals, to be precise."

"Are you sure a half liter's enough?" Alacrity asked eagerly. "He's got plenty. I could jump up and down on his chest for you. He's the only Earther you're ever going to see, after all."

"I guess I'll do it," Floyt decided.

Yumi smiled again, and they found themselves reciprocating. "Most puissant Governor Redlock has permitted me the use of a private compartment in *Blue Pearl*. If you'll follow me, most generous Citizen Floyt?"

Redlock caught the wary flicker that crossed Alacrity's face then and gave him a reassuring nod. That was good enough for Alacrity. *Worse luck*, he grudged. "Cash before splash, no IOUs," he cautioned his friend as Yumi slipped an arm through Floyt's. Floyt looked dazed but happy.

"Won't this hold you up?" Alacrity asked Redlock.

The governor shook his head. "*King's Ransom* won't rendezvous with us at the spaceport for another two hours, so I was planning on taking a roundabout course there. I wanted time for some uninterrupted talk with Seven Wars and Sortie-Wolf, among other things."

Alacrity understood. Things like giving Alacrity and Floyt a chance to pick up a little traveling money, where Tiajo couldn't interfere. "Thanks very much, Governor. I hope we can make it up to you, one day."

Redlock inclined his head. Then he looked up to where his wife meditated alone on the cold stars. The *Pearl*'s hull had been shifted to full transparency and her lights dimmed a bit. Alacrity spotted The Strewn, the open star cluster that was the brightest ornament of Epiphany's night, after her two moons.

"Make yourself comfortable," Redlock invited as he moved off to join Dorraine. "Why don't you begin by changing out of that drogue chute you're wearing?"

CHAPTER 2

RHAPSODY IN BLUE PEARL

THE COMPARTMENT IN THE *PEARL*'S LOWER HULL WAS JUST off the crew lounge, with a big, padded card table lowered to serve as an examining table.

Yumi was cordial but briskly efficient as she readied medical instruments. A superb little *bento* tray, holding four chocolates, had been set out. Floyt, sitting on the table, helped himself to one. It was delicious beyond compare, with a sweet, syrupy liqueur center. He couldn't resist a second.

Meanwhile, she scanned his heart and blood pressure, scoped his chest, and made similar assessments. Then she drew the robe from his arms and upper torso and pressed him down flat on his back.

The thing she used to draw the blood was like nothing Floyt had ever seen before, a flat tube with a shrunken sac the size of a walnut at its far end. It had a veined, organic look to it, nothing like a man-made object, and glistened wetly.

Yumi laid the open end of the tube into the hollow of Floyt's right elbow; it made itself fast, numbing the surrounding flesh. A few moments later the sac began to swell, and Floyt could actually see the tube—blood vessel, whatever—pulsing with his blood.

He shifted uneasily. "Is it alive?"

"Not in any significant sense, except in that it serves this

16

purpose very well." She moved to stand behind him. Closing his eyes with soft fingertips, she began gently massaging his forehead and temples, her small hands cool, strong, and skilled.

At length Floyt said, "I saw you in your kimono too, Yumi. It was rose red, with big hibiscus on it."

"Yes. Your own traditional regalia caused much, much talk in Frostpile. My Daimyo is having a suit such as that made for him. What do you call such garments?"

"A tuxedo. White tie with black tails."

"You were a splendid figure, like a man from legend. You were the envy of Frostpile."

That came as such a revelation to Floyt, who'd been treated more like a gatecrasher, that he was silent for a time.

"Do you believe it, Yumi?" he asked dreamily after a while, the slow massage having set him drifting. "Do you believe that Terran blood is something magical?"

"I know that my master believes so." Her fingertips caressed his temples. "And if it makes a dear old soul imagine he is a strong young man instead of an aged, infirmed one, then it is worth any price, and I am happy."

The fingers went to the muscles of his neck. He felt as if he were floating, but at the same time he could feel every nerve ending in his body.

"Then I suppose he's disappointed he couldn't get a younger donor?" The scent of jasmine had Floyt's head swimming.

"Younger?" Her laugh was musical. "Oh, Citizen Floyt—"

"Hobart."

"Oh, Hobart! Why would my Daimyo want the blood of a stripling!"

The deft fingers were at his shoulders now. He felt his muscles relax. Immersed in the sensuality of it, he wondered fleetingly how long such tension had been in him.

The lilting voice said, "My Daimyo hopes to feel the spirit of a man who has led a full life on Manhome, who has had time to experience the nuances and extremes of existence there."

Floyt thought back through his life. "I doubt I'm what he had in mind."

"You must not say that! You are the first Terran I have ever met, but I sense that it is true of you. I sense that most clearly, Hobart."

Her hands rested over his drumming heart now; he felt her small, firm breasts against his head as she half cradled it. Instead of leaving him weaker, the drawing of his blood left him preternaturally alive, as if a light charge were passing from cell to cell throughout his body. A voluptuous heat seemed to radiate from his face and neck, chest and loins. His body, ignorant of etiquette, responded eagerly.

Taking her wrists, he drew her hands hands to his mouth, ignoring the tube in his arm. Yumi's breath caught, then became quicker and deeper. He kissed her palms softly, bit gently at the fleshy mound of her thumb, traced her heartline with the tip of his tongue, and tasted the skin between her fingers.

Yumi moaned and bent over him, drawing the midnight curtain of her sweet-smelling hair around them both, pressing her lips to his. He eased his fingers deep into her hair, inhaling great, long, dizzying breaths of her as they kissed. Her mouth opened to an aroused, unhurried dialogue that became their whole universe.

After an unmeasured time, she broke away, panting. "A moment, Hobart . . . No! Only a moment . . ."

Floyt was a little surprised to find himself back in the compartment inboard the *Blue Pearl*. Yumi detached the tube from his arm quickly but carefully, spraying his elbow with something that prevented bleeding. He felt no pain.

She placed the bloated sac containing Floyt's blood—the Daimyo had gotten his money's worth—into a small refrigerated cannister. Then she crossed to the compartment's hatch, to make sure it was secure. Floyt, up on one elbow, watched her movements hungrily, the sway and flex of the lissome body and the answering swing and ripple of the glossy mantle of hair.

Yumi lowered the lights to a glow. Walking back to Floyt, she discarded the bandeau in one direction, the hip-yoke in another. The golden skin over her heart bore a straight white scar that for some reason she'd chosen to leave there; her breasts were high and dark-nippled, her pubic triangle a slender delta.

Yumi bent over the table, breasts flattening against his chest, hair trailing across them both, as she loosened the thongs of her scandals with one hand and kicked them away, supporting his head, with his lips to hers, with the other. She gasped at the contact with the cold Inheritor's belt; he unbuckled it and dropped it to the deck.

Floyt lifted her onto the table alongside him, holding her in long, slow kisses and conforming his hand lingeringly to her shoulder, her breast, the small of her sinewy back, an upthrust hip, the moist warmth where those slim legs met that made his breathing suddenly require conscious effort. The blood pounded at his head, his neck and chest.

Yumi helped him slide out of the robe, and he wafted it away dramatically, making her giggle. They explored with hands and lips and tongues, breathed one another's breath, tasted jasmine and sweat, united their flushed heat.

Floyt embraced her to him, beneath him. Yumi drew her fingertips across his slick back, pressing into his buttocks, pulling him deeper into her. A sustained sound, by parts coo and outcry, came from them both.

And, later, she was on top, tenting their faces again with the raven's-wing hair, hips pumping, rocking, orbiting. Her mouth clung to his throat as he threw his head back and cried her name . . .

"So what's your name?" the barmaid asked.

"Alacrity Fitzhugh."

"Sounds like a sneeze."

"Ho-ho. As a matter of fact, it's an ancient, foolproof tantric sex mantra."

She finished polishing a snifter and set it in the dispenser, making sure it was secure. People tended to forget, but the *Blue Pearl* was a spacecraft.

She was a mildly *zaftig* brunette with engaging green eyes, wearing her hair in the "drop-away" fashion, lower part of the strands stiffened, upper relaxed to the point of lethargy. She wore an outfit of cascading, almost microscopically fine gold chains, like waves of rippling metal down her body, plunging in deep parabolas between some of her more spectacular topological features. It provided for absolutely riveting, if brief, glimpses of various portions of her lily-white form.

"You were the one in the airbike race, right?" she said. "Are you the Terran? You don't look Terran."

"No. That's my pal Hobart."

"He's the expert on genealogies, right? Y'know, Acrimony—"

"Alacrity."

"Alacrity. Y'know, I'd really like to talk to him. I was doing a little family tree of my own."

I am curséd, Alacrity decided sourly, though he gave her a suave smile. "He's really in demand, I'm afraid. But I'll do my poor best to divert you."

"Try that again?"

"Amuse. Entertain."

"Whoa, lucky me. Well, what're you having, mantra-man?"

He slid his goblet away. "No more of that wine. What've you got?"

She studied him for a moment, lower lip outthrust, then began putting crushed ice in a glass. As she worked she said, "So, your sidekick left you high and dry, hm?" She was pouring, squirting, shaking, dabbing. The light seemed to adore her, glimmering and rippling across her finery.

"Naw, that's just business." *He* can't *be down there layin' commo cable! Not Ho!*

That's what Alacrity had been trying to tell himself for the better part of an hour. He wanted very much to believe things were taking so long because Yumi was drawing Floyt's blood drop by drop. Each from a different spot on his body. The dirty, lucky . . .

"Business, sure." The barmaid scoffed, setting a columnar glass before him. "And next I'm supposed to swap you two tens for a five, right?"

Alacrity considered the frosted glass and its orange contents. "What's in this thing, pet? And to what alias does it answer?"

"Orange juice from Satori—see the pulp?—ouzo we picked up on Hellas, ice I made myself, and a few odds and ends. I call it an Archimedes' Screw."

He sipped warily, then drank. "Woo! You oughta patent this phlegm loosener!"

"Thanks. But then, they always taste better when they're on the house, don't they?"

"I'll drink to that." But he went easy on it; there was no telling what sort of complications he and Floyt might face at the Epiphany spaceport.

The barmaid's name was Charivari. They got into a more or less standard bar volley about what it was like to work in the *Pearl*, how he'd gotten there, where she came from, and where he'd visited. Elsewhere could be heard the Severeemish, slightly the worse for alcohol and whatever else, trying to teach the very amused young women of the Daubin' Band one of their *a cappella* battle dirges.

"For a breakabout, you look like you expect to be doing an awful lot of walking," Charivari observed.

He'd changed to a frayed and faded flying suit, with its abundant pockets, pouches, loops, and tabs. It was bare of insignia, ship patches, or badges of rank. Around his neck under his collar, knotted in the style of the cowboys, was a blue bandanna. He also wore the prized pathfinder boots he'd had made on So Far. The pathfinders were versatile and tremendously durable, of fascia, vertical reinforcements and elastic joints, with knee-cupping shields like a knight's *genouilleres*. They showed a good deal of hard use.

"It wouldn't be the first time." He shrugged. The Daimyo's fee was a terrific windfall, but a pittance against interstellar passage. Alacrity, member of any number of spacers' unions and guilds, might be allowed to deadhead if a starship had room, but for Floyt they must come up with lots of cash. *At least deadheading's been getting easier these last few years*, he thought. The increasing speed of travel and volume of traffic, as the Third Breath of Humanity swung into high gear, made the difference.

"Here's to a new day," he proposed as the *Pearl*'s roundabout course brought her up on the dawn line over a tranquil green ocean. Charivari toasted with an Irish coffee he insisted she drink. *As for you and your Jinx, Dincrist—go twirl on it!*

"Here's to luck and the Breakers," she said.

Alacrity left off contemplating the dawn to look up at Redlock and Dorraine. The Queen of Agora was much taller than
her husband, supple but erect. Her hair was as dark as Yumi's,
and longer; her brown skin seemed a fiery orange with the
rising of Halidome, Epiphany's sun. Dorraine, too, wore an
Inheritor's belt. Draped around Dorraine was a divided, over-
lapped cloak with exaggerated, upcurving shoulderboards. It
was silver-veined and translucently gray, like the folded wings
of an enormous insect.

Charivari had told Alacrity that the porcelain box on the
pedestal held Lord Inst's ashes.

As the couple talked, a Celestial stepped up, interrupting
very respectfully but very quickly. Alacrity was looking on
with full attention now; it was always worth knowing if something was happening in a ship where one was a passenger.
Charivari, forgetting that she'd been polishing another snifter,
watched too.

Redlock heard the Celestial out and spoke a few quiet words.
Dorraine, still remote, was nevertheless listening, drawn back
from her mourning. The Celestial relayed something over his
military proteus and left. As he went, Alacrity sensed a change
in *Blue Pearl*'s heading despite the fact that maneuver forces
couldn't be felt within the ship.

Epiphany's dawn quickened, as Halidome began a percep-
tible slide to port. Alacrity straightened from his barstool and
hurried to intercept his host and hostess as warning hooters
sounded.

Dawn became high-altitude early morning, the light streaming through the *Pearl*. The shuttle was picking up speed as
scraps of cloud tore swiftly past and around her.

A change coming over the young women with the sounding
of the alarm, the Daubin' Band had stopped their friendly sing-
along with the Severeemish. Suddenly impersonal, they excused
themselves and rapidly stowed their instruments. Then they
headed below decks in an orderly column of twos, leaving the
Severeemish alert to some danger they couldn't sense yet. The
prospect put the towering creatures in a bluff, slightly skished
good humor.

Alacrity stepped into Redlock's path resolutely. "Governor,

I know you've got a lot on your mind right now, but I'd just like to know—"

Redlock didn't even slow as he barked, "Go to the main lounge area and wait with the others." Alacrity had to backstep out of his way.

But Dorraine paused. "An alarm sensor was triggered in one of Epiphany's restricted areas. There's only one patrolcraft in the area, an Invincible aircutter, the *Scimitar*. We rendezvous in a few minutes."

"Oh." His midsection tightened.

"*Scimitar* will recon and land, while the *Blue Pearl* flies high cover and backup. No outsiders are supposed to be in this part of Epiphany, so we'll take all precautions, Alacrity."

"Uh, good. Thanks." He glanced out over green seas; the shuttle was closing quickly on a southern continent. He made a rough estimate of the course the *Pearl* had taken and potshot, "It's a Precursor site, isn't it? That's what you're worried about."

The cant of her head as she studied him told him he was right. "I think you'd better follow the governor's instructions. My husband's putting the ship on full alert; you and Hobart will have your sidearms returned to you sooner than you'd expected."

Floyt and Yumi were lying together on the card table when the alarm sounded. Floyt had recovered his robe, draping it across them both, after they'd made love a second time.

They lay with her head resting on his arm, her legs held between his. They were both pretending, a little, that the flight of the *Blue Pearl* wouldn't end. They talked of Earth and Shurutzu. He laughed when she told him that the planet's original name had been Shultz. Then the *Pearl* went on alert. Yumi was on her feet while Floyt was still trying to figure out what was going on. She made certain the container with his blood was safe, then began dressing quickly as he donned his robe.

"Maybe you'd better stay here while I see what's happening," he was suggesting as someone rapped at the hatch. He opened it on a comely young member of the Daubin' Band. She still wore her shimmerskin and whiteface, but now she carried an over-under military rifle at sling arms, looking quite accustomed to it.

"Both of you report to the main lounge immediately. Governor's order." She pushed Floyt's bag into his hands.

He paused long enough to dig out and pull on brown bush fatigues; the robe no longer seemed adequate. He wriggled his feet into soft shoes.

When they reached the lounge, Floyt and Yumi found Alacrity and the Severeemish being given weapons by the bandswomen.

"It turns out they're really Celestials." Alacrity grinned. "I'm trying to sign on." He was buckling his Sam Browne–style belt.

He saw right away what had happened and came close to teasing Floyt and Yumi about it. After all, if the Daimyo was so hot about a little tellurian hemoglobin, he could have put her up to collecting certain other substances.

But Floyt's expression told Alacrity it wasn't a subject for jokes so he said only, "Welcome back to real time, folks. I'm truly sorry about the rude interruption."

The return of their combat harnesses overjoyed the Severeemish. They shrugged into the complicated tackle, checking knives, handguns, and other equipment, laughing and joking like jolly trolls. Charivari sat to one side, affecting a bored look, but her eyes were wide with fright.

"What's going on, Alacrity?" Floyt puffed, dumping his luggage on a couch.

Alacrity explained, adding, "*King's Ransom*'s supposed to join up with us too, and there're more aircutters on the way, so there's really nothing to worry about. So they tell me." He handed Floyt a pistol. "But it's Standard Operating Procedure that everybody's armed, just in case we have to set down." He smirked again.

Floyt sighed. Sometimes Alacrity didn't so much break bad news as share great new comedic material in the ongoing joke that was life.

The pistol was a reproduction of the archaic Webley .455 Mark VI revolver; they'd picked it up at a Forager lashup on Luna. The lanyard ring fastened to the bottom of its grip swung and clinked. Floyt accepted it carefully, along with a pouch of amazingly heavy little bullets. They were fat, soft, slow Dum-Dum rounds known, for some reason lost to time, as "Chicago popcorn." They were notched all the way down to the case mounts, and cast of something different from lead or the conventional alloys.

Floyt opened the top-breaking revolver and, tongue protruding in concentration, began fitting bullets into the chambers. He remembered to leave an empty chamber under the hammer. Closing it, he tucked it into his Inheritor's belt.

"A good, simple arrangement," Seven Wars boomed. "Nothing fancy or complicated. May I ask where you came by that piece?"

"From some Foragers," Alacrity supplied, checking the charge level in his father's sidearm. It was a big, matte-black pistol with a basket handshield. Its yellowed ivory grips were mounted with black crests, a cross-and-arc design. He slid it into its holster. "They got it on Raj, from a shipment of Webleys that ended up there from Halcyon." The Severeemish gathered round like a palisade of muscle and bone.

"Oho! I have heard that tale!" Seven Wars grinned, showing teeth that looked like they could bite through a crowbar. "So; this is the gun that won Halcyon."

"One of 'em, anyway," Alacrity answered casually. Floyt busied himself making sure the Chicago popcorn wouldn't fall out of his pocket, then glanced around to locate Yumi. He resolved to find out where Halcyon was and how a primitive revolver had won it.

Just then the Daubin' Band—Celestials drew the attention of the Severeemish as the young women divvied up extra charges for their energy tubes and rocket magazines for their launchers. The four amiable monsters ambled over that way.

"Where did Yumi go, Alacrity?"

"While you were adjusting your hardware, she went below-decks with Charivari and the other noncombatants."

"*Huh*? You mean we're *combatants*?"

"Would you mind not shouting, Ho? You're making my conditioning queasy. Anyway, no. Under local procedure, we're just classed as part of the trained, able-bodied ship's complement, that's all. And anyway, we'll just be hanging around overhead while that Invincible aircutter does all the work. Dorraine said so."

That made Floyt feel better, but he still wanted to be with Yumi.

At that moment a swift, deadly shadow streaked up alongside *Blue Pearl*. The *Scimitar* was exactly like the aircutters that had shown up to rescue them and arrest them less than a day before, after the airbike crash and just as a hungry fangster had nearly breakfasted on them.

"I want to see this. Come on, Ho." Alacrity led Floyt up short staircases and across various terraces and mingling places. Floyt, hesitant to go poking belowdecks, especially with members of the band posted as guards, was content to follow. He was also eager to see what was going on, but commented, "It's rather a helluva note, isn't it, Redlock's dragging diplomatic envoys and civilians and irreplaceable us into something like this?"

"Local conventions," Alacrity replied as they reached a spot by a red plush loveseat, near where Dorraine had stood. "The Domain's been a war zone more than it's been at peace, so they figure everybody who's not on active duty is in the ready reserves. There goes the *Scimitar*."

The two ships had descended into a broad valley where a fast-moving river widened out into silty sluggishness. The valley walls were steep, with cliffs breaking through facades of green, gray, mauve, and rust-red vegetation. The familiar, glassy glitter of ice-trees made a bright background for the few flocks of darting tarwings and jackflyers that scattered with the ships' approach.

The aircutter began circling an area in the center of the valley several kilometers from where the *Pearl* took up her station. "What makes you think it's a Precursor site, Alacrity?"

"Has to be. The alarm came from a ground sensor. Why would they have one planted out here in the epicenter of no place, and why get apoplectic about it, if it's not something pretty important, like a significant Precursor find?"

"Mmm—maybe." Floyt watched carefully as the *Scimitar*

banked and began low fly-bys, each a little closer to the ground, coming from different vectors.

"Remember the hunt?" Alacrity said. "The staff had hunting parties spread out just about everywhere on Epiphany except here, on this continent. I noticed that on the staff maps the other morning when we set out from Frostpile."

"A Precursor site . . ." Floyt mulled that, even as the *Scimitar* started spiraling down for a close look. Certainly there were no visible aboveground installations to warrant alarm sensors.

Or, Floyt thought, *Alacrity's guess might just be a product of his preoccupation with the Precursors. He always keeps his own counsel about that.* Some contended that there'd never been any such thing as Precursors; Floyt, like all Terrans, gave the matter as little thought as possible. "Well, it might be," he conceded, only to make Alacrity feel better.

"Except that Precursors almost never built anything on or under planetary surfaces." Alacrity *tch*ed.

Scimitar made another approach, preparing to land some recon troops. Reinforcements were due within minutes.

"For all we know, this might've been some kind of false alarm."

"Precursor site, Ho." Alacrity shook his head slowly. "And we know it because we've already seen an artifact from it."

"An arti— What artifact? Are you all right, Alacrity? What are you— *God in the Void!*"

Alacrity yelled aloud too, and heard other cries, and howls from the Severeemish. *Scimitar* vanished in a hellish explosion, lighting the valley walls and the *Blue Pearl*'s interior with an unbearable white glare.

CHAPTER 3

ZAGGING IN THE ZIGGURAT

THE *PEARL*'S ATTACK ALARMS WERE MUCH MORE SHRILL AND unnerving than her alerts. The hull darkened instantly against the glare, sparing those inboard it blindness. There was a confusion of half-begun shrieks, bellows, and exclamations.

The ship pealed and skirled as the roiling globe of the explosion ballooned. There was a subtle change as the shuttle's artificial gravity stood in for the real thing, anticipating maneuver forces.

The *Pearl* began to descend slowly, indecisively. She'd assumed position well out of what her Celestial captain estimated to be effective light-weapons range, but *Scimitar*'s vaporization proved that someone had misread the situation entirely.

The momentary debate hung almost tangibly in the air: withdraw or attack?

Alacrity was hoping Redlock wasn't the kind to charge hellbent into battle hungry for revenge. There was the well-being of the passengers, Yumi and the others, to consider, even if the health of a rootless breakabout and a Terran functionary didn't exert any gees.

A moment later there wasn't any point wondering about Redlock's caution. Fireballs arrowed up at them, leaving blazing trails behind.

"Mis—" Seven Wars started to yell.

There were giant detonations and the *Blue Pearl* attempted to turn turvey.

—siles, Floyt finished to himself automatically. He fully expected to be immolated, his particles swept along by the irresistible forcewall of an explosion. He should've known that Governor Redlock wasn't the type to travel in a fragile, defenseless gaud.

Alacrity wouldn't've been terribly flabbergasted to be demoted from rational being to elementary particles either. But he was surprised when, concussed by near misses, the shuttle's artificial gravity was knocked out. He wanted to say, *I really prefer ersatz*, as the actual item sent him windmilling through the air. All he got out was "Shhh—"

All the things that people, however careful, had forgotten, physics remembered, and didn't miss a trick. Though plants had been anchored in their bunkerlike planters, branches and fronds whipped, some breaking loose. The air was a whirlwind of leaves, petals, flying soil that had sifted through retention nets, fragments of bark, and projectile fruit. Loose glasses and a bottle overlooked by Charivari shattered into splinters.

The furniture had remained secure, but cushions went sailing. Weapons, ammunition, and various pieces of clothing and equipment flew. Sortie-Wolf nearly lost an eye to a stylus from an inner pocket of his own uniform tunic, which he'd set aside.

The passengers themselves set up an ululation of concerted wails, roars, and howls as they tried to protect themselves even while they whirled and fell, tumbling.

Alacrity and Floyt slammed against the convex of the hull. Redlock, seizing a well-mounted sculpture, saved both himself and Dorraine. One of the Severeemish bodyguards tore through a section of railing. The porcelain funeral urn containing the remains of First Councillor Inst remained firmly in place, but a hurtling rocket magazine hit it squarely, bursting it apart. Gray-white ashes were scattered across the passenger space.

The *Pearl* swung back, righting herself. Alacrity and Floyt slid down the curve of the hull to land in a heap on the deck, stunned. The shuttle was shaking and bucking; they did their best to cling to the deck carpeting.

The ship began to stabilize. Alacrity wondered where *King's Ransom* and the other aircutters were, then realized that very little time had passed.

"There! Open fire!" Redlock yelled into his proteus. He was standing in the middle of the main lounge area, the Severeemish and others getting to their feet all around him.

Shaking the pretty lights and restful fog out of their heads, Floyt and Alacrity saw what he was pointing at. Down where the *Scimitar* had been circling, a dark shape was rising with gathering speed. It was larger than the *Blue Pearl*, a cluster of bulbous, pendulous shapes, spiny with commo and detector vibrissae and armament. In the fleeting glimpse they got of it, they saw the intruder ship changing color, beginning to match Epiphany's sky. Alacrity registered numbly that it must be some new stealth system he'd never heard of before. The stealth ship fired another flight of missiles.

The *Blue Pearl*'s defenses had barely saved her from the first, unexpected salvo, with a flurry of jamming and counter-measures aimed at the missiles' guidance systems. Those systems had been analyzed; the shuttle merely rose a bit and the twin fireballs streaked red annihilation beneath her. They failed to detonate.

Redlock's ship opened up with an answering volley. A long, straight bridge of blinding yellow-white light connected the intruder and the *Pearl*'s underside for a moment. If the intruder had shields, they failed; part of her upper hull disappeared.

A doomsday crack shook the sky, air rushing into the vacuum created by the cannon bolt. The stealth vessel jolted and wobbled, then, trailing thick blue smoke and windblown flames, began an emergency descent that threatened to become a crash.

The *Pearl* followed her kill down. For the first time Floyt noticed the long, silvery seam of a crack in the shuttle's crystal hull, curving from the level of the main lounge area almost to its apex. He also noticed how sluggish the shuttle was.

"What's he landing for?" Floyt sounded angry. "Why doesn't he wait for reinforcements?"

They became aware of Redlock's mustering the band members, a few other Celestials, and the Severeemish, including the giant who'd taken out the span of railing and now seemed none the worse for it. Dorraine was standing by the remains of her father's funeral urn, silently studying a shard she'd picked up from the deck.

"I don't want them back in possession of that site," the governor was saying, "not even for a few minutes."

Alacrity nudged Floyt. "See? What'd I tell you?" Floyt made a sour face.

"But, my lords Seven Wars and Sortie-Wolf," Redlock was saying, "I still think it might be best for you both to remain in the shuttle."

Under the heavy bone cliff of his brow, Seven Wars' dark, close-set eyes widened a bit. He answered in a hearty, good-natured tone.

"And miss a good fracas? Don't you think you owe your allies better treatment than that, Governor?" His son and their bodyguards made laughter resembling steam locomotives leaving a station. Redlock gave one of his rare, brief smiles.

Dorraine let go of the shard; it shattered to fragments on the dance floor. They all turned to her.

She went to join her husband, flinging back her resplendent robe and opening the heavy brooches, one the tragic mask and the other the comic, set at either shoulder. Letting the robe fall, she drew two silvery little guns from the folds and overlaps of her tightly cinched gown. They were modeled after antique derringers.

Redlock didn't object to her tacit insistence on coming along. Floyt had already seen the Queen of Agora use a handgun; she was good at it.

"I'll be going too," Alacrity called down, and started picking his way through branches, broken glass, fallen fruit and melting ice, dirt and debris. Redlock glanced at him but didn't answer, going back to his council of war.

Floyt caught Alacrity's shoulder. "This doesn't have anything to do with us, you know, or with what we came here for."

"Ho, I have to get a look inside that Precursor site."

"Is there any point in asking you *why*, goddammit? No, never mind; you'll only get vague on me again." Floyt was also puzzled that the Earthservice conditioning didn't force

Alacrity to hold back from becoming involved. Something deep within the breakabout must have overruled it on this subject.

"I'll explain it some time, Ho."

"Don't put yourself out. Let's go."

They were both hobbling a bit. Alacrity showed only an instant's surprise that Floyt was coming along. Floyt himself didn't understand it too clearly. Alacrity was still a major factor in accomplishing the mission, so that was a rationale to use against the conditioning. More to the point, Floyt, on his way to receive his bequest a few hours before, had realized that at some time in their misfortunes they'd become friends.

"We volunteer, sort of," Alacrity declared as they joined the others near the *Pearl*'s main hatch.

"Wallflowers at the landing party," Floyt muttered. One of the bandswomen laughed.

The shuttle descended. Below, the stealth vessel had grounded lopsidedly, smoke and flame still rising from her. Seven Wars, studying the craft through a pair of outsize vision enhancers, said, "They're abandoning her. It's difficult to tell who they are through the smoke."

"What if they're faking?" Floyt wondered aloud.

"All their systems appear to be out," Redlock observed. "Still, I don't plan to board the intruder. I only wish to secure the site and post guard until the *King's Ransom* and the other aircutters show. I want to make sure they don't get back in, and that they didn't leave anyone inside."

He consulted his proteus. "That shouldn't be more than another few minutes."

The *Pearl* settled in some distance from the downed ship, with a ridge of ground between them for protection just in case. Alacrity and Floyt followed the others down the ramp, then the shuttle rose again, to stand off and make sure the intruder vessel remained where she was.

The landing party had been set down near a hill, half of which had been removed. A tunnel mouth, a precise equilateral triangle ten meters on a side, angled down into Epiphany. There were construction lights, apparently rigged by Weir research teams.

"Underground site," Alacrity murmured to Floyt. "I never heard of one before."

"Is that why they wanted to keep it to themselves? Weir's people, I mean?"

"Ho, *nobody* shares a Precursor find, not if they can help it."

"Citizen Floyt; Master Fitzhugh." Redlock spoke in the easy, listen-up voice of an experienced squad leader. "If you gentlemen will be good enough to mount guard here, the rest of us will proceed. Our proteuses aren't integrated and they'll be of no use once inside anyway. Recognition signals will be verbal and visual. Our challenge will be 'interlock,' and the countersign, 'downcheck.' Understood?"

"Got it," Alacrity replied. Floyt was bewildered.

The others already had their instructions. The point man was a Celestial sergeant from the *Pearl*'s crew, wearing vision enhancers set for night work. The officer who'd greeted Alacrity and Floyt when they'd first dashed inboard was next, with two more of Redlock's elite. After them would go the governor and Dorraine, along with the Severeemish. The four musicians would bring up the rear and do flanker duty as necessary.

"About two hundred and fifty meters in, there's a chamber at the end of this adit that our research team used as a base of operations," Redlock said. "We'll proceed to that, then check other areas if it seems appropriate. Everyone is to stay within sight of those ahead and behind them. Fitzhugh and Floyt, make sure to relay the passwords to my troops when they arrive."

The main party moved out. The Celestials were silent and wary, the Severeemish methodical and rigid, looking as if they were just waiting to open up on everything in sight. Everyone in the group seemed to be old hands at what they were doing, even Dorraine. The adit curved gently to the left.

"*King's Ransom* ought to be here inside ten minutes or so." Alacrity frowned. "Now what d'you think's so important Redlock couldn't wait and send a whole friggin' armored column down there?"

"If you want to tell me, tell me," Floyt prompted. "I hate being a rhetorical sounding board."

"I can't. Yet."

The main party followed the bend in the tunnel, the last rearguard musician finally disappearing. Alacrity started forward, into the tunnel mouth.

"Hey!" squawked Floyt.

"Ho, I'm going to take a look around, and it's not going to be on Redlock's guided tour. I'm not going to steal anything, and I won't run into any trouble because Redlock's marching band will be out there in front. So don't lecture me."

"That was 'Hey' as in 'Hey, wait up!' you ass."

"Sorry, I can be a jerk sometimes. Next tour group leaving right now."

They stayed close to the wall, easing through the semi-darkness as quietly as they could, but not trying to copy the nightstalk tactics of the governor's bunch. Their footsteps echoed softly. The incline grew steeper.

"Is this a typical Precursor construction?" Floyt whispered.

"There's no typical Precursor anything."

The walls were flat and smooth, but seemed to have a fine grain. Every thirty meters or so a buttress ran along both walls and across the floor, so the two were obliged to hike themselves over a waist-high barrier. In their worse-for-wear condition, it was a complication they didn't need. It was also proof the place hadn't been built for foot traffic, at least not the human kind.

"Redlock forgot something," Alacrity realized. "Earplugs."

"What for?"

"If one of those honeys lets fly with an H.E. rocket in this place, you're gonna know what for."

The worklights had apparently been turned off at some central point. Soon the two were feeling their way along the left side of the tunnel with their left hands, right hands on their weapons. As their eyes adjusted, they saw that the tunnel walls gave off a dim glow, a ghostly green-white that came from what appeared to be a whorled grain in the walls, but the material felt icy cold.

"Heat sink?" Alacrity puzzled as he led the way. "Redlock called this an adit. I wonder just how big the place is."

The barriers were a good spot for an ambush, or for one of Redlock's crew to shoot them accidentally. They crossed with all caution, guns drawn. Floyt repeated the challenge and countersign to himself several times to make sure he had them straight. Their conditioning was bothering them less than their own apprehensions but, having started, they were drawn on by the mystical feel of the Precursor site. There was a sharp, not human or even organic smell to the place—not mustiness but definitely *old*.

"All right then, who *were* the Precursors?" Floyt had once asked Alacrity during the voyage to Epiphany.

"Ask anybody; they'll tell you. Then ask somebody else and you'll get a different answer. It's the biggest guessing game since religion."

They crossed still another buttress, almost two hundred meters into the tunnel by Alacrity's calculation. He went over first, then motioned Floyt on, a motion barely visible in the glow of the walls.

But now they could make out a brightness up ahead. Human-style lighting was part of it, but so was something else, something irregular. And they could hear deep, distant sounds, unintelligible yet somehow familiar.

The incline was very steep. Floyt was worried about losing his footing; Alacrity's pathfinders still gave him good purchase. The glow before them grew brighter, outshining the walls. Its source was somewhere close, around the bend.

Suddenly they heard yells, Severeemish roars, the chatter and hiss of weaponry, and the concussion of a rocket. Floyt understood what Alacrity meant; even at a distance, the report slammed their eardrums.

The firefight died away abruptly, raged again for ten seconds, then became sporadic.

"Now what?" Floyt asked, his heart hammering.

Conditioning and instincts told them to get out, but they were indebted to Redlock, perhaps even more so to Dorraine. Alacrity bit his lip. "You ever feel like everybody else's problems are simpler than yours?"

Floyt thought about how Redlock had intervened on their

behalf and the look on Dorraine's face when she'd found out that her father was dead. "Not right now, for a change."

"Yeah? Okay, Ho; keep your head down."

They made their way to the next buttress, crouching low, then crawled behind it to the adit's right wall. From there they could see the end of the tunnel.

The Precursors hadn't any use for landings or ledges; the adit simply ended at a sharp angle, plunging into a vast underground chamber. They couldn't make out much except that they seemed to be looking into the upper reaches of the place. Brief shadows flickered against the ceiling and there were the sharp sounds and echoes of the battle.

Someone—Weir's research teams, presumably—had built a stairway down the last, steepest stretch of the adit, bracing it with suction disks and tension members. The steps led to a catwalk grating where the adit simply emptied into the artificial cavern.

There one of the Daubin' Band musicians lay unmoving, badly wounded or dead, blood darkening the white stripes of her shimmerskins. Her over-under infantry rifle lay nearby.

"Ambush," Alacrity guessed.

"Could she still be alive?"

Alacricty made a *who knows*? face. They began to ease up over the buttress, then ducked back as they heard running footsteps on the catwalk. A figure came into view, pounding up the steps in silhouette, crouching low, impossible to identify.

Alacrity braced both arms across the barrier, aligning the barrel of the Captain's Sidearm. "Halt! Stand fast!"

The figure froze almost comically, posed like a statue of a cat burglar.

"Interlock," Alacrity called out. Floyt glanced at him. His face, merely shiny with sweat a few moments ago, streamed with it now, catching some of the glare of the cavern.

"Interlock!" Alacrity repeated. "Gimme the damn countersign; I'm not asking you ag—" He threw himself sideways, taking Floyt with him. They heard the enraged buzzsaw of a flechette burpgun, the reports of the rounds battering their ears, the metal slivers whining and ricocheting off the floor, barrier, and walls, nearly as much of a hazard to the marksman as to his targets.

All the tension and resentment in Alacrity—some of it dated back to Terra and the underhanded way he'd been framed and recruited—exploded. With a curse in some language that didn't sound quite human, showing his teeth and the whites of his eyes, he scrabbled back to the barrier, staying below the line of fire, and waited for a lull in the swarming of flechettes. Lying asprawl, he eased the muzzle of the Captain's Sidearm up, barely over the buttress, and let fly.

Floyt, who'd been present on a previous firing, already had his fingers in his ears.

The bulky old handgun overloaded the adit with thunderflash, heat, and death. It had been designed for use against the dangers a vessel's skipper might face: boarding, riot, and mutiny. Its discharge was attended by almost overwhelming visible light and sonic energy.

Alacrity fired again; the shot boomed, reverberating through the place.

The flechette burpgun had fallen silent. Alacrity pushed his hip howitzer up higher for a better angle on a third shot, still without so much as raising his head. Then he swiftly wriggled to a different firing spot elsewhere along the barrier, using shoulders, heels, one hand, and the back of his head.

In the wake of the concussion and glare, he was up, forearms once more steadied across the barrier. The man was backing toward the catwalk, nearly on all fours, the burpgun aimed where Alacrity had been.

Alacrity cut loose again, just as the burpgun muzzle swung to bear on him. The fierce blare of energy caught the intruder squarely, knocking him backward through the air as it simply vaporized his middle. For an instant Alacrity saw the disbelieving look on a face that seemed to be all bulging eyes.

The body hit the catwalk and lay smoking and crackling. Alacrity was up and over the buttress, sprinting for the catwalk. Floyt brought up the rear, the Webley in his hand, it's lanyard ring flapping and clinking.

Floyt fetched up against Alacrity's back, almost toppling

them both. They were gagging on the smoke, breathless and nearly spent.

"See?" Alacrity asked in a remote voice as they gazed down into the chamber. "Didn't I tell you we'd seen a Precursor artifact?"

"Hell, no, you didn't," Floyt answered softly. "All you did was hint. I wonder if the one on Weir's terrace is an egg. A *nit*."

The causality harp they'd seen at Frostpile was small and uncomplicated compared to this shifting, churning titan. The Precursor chamber was wide and high—fifty meters or more through its long axis, the vertical—and most of that was occupied by this fuller, terribly complex looking nebula. The primeval smell they'd noticed was all-pervasive.

The half-familiar sounds came to them clearly, the tonalities and near-subsonic hum, the great baritone chiming of the thing. It was more alive-seeming than the first; the adumbrations and eddies, brume-shapes and hazy images seemed much more immediate, nearer to resolution.

"Quit goggling and help me," Floyt panted, snapping Alacrity out of what was becoming a trance. Floyt was on one knee by the fallen woman. A few minutes earlier she had laughed at his wallflower joke.

Alacrity leapt to help. Both could hear the sounds of the fighting below. Levels of catwalk had been set up surrounding the harp and beneath it. The vault itself didn't have a level floor; it was as concave as an egg cup. At several levels, gantries had been installed.

All around the Precusor artifact were detectors or sensors of a kind Alacrity had never seen before, something Weir's people must have developed. Some were spherical, resembling tufted dandelions three meters across, others were like metal barnacles.

Alacrity's jaw had dropped. *My god! Did Weir actually figure out a way to* interface *with that thing?*

Beams and projectile shots ranged up at the catwalk where Floyt and Alacrity knelt, flaring and spanging off it. The combatants were keeping to cover; the engagement had settled into sniping and jockeying for position.

The musician-Celestial had been caught below the waist by a burst of flechette fire. There wasn't much left of her pelvic area at all.

"Ho, she's dead."

"Give me a hand here." Floyt was trying to compose the body so that he could move it without losing part of it.

She's about the same age as his daughter, Alacrity realized. Energy bolts were exchanged below; beams in various hues and intensities lanced up at them, making molten metal run and spit from the railings and grating.

"Ho, she's *dead*."

Floyt got his arm under the blond head, trying to gather her up. A brief burst of flechettes from below spattered against the adit ceiling behind them. "At least let's get her out of the line of—"

A mixed barrage of solids and energy hit the catwalk, and Alacrity, amazed in its aftermath that they were untouched, saw when arguing was no good any more. He wrestled Floyt loose and propelled them both back up the steps.

"I'm all right. I'm all right." Floyt clapped Alacrity's shoulder tiredly. "We have to help Redlock and Dorraine."

"Ho, we owe Redlock for his help, and I guess we both have kind of a crush on Dorraine, but *King's Ransom* ought to be here any second. We're only gonna get in the Celestials' way."

"Then why didn't Redlock wait?"

"Huh? I guess he—I—damned if I know."

"They're going to blow the place up. Maybe if you'd looked around a little more instead of gaping at the harp, you'd have noticed."

Alacrity let loose his hold on his friend as the enormity of it hit him. "No! They can't!"

Charges were plastered all over the vault. "Probably the only reason they haven't been detonated's because the governor's got the intruders bottled up in here. The only way Redlock can win is keep them pinned down till help comes. I wonder how he knew?"

Alacrity glanced over the woman's body. "And his rearguard's dead."

Floyt hiked himself up. "I think two of the Severeemish are dead or wounded down there; I couldn't get a good look, with all the firing and the obstacles."

They studied their options. Floyt thought he caught a glimpse of Dorraine; Alacrity saw a dark figure in a chinstrapped battle helmet—not one of the *Pearl*'s landing party—who snapped off a round with an energy rifle of some kind, then ducked back under cover, all too fast for Alacrity to get off a shot.

There were coruscations of crossfire and ricochet; panels blew out in showers of sparks and liquefied metal and glass. Bullets sent fragments whining. The noise was appalling.

A number of triangular passageways ran from the vault off the lowest level of catwalk. It looked like the surviving intruders were withdrawing into two of these.

As Floyt watched, Dorraine fired down a tunnel with one of her lovely little imitation derringers. It gave a high report and a more powerful beam than he'd expected. Redlock was by her side, and they advanced into the tunnel, from which came sounds of more shooting. A quiet descended on the vault itself.

"We can at least give the wounded a hand," Floyt said, starting to get up. Alacrity, who'd been making frantic adjustments to his pistol, caught Floyt's sleeve and pointed to a lift. In seconds they were dropping to the bottom level, crouched behind the lift's gates.

A hasty scatterbeam shot splashed off the vault wall near the lower catwalk. They couldn't see where it had come from, and could only hope it had been stray fire from an intruder in one of the tunnels.

When they reached the bottom, they found that one of the wounded Severeemish was Seven Wars. A short distance away lay the body of one of the Corporeals—the Severeemish bodyguards. A flechette burst had ripped his tough skin; his blood looked altogether human.

Floyt and Alacrity, weapons ready, squatted next to Seven Wars. He was barely conscious, clutching a deep wound in his side.

"See what you can do," Alacrity said. Extremely jittery, he went to make sure the immediate area, at least, was safe. Even so, he spared a few intrigued glances for the piles of research equipment.

Seven Wars came around a bit, his craggy head resting on Floyt's knee. He pawed feebly at a big, bulky pouch on his harness. Before he could get it open, he drifted off again.

Floyt worked the piece of equipment free of its pouch. It was bell-nozzled, with small fittings and manipulators retracted up inside the bell. It had a reservoir of some kind and a hand-grip. Floyt hadn't the first idea how the thing worked, though the controls looked very simple.

He turned to the corpse of the Corporeal, laying the muzzle of the medical instrument over one of its wounds.

The device buzzed his palm silently, which, Floyt con-cluded, was meant to let him know this patient was dead, without giving off light or sound that might attract enemy fire.

Floyt pressed his thumb against a button. The device vibrated a little, growing warmer. When he removed it, the machine had irrigated and sterilized the wound and covered it with layers of sticky webbing, some sort of battlefield dressing.

Floyt pried Seven War's powerful fingers away from his wound and used the envoy's combat knife to cut away the fabric of his uniform. Blood ran freely, and Floyt's hands began trembling. He laid the muzzle of the medical kit over the wound and triggered it. The unit became warm under his hand until a measured pulsing of its grip gave him what he supposed to be a treatment-completed signal. When he removed the unit, Seven Wars' wound was thick with spun dressing and no longer losing blood. Floyt began checking him out for other wounds.

Alacrity reappeared. "How is he?"

Floyt looked at the medical instrument doubtfully. "I found a switch to take readings, but I don't know what any of them— *look out!*"

Alacrity spun, holding the Captain's Sidearm at waist level with both hands. He was facing a man in a mottled battle suit and chinstrapped helmet holding a flechette burpgun slung from one shoulder.

Got me cold . . . Alacrity knew it would be his last thought. He tried to fire anyway; he didn't realize that he was shouting at the top of his lungs.

The burst never came. The intruder's expression was stunned disbelief as he squeezed the trigger without effect.

Showdown syndrome, Alacrity registered with a stopped heart. *He must've emptied his magazine without realizing it.* The crash of Alacrity's shot took the man squarely in the chest, driving him back off balance, riddling and igniting him. The intruder shrieked once, then collapsed, clothing aflame, tissue smoldering, marrow gone to ash.

Alacrity fired again to make sure he wasn't suffering, but it produced only a weak, pale ray. As charnel smoke mushroomed into the vault of the Precursors, he tried again with no result.

Coughing and choking, he pulled the blue bandanna up over his nose and mouth, stepping over the corpse, fumbling for a new charge even though the gun still read full. Another intruder rushed him from one side, raising a thing that looked like a combination war axe and carbine.

That one didn't fire either, but knew he was out of ammunition. He'd attacked because he saw no other alternative to being burned down. Alacrity tried to throw himself out of the way, slamming into a wall of Weir machinery, setting off agony in his elbow and ribs. He brought his father's weapon around and up with all his might, left hand reinforcing the grip of his right.

The blade of the gun-axe met the long, thick rib beneath the pistol's barrel, adding a new dent and nearly knocking it from Alacrity's hands. The man closed with him, sending them both toppling sideways against a console.

Alacrity freed up the pistol long enough to slam it against his opponents helmet, but that didn't do much good. He just warded off another blow of the axe with the pistol's deflector and basket handguard. Then he and the intruder grappled awkwardly for their lives.

A third enemy had arrived, holding a bayoneted rifle at low port, his ammunition, like his buddies, used up in the firefight and skirmishing. He was headed for the whirling tangle of his fellow and Alacrity.

The bayonet looked odd and cruel to Floyt, rather like an upside-down Bowie knife. Floyt had let Seven Wars' head slide from his lap. Having struggled to his feet, he dragged at the Webley while straddling the body of the Severeemish.

The intruder came to high port, whirling on him, ready to attack. The man appeared to make a quick calculation, from Floyt's expression and the fact that he hadn't fired to save Alacrity, that the revolver, too, was empty. He advanced.

Floyt raised the revolver in both hands, as he'd seen Alacrity do. The muzzle shook and quavered. An awful, abrupt doubt crossed the intruder's face. Floyt tightened his right index finger in a spasm, tightening his other fingers as well, thrusting the Webley at the other.

The revolver leaped and roared, shooting smoke and a tongue of flame, making Floyt shut his eyes involuntarily. Both Alacrity and his enemy, locked in their struggle, ignored it.

As for Floyt, he saw in shock that he'd missed clean. At perhaps five paces. It was no less of a surprise to his target. *Misfire?* It seemed impossible. With the pistol leaping in his convulsing grip, he yanked off another round, and two more after it, flinching, wincing his eyes shut each time. The recoil wasn't overwhelming, but it was something he had never dealt with before; the reports were unnervingly loud. The burnt propellant had a sharp smell.

The intruder stood unscathed. Worse, he dropped into guard and advanced. Floyt tried to back up, but his heels came up against Seven Wars. For some reason that reminded him of the Severeemish looking at the Webley earlier, and Floyt recalled that the pistol was a double-action design.

Tongue in the corner of his mouth, sweat running down his face, Floyt carefully kept his finger off the trigger while he put both thumbs on the hammer spur and cocked it. Only the one round was left.

His enemy came with a stamping assault, to open Floyt longitudinally. With great and delicate care, Floyt steadied the gun and squeezed the trigger. Smoke and flame and metal spat from the barrel.

The intruder howled and dropped his rifle, staggering backward trying to stop the blood from spurting from the entry wound at the base of his neck.

The man regained his balance for a second, then pitched

forward on his face, blood spurting from entry and exit wounds to drip through the perforations in the catwalk decking. Floyt had no time to gape; Alacrity, forearm bleeding where the axe blade had caught it, was still locked in a frantic struggle with the remaining intruder. They were rolling back and forth on the console, the intruder was getting the upper hand, levering the shaft of his weapon across Alacrity's throat; Alacrity's face had gone dark. He was carrying the fight with his left hand now, while his right shifted its grip on the Captain's Sidearm.

Floyt took an uncertain step toward them; reloading would take too long, and they were far too close together. The intruder's head and neck were well protected by his battle helmet; Floyt tried to decide where best to strike the man with the Webley.

But Alacrity did something to his pistol; a long, gleaming blade snapped from concealment in the deflector rib on the Captain's Sidearm.

Alacrity jammed the pistol bayonet into his enemy's side. The man made a sound halfway between a grunt and a squeal, eyes huge and round with horror, as the air rushed from his lung. Alacrity stabbed twice more, blood splashing across the gun's handguard. Pressure on the axe shaft fell away. As he pushed the man's body off him, Alacrity smelled death in the intruder's exhalation.

He massaged his throat, sucking in great lungfuls of air, as Floyt helped him up, demanding to know if he was all right although Alacrity was gasping too hard to answer.

At last Alacrity got out one word. "Reload!"

As Alacrity began digging a fresh—he hoped—charge from a belt pouch, Floyt shakily opened the Webley. The extractor sent empty shells flying. He fumbled in his pocket for more cartridges.

His hands were shaking so badly that he could barely fish out a handful of bullets, dropping two of them, which promptly rolled and fell through deck perforations. Floyt took another deep breath, focused himself by an act of will, and, bringing all his concentration to bear, began fitting bullets into the cylinder with exacting patience. Every few seconds he would glance around nervously. No noise or sound indicated any more intruders.

Ashen-faced, hands jittering, Alacrity had returned the spring-loaded bayonet to its place in the deflector after replacing the pistol's spent charge. The charge indicator was indeed malfunctioning, reading full even when the gun was empty.

Floyt left no empty chambers this time, and kept the Webley in hand. He checked Seven Wars again, finding that, while the envoy was still unconscious, his pulse rapid and rather weak, the field dressing was still containing the bleeding.

He heard footfalls on the catwalk and very nearly fired as he turned. Alacrity was prowling, gun ready, through the maze of equipment, up a short flight of steps, in the direction of the harp. Floyt turned back to the medical device, to see if it could tell him any more about Seven Wars' condition.

Most of the research apparatus seemed to be on and functioning; Alacrity figured the intruders had activated everything to cover their movements. He came to a central bank of displays, picking out bits and pieces.

SYNCHRONISTIC PATTERNED SET ANALYSIS

FEYNMANISTIC EVALUATION

KOESTLERIAN EVENT CONFLUENCIALITIES

STRANGE ATTRACTOR INFERENCES

Weir's researchers had apparently been using the gantries for some sort of direct observation or testing, going out to the edge of the harp itself. He found a screen with a red indicator over it. It read:

ENTER NEXT TEST RUN SUBJECT:

Floyt was still looking after Seven Wars. Alacrity studied the touchpad and entered an inquiry that meant everything to him. The screen changed to read WORKING and its indicator changed from red to green. The indicator on the next screen along lit up red, as it displayed ENTER NEXT TEST RUN SUBJECT.

Computers and inference engines came to full life; the dandelion and barnacle interfacers glowed and glittered.

The gantries had smaller interfacers on them; he extended the nearest until it nearly entered the eerie maelstrom. He walked the gantry with a feeling of unreality; reaching the end, he moved between the interfacers. The causality harp roiled.

Well? What's the answer? He pulled down the bandanna.
"Out with it!"

A sudden, almost unbearable increase in the humming and
toning of the harp drove him back a step. Hissing discharges
rippled through it; the harp was all flame and turbulence, making the vault vibrate with its peturbations and pitch patterns.

Alacrity threw up one hand to ward off the fierce light,
laughing shrilly. He slowly extended his other hand into the
star-brume.

He was lost in a storm of thought-fillips and surges from
his overloaded nervous system. He lowered his hand again,
watching the dance of the phase-portraits and the grand proces-
sions of the adumbrations through slitted eyes. Lost to the
normal passage of time, he wavered, wrist entering the harp's
turmoil. Dimly, he heard alarms and bells.

"Alacrity! Get back here!" Floyt stood at the other end of
the narrow gantry, unable to force himself out to the alien
starfoam. Alacrity, silhouetted against the majesty of it, was
roaring, glorying. Some of the damaged equipment had begun
sputtering, smoke wreathing from it.

Alacrity couldn't resist wondering what would happen if he
leaned over just a little further; if his head entered the causality
harp. If it swept through his skull and into his naked mind.

He bent forward, but the harp seemed to be withdrawing
from him. Alacrity took a deep breath, preparing to swing
himself out further. Then he realized perplexedly that the harp
wasn't withdrawing; the gantry was moving backward. Arms
grabbed him from behind and dragged him down to the gantry
surface. All in a moment, the harp subsided, becoming an
almost invisible, almost silent ghost.

Floyt was on top of him, holding him. Alacrity's out-
stretched hand pulled further and further back from the harp.

He didn't struggle. Craning his head, he saw Redlock arrive,
Dorraine and the rest following. Alacrity looked at the darkened
harp sadly, but told himself it didn't matter. He had his affirmation.

When the gantry was fully withdrawn, Redlock helped them
both to their feet. "Snap out of it, Fitzhugh. There's no time
for this!"

Floyt noticed woozily that, down below, Sortie-Wolf was kneeling by his father's side. The surviving Celestials and the Corporeal were checking the bodies of the intruders. Several members of Redlock's party were missing.

"What—what's wrong?" Alacrity slurred.

"We can't disarm all the explosives in time. This entire place will go in minutes."

Others were already crowding into the lift, bearing Seven Wars. The slain Corporeal was left behind, for lack of room and time. Alacrity came around enough to support himself on Floyt's shoulder.

As they hurried past it, Floyt caught a look at the screen where Alacrity had entered his question. The red indicator light still shone.

Alacrity watched the seething nebulae of the causality harp as the lift rose past it, gazed back at it over his shoulder as Floyt pulled him back from the edge.

At the top they were met by heavily armed Celestials in company strength. After some initial confusion, Redlock got everyone moving for the exit.

Just as they came to the mouth of the adit, ground-shaking explosions rolled up from the vault of the Precursors.

CHAPTER 4

THE VERY STUFF AND PITH

WHEN THE SURVIVING MEMBERS OF THE LANDING PARTY struggled from the adit, they were still under cover. Floyt looked up to see *King's Ransom* hanging low overhead, blocking out a good deal of the sky.

To Floyt, Governor Redlock's flagship would always resemble the fabulous jeweled eggs Carl Fabergé made for the czars centuries ago on Terra. But this bauble was six kilometers stem to stern and, all the sparkle and trimming aside, a superdreadnaught that had trounced whole fleets of conventional warcraft.

Landing boats from *King's Ransom* had encircled the adit's entrance, the *Blue Pearl*, and the wrecked intruder stealth ship. Aircutters and other vessels from Frostpile maintained close surveillance over the valley; the landing zone was crawling with Invincibles, Celestials, and Redlock's space marines.

Over by one big Celestial landing boat, Charivari and Yumi and some others from the *Pearl* waited. Floyt went over to speak to Yumi, but a pair of Invincibles, a lieutenant and a captain, barred his way.

Yumi said softly, "Kindly let him by, please."

The Invincibles stepped aside at once; Floyt went to her. Medical personnel closed in on the others who'd emerged. More explosions rumbled from the vault.

It came to Floyt with a jolt that only minutes had passed

since he and Yumi had been in each other's arms. It felt more like days, making their time together seem even more unreal. In the middle of the martial confusion of the landing zone, he hesitated to throw his arms around her.

Yumi read it on his face; she hugged herself to his chest, pressing her cheek to his. "You are unhurt? No—you have injuries!"

"What? Yes; Alacrity too. We'll be all right, though. He's just a bit, um, fuddled."

"I feared for you, Hobart. I am glad you're safe."

He was jarred, to inhale the jasmine in her hair again after the smells of gunpowder and burning machinery and blood, and the indefinable odor of eternity in the vault. He glanced around the landing zone. "But what about you? They should've gotten you out of here right away, up to *King's Ransom.*"

She resisted when he would've led her to one of the landing boats; he was surprised at her strength. "I will not be going inboard the governor's ship, Hobart. I must return directly to Frostpile, to rejoin my Daimyo."

"Oh. I'd been hoping—"

"It is his wish. But I couldn't leave until I knew that you were safe."

She pulled his head down to her and kissed him again, a grace note and a good-bye. She pressed something into his hand. "I will always keep you in my prayers, Hobart Floyt." Then she broke away from his embrace. Yumi picked up the small case that contained his blood and said, "I am ready now."

More Invincibles appeared from somewhere. The captain was back with the lieutenant, to salute her smartly, saying, "At your service, Lady Nakatsu," while his men came to present-arms.

She looked tiny and fragile among them, but regal and accustomed to command. She was conducted aboard an air-cutter with a great deal of military courtesy. Floyt watched it lift into the sky.

When he opened his hand, he found she'd left him a small woven wire sack, like an old-fashioned reticule. It was heavy, and clinked as he tossed it on his palm. Tucking it indifferently into a bellows pocket, he kept his gaze fixed on the aircutter as it slid across the sky in the direction of the Weir stronghold, vanishing from sight.

Someone was talking to him; a jowly Celestial field surgeon stood at his elbow. "I've been ordered to examine you, Citizen Floyt. The governor will be very vexed with me if you don't comply. And if I may say so, you look as if you could use it."

Floyt capitulated; his gaze left the sky. "Why, that's very kind of you, Colonel." His nose was grotesquely swollen again, hurting like hell. And the parts of him that weren't bleeding were sore. The colonel held up a medical scanner.

"Just pick a spot, any spot," Floyt invited. "Has Alacrity— Master Fitzhugh—has he been treated?"

"They're working on him, sir. Nothing very much wrong with him but a slice, some contusions, a bit of shock. I'm going to give you both a thorough going-over inboard *King's Ransom*."

"I'm afraid we're bound for the spaceport."

"Not anymore." The colonel eyed his scanner. "How long have you been anemic, Citizen Floyt? Sir? *What's so blasted funny?*"

The *Blue Pearl* had already been limped back to the flagship. Floyt found himself in a landing boat with other members of the original party.

Alacrity, who'd come out of whatever state the harp had sent him into, moved off to one side with Floyt. "Do you have any idea what's going on?"

"I was going to ask you that. Do you think Redlock would go back on his word? That doesn't sound like him."

"No, but now isn't the time to pester him." The governor sat with Dorraine, watching as his medical people ministered to Seven Wars. The other landing party members were silent; *Mourning their losses*, Alacrity decided.

The breakabout insisted he wasn't much the worse for wear. "Which is probably more than you can say for the causality harp," he added. "All those explosions."

"What got into you down there, Alacrity?" Alacrity's face went into neutral, and Floyt knew better than to pursue the matter. "All right, then. Tell me who you think those people

were—the intruders." There was a slight vibration as the landing craft lifted off. "Redlock doesn't seem to be sure yet,"
Alacrity said. "Could be almost any government or independent
group, one of the big cartels—almost anybody with real
resources behind them. That stealth ship—that's a new one on
me."

"But how did they get here? The whole Halidome system's
awfully well guarded."

"There was so much traffic coming in for the funeral, maybe
they were dropped off by one of the big, legitimate ships. Took
guts, you have to give 'em that. They found out about the harp
somehow and made up their minds they were going to steal it
or study it, duplicate it, whatever."

"But whoa, then they blew up the vault."

"Samson in the temple? I dunno; people play for keeps when
it comes to Precursor stuff. They took out the regular guard
detail. Redlock said they might've pulled it off if they hadn't
tripped that sensor."

The landing craft entered a hypaxial lock and made fast to
the flagship. As Alacrity and Floyt moved to the hatch, they
were met by Seven Wars. He was on his feet, looking amazingly
well, impressing them with the vigor of Severeemish recuper-
ative powers. "I understand I have you lads to thank for slapping
that patch on me," the minister boomed. He was wearing a
more workmanlike dressing applied by Redlock's people.

Alacrity jerked a thumb at Floyt to clarify the matter.

"There wasn't all that much to it, actually," Floyt assured,
feeling heroic for a moment.

"A *little* less modesty, please, Citizen Earther," Seven Wars
implored. "The rescue of a Severeemish envoy is worth a certain amount of fuss and ado." He clicked claws like black iron
against his heavy red-gold Inheritor's belt, then indicated Floyt's.
"We perhaps owe one another a little something anyway, but
this makes the debt rather heavier on my side, eh?"

He winked one dark little gleaming eye, then hobbled through
the lock leaning on his son's shoulder, the surviving Corporeal
trailing behind.

"You can translate that?" Alacrity inquired.

Floyt shook his head, but Redlock, who'd come up behind,

promised, "I'll clarify it for you both later. First, you can clean up and rest, while my wife and I attend to some other things."

"But—" Floyt foundered. His conditioning was stirring within him again.

Dorraine approached, favoring them with one of her most disarming smiles. "Why bother with the Epiphany spaceport when you can ride to Palladium with us?"

"But Dame Tiajo said—you—we—" Alacrity fumbled.

"I told the Grandam that I would dump you two at my first port of call," Redlock explained. "This site isn't a port of call, and we're no longer stopping at the spaceport. Now, if you'd be gracious enough to permit my wife and myself to pass, Fitzhugh, perhaps I can get us underway."

Floyt yanked Alacrity aside with his good arm, sparing his rib. Redlock exited into the flagship, an amused Dorraine on his arm. Several high-ranking Celestials entered to welcome their subordinates who'd been on the raid. The bandswomen-Celestials were very proper and proud.

A ship's steward showed up in the wake of the brass and braid. "Pardon me, sirs, but are you the two who'll be needing temporary billeting? Food and bath and so forth?"

"We'll come quietly, officer," Alacrity pledged gravely.

On their previous voyage in the *Ransom*, the immense Easter ornament of a ship made the intrasystem trip from Palladium to Epiphany in less than three hours. On this voyage, though, there was more time. Departure was delayed until the flagship's role in ground operations was ended and her forces back inboard.

Alacrity and Floyt were shown to a stateroom equivalent to a first-class suite in a five-star hotel. The steward unloaded their baggage from the passageway tram, acquainted them with the appointments, and left.

Floyt began digging through his toilet kit. Alacrity stepped over his warbag, bound straight for one of the two big, soft, turned-down, ground-style beds. He paused only to undo the double buckle and shoulder strap of the Sam Browne.

Flopping on the bed, dirty boots and all, he groaned ecstatically, dropping the gunbelt with a heavy thud. "*Chinga*, I forgot how heavy that thing is to lug around. Possible hernia. Don't let me sleep through Judgment Day."

"At least take off those bog flatteners." Floyt removed the Webley from his Inheritor's belt and gazed at it. It smelled strongly of propellant and he could still feel the impact it had made on his ears. An hour ago, or so, he'd been in Yumi's arms.

He was aching with fatigue too, but strangely depersonalized, waiting to feel some emotional reaction. He doubted he could shut his eyes. He shook off the memory of the man he'd had to shoot. Concentrating on the smell of jasmine, he headed for the luxuriously appointed head.

Floyt tried to mark the distance in space and time and internal changes since his first lift-off, in the Luna shuttle *Mindframe*, from Nazca spaceport to the Moon.

Novel plumbing no longer intimidates me, for one, he thought, looking around. He began hunting for instructions and experimenting carefully. He was soon lazing in a hot, foaming bath with concert-hall water jets. He had the scent system add the fragrance of jasmine to the air, then angrily commanded it to stop and change to attar of roses, a scent favored by Balensa, his estranged wife.

Floyt finally emerged clean in pore and follicle, crevice and tooth and nail. *If not in thought*, he sighed to himself.

Alacrity was sitting on a portable examining table that hovered several centimeters over the wood-plank deck, being attended by Colonel Chase, the surgeon, plus quite a number of fetching distaff medical techs. Floyt guessed that someone— Dorraine?— had passed word that there was one good way to get Alacrity's uncompromising cooperation.

"Intensive care?" Floyt asked mildly.

Alacrity grinned. "We can't pass up a chance like this. The good doctor says he'll update our immunities, *free of charge!*"

"You don't find deals like that much anymore," Floyt admitted. *Particularly if you're an Earther*. He had no idea how good or comprehensive the immunization treatments given him by Earthservice had been; that sort of thing was seldom called for on Terra.

One of the techs eyed him calculatingly. "We do noses, sir." It sounded flirtatious.

Several hours later the two rode a tram to an interview with Redlock and Dorraine.

Floyt had accepted repair work on his nose and, once the surgeon had promised that they'd cause no aftereffects, immunizations.

Colonel Chase had also called in a colleague, a specialist named Captain Twain, a very handsome middle-age woman who eclipsed the female techs in her own subtle way. Twain brought a dental unit with her and, in an astoundingly short time, initiated the growth of teeth to replace the ones Alacrity had knuckled loose. She also fit Floyt with a temporary retainer to keep the space open and the surrounding teeth in place until the new ones came in.

Alacrity settled for the immunization updating and another check of his rib. It was doing fine. He cleaned up while the team was seeing to Floyt. Then the two companions tried to doze, but in spite of all they'd been through—"Because of it," Floyt grumped—they hadn't managed to sleep.

Eventually the steward reappeared. Wearing the last clean clothing they had, they trailed the man to a large hatch. He handed each of them a voluminous blue-red fur greatcoat, saying, "His Excellency and Her Majesty are waiting for you in the winter garden."

They already knew *King's Ransom* was filled with surprises. "But, 'winter garden'?" Alacrity pondered. The steward worked the hatch and stepped aside.

They entered an antechamber paneled in some highly polished wood that looked like pink maple. The hatch closed behind them, leaving them alone. After a few moments— they'd both begun sweating again—the other side of the foyer swung away.

Neither of them could do anything but bug-eye and laugh with delight. They were in one of the environmental domes that blistered the *Ransom*'s hull, jewels of the Fabergé egg. This one looked to be about sixty meters across, but it was difficult to tell, because the center was occupied by a little hill crowned by an octagonal gazebo. Foliage and landscape features hid the dome's base.

Besides, the snow was falling rather heavily.

"Please join us," a voice called. Dorraine and Redlock were sitting together in the gazebo, watching white flakes lazily drifting down.

"It's so *quiet* here," Floyt said softly. He could just about hear the infinitesimal hiss of snow.

"Everybody knows I have been here and there," Alacrity breathed, "but this is just the cat's posterior!"

Pulling the greatcoats tighter, they picked their way up the hill, their breath fogging in the cold air. The snow was ankle deep but they both had boots on. Their footsteps and breathing sounded unnaturally loud.

Floyt couldn't make out what mechanism produced the snow; though stars were visible out the sides of the unclouded dome, overhead was only blackness. The lighting that softly illuminated the gazebo, the hill, and the rest of the place was so subtly arranged that Floyt and Alacrity couldn't see any of its sources.

And what was falling was genuine snow, big fuzzy crystals of it, not simply sleet or frozen chemicals. Alacrity caught a few flakes on his tongue; they tasted wonderful.

The landscape was winter-stark. There were a few green perennials that neither of them recognized; the rest of the foliage was bare bushes and trees layered with white. There were rocks and even a stump, and what looked to Alacrity like a low stone prayer wall carved in the style found on Llahsa.

The gazebo was draped with withered vines and ivy. It was open to the air, its sides low dividers of white latticework. The roof was low-peaked, covered with several centimeters' accumulation of snowfall. Wooden benches lined the walls, the only furnishings in the place.

The governor and the queen sat close together under a thick fur coverlet the color of their winter garden. Dorraine was all in white as well: stole, cossack hat, and a muff big enough, it occurred to Alacrity in passing, to hold those cute derringers plus a few landmines for luck.

Her husband's greatcoat was a deep, silver-gray; he was bareheaded. He was more at peace than they'd ever seen him.

"Don't ever sell this place, folks," Alacrity pleaded. Dorraine and Redlock didn't seem to mind the familiarity.

"Yes, you can hear yourself think in here; that's why we like it," she said. "In some matters the previous tenant had good taste."

The previous tenant, as Alacrity and Floyt had had it explained to them, was a planetary monarch with the bad judgment to provoke the late Director Weir and his good right arm, Governor Redlock. The vessel had been called the *Versailles* in those days; Redlock claimed her as part of the terms of surrender.

"You both look much, much better," Redlock greeted them. "Won't you sit down?" He pegged a snowball out one side of the gazebo. It flattened against a denuded tree with a *pok!*

"About what happened at the harp—" Alacrity began.

"If you start asking us questions or telling us things you shouldn't, you'll only force us to take official notice," Dorraine warned. "That would ruin everything. Please, seat yourselves."

There was no lap fur for the two companions, but stray snowflakes dusted off the benches easily, and the greatcoats made sitting comfortable.

"We're running out of fingers and toes, counting up what we owe you both," Floyt said.

"Do keep your shoes on, Hobart; you've done us a few good turns too." Dorraine smiled. Alacrity and Floyt couldn't help smiling back; that was just how they felt about her.

"I don't know how those intruders outflanked us," Redlock resumed, "but—am I wrong in saying things would've gone for the worse if you two hadn't been there?"

They both shook their heads vigorously: *oh, no-no-no.*

"But we really didn't have much choice, once the spitting started," Alacrity pointed out, honesty triumphing for once.

Floyt tried to suppress his excitement, asking himself, *Could they possibly be planning to take us to Blackguard? Please, please!* He felt a little faint; it seemed too much to hope for.

"I wish we could do more for you," Redlock said evenly. "I have obligations that demand my immediate attention."

"We know how important your alliance with the Severeemish is," Floyt assured him, trying to sound sincere, quashing the impulse to plead for the loan of one piddling little starship, or money for the fare. His conditioning had him queasy, his head was throbbing, impelling him to do just that.

"My options are also limited by certain promises I've made to Grandam Tiajo," Redlock continued. "I cannot give you money. I cannot permit you passage in a Weir ship beyond this point. I cannot offer you assistance of any kind once you debark *King's Ransom*."

Alacrity scuffed his boots on the gazebo floor and looked at Floyt, who shifted uneasily and began, "We understand, really we do—"

Dorraine wore a faint grin. "*Tch!* Don't look so glum! We arranged for you to earn a little traveling money, didn't we? Bear with us, fellows, and maybe you won't have to walk all the way to Blackguard, however far that is."

Alacrity, eyes closed, had risen a bit and leaned his head back over the bench and divider, catching fleecy white hex-lattices on his face.

"I haven't been able to discover any explicit information on the place," Redlock said. "Director Weir apparently kept everything he knew about it in his head, or banked somewhere inaccessible to the rest of us. How did you plan to tackle the problem, Alacrity?"

Alacrity opened his eyes again. "Everything's happening so fast. Our only choice was to go to the spaceport and start asking. I thought maybe we'd try to locate a Forager lashup."

"Not very promising."

"No. Governor, you're looking at two guys who're open to any and all input. Fire away."

"You're trying to track down a rumor, essentially. I'd say to begin with the kind of people to whom that rumor's important. You have money to pay for information now. Why don't you begin at a Grapple?"

Floyt held his tongue, not wanting to sidetrack the conversation with "What's a Grapple?"

Alacrity's brows knit. "It's not so easy to find one of *those* either."

"Have you ever been to one?"

"A *real* Grapple? Well, no. I mean, I've been to some Turnouts, some fairly rough ones. And lived in boxtowns, Forager lashups. But still—"

There was a chime from the direction of the entrance. A tall man in a parka appeared, gawking around him in amazement. Redlock hailed him and the man started up the hill.

"You'll kindly allow me to do the talking," Redlock ordered pleasantly. He got no argument from them.

"Who's he?" Alacrity inquired softly, out of the corner of his mouth.

"Amarok, an Innuit-Esker from Quaanaaq-Thule," Dorraine said in a hushed voice.

Amarok stopped at the gazebo's entrance, studying those within. He was youngish, perhaps two years older than Alacrity. The Innuit-Eskimo descendant was also taller, a good bit over 200 centimeters. He had to bend forward to enter.

Amarok bowed low before Redlock and Dorraine. "Your Excellency; Your Majesty. This One is very grateful for your kindness to a poor traveler. One hears tales of the winter garden, but those are far short of the mark. Someone deems Himself most fortunate to see it with His own eyes."

"Does it resemble your homeworld?" Dorraine asked.

A tiny smile touched the broad face. "That's somewhat like comparing a perfect little *bansai* to the jungles of Last Ditch, Your Majesty. Still, Quaanaaq-Thule is beautiful to those who live there."

"Ah; I see."

There was a bit of silence, Redlock not yet choosing to speak, Amarok not daring to move his eyes from the august personages to scrutinize Floyt and Alacrity. It gave them a chance to look him over.

He had the flat Mongol features of his Terran forebears, dark oriental eyes, and fine, straight hair, black as the night outside the winter garden, worn in bangs low across his forehead. He had a thin down of mustache and a complexion that reminded Floyt of Yumi's.

The governor broke the silence at last. "Your trading venture goes well?"

Amarok tried to make his hesitation as short as possible,

but he gave that one a little thought. "As Your Excellency may already know, yes, Someone did quite a bit of trading. But He is afraid His profit margin will only barely cover the cost of the voyage this time out. If that."

Redlock gave him a frank look. "I'm aware of your business skills, Amarok, and that you've already made your family wealthy several times over. But your humility is praiseworthy."

Amarok showed the distress any trader feels when a government official talks knowledgably about his balance sheets.

"After all," Redlock went on, "we'd hate to have you suffer losses through your dealings with the Weir Domain."

"Hee! This One never meant to give that impression, Your Excellency! Things have been most propitious, indeed, to be sure."

"Fine, fine." The governor nodded slowly. "I would certainly wish to know if there was anything we could do to help our friend Amarok."

"Someone is most honored and beholden for your generosity, Your Excellency."

Redlock waited expectantly. Amarok was too good a trader to miss the point.

"And of course, presumptuous as it may be for This One to say this to the lord of nine stellar systems, if there is anything, any favor that lies within Someone's modest powers—any way in which He might show gratitude and His boundless admiration for Governor Redlock and the Weir Domain—"

"Now, that's a very decent thing for you to say, Amarok; how kind!" The governor seemed to consider the concept for the first time.

"And since you raise the point, there's something—oh, but it would be too great an imposition . . ."

Amarok grew distressed. "Please don't give that any thought! It is Someone's honor and His delight! How many times One has wished to make known His esteem for Your Excellency!"

"If you insist. These two here beside me are Citizen Hobart Floyt and Master Alacrity Fitzhugh. For their own reasons, they wish to attend the upcoming Grapple."

"Grapple, Governor Redlock?"

"Grapple. I thought you might advise them as to how to get there."

"*This One*, Lord? But Grapples are iniquitous gatherings. What would Someone know of them?"

"Ah, my error. I'd heard that you've been known to attend them. So I was told by Deputy Minister Nightweather—who's in charge of commerce regulations and, oh, preferential trade agreements."

"A splendid and noble man to be sure, Your Excellency. Does This One take it then that these gentlemen here wish to book passage or charter His *Pihoquiaq*?" Amarok asked without much optimism.

Redlock's response was flat. "They don't. They want to attend the Grapple and perhaps receive some guidance there. Naturally, if it is in the least inconvenient for you to suggest anything, dismiss it from your mind altogether. Deputy Minister Nightweather informs me that the trader *Munificent* of Tillman Quendal is due soon. Maybe Quendal will have a helpful thought."

Amarok took the plunge with a completely believable smile pasted across his wide face, Alacrity had to grant him that.

"Ooo! An idea occurs! This One can transport these two intimates of the Weir Domain to the Grapple in the *Pihoquiaq*, and be their advisor and guardian!"

Redlock contrived to look surprised. "That is truly a noble gesture, Amarok," Dorraine said elatedly. "We'll have to remember to mention it to Deputy Minister Nightweather."

There was a little more of the same, then Amarok begged leave to go make ready to depart. He was scheduled to get underway in a little over an hour.

Before the trader left, Alacrity managed to get in, "What kind of ship is the *Pho*—the *Phio*—"

"*Pihoquiaq*," Amarok supplied. "It means *Ever-wandering one*. That is what Someone's ancestors called the white bear on old Earth. *Pihoquiaq* is a converted monitor."

Alacrity's face fell. "Real fine. Looking forward to it."

When Amarok was gone, Redlock said, "I take it you've shipped in a monitor?"

Alacrity sighed. "Uh-huh. But don't get me wrong! We've

got a ship and a destination now; wouldn't have either, or any money, if it wasn't for you."

"Yes, and I don't quite see how we can ever hope to pay you back," Floyt put in.

"Don't mention it." Redlock waved a hand. "Belt-favors come in assorted forms, from pulling a few strings to, oh, lending a hand in a landing party, for instance."

That wasn't the first time Floyt had heard the Inheritor's belts referred to that way. "What is a belt-favor?" Perplexed, he fingered the ring of plaques around his middle.

"We wanted to make sure you understood the custom surrounding Inheritors—that they can call on one another in time of need," Dorrainc said.

"No one bothered to tell me about that," Floyt said slowly. "Thanks."

"I thought that Tiajo might neglect telling you," Redlock added. "Hang on to that belt, Citizen Floyt."

Alacrity was already running down the list of other Inheritors in his mind. They were spread all across that part of human space, and in many places beyond.

Who might be willing to do us a favor if we—Ho—needed it? Stare Skill and Kid Risk, I'll bet. And Maska, if we ever run into him again. Sir John? Seven Wars and Sortie-Wolf, for certain.

"I hate to seem abrupt," Redlock said briskly, "but you two haven't much time."

"I am bound by the same proscriptions as my husband," Dorraine announced, "but they wouldn't apply to a few going-away presents. Perhaps something to make a long voyage in a monitor more bearable?"

"Alacrity," Redlock said, "surely you can think of a few things. Speak up; don't make us drag it out of you."

"Books," Alacrity replied promptly. "Vitamins and diet supplements. Some recreational substances. Soap and air fresheners; spices, condiments, and sauces. A few games and diversions would be nice, and snacks and a supply of potables. Oh, yeah: and a hammock or sleepsling; the bunks in the cuddy are always short in those monitors—every time."

Dorraine had started laughing halfway through the shopping

list. "You really have shipped in them, haven't you? What about you, Hobart?"

Floyt was looking thoughtfully after the departed Amarok. "He comes from a cold climate, and he'll be in charge of the thermostat. Um, is there any chance of getting some warm underwear?"

CHAPTER 5

GUESTS OF THE
EVER-WANDERING ONE

"THE SECRET TO CUTTING IT AS A BREAKABOUT, HO—A *REAL* breakabout, that is, not a trained flea on a yacht or a liner— isn't resourcefulness or job proficiency. Or I.Q. or even wanderlust. Watch your head now."

"What is the secret, Alacrity?" Floyt asked, playing audience amiably. The inner hatch of the *Pihoquiaq*'s main airlock began to open.

"Putting up with shipboard life. Boredom, routine, and especially—"

The inner hatch swung away and they were looking into a passageway.

"—cramped quarters," Alacrity finished.

"Great Suffering Martyrs!" Floyt cried. He'd assumed the ship's interior would be a bit close, having seen her through a viewpane. Monitor-class vessels, named by some history buff of long ago, had been aptly tagged. *Pihoquiaq* did indeed suggest, in a streamlined, sweptback way, the cheesebox-on-a-raft federal ironclad of the American Civil War.

She wasn't very big, some forty-five meters long, if a bit beamy. Floyt had figured that all available cargo space would be used; running a starship was very, very dear but the profit to be realized equally high. But he hadn't expected that most of the living space would be usurped too.

The main passageway had become a low tunnel, its sides lined with packed storage shelving, its dropped ceiling of tranverse metal lathes holding cases and boxes, bales and crates. There was barely room to crawl and duckwalk along.

"Does this mean there won't be a Welcome-Aboard Cotillion?" Floyt wondered aloud.

Amarok showed up just then, stylus behind his ear, a readout in his right hand and another tucked in his belt.

"Welcome aboard, gentlemen. This One has shifted most of the cargo out of the cuddy." Alacrity gave a stifled groan. "So you can bunk in there. *Is all that ballast yours?*" he cried, staring at their luggage—Alacrity's warbag and attached umbrella case, Floyt's travel bag, and the parting gifts from Dorraine and Redlock, a not-excessive pile of this and that bulging in a large backpack. Amarok made it sound as if they'd lugged along an engine block collection and a wet bar.

"That's right," Alacrity answered. "Redlock said if there wasn't enough room, the—what'd he call her, Ho?—oh yeah, the *Munificent* is a roomy little tub and we could hang around Palladium until she shows up."

Redlock had said no such thing, but Amarok didn't know that. With considerable worming effort, he turned around in the narrow passageway and led them forward.

"The man's part squirrel." Floyt snorted, grabbing his stuff.

"Just be glad he's not a midget," Alacrity advised.

As they made their way aft, Floyt noticed that the ship was chilly.

If Amarok had cleared the cuddy, a tiny compartment below and abaft the round deckhouselike structure, it must formerly have been packed solid. He didn't try to enter with them, but squeezed beyond the hatch and ushered them in. It was noticeably warmer than the rest of the *Pihoquiaq*. Sure enough, the bunks were short.

Alacrity, his worst fears realized, entered first, obliged to stoop, shoving all his gear onto the upper bunk. He wedged himself in after, in a sort of modified fetal position. Floyt followed awkwardly, pushing his luggage into the lower bunk, which had less than fifty centimeters' clearance from the top. There wasn't quite enough room in the space between the bunks and the opposite bulkhead to scratch.

The trader hastened off to finish restowing cargo and make final preparations, saying they'd be leaving shortly. Floyt turned his head and met Alacrity's gaze, since turning his whole body would've been too laborious.

"Let's hear it, Ho; what d'you think?"

"I was trying to make up my mind if it would be better to wait until we're in Hawking before we mutiny and shove him out the lock."

Alacrity chortled. "He's probably thinking more or less the same thing about us. Every little widget and thingie you can cram into a ship can mean a boodle, if your luck's right. And we're taking up the equivalent space of an awful lot of widgets."

"What's our next move?"

"Stow our stuff in those lockers; that'll give us a little more breathing room. Check 'em, would you?"

But every locker was tightly packed, not with Amarok's precious cargo, but with oddments of ship's gear, spare parts, tools, repair materials, and so forth.

"Alacrity, if we hurry, we can get back out of this thing before this packrat casts off from the *King's Ransom*. We'll wait for the *Munificent*. I don't care if my conditioning kills me."

Alacrity was shaking his head. "The *Munificent* is from Illyria, in the first place. That means the ship's complement is an extended polymorphous pansexual ménage."

"So?"

"So anyone else is obliged to participate, *de rigueur*."

"But we can't live under these conditions! We'll never make it!"

"Easy, shipmate, easy. Here—" Struggling and grunting, Alacrity dug something out of the backpack. "Here's the hammock I got from Redlock. We can rig it and I'll slide in. Then we cram our stuff into the lower bunk, and you get the penthouse. I can stick my feet into the end of the bottom bunk and lay the rest of me in the hammock."

Floyt thought for a moment. "Alacrity—those recreational substances and potables Dorraine gave you—"

"Yes?"

"Did she give you plenty?"

She did. Once they'd thrashed out a compromise with the laws of mass and space as applied to the confinement of the cuddy, Alacrity brought out a container that looked like a big onyx kidney bean. He hadn't found it necessary to stick his feet into the end of the baggage bunk; rigging the hammock from the side of the hatch frame had given just enough room to sleep as long as he wasn't too active.

Just now he was sitting up, feet hanging off to either side of the squeezed-together hammock. He carefully tapped out onto his palm two tiny granules that glittered like prisms.

"Nirvanitol! Redlock and Dorraine really know how to entertain."

"Is this a good idea in the state we're in, Alacrity? How long is it since we slept? Thirty hours?"

"Something like that."

"What will that stuff do?"

"We'll feel awfully nice for a while; quiet, perfectly content to lie right here in this cocoon without moving around."

"And then?"

"Out like a light, probably. It's just as well; Amarok wouldn't mind not having us underfoot for a bit."

"Alacrity, I'm practically out right now. Why waste it?"

"You won't get any argument out of me." He carefully put the nirvanitol back in the kidney bean and reached up with his toes, the most practical way to reach the light controls. He experimented and got the illumination down to something like a low nightlight. By that time Floyt was asleep.

Floyt dozed a little fitfully. Alacrity half sat in his hammock when Amarok cut in the Breakers, activating the Hawking Effect generator. Hearing nothing amiss, Alacrity went back to sleep without even realizing he'd wakened.

Floyt came around much later, tried to edge around Alacrity in order to visit the head. Alacrity woke up in the course of the struggle. They both felt famished and were beginning the battle to collect their clothes when Amarok showed up.

He brought two trays of ship's rations straight from the warming unit, explaining that they'd have to eat in the cuddy, the passageway, or the head.

Alacrity waved a hand around the cuddy. "This just isn't going to do, Amarok, and you know that. How long before we get to our next stop? Fifty hours? A hundred?"

"More on the order of one hundred twenty."

"Merde alors! You don't expect us to sit in this coffin that whole time, do you, shipmate? Better not."

Amarok bridled. On someone his size, it was rather scary.

"This is Someone's ship. He doesn't care who got you two inboard, or how important you are; nobody tells One how to run His ship."

"Ah, but nobody *helps* you run it either, right? You've got this whole crate automated and you're a one-man crew. Well, we can bear a hand. Stand watch in the control room. Turn to in the power section. Run standard maintenance. All we want is a chance to stretch; you look like you know what that means."

The flush was leaving the Innuit's cheeks. He motioned to Floyt. "He's not a high-mover." Like "go-blood," it was another name for a career spacer, a breakabout.

"I'll keep an eye on him. But listen, there's something else: prepackaged food isn't this bad by immutable natural law. There're things that can be done with it."

Amarok's face looked like a displeased graven idol. "Men of Quaanaaq-Thule don't cook, freeloader."

"Keep your boxtop on! I didn't mean you; I mean *me!* Redlock gave us flavorings, spices, mixes—lots of stuff. You won't be sorry. I've cooked before."

Amarok's anger left him. "One has no objection to that. But stay out of Someone's way. And neither of you enters the bridge or power section unless This One is there, do you understand, Fitzhugh?"

"Aye, sir," Alacrity responded, dead on the level, without a trace of sarcasm.

When Amarok was gone, Alacrity beamed at Floyt, who still wore a sour look. Nodding toward the departed Amarok,

Alacrity said, "Don't let him get to you. He's a skipper with lots on his mind, and a real young one at that."

"How could you be so—genial?"

"It works better this way. You should start seeing things from his side. After all, you're a starship owner now."

"Don't remind me." Floyt sighed, opening the meal tray and sniffing dispiritedly at the contents. "On Earth it's bad form to show any interest in offworld things. An offworld print on your wall would make you a pariah. Do you have the slightest idea what owning a starship will mean? A child molester with the plague would be more popular. Uh, do you really think anything can make this goo taste better?"

Alacrity dug into the pack, fetching out a large plastic bottle shaped like a grinning Buddha. Its metal-foil label glowed and pulsed in primary colors, seeming to project characters into the air—EPICUREAN MYSTERY SAUCE—FINEST CONDIMENT IN THE KNOWN UNIVERSE!!!

"You could feast on compost with this stuff," Alacrity proclaimed. "Try it."

Floyt put his thumb on the bottle's trigger and tentatively sprayed a fine mist over a small section of his food.

"That's the way! Goom it over, goom it over, Ho."

Floyt tasted charily. His cheeks inflated and his eyes bulged out. "Tell them back on Earth that I went out gamely." He collapsed.

Alacrity clicked. "*Come* on!"

Floyt straightened. "No, really. No more, I beg of you; I'll tell you where my unit is located, you fiend."

Alacrity was happily strafing his tray. "*Your* problem is you haven't tasted this spew-up *without* the sauce."

Their tour of *Pihoquiaq* put Floyt in mind of a crawl through a kids' play-fort. There were only three places with no excess cargo stowed in them: the head, power section, and bridge, the last of which Alacrity, like most breakabouts, referred to as the Fuckup Factory.

Even the ship's escape capsule was packed, hardly leaving room for three bodies. Alacrity couldn't really fault that, though, since most of the stuff was food concentrates and other emergency supplies.

Amarok dogged their track for a while, but he was reassured by Alacrity's brisk, spacemanlike manner. When the Innuit was content that Alacrity knew his way around a monitor, he left the two friends to their own devices.

The bridge was located in the turretlike roundhouse. It was still a two-seat affair, despite all the automation, but nevertheless too confined for even Floyt to stand upright.

It offered a feeling of space, however; Amarok had left the forward viewports uncovered. They looked out at an infinite nullity. Floyt was never quite sure what it was he was seeing, though at times it seemed to suggest parts of the causality harp. He did know that none of those images registered on cameras or any other image-recording device.

The head, a mere stall combining several functions, was cramped for Floyt, torturous for someone the size of Alacrity or Amarok. Monitors had originally been designed for a crew of six, and nobody had been lavish with living arrangements.

The power section had been decorated with incised *angatkua*, ritual images, Quaanaaq-Thule style. There was standing room and more; even the profit-fixated Amarok didn't dare block access to various systemry and the Hawking Effect generator.

It was the first one Floyt had ever seen, a wide cylindrical metal casing standing almost as tall as himself, painted whocares green.

Alacrity took hold of one of the housing's grab irons, put his foot on a step, and hauled himself up to an imaging scope. The light from it made a faint bandit's mask across his face.

He descended again, making way for Floyt. "Want a look?"

Alacrity helped with the scope controls. Floyt had heard Alacrity refer to the "chandelier guts" of a Hawking generator. The scope's image of this one looked more to Floyt like an incandescent carousel of strung light, difficult to focus on for long.

It was hard for him to believe that this was—for humans and many of the nonhuman races, at any rate—the key to fast

superlight travel among the stars. He felt overawed and disappointed at the same time.

Floyt pulled back from the scope to look around the rather
grubby power section. "And it's just, just *here* like this? Where
anyone could tamper with it? What if somebody bungles, or
something?"

"What happens if you decide to stroll out a five-hundredth-
story window?"

"Mmm."

"Only, in this case, it happens to everybody inboard." Alacrity checked the readings on the casing's instrumentation, which
were also patched through to the Fuckup Factory.

"On a military vessel, a good one, the Hawking and its
backup—which we haven't got one of—are usually a No Lone
Zone, Deadly Force Used. In a one-man circus like *Pihoquiaq*,
things get pretty casual. Don't let it bother you though; it looks
like he takes good care of this crate."

"No, it's not that. I was just thinking; there's plenty of
headroom in here."

"Only place in the ship. So what?"

"You'll see. It's easy to tell you never spent any time in an
Earthservice urbanplex. What's next?"

While they wormed their way through the ship, visiting the
galley-booth, lifeboat station, main gun turret—which had been
hung with a *Kikituk* killing effigy—and the rest, Alacrity told
Floyt the story of the monitors.

The ships had originally been sublight vessels, no-frills
workhorses of the Spican fleet. Thousands had been built for
the First and Second Spican civil wars; more for convoy duty
during the Beguile spacelift. They'd been used for patrol purposes and, in many cases, pressed into action as ships of the
line.

Development of the Hawking Effect coincided, for Spica,
with invasion by a neighboring system. The Spicans had only
the time and resources for retrofitting with simple, mass-
produced Hawking generators and astrogational gear.

After winning the war, Spica phased out the monitors, dis-
posing of something like fifty thousand of them as war surplus.
The vessel became the Model-T of the Third Breath.

"So, you still find 'em all over the place, especially in the backwaters," Alacrity told Floyt as they hunkered along.

"But how old *is* this thing?"

"Whew, maybe a hundred, hundred and fifty. But don't lose your grip! She'll get us where we're going. Still, I'm surprised Amarok doesn't give himself a *little* more breathing room. Quaanaaq-Thule probably hasn't had a starship for long."

"It looks to me like he's poor."

"*Nobody* with a working starship is poor, Ho. It's just about impossible. You might be a little marginal if you owned a sublight scow in a poor star system, but a starship, uh-uh."

Alacrity tried to sound casual as he came around to his real point.

"In fact, if you've got your own starship, the only way you can be poor is by trying real hard."

"Alacrity . . ."

"What I'm saying is, every little gew-gaw Amarok's got stashed away in every cranny is worth a lot more, someplace, than he paid for it. He probably lives like this because he's only been in business a short time, has to pay off his backers or keep his family or tribe afloat or whatever. But at this rate it probably won't be long before he pays off the *Pihoquiaq* and starts trying to pick up another ship, especially with Redlock granting him trade concessions. That's how mercantile empires get started."

"Yes, that's all well and good, but—"

"I'm telling you, you give it another ten, twenty years and things'll be all different. More and more planets will be launching their own starships; competition will be murder. Oh, it'll always be a good life, don't get me wrong, but now is the time—"

"Alacrity, forget it."

"—when unlimited opportunities—"

"*Will you kindly slap a seal on it?* The *Astraea Imprimatur* goes straight back to Earth. Directly. No detours."

Alacrity felt a twist in his stomach and a sudden flash in his forehead, Earthservice conditioning endorsing Floyt's words in no uncertain terms. Floyt was rubbing the bridge of his nose with thumb and forefinger; his own conditioning had bedeviled him all through Alacrity's pitch.

"I'm sorry, Ho. Straight to Earth, aye. Once we find the damned thing. Um, is your conditioning going to keep you from learning about standing watch and helping run a ship? Because you might need to, once we've got the *Astraea*; I might need help."

Floyt considered that. He'd been warned by Earthservice bureaucrats that unnecessary exposure to offworld ways might mean radical reorientation and more behavioral meddling. Regardless, it wasn't fair to expect Alacrity to shoulder all the work if they had to ferry the *Astraea Imprimatur* themselves. Floyt felt no twist of negative reaction. He decided, *To hell with the injunctions* and resigned himself to Earthservice reorientation, if that's what it was to cost him. "Of course I can learn, Alacrity. How do we start?"

"First let's look over the food supply. I'll throw something together—something impressive—then we'll hit Amarok for permission to train you on the job." He paused, halfway into the galley-booth. "Can you cook, by any chance?"

"Alacrity, in an urbanplex you don't cook; you unwrap."

"Stick with me. Astrogation will take you a long way, but a really good slumgullion will make you *popular*."

They found Amarok sitting up against a unit for the manufacture of photovoltaic shingles. He was beginning a new voyage letter, having handed off his last one during his stay at Palladium to a captain bound for Quaanaaq-Thule.

The Innuit was reserved but pleased when he saw and smelled what Alacrity had done with the processed, irradiated, canned, and powdered foods from *Pihoquiaq*'s galley. As they supped on *muktuk bouillabaisse*, Floyt asked about the voyage letter.

"It is a kind of extract of the log and commentary on the trip thus far," Amarok explained. "This One keeps it up to date as much as possible, so that when He meets another skipper going in the right direction—and that person seems trustworthy—it can be dispatched. When the letter is delivered at home, This One's people will know how the voyage proceeds."

He showed Floyt the screen he'd been using to compose. The voyage letter was couched in an indecipherable jumble.

"Our trading code," Amarok clarified. "The *Pihoquiaq* really belongs to Someone's family."

"You sure don't waste much operating money on hired help," Alacrity observed. "Did you ever think of going all the way and changing over to a headboarder setup?"

Amarok shook his great head vigorously. "No; getting a cranial switchboard doesn't appeal to This One. He does all right by Himself, just the way things are. In His homeworld tongue, Amarok means 'Lone Wolf.'"

Alacrity wondered privately if the big trader would feel the same way after, say, his twentieth voyage, or his hundred and twentieth, but didn't bother saying so.

It turned out Amarok had first shipped as a boy, with his uncle, learning the breakabout's trade on commercial vessels from other planets under Quaanaaq-Thule's trade-assistance agreements. The uncle was to have captained the *Pihoquiaq*, but was badly injured in an incident on Pesthole. Amarok took up mastery of the converted monitor.

"But with all this time on your hands—" Floyt broached a subject he'd been wondering about. "I mean, don't you sometimes wish for an induction helmet?"

Amarok was shaking his head again. "No, nor cachesleep unit, nor a sensory capsule. One has to keep His wits about Him. Someone spends most of His time during Hawking cataloging purchases and writing up sales descriptions and price guides. Then there are the ship's log, maintenance to run, the trade situation at the next port of call to study, appropriate trade items to select. This One plays chess against the computer when he gets the chance, which isn't often, and has a very interesting postage stamp collection."

A thought crossed his face. "Someone doesn't suppose by any chance that either of you know any cat's cradle? Too bad. Let's see, what else? Well, there's always cargo to be restowed and checked—" Here he gave them a rueful smile. "Especially since you two came inboard."

"What about exercise?" Floyt inquired.

That took Amarok a little by surprise. "Oh, a little dynamic tension, yoga, *very* restricted calisthenics. There's no room for

Tai chi or martial arts, or for much else. Someone hopes you two weren't thinking of jogging."

Floyt grinned. "No, but I can show you something almost as good."

"Very well—within reason."

After Amarok brought his new voyage letter up to date and Floyt and Alacrity made minor adjustments to their meager living space, the three met in the power section near the Hawking generator.

"This One warns you, there'll be no nonsense with the Hawking," Amarok announced ominously. "No chinning on it or running round it or—in fact, maybe you'd just better forget whatever it was you—"

"Aw, give him a chance, Rok," Alacrity chided.

Floyt moved to the center of the maximum-headroom spot between the Hawking generator and the power-section hatch. He drew from his pocket a length of rope.

Shaking it out and taking it in both hands, he poised dramatically, then began jumping. He started slowly, not having done it in a long time.

"Yes? *And?*" Amarok said expectantly.

Alacrity intervened. "Um, Ho, is this your idea? Your *whole* idea?"

Floyt was jumping more confidently now, getting the rhythm and the feel of the rope. "Actually, I'd like to see either one of you do this for just fifteen minutes." The rope slapped the deck; Floyt skipped lightly, changing his lead foot.

"But if you can, you might give this a try."

Floyt began doing matador crosses so fast that he feared for a moment that he might get tangled up. But the skill he'd picked up as a kid came back quickly. He did some cross-jumps for them, and a few 180-degree turns. Despite the chill, he was sweating.

"Hmmm," Amarok said, reconsidering.

"I didn't know you could do that," Alacrity told him admiringly. "Let me try that."

"In a minute," Floyt answered blithely. He did a few can-can steps, some side taps, and went into double jumps. He was getting a little winded and his timing became ragged. The rope snagged on his feet.

Alacrity wanted to be next, but Amarok exercised captain's prerogative. It took a couple of seconds for him to discover it was tougher than it looked.

"On Quaanaaq-Thule the children sometimes do this in big groups, with long ropes, several at a time. Someone never heard of doing it solo in a starship for exercise."

He tried again, catching himself in the shins on the second jump.

"C'mon, Rok; give somebody else a turn."

"Be patient, be patient." Amarok panted, trying not to fall over as he tangled his legs again.

"'S that a joke, or what? You'll never get it."

"Would you care to make a wager, Master Fitzhugh?"

"Sure. You make fifteen jumps without a miss and I pass on my next two turns."

Amarok considered. "And if This One loses?"

Alacrity thought it over. "You lose, you have to start using first-person singular pronouns."

Jumping rope in the power section and Alacrity's cooking, what he called the "bombs away" school of cuisine—livened by things like Red Shift Chili Peppers and Core Explosion Hotsauce—became fixtures of the voyage.

Alacrity and Amarok picked up jump rope skills quickly, coming to appreciate what Floyt had said about fifteen minutes' solid jumping. Amarok fitted the rope with revolving handles, built to Floyt's description of the ones used on Earth.

In the meantime, Floyt learned about running a monitor. He received instruction from both Alacrity and Amarok, who warmed to his passengers as he got to know them.

But one thing on which the trader was adamant was the temperature at which he kept most of the *Pihoquiaq*. He maintained that the dry chill was good for the cargo and ship's systems and beneficial to health. Alacrity disagreed, but not in their host's presence. Though the minuscule cuddy was warm, the rest of the ship was uncomfortable to the two friends if they weren't exercising or warmly dressed.

And so they dug out shawls that Dorraine had pressed on them, fringed ceremonial garments from Dunrovin', of rich twill-weave and patterned in eye-grabbing colors with stylized DNA chains and fractal diagrams. A shawl was much more convenient than a jacket or sweater, Floyt discovered; very comfortable, especially when standing watch—in an acceleration chair—in the coolness of the bridge. It was, like Alacrity's umbrella and the big bandannas he wore, more practical than it first appeared to Floyt.

The Terran became proficient as watch-stander, in that he knew in general what the indicators meant and when they said something was wrong. As an information accessor from the Earthservice bureaucracy, he showed skill at pinpointing something Amarok or Alacrity wanted to know. He absorbed just enough to be able to guess at how very much more there was to know.

"Alacrity, is there really any reason for me to stand watch? Or you either? Other than as backup in case all the automatics fail?"

"Affirmative; Rok's entering your time in the ship's log, Ho. That and the help you give during maintenance and repair work."

"And so I've learned which dial to watch and which tool to hand you two. But what of it?"

They were in the cuddy, relaxed as much as room allowed. Strangely enough, it was beginning to feel like home. Floyt's fingertips were a bit shriveled; it had been his turn to do their laundry, which involved stripping down and tackling it in the head stall.

Alacrity had pulled out the onyx kidney bean again. Most of the maintenance and repair work was caught up, and Amarok wanted to take watch for the next ten hours or so to double check everything personally.

Alacrity wasn't exactly ecstatic over the labyrinth of automated equipment Amarok had installed in order to crew *Pihoquiaq* alone. But having satisfied himself that it seemed to be working, he had made his peace with it. So, to stave off what he referred to as "an imminent attack of bulkhead fever," Alacrity convinced Floyt to join him in a time-honored breakabout tradition known as the Eight Hour Vacation.

Now he tapped out two shimmering granules of nirvanitol, rolling them in his palm.

"Look, m'friend, we'll get a certified abstract from the log, proving you've put in time in crewmember capacity. After all, you *do* know your way around; in a monitor, anyway. We still might have to deadhead or work for passage before we're through; this would count in your favor."

"But what do I really know? Which dial to oggle, is what."

Alacrity shook his head. "Will you please get a good attitude? You proved you can get along in confined space, cooperate, take orders, leave the bridge before you break wind—"

"I see; a passing grade in deportment."

"If you like, yes. Listen, nobody's saying you're a certified crewman yet, but you already know more about starships than most people in the galaxy are ever going to learn in their life. Here."

He gave Floyt one of the granules and popped the other. Floyt let his dissolve slowly on the end of his tongue. It tasted sweet and sharp. "How soon will I feel something?"

"A minute or two. Look, Ho: if you don't want to play breakabout, you sure don't have to. I know it could make things tougher when we get back to Terra. But it might come in handy for a variety of reasons. It sure as Shiva looks like we're not going to be able to hire a crew."

"In fact, we haven't really talked about this at all. Even if *Astraea Imprimatur* is spaceworthy, mightn't it cost a great deal to get her home?" Floyt asked.

"Home" suddenly summoned up a recollection of the unique blue-and-white ball of Earth as he'd last seen her; it set off an unlooked-for longing and homesickness in him, an attack such as he hadn't had since his trip out, in the *Bruja*. It wasn't so much distress as a poignant and almost infinite yearning, ill-defined, all-consuming. Then he realized he could feel the steady, dependable beat of the blood in his veins and a connectedness between who he was, the things that had happened to him, and what he must do—and the greater universe around him.

Alacrity was chuckling. "Cost? We don't know if there's money owed for docking fees or defaults, or if she's been impounded—and there's no point worrying about that now. We'll just have to deal with what we find when we get to Blackguard, but..."

"But?"

"But two breakabouts would improve our chances over a breakabout and a groundling—no offense."

"None taken. All right; what's next?"

"Well, I was thinking we could check out the airlock and at least teach you how to get into a suit. Then maybe run through escape capsule procedures."

Alacrity was sprawled in the hammock belly down, like a large, sedated cat.

"Very well." Floyt looked around the cuddy, feeling a calm, quiet sense of energy and inner reserve, and of tranquility. "Alacrity, did they move the bulkheads back, or, um..."

"Classic nirvanitol reaction. All that elbowroom is a nice feeling, isn't it?"

"It is indeed; it is indeed." And the harsh cuddy lighting seemed more benign too. The gnawing of the Earthservice conditioning that was usually at the back of Floyt's awareness like a trickle-current was now distant and dim. He could recall all the details of his problems; he'd simply relaxed before the fact that there was nothing more he could do about them right then and there.

Alacrity reached under his hammock and came up with a square, blue glass bottle. The cap unscrewed and popped off when he set his thumb against it. He took a very small sip and passed it to Floyt.

Floyt had just reminded himself that even if by some miracle everything was to work out and they got *Astraea Imprimatur* back to Earth, were deprogrammed, and Floyt avoided radical reorientation, some new set of troubles would arise and run its course in one fashion or another. He knew that wasn't particularly sage, but made a mental note not to worry so much.

"Sufficient to the parsec the evil thereof." He sighed, accepting the bottle. It felt cold.

"Inshallah!" Alacrity seconded, hands behind his head now, staring up at the overhead.

"Inshallah!" echoed Floyt, good old Earther word. He took a sip and found that the stuff was heavy, almost sludge, but warming and fragrant. He took a second sip, barely a wetting of the lips, and passed it back.

"Alacrity, all this Precursor business—it's just a variation on everything from Delphi to Jung—trying to get in touch with something that'll answer all questions."

"I guess that's fair enough. So what?"

"So what happened to you up there on the gantry at the causality harp?"

Alacrity gazed at him. "You still have to go through reorientation. If I tell you, it'd be like telling Earthservice, wouldn't it?"

"I hadn't thought about that. You'd better forget I asked." A little time passed. "This is very pleasant, but it isn't Nirvana the way I heard it described."

"Increasing the dosage increases the effect. Believe me, if you want to see the White Light, you can do it right here."

"Not necessary; this is fine. Besides, duty might call. Can we *function* on this stuff?"

"Well, I wouldn't want to do any neurosurgery right now."

"What happens if we get hit by a meteorite right now and the space pirates attack?"

"We give them a few granules and a drink and they help us patch the leak."

"Seriously."

"Crisis management isn't too hard; a load of adrenaline makes this stuff go away pretty fast. If you really needed it, I suppose you could take a quarter dose of Engine or something.

Floyt lay fiddling with his proteus. "Just asking. So, it's spacesuits next, eh? D'you want to know the unifying element of everything that's happened to us since we lifted out of Nazca spaceport? The flights and murder attempts and ceremonies and airbikes and all the rest?"

Alacrity brought out a little sound unit Redlock had given them. He picked something roomy, Bledsoe's *Forever Endeavor, Amen,* a piece inspired by Precursor artifacts.

"Yeah, tell me," Alacrity said, securing the unit to a wall clip.

Easing himself out full length, Floyt had found, brought the soles of his feet flat against the end of the bunk. He did so now. "It's that I haven't learned one damn thing that will help me make Earthservice Functionary Second Class."

"Which in turn tells you what?"

"Adventures and career goals seldom mix."

CHAPTER 6

HIRELINGS

ALACRITY AND FLOYT ESTABLISHED A BUSY, ABSORBING rhythm of shipboard life so quickly and thoroughly that it came as a surprise when, early one watch, Amarok showed up to say that they would soon make planetfall.

They both blinked as if awakening, having immersed themselves in details of life-support systems, basic combat procedures, the monitor's astrogational apparatus, waste disposal drill for the model V-B Clarion EVA suit, and who could do more matador crosses without lassoing his own ankles.

They'd also spent a lot of time resting up and mending. Alacrity's side felt fine, Floyt's nose had only a slight ridge to show where it had been broken, and the Earther's teeth were coming in with amazing speed. They'd also further researched the various substances they'd brought along with them—synaptiflake, neurobomb, metajolt, hypnozap—but found that sleep and work often seemed preferable. Alacrity said it was possible to spend most or all of a voyage in an altered state, but unwise. The unexpected had a lethal way of cropping up.

"Besides," he'd said, "prolonged *anything* takes its toll."

Then too, there was Carbon Dioxide College, a breakabout euphemism for marathon bull sessions. Of course, the bigger the crew, the broader the curriculum, and there were only two of them sharing the cuddy—though Amarok sometimes joined in. A certain amount of mutual aversion had kept the two from talking much on the voyage from Luna to the Halidome system, and they were still catching up.

Alacrity talked about his first encounter with the Foragers and about the time he'd shipped in a freighter where everyone inboard came down with a form of superjardia. Floyt reminisced about growing up in the Terran urbanplexes and recounted chapters from the planet's history.

Then, almost before they knew it, Amarok was standing before them in a loose-fitting groundsuit, announcing that they were about to make planetfall on Way 'Long, a dry, temperate place as comfortable to *Homo sapiens* as it was to its inhabitants. The natives' name for the place was immune to pronunciation. The locals called themselves the Croi.

It was an old, complacent planet ellipsing an aged main-sequence star. Way 'Long—or at least that part of it near the spacefield—smelled a little like the inside of an old sock, but aside from that it was actually quite pleasant. Even airlessness and volcanic upheavals would've been welcome after the confinement of the cuddy.

The Croi were reasonably peaceful, complacent and pre-technological. Blessed with a benign ecosystem, they'd taken a slow, unhurried climb toward sentience.

Their spacefield wasn't very impressive: a few bunkers containing sealed automatics—guidance and commo systems, mostly—fronting about two hectares of glue-fused soil. Their nearby village put Floyt in mind of a jumble of terra-cotta acorns. The Croi were gregarious creatures but not prolific; their small communities were scattered widely across Way 'Long.

Alacrity and Floyt were looking around, blinking at the local star, enjoying the opportunity to stretch and do little loosening-up moves. Floyt had originally chafed at the news that there would be a brief detour en route to the Grapple, but right then the idea seemed brilliant.

Amarok had set down to trade data, technical instruments and tools, and an array of seeds, cuttings, and plants. In return, he was to receive some novaseeds, extraordinary gemstones that accumulated in the gut of a creature native to Way 'Long's wastelands.

The trading had taken place so straightforwardly, been so devoid of red tape and formality, that Floyt, who'd grown up under Earthservice, was scandalized. The Croi expected Amarok's arrival and had his payment waiting. Offloading the appropriate cargo took only a few minutes, no bureaucracy involved.

("No quarantine either," Alacrity had pointed out in an aside to Floyt. "The Croi are safe for now; Rok's the careful type. But that'll have to change. I hope somebody tells 'em.")

"Where is everybody else, Rok?" Alacrity said, looking around. "What is this, election day?" Spaceship landings were very rare occurrences there; he couldn't believe the natives were so blasé.

The *Pihoquiaq*'s skipper had been talking to the little gaggle of locals who'd come out to treat with him. "It seems we've been upstaged by a funeral, Alacrity. A very important states-being has gone on to glory, so to say."

"What's it about us, Ho, that we're so good at coming across big-time funerals?"

Floyt shrugged, scrutinizing the Croi, loose-limbed creatures who stood three and four meters or more, all reedy limbs and angular sensory appendages, meeting in leathery hassock torsos. Their fantastic coloring ran the spectrum, combined in swirls and zebra patterns, dots and mottling. Their hides gleamed as if powerbuffed.

The Croi had no central organ display that could rightly be called a face, and their various extremities were in almost constant, if leisurely, movement. It made talking to them a bit like a conversation with a very large floral arrangement.

"So the ceremony is that important to them, Rok?" Floyt asked. He was fascinated despite the fact that he'd kept a cautious distance from the creatures, a very few of whom spoke a measured, surprisingly good Terranglish, though they were given to redundancy.

That probably makes sense, he thought. *Certainly their limbs and other appendages seem to provide for redundancy-in-depth.*

Amarok nodded. "That's the way Someone understands it. Death is the culmination of life; an individual is judged by his or her or its funeral, and the Croi spend a good deal of thought and time arranging for their own. They even hire mourners, as a matter of prestige."

"Professional mourners, like the old-time Chinese," Floyt said.

"One supposes. The final rite, locally, consists of taking the remains of the departed to that cliff up there and casting them into the sea." He pointed to a summit above the spacefield.

"Right now they're getting ready to heave some august old chappy after eight solid days of memorial drinking, testimonial orgies, inheritance soirées, and commemorative gluttony."

"Not too different from Frostpile." Alacrity pondered. "Can we go look? Just for a few minutes? I know we're short of time and all, but—"

"This One isn't sure that would be such a good idea. These are very amiable beings, but still, we haven't been invited."

Alacrity *tch*ed. Floyt, to his own surprise, found himself disappointed as well. Way 'Long was only the second XT world he'd ever been on, not counting the sealed environment of Luna. Even his terran aversion to nonhumans didn't make it any easier to pass up on a chance to get some exercise. And he was, though he tried to minimize it to himself, curious.

Alacrity and Floyt had done what looking around they could from the immediate vicinity of the ship, using Amarok's electroimager. It only whetted their curiosity and reminded them that the confinement of the cuddy was right behind them.

"Best we were going," Amarok decided.

"Hey, hang on a minute; what's that?" Alacrity asked, squinting.

A local was approaching across the field, having just come up from town. The Croi moved with a speed they hadn't seen from the creatures before.

"Trouble?" Floyt wondered at once, missing the feel of the Webley against his midsection. There'd been an unfortunate incident earlier on in human-Croi contact, entirely the fault of *Homo sapiens*. As a result, these peaceful giants forbade their visitors any weapons.

"This One doesn't think so," Amarok said slowly.

The Croi drew to a stop before them, fluttering and swaying. It was one of the largest they'd seen, with more appendages and a thicker growth of sense nodules and substructures than most.

"People-persons of the human race species!" the thing began eagerly in the register of a bass fiddle being bowed. "How pleasantly fun it is that you didn't exit into departure prior to the start of my arrival!"

"Interpreter!" Alacrity yelled playfully over his shoulder to a nonexistent diplomatic corps. Croi sensory apparatus tilted and swiveled toward him, and Floyt gave him a disapproving frown.

"I have the identity of being Caut'Karr," the thing resumed to Amarok. "I am very nice to meet your acquaintance."

"And what can This One do for you, Caut'Karr?"

"Well, we are about to funeralize the last rites of our bereaving leader, the High Meddler, with the solemnly dolesome flinging-forth of his extinct corpse," the Croi explained. "Such observances are about to begin on the dot of now."

"Yes, we'd heard. Our deepest sympathies are with you."

"Too bad you missed the sadly forlorn gorge-cramming of the epigastria-cavity stomachs. It was an admirably fed meal.

"At anyhow, the reason I have come is to ask you if you'll do us the overpowering thrill of walking the last final steps in the funeral cortege procession. Status rank is evaluated on the basis of mourners: their number, prestige, and hysterical unreservedness."

"See, now," Amarok began, not wishing to offend a customer, "it deeply grieves Someone to tell you this, but there are pressing demands on our time and—"

"Compensatory money payments would of course be of generous largesse, in keeping with our customs," Caut'Karr interjected anxiously.

"Money?" Alacrity jumped in.

"Affirmatively yes! Your presence would be so gratefully appreciated!" gushed the Croi. "To have the first offworld aliens in a funeral train—think of it!"

They did.

"Paid mourners, hmm?" Amarok said, rubbing the skin of his throat thoughtfully. "May Someone ask the amount of the, um, compensatory money payments?"

"As to that, for this great innovative modernism, our Botherers of the Privy have agreed that honor demands the sum of novaseeds be not less than one amber Perfect and four azure Primes per each apiece.

"Of course, common sense demands that it be no more," he added.

"Per each apiece *what*?" Floyt inquired.

"Per every inconsolably sad human mourner, per capita all," Caut'Karr clarified.

Alacrity worked it out in his head. An amber Perfect and four azure Primes was a tidy sum—several thousand ovals, or nearly a thousand ducats, depending on current prices.

Amarok turned to the two companions. "What about it? Would you two boys like to earn a little pocket money?"

"For a few minutes' work?" Alacrity said slyly, glancing to Floyt.

Floyt's conditioning was giving him only a mild tussle, in view of the need for money with which to carry out his mission.

"Do we caper, or roll in the gutter, or what're we supposed to do?" Floyt asked laconically.

"Isn't there a custom of lachrymose weeping and wailing?" Caut'Karr asked anxiously. "A completely bizarre bodily function like that should serve with altogether nicely admirability. Er, just what does it look like in any chance?"

The funeral procession was a long one, the three were told, even for the teeming megalopolis of the spacefield, which comprised some thousand or so Croi.

It came out of town a few minutes behind Caut'Karr. Musicians were playing, with a sound like kilometers of catgut being drawn through assorted holes. Croi lamentations reminded Alacrity of the noises he'd once heard in a warship's SIGINT section.

Hundreds of the creatures approached in a sloppily organized column. At the front was a large Croi borne along on a platform.

After a few moments the humans figured out that it wasn't some leader striking a noble pose, or a statue, but the late High Meddler himself, propped up by inobtrusive supports and gleaming with what looked like a generous application of shellac.

Gathered around him on his platform were flowers and food and drink, works of art, and memorabilia. Caut'Karr explained that the swag would all be recycled to heirs and mourners after the ceremony, making everything that much merrier.

Directly around the departed were his heirs and various Very Important Croi. After them came family, then close friends of same, then employees, associates, *their* friends and relations, and other amateurs.

Behind these came the pros.

It was the biggest funeral bash in memory, so Caut'Karr claimed, and the only unfortunate aspect was that virtually the entire town was involved, leaving very few spectators.

The professional mourners were receiving a pittance compared to the humans, but they put on a show that was beyond reproach.

They ululated like banshees and swayed like willows in the wind. They flayed themselves and one another with their various extremities, and whipped the ground. They twirled and flung debris in the air. Many appeared to have damaged themselves; as the human's watched, one Croi broke off a whiplike limb against a stone.

"Going a bit far, isn't it, Rok?" Floyt said.

"He or she or it will regenerate in no time," Amarok answered. "The Croi are good at that. And if they're really short of something, other appendages change specialties to fill in."

"This could be a tough act to follow," Floyt said dubiously.

"Are you kidding, Ho? Just do what I do; we'll have 'em fainting in the back rows." For the excursion, Alacrity had strapped on a chest-pack and stuffed into it three cold bottles of champagne from Haj. As the strange procession drew near, on its way up the mountain, he popped the cork on one and took a deep chug, foam squirting out of his mouth around the bottle.

Caut'Karr swung in Alacrity's direction an optical organ like a sundial. "And what is the identifying name of this act, will you please?" the Croi inquired.

"Ancient time-honored human customary habit," Alacrity responded, champagne running down his chin. "We'd offer you some, Caut'Karr, but—biochemistry, y'know . . ."

"Tradition?" The Croi marveled. "A traditional habitude? Oh, well; that's more than all right, then! But, ah, would your repertoire include anything perhaps by any chance a maybe-bit trifling smidgeon more *demonstrative*?"

"Like what? Name it."

"Well . . . we of the Croi-type sort of person are most preoccupied with your customary practice of the elegy. This *poetry* stuff is quite beautifully attractive, though for some obscurely hidden reason it seems to be apparently difficult for us to formulate things like rhyme and scansion."

"Yeah?" Alacrity took another sip. "You bet; we'll do what we can!"

"How very excellently fine! Now, if you'll just accompany me into coming along . . ."

He led the way toward the front of the procession. The other Croi were paying them a lot of attention by then.

Amarok warned Alacrity and Floyt *sotto voce*, "Now, this may be a lark to you, but these creatures are good customers and Someone doesn't want to see them offended or short-changed. Fair is fair."

"Hey!" Alacrity protested as Floyt took a cautious sip of the champagne. "We never stiffed anybody yet, Rok! But if you don't trust us, just say the word and we'll stay behind."

For the first time since they'd met him, Amarok laughed. "That's what This One thought, but He just wanted to be sure." He pulled forth an engraved Perkup inhaler, taking a deep breath from it.

They fell in with Caut'Karr at the very head of the procession. The carryings-on of the mourners, especially the career types, redoubled. Amarok took a pull on the champagne while passing the Perkup to Floyt.

"Everybody ready?" Alacrity sang.

Caut'Karr gave a long sonority then and, in a polite translation for the humans, wailed, "Ah! For the love of goodness! The High Meddler leaves into his good-bye! The delight of our organs of visions was he! The song-tune of our auditory senses!"

"This'll be a cinch," Alacrity muttered to Floyt.

Caut'Karr angled expectant receptive organs in the humans' direction.

The High Meddler has left us! Amarok roared up at the sky, out of nowhere, causing Caut'Karr to withdraw his extremities to a safer distance, and making even Alacrity and Floyt jump a little in startlement.

"He's gone!" Amarok shrilled, taking another long pull on the bottle. He flung his arms wide. "Gone! Gone! Ahhhh—" He pressed the back of his free hand against his forehead, desolate.

"Jeepers! How engagingly marvelous!" Caut'Karr brightened, ruffling his extremities in display behavior like a shiver, and all four of them felt a lot better.

"Why did he have to leave us? Oh, why?" Floyt keened, having taken some champagne and a wheeze or two on the Perkup. "Our beloved, irreplaceable High Meddler; our dear, dear, de-ee-ee, hee, he, he, he . . ." And he broke down into shuddering sobs.

That of course left nothing for Alacrity but to stagger around tearing at his hair, frightening a few Croi and screeching, as the cortege wended its way up the hill. The locals were awed and not a little unnerved by the humans' performance.

The High Meddler's glorious coat of shellac and his noble pose threw back the rays of the late afternoon sun bravely. Morale was very high.

As they ascended a series of sharp switchbacks toward the heights, Amarok, Alacrity, and Floyt, taking turns sipping and inhaling, entered into an unspoken contest to see who could give the most dramatic demonstration of his grief. They worked their way through the first bottle and got deep into the second, improvising.

Amarok rubbed dirt on his face. Alacrity and Floyt fell, bawling, into each other's arms. Floyt rolled in the dust of the road and was nearly trampled by a ponderous Croi female lost in her own grief. Alacrity beat his chest and ripped open his shirt. The three had been cooped up in *Pihoquiaq* for a long time, and it was beginning to tell.

At a bend in the road Amarok, declaring that he simply couldn't bear it one moment more, made ready to hurl himself off the precipice. The other two had to wrestle and drag the giant back from the edge, an impressive struggle if there'd ever been one. The locals were delighted beyond words. Their own mourning showed it as they spiritedly kept up their end of things, swaying and whooping, flaying the air and the ground and themselves and one another.

Alacrity suspected that he and his companions were writing a new page in Croi history. He ripped off the shreds of his shirt and, well aware of how many new ones he could buy with an amber Perfect and four azure Primes, cast the rags off one end of a switchback.

Floyt, not to be outdone, shrugged off his blouse and tore off the legs of his pants and discarded them in like wise. Amarok opened his groundsuit and, stepping forth unsteadily, flipped it into space.

At the top of their form now, Croi were mourning with wild enthusiasm, worked into a frenzy by the dedicated antics of the humans, not understanding but ecstatically appreciative. Floyt and Alacrity threw the last of their garments away, emulating Amarok. With nothing on but their shoes—and Alacrity's empty chest-pack—they marched on, howling and sporting and imbibing.

"You are being most Croi!" Caut'Karr proclaimed in a palsy of delight. "You've made our sadness so *giddy*!"

The entire strange caravan drew to a halt on the open flatland near the edge of the cliff. Reddish water surged against the gray and green rocks far below, whipping up a pink froth.

It was plainly a ceremonial place; all around were huge sculptured boulders that looked like they'd been carved by the wind, each covered with symbols and insignia.

The High Meddler was set down and the Croi gathered around. They made a space there near the edge of the cliff, so the humans could be in the center of things.

The three were tired, dirty, and sweaty, but altogether pleased with what they'd done and how happy they'd helped make the Croi.

Caut'Karr signaled for silence and, when he had it, made a brief speech in his own language that seemed to meet with the unanimous approval of the Croi.

He translated politely for the offworlders.

"I have said that this is a day to go down into the anus of history!"

"Annals?" Floyt suggested delicately.

"Affirmatively just-so! The High Meddler has received the most glorious funeral procession column ever held! All of those of us who are here share in the exalting honor!

"Now, as a last tribute to our beloved leader, we will all render the ritualistic sacrifice!"

So saying, Caut'Karr took the end of one reedy extremity in a manipulative tendril and, giving it a mighty yank, pulled it loose. It seemed to cause him no pain or distress.

Of course! Alacrity realized. *He'll just regenerate a new one. It's all right, then.*

Caut'Karr held the sacrifice aloft, waving it at the bold figure of the High Meddler. He said something in Croi, then reiterated it in Terranglish.

"This tribute I send before thee, as proof of my reverance and devotion!"

With that, he tossed the appendage far out off the cliff. The other Croi set up a wierd caterwauling and, as the three humans watched, dumbfounded, began plucking extremities of their own in an outlandish harvest of devotional tokens, showering them into the pink surf.

The three humans expected to see the departed follow his offerings over the side, but instead an expectant quiet settled over the Croi. All attention seemed to center on Amarok, Floyt, and Alacrity.

"Well?" prompted Caut'Karr after a few moments' silence.

"Well what?" Alacrity shot back.

"We are tarryingly waiting. The ceremony is nearly terminated to completion, and we're all famished for the post-obsequies ingestion competition races. If you three would be so goodly compliant as to finish and have done with your tributes, we'll just give the noble dead cadaver, here, a jolly old tilt into the briny oceanic sea and be off on our path of route."

"Tributes?" Floyt repeated, with an abrupt feeling of apprehension.

"Well of course naturally, tributes," Caut'Karr rapped with a trace of impatience. He mimed the ripping off of another of his extremities. *"Tributes."*

"Scheisse-mensch!" Alacrity proclaimed softly. "Y-you mean to say you expect us to—"

"Ah, look here now," Amarok interrupted smoothly. "That's just not the sort of thing our species *does*, don't you see, Caut'Karr. We're different from you Croi."

The rest of the Croi were pressing around, chittering and tweeting agitatedly at Caut'Karr and the humans. Some few who understood a little Terranglish were trying to translate.

"You mean to intend to say," Caut'Karr said balefully, "that you three negatively refuse to render this basic respect? A minor act like plucking off one lousy limb? You do commit upon ourselfs this intolerable provocational insult?"

The other Croi, hearing that in translation, set up a sound like untuned guitars being rubbed together.

"It's not that exactly," Alacrity was quick to protest. "For you, it's nothing to do something like that. But it's a lot more drastic for—"

He broke off as several Croi in the crowd lost their tempers over the humans' pettiness in welching on fundamental good manners like self-mutilation. Outraged, two of them charged at Alacrity, while Floyt yelled, "Wait! *You don't understand!*"

Which was pretty much the phrase Alacrity had once submitted in a contest for the slogan of the Organization for Interspecies Understanding. It did no more good than it had during the contest.

The trio of humans was standing near one of the giant stones, at the very edge of the cliff, with Croi dozens deep to every side and the precipice at their backs. Alacrity ducked one of the creatures, but the second began looping and angling various appendages about him. Scared for his life, he somehow got in close to the small hassock torso.

The Croi were tall and fairly strong, but not as heavy or as stable as they looked. Alacrity got a grip, pivoted, and hauled; the thing came over his shoulder, though he went down with it. Two more of the creatures rushed in, and he was entangled among them.

Amarok had dropped into an unarmed combat stance that was fearsome to behold, the tight ropes and long hawsers of his muscles standing forth. The Croi eluded by Alacrity turned toward him but, astoundingly, Amarok drove it back in a blur of leaps and flat-handed chops.

Floyt, eyes bulging, could see no way out as the incensed Croi closed in. His back to the huge rock, he felt one of the apertures in it, like a hole wind-carved in stone.

In an instant he'd turned and wriggled into it. It was a tight fit, leading downward, the stone abrading his skin, but he shinnied through like a squirrel through stacked cordwood, as Croi began reaching and snatching after him. Floyt went through so fast that he nearly plunged straight out the back of the monument and fell to his death on the wave-pounded rocks below.

But he managed to dig in, scraping knees and elbows bloody, halting himself. As he did, he felt the long limbs of the aroused mourners reaching for his feet.

Amarok, meanwhile, had somehow extricated Alacrity. Their protestations did no good. Determined to make a final stand, Amarok began swarming up the great stone; Alacrity tried to swarm up Amarok.

They were plucked from the stone and, struggling wildly, borne away.

Floyt, angled head-down toward the sea in the cramped hole, kicked out at the grasping Croi. His fumbling hand found a weathered crack above the hole, on the crumbling sea face of the stone. Driven by Terran loathing of nonhumans and a wild fear for his life, he got his fingertips into the crack for a risky hold and hauled himself out of the hole, scrabbling and kicking for purchase. He looked around hopelessly; there was the sound of the crashing water and of Croi on the other side of the stone groping around like cats at a mouse hole.

Something touched his calf, and he screamed.

Alacrity and Amarok were being restrained by an angry

mob. Caut'Karr, with threshing blows and enjoining cries, managed to bring back a little order. The two captives were spread-eagled on one of the smaller stones, bent backward, heads hanging over the booming surf. Alacrity's skull ached and a knot was beginning to swell where he'd clipped his forehead against the boulder.

Except for a few frustrated individuals still fumbling around at the hole trying to catch Floyt, the Croi thronged around the two captives.

"Despite of your rude truculence and intemperate discourtesies," Caut'Karr announced, "we will be lenient with you, foreign aliens. You will make your tribute, then be allowed permission to depart."

"Don't you understand?" Amarok bellowed. "We have a different physiology from you!"

"That is scarcely our fault, is it?" Caut'Karr riposted reasonably.

A lost arm or leg could be regenerated or replaced by graft if necessary, but if the humans were to lose it up on the cliff, they'd have no hope of making it to *Pihoquiaq*, much less advanced medical help. Alacrity and Amarok struggled.

"If you tear off our arms or legs we'll die!" Amarok roared.

"Umm, ha," meditated Caut'Karr. "I suppose we could settle for a minor appendage." He pointed to their midsections. "Those rather modest protuberances down there would suffice."

The Croi were somewhat surprised at how vehemently the two *Homo sapiens* began to fight and object.

"STOP!" a human voice thundered.

Floyt stood atop the great stone, panting and bleeding from the climb that had nearly cost him his life a dozen times in less than a minute.

Before the Croi could recover from their surprise, the Earther placed one hand over his heart and swept the other at the figure of the High Meddler. In stentorian grandeur, he declaimed:

> *The Croi stood on the burning deck,*
> *(uh,) his honor now I garnish,*
> *drape laurels round his nonesuch neck,*
> *and on his coat of varnish!*

Adrenaline had helped him condense a lot of thinking into the endless seconds of his climb; verse was the only thing he'd been able to come up with.

The Croi watched and listened, motionless. They could tell Floyt was doing something profoundly out of the ordinary, even for a human. There were rapid-fire questions to and answers from the few Terranglish speakers among them, including Caut'Karr. *Poetry? Poetry!*

Alacrity and Amarok, straining to raise their heads a bit, saw Floyt posed on the carved boulder, the sinking sun outlining him. He pointed to the High Meddler, trying to recall what he could of *Casabianca*, the only thing he'd been able to bring to mind (and that rather dimly). Thrusting a forefinger toward the heavens, he extemporized:

> *Yet beautiful and bright he stood,*
> *as born to rule the storm,*
> *Of limbs he had more, many, than*
> *the common human norm.*

Caut'Karr gasped. The other Terranglish-speaking Croi understood, too, that this was an elegy to their own High Meddler. Even the nonlinguists had caught the reference to their species. It was little short of miraculous to them that Floyt was composing on the spot.

They listened to his rolling recitation and the alien precision of rhythm and rhyme. The pressure restraining Alacrity and Amarok let up a bit. There were thrilled shivers among the creatures.

Floyt, having come to the end of what he could force to mind from *Casabianca*, took the gamble that the Croi couldn't tell poetic meter from a camel auction or, for that matter, really catch much of what he was saying. He spread his arms to the awestruck crowd:

> *He led and inspired the nation,*
> *this praiseworthy Son of Creation,*
> *but although we'll all miss him,*
> *it's time to off-kiss him,*
> *in the int'rests of good sanitation!*

The Croi were rustling and making noises like a flock of pigeons now, straining to hear, belaboring the Terranglish speakers for a running translation. They were missing almost all of it, but they were rapt.

Amarok and Alacrity were released, lying on their backs on the smaller rock, all but ignored. Alacrity felt sick from the knock on the head, the champagne, and the dizziness of being held head-down over the ocean. His stomach tossed in time with the waves.

Floyt had gone down on one knee, palms out to the High Meddler in a beatific gesture.

> *The High Meddler stands nigh the cliff,*
> *that splendid, beloved old stiff,*
> *and so, out of love,*
> *let us give 'im a shove,*
> *and end this ridiculous tiff!*

The Croi were rhapsodic, returning Floyt's gesture. Some had caught just enough of the last part to get the general idea. Willing limbs raised up the High Meddler and heaved his statuesque carcass out into the air.

Just then Alacrity, unable to fight off nausea any longer, crouched on all fours and vomited off the sea side of the rock after the High Meddler's plummeting form, thankful that the prevailing wind was behind him.

A great sound, like a universal grating of metal files, went up from the Croi.

Oh, Sweet Spirit of Terra! Floyt groaned to himself, dread stealing the breath from him and stopping his pulse for an instant.

"Imbecile! *We've had it!*" Amarok snarled at the pathetic, heaving Alacrity and began looking around for a way to save himself.

"You, you—" strained Caut'Karr as Floyt tried hysterically to come up with some viable excuse.

"You gave the High Meddler the *Grand Encomium!*" Caut'Karr went on. "Eversion of the epigastrian breadbasket, in the Return of Gifts! The Foregoing of the Eatable Gift-Victual Presents! *Zut!*"

He and a bunch of other Croi helped Alacrity up, patting and stroking his arms, making sounds of acclaim. The remains of the High Meddler, and Alacrity's lunch, were gone beneath the waves.

"That was rather actually above the limits," Caut'Karr remarked. "We were ignorant of any idea that you were thinking about planning such an intention. Er, I suppose internal damage will suffer your innards to expire to death, as is usually the case of things'?"

"Um, no." Alacrity grinned feebly. "I'm just as surprised about this as you are, you understand, but it looks like I'm gonna pull through."

"What a wonderfully pleasing, out of the ordinary rarity! How unflinchingly plucky! Ah, I trust you'll forgive our confused misunderstanding . . ."

"Oh, please, forget to remember it."

Amarok was next to Alacrity now, helping him soothe Caut'Karr's distress. Other Croi had helped Floyt down off the great stone; he rejoined his companions.

Caut'Karr paused to chastise several rash young Croi who were apparently considering imitating Alacrity in rendering the Grand Encomium.

"Their tender young internal stomachs would never put up with enduring it, of naturally," Caut'Karr explained to the humans. "Even we adults seldomly live through survival of it. Ah, but you humanity folks are creatures of ferrous iron, eh? No self-effacing modesty, now! Here; you have earned your payment sums!"

With that the three were given not one but *two* amber Perfect novaseeds each; not four azure Primes, but *eight*.

"Thanks!" Alacrity beamed. "Now we can get our mother that much-needed operation!"

"Never has there been so joyously sad of a funereal bash!" trumpeted Caut'Karr. "May I please have leave to declare the announcement that you *Homo sapiens* species types are hereby declared *winning champions of the bereaved mourning*!"

The three were borne aloft by deliriously happy mourners. They were carried back down the hill in triumph, through the slanting rays of the sunset, thinking how good it would feel to be back inside the *Pihoquiaq* once more.

CHAPTER 7

THE GRAPPLE

THEY FELL BACK INTO A SHIPBOARD ROUTINE QUICKLY AND comfortably, on friendlier terms after the debacle on Way 'Long.

Floyt had come to understand how Alacrity, who claimed to have been raised in spacecraft for much of his life, could've received a comprehensive education: there was plenty of time for it. Floyt learned to cook a bit, and Alacrity taught him some tradeslang without benefit of teaching tapes or mnemonic devices. Amarok came up with a new and better length of line to replace the jumprope, which the trio had managed to wear out. They bided their way across the gulf.

This time, when Amarok appeared to let them know they were nearing their destination, he had a holster on his hip. It was a splitfront, forward-throw model, and his sidearm a bulky hammergun with a stirrup grip. He was dressed in shiny indigo tights and a high-collared top that left his midriff bare, displaying the physique of a Hellenic wrestler.

The trader made no comment when, shortly thereafter, the two companions armed themselves as well. Floyt removed his Inheritor's belt and Amarok stashed it in the *Pihoquiaq*'s safe. The Terran substituted a webbed belt for it, tucking the Webley therein.

"Will everybody be carrying guns?" Floyt asked Alacrity. "Even with vacuum all around?"

"Guess so. It's a little risky, but most of the types who come to a Grapple wouldn't, if it meant going unarmed."

When the *Pihoquiaq*'s Breakers cut out and she resumed residence in normal space, the only celestial body nearby was an archetypical orange-red gas giant known only by an obscure catalog reference. The spot was of little interest to anyone, perfect for a Grapple and the cagey sorts who would gravitate to it: outlaws and contrabandists, underground leaders and *condottieres*, along with organized crime figures and fences, and all those who trafficked with them.

Floyt stared at the bizarre patchwork of the Grapple, which floated in space like a maze of mismatched plumbing. Vessels of all sorts were mated lock to lock or joined by tubes or other connectors, branching in all directions, moored by seals and tractor beams, cables, and magnetic anchors. At the approximate center was a titanic, much-repaired old attack transport.

Pihoquiaq's instruments registered commo signals—voice only, no visual—and weapons guidance systems coming to bear on her. Amarok was quick to transmit recognition codes. He was granted permission to approach.

Alacrity had explained that Turnouts, Rendezvous, and most other law-abiding versions of this sort of thing were usually open to all, or at least not overtly hostile, but the people involved in a Grapple were more particular about whom they admitted, and ill-disposed to interlopers.

Alacrity was crammed in the back of the bridge, yielding the copilot's seat to Floyt. Floyt used Amarok's electroimager to study the improvised labyrinth that was the Grapple. The aggregation included old and new craft, from disparate and divergent technologies. One ship reminded him of a pinecone, another a beautiful old samovar. He could see a ship—at least he assumed it was a ship—that looked as if someone had halved a geode, faced it with some transparent substance, and set up the interior as a terrarium. The craft next to it could have passed for a Franklin stove. Most of the ships were ablaze with flashing signal lights and holos.

"Where do we plug in?" Alacrity asked Amarok.

"That remains to be seen. There are protocols about these

things; it can be a bit tricky. After all, One will be using someone else's ship as a passageway."

Floyt handed the electroimager back to Amarok. "Do the authorities ever raid the Grapples?"

"Very seldom," Alacrity answered. "First, they're fairly tough to find. Second, there's a lot of firepower when this many rugged individualists get together, more than some governments could match. Besides, whose jurisdiction are we in right now? Nobody's, really."

"Granted, but surely there are fugitives here."

"At a Grapple you cannot take a deep breath without bumping one," Amarok agreed. "But then, you cannot really rely on a particular person or group to show up, so attacking a get-together like this to nail a certain target can be very counter-productive. Then too"—he lowered the images with a fey smile—"there are usually some semihonest folks attending. Killing them could raise repercussions and bad blood."

"They've sure got the party beacons lit," Alacrity enthused.

Floyt said, "I see just about every visual signal except for distress, right?"

"Very good, Hobart," Amarok answered. "Even here, nobody shows a distress signal unless they mean it."

He got back on the transmitter. "*Caveat Emptor*, this is *Pihoquiaq*. This One seeks docking arrangements. Is the *Rolling Bones* there, by chance, or the *Wotan*?"

"*Bones* is expected, *Pihoquiaq*," a voice responded. "Nobody here ever heard of the *Wotan*. There's still one lock available here in *Caveat Emptor*."

"There's always one left," Amarok muttered. "And they always want your dangles for a docking fee."

To the transmitter he replied, "Thank you anyway, *Caveat*, but This One was looking forward to seeing old friends. Have you had word of the *Magus*?"

Floyt was pointing out a large, openwork ship with other, smaller vessels fastened within her, inquiring what she was.

"That's a ferry," Alacrity answered. "Sublight tubs sometimes go from one system to another in 'em, and they transport damaged starships too, but it's chancy. The rates are stiff, and if you miss a connection, you're probably stranded. Then, sometimes you *can* go broke and starve, even if you have your own ship."

"Attention, *Pihoquiaq*," the commo was saying. "*Magus* is grappled to us, aftmost boatlock, portside. She has granted permission for you to make fast."

Amarok beamed, thanking *Caveat Emptor* and signing off. Easing his ship around the haphazard protrusions of the Grapple, he said, "Captain Merrywell of the *Magus* is a close friend to Someone's family; This One can simply chip in on his docking fee."

They closed slowly on a vessel several times the size of the old monitor. *Magus* appeared to be a frigate refitted as a swift, formidable merchantman, which was also a good configuration for a blockade runner, smuggler, or pirate.

Amarok deftly matched his ship to the *Magus*'s portside lock. As the three were making fast and shutting down, though, a polished, languid voice hailed the *Pihoquaiq*.

"Captain Sile, here, of the *Lamia*. How pleasant to hear your voice once more, Amarok my young entrepreneur!"

Amarok was scowling as he replied. "*Pihoquiaq* here. What is your message, *Lamia*?"

The reply was mellifluous. "I notice you're sealed to the *Magus*, so if you don't mind, I'll just make fast to your portside. It's very nearly the only spot left. I was just telling my associates how fortunate it is that we're old acquaintances, you and I."

Amarok thumbed the sender angrily. "Negative, Sile. Docking permission refused. *I say again*, docking permission refused! Stand away!"

There was a brief silence at the other end. Tension in the bridge made the air fairly crackle.

"Someone would rather not have offended him," Amarok admitted quietly, "but One will not give Sile and his pack of cutthroats access to this ship."

"There're other docking spots anyway, Rok," Alacrity said quietly.

They were all watching *Lamia*, a heavily armed carbon dagger of a vessel. Amarok's hand hovered near the firing grip of the monitor's single cannon. Knowing how outgunned they were, Alacrity and Floyt had begun to perspire, even though starting trouble at a Grapple could earn Sile stern retribution.

After time had stood still for a while, Sile replied, "Oh, dear; how disappointing! Well; do enjoy your stay, my boy! *Lamia*, out!"

The deadly lean shape drifted away. Amarok let his breath out. "This One bets that Sile has to take that last open lock on *Caveat Emptor*. Few people trust him."

"But does he hold grudges?" Floyt wanted to know.

Amarok's expression was uncertain. "If it doesn't place him in danger, he'll attempt to get even for a perceived wrong, but he won't risk being turned out of the Grapple and being barred from others. *I think*. Are you both ready?"

They passed through into the warmer air of the *Magus* and were there greeted by her skipper, Captain Juxtar Merrywell.

Merrywell might've been nearly Alacrity's height when standing upright, but he was in a perpetual slouch. That and a sad, bassethound face combined to make him seem one step away from terminal melancholy. He wore a formal blouse, cravat in need of adjustment, and voluminous green pantaloons with metallic brocade. In his cummerbund were tucked two long, slender, gold-plated Monzini stunguns, heavily chased. They were short-range, but powerful; *Just the thing*, Alacrity thought, *for a visit to a Grapple*. Merrywell's crew, mixed males and females with a sprinkling of nonhumans, seemed to dress pretty much as suited them.

Merrywell greeted Amarok with a flattening of his downcast look that wasn't quite a smile and a pat on the shoulder that seemed to take all his strength.

"Good to see you again, sonny. How's business?" He favored Alacrity and Floyt with a long-suffering look. "Amarok's a hotshot trader and captain now, but when he was cabinboy-apprentice with me, we had to teach him what went where in the head."

Amarok colored a bit and hastened to make introductions.

"Glad you had the sense to turn away that treacherous little degenerate Sile," Merrywell said when that was over. "You saved me the trouble. I never could stomach him or that wacko chippy he married."

"Married?" Amarok registered with surprise.

"You didn't hear? Yep, he and Constance are now joined in connubial bliss. Who else'd have either one of 'em?"

"What I'd like to know is where he got himself a ship like that," Amarok said.

Merrywell waved his hand and blew a curt raspberry. "Our little Sile is all jumped up in this life. He's got himself a rich patron is the word. Whoever it is must be either crazy or desperate; he's liable to wake up dead one of these watches. You and your friends be careful of Sile. *And* Constance."

Amarok said they would; Floyt and Alacrity both nodded.

"Well, come on; we'll go have a drink," Merrywell proposed. "You fellas got here late, you know. The Grapple's almost over."

He took Amarok's elbow. Floyt and Alacrity fell in behind as Merrywell led the way through the *Magus*. She was a fairly well-run ship, Alacrity saw, and while the atmosphere was somewhat casual, the crew was trained and disciplined. And just then they were all carrying weapons, and most of the interior hatches were secured.

"Got most of my business done already, actually." Merrywell wheezed. "Unloaded a lot of gemstones, small arms, and assorted, uh, medicines. Picked up some manufacturing equipment, AI matrixes, and detector gear." He coughed rather distressingly into a scandalously expensive kerchief of burrownymph silk from Masada; Amarok took no notice.

They cycled through the *Magus*'s well-guarded main airlock. A trio of Merrywell's crew fell in with them as escort as the outer hatch swung open. Two were tough-looking men with flaring mustachios, their long brown hair woven and intertwined in triangular wooden frames they wore atop their heads; the other a short, slender, auburn-haired woman who looked to be about Floyt's age or so and had a rather elfin air to her. All three carried short-barrelled shockguns with folding stocks, supported by shoulder slings.

The *Magus* was grappled directly to the central portion of the *Caveat Emptor*. Merrywell led the party into a much larger lock, which wasn't in nearly as good shape as his own ship's. As they entered, brothel steerers, pushers, vendors, all manner of commission men and women and several beggars began yelling and importuning. Apparently they knew enough about Merrywell and his crew to keep their distance, though.

A wizened little man with multicolored braids that reached past his knees offered Floyt a transparent sphere containing a tiny gossamer-winged spider with eyes like red coals. According to the hawker's spiel, the spider spun golden webs and laid clusters of golden eggs. Then two big huskies squatting by a sedan chair wanted to bear him around the Grapple in style.

Alacrity pointed out the commission men and women. "Percentage reps. They'll bring just about anything you want to you in your ship—food, drugs, dealers from the casinos, sex servants, whatever—at a ridiculous markup, of course."

They made their way through the *Caveat*'s lock, out into pandemonium.

They were in one of the attack transport's gargantuan holds, which had been converted into a thieves' market of booths and stalls, marquees and kiosks. A thick pall clogged the air, compounded of every sort of smoke, aroma, and stench. Humans and other beings were puffing without restriction on a wide variety of materials, unusual inboard a sealed spacecraft.

Light came from harsh overhead spots and beautiful biolume lamps, strings of elaborate lanterns and glowing deckplates. Condensation from pipes and conduits high above fell in erratic droplets. A variety of midges and other flying things circled and buzzed; Floyt was unnerved to think how easily these indifferent underworlders could infect new worlds with vermin, pests, and diseases.

"Oh; meant to ask." Merrywell frowned, fumbling in his cummerbund. "Do any of you boys want nose filters?"

All three declined. Merrywell shifted his search to his blouse and drew out a long gold cigarette holder, fitting a thin crimson cigarette into it and lighting up with a tiny heat-node. Puffing contentedly, he said, "Well; shall we go?"

Floyt was trying to look everywhere at once as they sallied out into the bedlam of the Grapple. He nearly collided with a flirtatious androgyne in a very revealing costume who gave him a brazen wink before continuing along.

The next thing he noticed was two men in intense, very

animated conversation. One, in robes of iridescent fabric, put him in mind of an ancient Berber. The man was chewing rapidly on something or other, pausing occasionally to spit into a small chalice of what looked like black iron. From the chalice came brief flashes and puffs of smoke, as the spittal was incinerated. The man kept his eyes to the deck, speaking angrily, with broad gesticulations.

The one he was talking to was unclothed but not naked. His pale skin was nubbled with fantastic ritual markings and scars, in swirling patterns resembling a Maori's. The end of his prepuce was pierced by an elaborate sexual fetish of feathers, excrescenses, wattles, and stimulators.

"The one on the left's from Desolation," Alacrity told Floyt. "He destroys his spit, nail parings, hair trimmings, feces—all that kind of stuff, so nobody can use it against him in clone voodoo. He's not allowed to look unbelievers in the eye."

"What about the other?"

"From Rock of Ages. The body markings tell everything he's done—right and wrong, brave or cowardly. Men who don't have a sexual fetish like that—well, they're just not considered very desirable husbands."

Floyt caught a snippet of their conversation.

"—nuance of *carn* in the hundredth part, *feoke* lacking; *ilm* recondite-suggestive . . ."

"They're dealing in perfumes and essences," Amarok told them. "That's scent-talk; notational-olfactory language. It takes forever to master."

Floyt's head was swimming already and he'd barely stepped out of the airlock. "There's a tolerable little cafe down this way," Merrywell announced, slouching off through the tumultuous bazaar with the rest trailing.

Floyt found himself in a world of unctuous flesh peddlers and slab-muscled enforcers, carousing mercenaries, swaggering go-bloods and a disconcerting array of strangely conceived nonhumans; he saw screaming hawkers and sauntering prostitutes of every sex and description.

A furious blur of blue-scaled lightning came broken-field-running through the crowded hold at knee level, weaving between bystanders and stalls, overturning bins and cannisters, squealing and honking. It ran on two short, thick legs, a bulbous tail raised high to balance it.

Hot on its pronged heels came a drugged and drunken mob of laughing, shrieking, swearing men and women. Onlookers jeered and catcalled. A small human—at least, Floyt *thought* it was a human; he looked like something out of a *hummel-werk*—made a dive for the prey and ended up bowling over a stilt-legged humanoid who resembled an ostrich.

The little quarry darted through the center of Merrywell's party. Alacrity and Floyt and the others sprang aside as howling, blaspheming, cleaver-waving pursuers stumbled and careened after it. The chase disappeared into the far reaches of the giant hold, but shouts of outrage and screams of frustration, complaints from concessionaires and profuse squealing and honking from the prey continued in the distance.

"They'll use up more calories catching it than they'll get eating it," Merrywell predicted morosely, drawing on his cigarette holder.

In his haste to get out of the way, Floyt had fetched up against a sign affixed to the bulkhead. A man standing close by leaned toward him, shooting back his floppy sleeves. His arms had instruments strapped to them, all the way up to the shoulders.

"First-rate proteuses, sir! Newest and most versatile models! Lifetime guarantee!"

Floyt grunted, shoving himself back on balance. "I don't think—"

The man got in front of him. "Telelinks! Accessors! Comaides!"

"No, really, I—"

"Very beautiful lady's multi here, sir! Necklace model!" The man was shaking it under Floyt's nose, an instrumented bauble mounted with too many fake gems. "Double your money back if not delighted! *Works anywhere!*"

"Oh, yeah?" Alacrity broke in. "What about some of the less popular bodily orifices, you scrote?"

The hawker's mouth snapped shut; he scuttled away.

"You all right, Ho?" Floyt nodded. Dusting off his hands, he turned to look at the sign against which he'd leaned. THE

ARES HOUSE OF BIOSYNERGIC DEFENSE—EXPERT SKELETAL AUG-
MENTATION—DIGITAL IMPLANTS OUR SPECIALTY—ONE-TIME
OFFER: FULL TWO-HAND BLADE ARRAY FOR THE PRICE OF ONE!!!

The two rejoined the others. The hold was fruited with a
bewildering assortment of signs, placards, and advertisements,
everything from crude hand-lettered shingles to floating holographic murals in full-spectrum colors with high-fidelity sound.
Floyt scanned what he could of the ones in Terranglish and
Tradeslang.

THE PHOENIX NEST REJUVENATION CLINIC. RELIGIOUS ITEMS
AND OCCULT SUPPLIES—FULL TIME SEER ON DUTY. NEW AND LIKE-
NEW HAWKING EFFECT EQUIPMENT. FINE WEAPONS AND AMMU-
NITION—EXPERT INSTRUCTION AVAILABLE. RELIABLE DEALER IN
IDENTITY CHANGE. HYDROPONICS & AEROPONICS UNLTD. OLDE
EARTHE NATURAL TELLURIAN SPRING WATER.

"That can't be true, can it?" Floyt asked, as he and Alacrity
were obliged to go around a crowd that was gathering to hear
a laser-eyed prophet spout armageddon. "Terran water, I mean?"

Alacrity was exchanging appreciative glances with a sultry
young odalisque who gleamed in scarlet dermal stain, sun vor-
tices glittering from her fingers, earlobes, nose ring, and navel.

"Huh? Oh, not a chance. But there's a huge market for that
kind of stuff—people who feel the way your buddy the Daimyo
does."

He kissed his fingertips to the woman as they moved on;
she reciprocated.

"Ho, if they ever opened Terra to general tourists, the trade
in health neurotics and people hoping for miracle cures *alone*
would make you folks rich. The whole place would be one big
what'd-they-callit—Lourdes."

They were both distracted, looking back at the odalisque,
and so nearly bumped into two men coming the other way in
the narrow, cluttered aisle. The two were huge, Amarok's height
but much burlier, more like Corporeals. Their skins were a
deep brown; they had great curling masses of brown hair and
beard. *Corsairs or mercenaries*, Alacrity figured. *Maybe
slavers. Or assassins.* Whoever they were, they were a lot
more than run-of-the-Grapple hired muscle or enforcers. Floyt
had never seen such cold empty eyes.

The two men were decked out in gaudy clothing that was now soiled and reeking. They were weighted with mismatched jewelry that smacked of plunder. Their faces and bodies were scarred and muscular, and they carried an arsenal of well-worn weapons. Around the neck of one was a necklace of small, wrinkled brown objects that were, Floyt saw, human ears.

Once the pair had passed, Alacrity murmured to Floyt, "Sintilla's trying to make us sound like square-jawed heroes in those penny dreadfuls of hers, but I'm telling you, compared to people like that, we're just a pair of parakeets."

Hurrying to catch up again, they ascended a circular ladderwell. The bulkhead had been cut away from a compartment overlooking the hold to form a sort of bistro with a view, the Prang Inn.

Merrywell had appropriated a large circular table of pitted gray plastic near the rail. As they all ordered drinks, they considered the activity and commotion below. Alacrity ordered something called a "meltdown," and Floyt elected to try one.

The *Magus* crewmembers kept casual lookout. "Merrywell, these chaps need some special help. They want to go to Blackguard," Amarok began.

That only made Merrywell sorrowful, but then everything did. "Do you two know anything about that place?"

"Nothing, really," Alacrity confessed.

Merrywell pondered that. "Then might I ask what your business would be? I ask by way of helping, you understand."

"We're very sorry, Captain Merrywell, and we don't mean to give any offense, but we're not at liberty to discuss that," Floyt got in before Alacrity could answer.

Merrywell held up a hand. "'S quite all right; I don't offend easily, boys. But you see, showing up as an uninvited visitor is very different from going there as a guest, from what little I've heard. Now, you two don't look to me like wealthy men."

"That's a good call," Alacrity conceded as the drinks arrived. "We're anything but."

Floyt accepted his meltdown. It was a softly bubbling, thick aquamarine fluid from which slow wreaths of smoke wound. Either the inside of the tankard was luminous or the stuff was reaching critical mass. He blew away the smoke and took a sip. It was viscous and too hot, highly spiced and excessively strong. Floyt couldn't quite pin down why he found himself liking it.

"There are two aspects to Blackguard," Merrywell explained. "The one's what you might call a private resort, a retreat for the well heeled, where they can have, shall we say, a little unsavory sport?" He gestured at the turmoil below. "Whatever else you might say about those sods down there, most of them do what they do to survive, or for profit, or because it's all they know or they hate honest work. But on one part of Blackguard, I hear, they play all the nastiest games there are, just for something to do. It's very exclusive."

"And the other part?" Alacrity asked.

"Just a little population center with limited offworld contact not all that hospitable to outsiders either, from what they say. Which would be the one where you have your business?"

"Not sure." Alacrity shook his head. "Which is the space-port?"

"I recall hearing that both places have one. One of your problems is that nobody talks very much about the place; it's not considered an important planet, but getting too curious about it is unhealthy."

Floyt had taken a deeper drink of his meltdown. "Smooth," he croaked.

"Cap'n Merrywell, do you know anybody who's actually been there? Anyone we could talk to?" Alacrity asked.

Merrywell scratched under his chin and coughed once or twice into his elegant kerchief, concentrating. "There's only one I can think of: Costa."

"Who's Costa?"

"You're in his ship, son. Costa owns the *Caveat Emptor*, and this is his Grapple. He's a cold-hearted bastard, and no one to annoy, but he keeps confidences, so if he agrees to talk to you, I think you can trust him."

Alacrity and Floyt were quick to thank him. Merrywell just slouched further and looked more downcast than ever. "I'm doing it for young Amarok here, because you're his friends. Do you two have money?"

They swapped glances, shifting in their chairs. "Some," Alacrity allowed at last.

"Good; you'll probably need it. I can—"

He was interrupted by a small warning gesture from his female crewmember. A little contingent was making its way in the direction of the table.

"Sile." Amarok grunted, indicating the man who led the way.

Sile had an air of bravado. He was clad in a purple satin blouse that was all pintucks, pleats, and darts; tight leather breeches of the same color; and a matching pelisse jacket, festooned with gold braid and *fourragères* draped dashingly from his left shoulder.

His Wellington boots were purple too, with massive triple-rowled spurs that clinked and clashed as he strode the deck. Sile had a pale, narrow face that looked young from a distance. Up close, the network of lines around his eyes contradicted that. His tonsured brown hair had been grouted and glossed into what resembled a ceramic bowl.

He led by the hand a woman who was nearly his own height, perhaps 170 centimeters, slender and lean-flanked as a boy, with a deep olive complexion. Her waifish eyes, heavily made up and almost comically long-lashed, were as blue as Spica, Alacrity thought, while Floyt compared them to cornflowers. Her lemon-yellow hair was barely long enough to hold a part; she wore a duplicate of Sile's outfit, spurs and all.

"And Constance," Amarok added softly.

As the two approached the table, most of their party held back a few meters, while the shockguns were casually held ready by Merrywell's crewpeople, not quite aimed at them but not far off target. Sile's gang consisted of breakabouts and portside goons of various shapes and sizes, mean-looking and armed but not in a class with the truly lethal types Floyt and Alacrity had already seen.

But one stayed up just behind Sile and Constance. He was a small man, sinewy and lean, with a yellow-brown complexion somewhat lighter than Amarok's and a lesser epicanthic fold to his eyes. He wore a dramatic black costume, with high tabi and a hood that allowed only his eyes to show. His long gauntlets left his fingers and palms exposed. He wore no weapons they could see, but the roomy attire might conceal anything. He carried a long staff of what looked like green glass ringed with silver bands of assorted widths.

"Pneuma-warrior," Merrywell said aside to Alacrity and Floyt dolefully.

"Well, well, Amarok, dear boy." Sile almost crooned. "Constance, my pet, you remember this brawny young scamp. He moored his *Pihoquiaq* to our vessel at the *Read 'Em and Weep* Grapple."

Amarok's lips tightened. "Yes and part of the *Pihoquiaq*'s cargo wound up missing."

Sile pretended not to hear. Constance pursed her lips at Amarok, seductive and scornful.

"And jolly old Merrywell," Sile continued, "happy-go-lucky as ever." He made a courtly bow; Constance curtsied. "You should make an effort to smile now and again; what if God freezes your face like that?"

"He already has," Merrywell drawled, blowing crimson cigarette smoke Sile's way.

Sile giggled, turning to Alacrity and Floyt. "And who might these two wayfarers be?"

"Shipwreck Mazuma," Alacrity shot back with an unfriendly smile, using his Forager pseudonym.

"Delver Rootnose," Floyt threw in, using the alias Alacrity had conjured up for him when they'd stayed with the Sockwallet Outfit.

"How adorable! How quaint!" Constance purred, clapping her hands. For Floyt she had a coy wink.

"I was rather hurt by your refusal to offer me hospitality, Amarok," Sile resumed. There was an edge to his voice.

"Hurt and *annoyed*," Constance added dreamily, still smiling, running a hand over Sile's chest. She wore long, mandarin-style fingernail sheaths, lacquered and set with precious stones.

"Your hurt is of your own devising," Amarok said tightly. "Your annoyance is best controlled." His eye met those of the pneuma-warrior. Something hypnotic glinted about the little man's black eyes, Alacrity saw; it was like matching stares with a cobra.

"*Pihoquiaq* is grappled to my vessel," Merrywell interjected tiredly, slumped in his chair. His drink was some sort of oily brown concoction with what appeared to be aluminum shavings floating around in it; he was stirring it with his hairy, beringed pinky. "And so you'll be understanding, naturally, Cap'n Sile, that Amarok and his shipmates are under my protection."

Sile laughed shrilly, head tossed back. "Merrywell, Merrywell, what *would* we do for a good joke if you weren't around, you precious old buffoon? Come, my dear."

He led his wife away, the pneuma-warrior falling in behind, with the rest of the entourage coming after.

"How come they're dressed like a couple of grapes?" Alacrity inquired.

"The little viper likes to pretend he's some kind of aristocrat," Merrywell answered. "It's also to advertise the fact that he'll be in the Regatta for the Purple; he has to change underwear three times a day, he's so happy about that."

"Regatta?" Alacrity repeated. "They're letting *him* in the regatta?"

Floyt recalled hearing something about that in the *Bruja*. The Regatta for the Purple was some sort of blueblood interstellar race, limited to a chosen few.

"Um-hmm," responded dour Merrywell. "He'll be captaining a new racing yacht for some bigshot. Although how a germ like that rated it is a bigger mystery than the Precursors."

"Cap'n Merrywell, what's a pneuma-warrior?" Floyt asked.

"A mystic martial arts sneak. Cat-burglar, assassin, ninja-swami, or whatever."

Amarok added, "They train to empty themselves, to become a vessel for their pneuma, their personal warrior-spirit, they claim. It's supposed to take them over and direct them. No pain or weakness, and all that rot."

"He was the first one I ever saw," Alacrity said. "You don't find many of them around, right, Cap'n Merrywell?"

"Nope." Merrywell's face creased even more. "They're supposed to be kinesics readers, miracle men in a fight."

"The best miracle that little cockroach can do for himself is to stay clear of One," Amarok grated.

"He stared at you in particular, Rok," Floyt commented.

"Someone warned him once to stay out of One's way, or have his head squished like a berry."

"Getting back to cases," Alacrity put in, "what about Blackguard?"

"I'll go see Costa," Merrywell said, "and try to get him to talk to you two. You go get your other business done, or look around, and I'll meet you back at the *Magus* in an hour or so. Some of my crew will go with you."

"Not necessary, thank you," Amarok declared, standing up and squaring his great shoulders. "Sile's nothing but a lying little rodent, no matter who stands at his elbow."

Alacrity wouldn't have minded a bodyguard, but he and Floyt were guests and that made arguing a bad idea.

Merrywell shuffled off with his people. Amarok, Floyt, and Alacrity went back to exploring the Grapple.

Floyt wasn't all that surprised that the drug dens, drinking places, and sex emporia were doing a brisk business. But it did take him aback to see that fresh fruit and vegetables, green salads, dairy products, and natural water were so popular.

"Lots of ships don't have gardens or good food storage," Alacrity explained. "After a few weeks or months of reconstituted meat paste, rerecycled water, and synthetic gruel, you find yourself thinking about fresh cold milk and bananas that are barely ripe."

Amarok and Floyt were back on the main deck, threading their way toward the next hold, which looked just as big as the first. Conspicuous teams of Costa's enforcers were in abundance. Amarok explained that Costa made some money off his docking fees, but in the main from owning a piece of every business based in the *Caveat Emptor*. Private deals struck between attendees were permitted as long as they posed no competition to *Caveat*'s industries. Costa payed lavish rewards to informers; circumventing the rules was dangerous.

There was surprisingly little bloodshed. Amarok had explained the rules during the voyage: no shooting unless attacked or otherwise certifiably provoked, and even then it was wise to be very judicious. Disagreements could be settled in a grappled ship or under Enforcer supervision in *Caveat Emptor*. No stealing, cheating, or conning.

There was a sudden furor ahead. An enraged crowd of mixed humans and nonhumans came their way. All were dressed in identical ship's coveralls. They carried and dragged a struggling, thrashing captive, a wild-eyed man wearing torn, blood-stained finery. Blood also seeped from a scalp wound.

The three got out of the way, like everyone else. Two teams of Enforcers bringing up the rear made no move to intervene. As the mob went by, Alacrity called out, "What's up?"

One of the humans, a female with iron-gray hair, paused long enough to yell back, "Caught him cheating, shorting the mixture in an air-sale."

"What are you going to do with him?" Floyt queried.

She stared at him for a beat, puzzled. "*Do*? Why, feed him out the airlock, of course, what else?"

Then she was off again to watch the short-mixer drown in his own blood.

A bystander, a Junoesque woman carrying a bundle of some kind poised on her head, remarked, "I heard they spaced a Langstretch agent a while ago."

Alacrity was too quick to ask, "Langstretch? Were they sure?"

"Sure enough to space him, brother." She proceeded on her way, hips swaying, head erect. It struck Floyt as a very graceful way to carry a burden, not to mention leaving one's hands free.

Alacrity was still preoccupied with the news. Operatives of the Langstretch Detective Agency, both full-timers and stringers, were active throughout human space and beyond. Floyt had noticed in the past that news of them always seemed to rivet Alacrity's attention.

No point in asking, though, Floyt decided. *He'll only sphinx up on me again.* Instead he asked, "What are the penalties for the other violations? The ones you were talking about?"

Alacrity clapped both hands around his throat, bulged his eyes, and made fishy mouthings.

"Pushing people out an airlock is about the *only* punishment they have around here?"

"It's the only one they need," Alacrity replied.

CHAPTER 8

PAYDIRT

THEY STOPPED AT A BOOTH TO BUY THREE MORE MELTDOWNS, these in plastic squeezebags with drinking tubes attached; there was a lot of jostling and elbowing on the main deck. The containers also kept out the winged insects and other flying pests that infested *Caveat Emptor*.

Sauntering along with Alacrity behind Amarok, Floyt tried to look nonchalant. They passed displays of smuggled pets and wildlife alongside stolen and forged antiquities and artifacts, and what was guaranteed to be the most artfully rigged gambling equipment available anywhere. Rare wines and textiles were set close by the latest in surveillance devices and burglary tools.

Hole-in-the-bulkhead surgeries that advertised transplants, implants, regeneration, and every other manner of procedure. Due to the short duration of the Grapple, though, it was strictly cut-and-pray medicine, with little postop time and no supervised recuperation.

"You can also find some very skilled physicians with well-equipped operations here," Amarok explained, "if you happen to have a *lot* of disposable income. The principle is the same, however: cash out front, and no such thing as malpractice."

Alacrity elaborated. "The usual drill is, you get your pore and retinal patterns altered and have new prints grafted on.

116

Then you go aft to the restricted area where the lifeswap shops are, or hit one of the cheaper identity-change booths if you can't afford that. Then you hope your fingertips don't slough off or blindness doesn't set in."

"And that the people who set you up don't sell you out," Amarok added.

Vendors were hawking cans of luxury cigarettes and phials of aphrodisiacs, pirated data and components, survival equipment and rescue gear. All around was the babble of strange languages—though many had Terranglish cognates—plus various forms of signtalk. The high and low cuisines of hundreds of planets, along with bastardizations and cross-pollinations added their smells to the air.

The three paused while Amarok looked over a display of weird musical instruments, trying one or two, chatting tentatively with the proprietor of the stall.

Glancing around, Floyt said, "Maybe that's what I need for the next leg," and indicated a booth advertising LANGUAGES TAUGHT—MNEMONICS!! SUBLIMINAL TUTELARY PROGRAMS!! HEURISTICS OUR SPECIALTY!! —AFFILIATED WITH PAN STELLAR COMMUNICATIONS INSTITUTE!!!

"Their affiliation with Pan Stellar's probably in the form of a lawsuit," Alacrity opined. "But we could pick up some tapes. Good idea; it'd probably help for you to learn more tradeslang and maybe some crosstalk."

Amarok passed on the purchase of a miniature glass harmonica, and they took up their way again. One side compartment was very quiet and dimly lit; it's modest sign said, TRANQUILITY BASE—HEADBOARDERS WELCOME. Floyt sneaked a peek through the inner hatch. Headboarders, old and young, male and female, were stretched out on bunks, their dural shunts hooked up, smiling blissfully.

Just beyond that the trio passed a smooth-skinned male teenage sextoy. He was dressed as an animal tamer, leading by a glittering leash a beautiful young woman wearing lizard makeup and grainy reptilian fleshpeel. Across the way a merchant advertised what were purported to be embryos cloned from a tissue sample stolen from a popular sensostar.

"Earthservice is going to lock me up and vacuum my brain,"

Floyt moaned. "They'll rip out all my synapses and bury my body at sea in cement."

"You've got to stop thinking that way, Ho. You'll be a big hero, after all. Supervisor Bear's gonna need you for psycho-prop. Keep your grip!"

That made Floyt feel a little better. The three wandered over to examine displays of weapons. There were edged, projectile and energy types, as well as razorwhips, molecular garrotes, and artificial claws with built-in injectors. It made an ordinary pistol seem terribly passé.

While they were looking, a bright-eyed little man approached them. "Undertow? Finest anywhere. I can even arrange a doss for you if your skipper objects. How about it?"

Floyt shook his head, thinking nothing of it; they'd already been offered dozens of drugs and other substances. But then the man yanked Alacrity's sleeve. "Hey, boss! *Mijneer!* Undertow?"

A change came over Alacrity's face. He shook off the grip, gathered up the front of the man's doublet, and lifted him off his feet with his left fist, his right fumbling at the Captain's Sidearm. All the blood had left his face.

"*No!*" cried Floyt, throwing himself into the struggle. Amarok intervened too. In a moment they'd pried the two apart.

Alacrity came back to himself, but stood glowering. The little pusher shook off momentary fear for his life, becoming indignant. Floyt pressed a one-oval piece into his hand and drew his two companions away before a crowd could form.

Floyt demanded, in the lee of a bookstall, "What was that all about?"

Alacrity puffed his cheeks, blowing out his breath. "Sorry, Ho; he took me by surprise. It's just an attitude I have about undertow."

"It is no worse than many of the things for sale here," Amarok reasoned.

Alacrity shrugged, glaring at the deck, not leaving room for much argument. The trader said, "Enough; let's browse in here."

Alacrity was agreeable, apparently past his sudden rage. Floyt filed away a new word: *undertow*.

For a brief time in the late twentieth and early twenty-first centuries, humanity had been all but indifferent to distance. But now, once again, human settlements were weeks or months apart by the fastest communication available, Hawking Effect travel. Then, too, some communities might not receive visits for years.

And there was the sheer size of human space, the vast number of people and of things going on. Except for isolationist backwaters like Earth, there was a universal hunger to know what was going on, what was the latest, what was *new*. At no time in history had travelers' journals and personal diaries been more popular.

Even at the Grapple it was a rare bar or brothel that didn't have at least one newsfeed. The same went for eating and gambling spots, and even some of the drug dens.

The bookstall-infocenter the three had chanced across was less given to current events than to tapes and books, but several large screens and displays competed for the attention of passersby. Paying the entrance fee, they paused to find out "what's new on the Rialto," as Amarok misquoted.

They skimmed the local "Whereabouts," a personals-locater media bulletin board, through which people tried to find loved ones, advertised for mates, posted legal notices and so on. One ad showed a bearded man with a slightly fanatic gleam in his eyes, who reminded Floyt of oldtime photos of Rasputin.

Alacrity saw, and laughed. "The contact-address must be a cover for some some police agency, or Langstretch. They've got him listed as a missing heir here, because Grapples don't post Wanted bills, but that's Janusz."

"A criminal?"

"Pirate, bank robber, con man; Janusz's done it all. The guy's been cornered but never caught. A lot of people think he never will be."

The three checked out current events. Aside from the usual wars and rumors of wars, Spican Amalgamated had announced that a new technique promised near-instantaneous interstellar communication.

"How many times have I heard *that* before?" Alacrity scoffed. "More likely, their stock's in trouble."

Unconfirmed word had come that contact had been made with a vastly advanced nonhuman culture whose borders were gradually approaching those of the human race. Leading philosophers, clergy, and scientists were expressing deep concern that *Homo sapiens* wouldn't measure up to the standards of a species so technically, intellectually, and spiritually superior.

That gave Floyt great pause. Amarok's reaction was "Let us see them prove it before we worry."

The Earther turned to Alacrity, who raised both eyebrows and said, "The last time this happened, it was the Kindurii. It turned out the snobby little highbinders owned four lousy star systems and looked down on anybody who couldn't reproduce by fission."

The place was surprisingly large and they fanned out among the amassed scrolls, hardbounds, capsules, magazines, lozenges, faxes, chips, paperbacks and magazines, tablets and codexes.

Amarok was studying an ancient folio of Edwardian prints. Floyt and Alacrity rounded the corner of a row of high stacks, Alacrity in search of Precursor material. The breakabout moved quickly, scanning up and down and back and forth, already familiar with most of what he saw.

Rounding the corner, they found they'd crossed over into another subject entirely. In a cul-de-sac, they discovered they were surrounded by a circus of bright cover illustrations, holoimages, and advertising flats depicting scenes of derring-do and raw passion, horrible predicaments and turgid romance.

Penny dreadfuls, Alacrity realized, amused.

Seated on the deck in the midst of a smorgasbörd of books, info caps, tapes, and so forth, was an odd little creature who put Floyt in mind of a golden-lion tamarin monkey, except that it was a little bigger and bulkier, more ground-dweller-looking. It wore a yellow garment like a tabbard, finely embroidered in red, green, and black, from beneath the rear hem of which a regal, flaxen banner of prehensile tail curved up it like a question mark.

The thing had a magnificent, curling mustache and large, startled-looking brown eyes. From its thick brows, darker filaments, like long antennae, swept out to either side. Its ears were tall and tufted; it had a book in its clever little hands, a viewer in its lap, and other items in various formats under its feet, which had opposable digits at either side.

"Alacrity, do you see what it's reading?" Floyt said out of one corner of his mouth, elbowing his friend.

"Hoo! Bombastico Herdman!" Alacrity snorted softly.

Bombastico Herdman was the pseudonym under which Sintilla had written penny dreadfuls about Weir. They were scattered around: *Cazpahr Weir and the Voodoo Virgins of the Vengeance Vector*; *Cazpahr Weir Faces the Zombie Cannibals of the Whistling Asteroid*, and the hardcover the little one was skimming, something filled with computerized images of unlikely sailing ships, voluptuous mermaids, and swashbuckling freebooters, entitled *Cazpahr Weir Meets the Vampire Teddybears from Hell*.

The little being looked up from its deep engrossment, fixing them with big brown eyes. "Prepare to jettison the supercargo!" it squeaked suddenly, tail quiveringly erect, mustache and antennae flaring, its mane standing out in display behavior. "Hoist the Gibsons! We don't know the *meaning* of the word 'guts'!"

"I believe that's supposed to be 'fear,'" Floyt corrected gently.

The creature looked very chagrined, its tail drooping as it gave them an embarrassed showing of teeth. "Oh? Ooo, sorry, humans. Your various idioms are betimes illusive." It held up the book. "But so vivid! Such high adventure! Such *hormonalism!*"

"You like that, do you?" Alacrity smiled.

"Great gosh, yes! And *Kim*, the Old Testament, *The Three Musketeers* . . ."

Just then the manager of the place, a big bruiser who looked more like he ought to be bouncing in a starport dive, stuck his head around the corner and said, "Perfessor, yer gonna get me in trouble; this ain't a liberry. I know how you feel, but you been nosing around back here for two hours now, fella!"

"In a moment, in a moment," the being chirped. "Am I not allowed the opportunity to be selective, at these scandalous prices you charge, Cully?"

Cully made a halfhearted gesture of disgust and went away.

"You have an interest in these stories too?" The creature blinked at Floyt, Amarok, and Alacrity.

"Kind of," Alacrity answered, thinking of *Hobart Floyt and Alacrity Fitzhugh Challenge the Amazon Slave Women of the Supernova.*

Floyt grinned.

"Personally, Someone doesn't have much time for that sort of tripe," Amarok declared, having come up behind.

"*Tripe?*" the creature piped, leaping to its feet and scattering the books, the tip of his tail vibrating over his head.

"As an affiliate of the Pantalogical Institute of *Ch'k*, I can assure you, sir, that they are neither tripe nor trivial! Look to the history of your own species for telling precedents!"

The fur of his tail began to lay flat again as the creature calmed. "It's incumbent upon me to introduce myself: Professor *K'ek-k'ek-k'ek.*" There was a trill to it.

They introduced themselves in return, Alacrity and Floyt using their Forager *noms de voyage.* Professor K'ek, as he invited them to call him, not only clasped their hands in human fashion, but sniffed at them, memorizing their odors, while his antennae bobbed in their direction.

"I'm on sabbatical," he explained. "I was on a tramp freighter that docked at the Grapple to do some sort of business the captain didn't want to explain. It's all very colorful, isn't it?"

"In some ways," Floyt confessed. "But you'd better watch yourself, Professor K'ek. It can be dangerous here."

"Have no fear," K'ek answered, flashing some shiny thing in the palm of his long hand. "I've no intention of ending up in a menagerie."

Floyt was about to say something else when he realized that two of Merrywell's bodyguards had caught up with them and were talking to his companions.

"I have to go meet Merrywell," Alacrity told Floyt quietly. "He's gotten Costa to agree to a meet."

"You? Not us?"

"That's what Merrywell says. Costa's the suspicious type."

That being the case, Floyt had to admit that Alacrity was the logical one to go; he knew what questions to ask.

But Professor K'ek had picked up some of the conversation with those big, swiveling, tufted ears. "Captain Costa? What a mine of information he would be! May I come? Please, *please?*"

"Sorry." Alacrity tried to pat him on the head, which K'ek shied away from. "Impossible, Prof."

"How too bad!" K'ek surrendered glumly. Then he brightened. "Do you know the cafe called the Oasis? Over near where the *Rantipole* is grappled? I'll be there a little later. I'd be delighted to buy you and your friends a drink, and perhaps you could fill me in on certain local customs."

"*Rantipole* enjoys a certain . . . infamy," Amarok said. "She'll be easy to find."

"Sounds good," Alacrity decided, "if we can spare the time; we may be moving fast. Ho, I'll meet you two there or back at the *Magus*, depending on how things go."

Once Alacrity had left with Merrywell's people, K'ek gathered up his selections and went to make his purchase. Floyt browsed for some light reading to occupy him on the next leg of the journey, feeling a guarded elation and hoping there'd be no more major obstacles to laying claim to *Astraea Imprimatur*. He picked out a few items while Amarok chose a tape about creative accounting.

The two decided to proceed with the tour, wending past hip-pocket tool-and-die shops, sex arcades and dealers in life-support systems and environmental suits.

Amarok paused at one of the latter, in a mind to fill out the *Pihoquiaq*'s inventory. Floyt was amazed at the variety in suits, every sort from armored monsters that were virtually one-person spaceships to a minimal thing disturbingly like a body bag, in which people could be transported or evacuated like luggage, or corpses.

The place was also stocked with mounds of supplies, gear, and gadgets. Floyt looked over collapsible shelters that folded to a wad the size of a playing card, dermal misters for staving off itches while suited up, and portable hygiene chambers of dubious design.

He picked up a purportedly all-purpose survival tool that combined the functions of knife, brass knuckles, file, saw, firestarter, transit, microfiche viewer, radiation detector, water purifier, and a number of other things. It also had a compass mounted in its hilt.

Amarok, deciding not to make any purchases, came over to see what it was.

Floyt showed him the whatsit proudly. "It's even got a corkscrew here, see? Also, you can scale fish!"

Amarok looked it over condescendingly. "A *compass*? Not even an inertial tracker or telelink locater? Hobart, that object ought to be in a museum!"

Maybe it was Floyt's reflexive Terran reverence for the archaic, maybe the giveaway price, or perhaps just that he liked the weight of the thing. He pulled two single-oval pieces and handed them over.

The owner of the establishment inspected the money carefully, passing a small detectorwand over it; there was no Bank of Spica or other verifying agency within light-years, and Grapples were bread and butter for some of the more daring forgers.

Satisfied, the man passed back Floyt's change in Centauran deciducats.

"Just a sec," Amarok said. He brought out a veryifying unit of his own, even though the amount was very small change indeed. The shopkeeper scowled but made no objection. Amarok let Floyt accept the specie. "The least you could've done was haggle," he grumbled, as Floyt admired his prize.

Again they wandered, until they came to another concession, a shop like a section of transparent Doric column. It held trays and cases of odd jewelry and pharmacopeia. They'd chanced on a booth selling poisons, love potions, knockout drops, truth serums, and kindred substances, along with sinister devices for administering them to the unsuspecting. They saw rings and bracelets, brooches, belt buckles and anklets, hairpins and walking sticks, all fitted with various secret compartments and hidden injectors.

Floyt stared at those a long time, thinking how different things would've gone if the woman who'd been sent to waylay him on Earth had used something like one of these instead of an autostyrette. Lost in thought, he focused on a beautiful Ouroboros ring.

"Absolutely guaranteed to pass any inspection," the shop-keeper, a garrulous little Eried tub of lard, said slyly. Over his head floated the traditional halo of an Eried trader, its projector hidden somewhere on his rotund person. From his voice, he'd been neutered; all really good Eried merchants were.

"That ring holds four separate doses of whatever you care to choose, would you believe it?"

"Hobart, what would you want with that?" Amarok challenged. "That's no honest person's implement."

The Eried was loathe to lose the sale, but not about to argue directly with Amarok. "Tell you what, I'll throw in a starter kit, free of charge: twenty assorted doses, one hundred ovals for everything. I don't know why, but I feel generous today, so catch me while you can. Toxins, sleeping draughts, love potions—"

Floyt looked up. "Love potions?"

"Any and every sort! Well, aphrodisiacs, really. Erotimax, hedonol, cantharidone, stimulex—and for you, sir, I reduce my price. To ninety ovals."

Floyt was thinking of Yumi. "What about candies? Choc-olate ones with liqueur centers?"

The shopkeeper canted his head so that his halo was tilted, giving Floyt a dismayed look. "I suppose I could throw some in; Angle's Kiss, a box of four, free, and you can have the whole pot for seventy-five ovals!"

Amarok was puzzled. "Why would you need such things, Hobart?"

Floyt's first reaction was shock, then anger; the chocolates the Eried showed him were the same sort he'd eaten with Yumi, before they'd made love. *So it was an assignment from her Daimyo and she couldn't bear being with me without it? But . . . a box of four; there were four on the bento tray. She may have been unsure of me, but Yumi didn't feel the need of one.*

But then he remembered her parting kiss, her grace note. The preliminary motives didn't matter then. Floyt brightened as Amarok's words sank in.

"You're right; why should I need 'em, Rok?"

The Eried was nearly weeping. "Sixty ovals, my final offer!"

He was down to forty by the time they passed out of earshot. At Amarok's suggestion, he and Floyt exited through one of *Caveat Emptor*'s aft locks into another concession ship, a smaller one, the *Rantipole*, which was set up for contests, competitions, and other betting events.

Rantipole was joined to the attack transport by an elbow of temporary passageway with a contoured gravity field. Floyt found great novelty in watching the far bulkhead become the deck as he walked. *Rantipole*'s main lock was marked with symbols indicating, Amarok clarified, a slightly higher gravity and a somewhat thinner atmosphere than Standard, which was, more or less, Terra's. Admission was ten ovals each.

Inboard, they found polyspecies crowds wagering and screaming over various bloodsports. Pit-fights were being staged between animals from assorted worlds; target and fastdraw contests were fought with stunguns and more permanent firearms; duels saw carnage wrought with razorwhip, knife, combustorbags, and biosynergic weapons.

In one arena, a small, transparent dome, two heavily drugged men were having it out with blistermist projectors. Floyt averted his eyes.

"Why did we come here?"

"Mostly so that I could remind myself why I don't like Grapples, Hobart."

"If you've had enough, let's go."

They made their way past a compartment with contests in geeking—swallowing XT creepy-crawlies whole—and heavy-gee arm wrestling and more, headed for the *Rantipole*'s bow lock for a shortcut back to the *Caveat*.

On the way they passed a small hold where unarmed combats were being fought. The place reeked of sweat, blood, and hatred. Amazing amounts of money were changing hands. Floyt thought he detected a feral enthusiasm under Amarok's reserve.

"If you want to enter, Rok, I'll hold your shirt."

Amarok spit on the deck. "With those bunglers? It would be a betrayal of Someone's training and teacher."

They came across another commotion in the next hold along. A crowd of raucous, besotted, and overmedicated onlookers was gathered along a marked-off area like a tenpin lane or a fencing *piste*, howling bets and putting up cash. Off to one side, some standing upright, some scattered about, all dented and crumpled from impact, were what looked like ordinary lockers of sheet metal.

At one end of the lane were men and one or two women, a few of them bleeding from scalp wounds, most drinking or taking deep breaths from inhalers, puffing on pipes, or popping pills.

As Floyt and Amarok watched, two intoxicated officials set one of the lockers up at the far end of the lane, a meter past the foul line, squaring it carefully. One yelled, "We've got another challenger for you here, Lugo!"

From among the contestants stepped a squat, powerful-looking man who resembled a champion shot-putter gone to fat. His shaved skull, like a pink bullet, bore livid marks but was unbloodied. Thick swirls of black hair grew like fur on his chest, back, belly, and shoulders.

Intrigued, Amarok slipped quietly into the hold, headed for the sideline. Floyt tagged along watchfully.

The squat man—Lugo—waved to acknowledge news of the challenge, drinking slugs of pale-blue rum from a glass cylinder like a long, wide stylus.

"This looks like something This One has heard about. Let's see how Lugo does, Hobart."

Floyt wasn't really in the mood, but could hardly refuse, given how Amarok had accompanied him around the Grapple. Officials of the strange contest loaded metal plates into the locker under the inspection of seconds. Another contestant, a powerful young man put together like a heroic statue, wearing only soleskins and a loinstrap, toed the starting line. Lugo didn't seem in the least worried.

Floyt, since he didn't know what was coming, wasn't looking, and missed the new opponent's take-off. He was playing with his survival tool, getting the hang of the blade releases and various features.

As Amarok watched, the challenger started down the lane at a fast walk that quickly became a trot, then a full run, his head lowered like that of a charging bull, arms pumping. He left the deck in a tremendous dive just at the foul line, arms held stiffly behind him, to ram dead center into the locker with a fearful crash.

The locker went flying back from the collision, but not as far as Amarok had expected, given the circumstances. It hit the deck with a resonant crash, disturbing an area of white powder that had been dusted there. The human battering ram caught himself in a semisprawl on the deck. There were whines and moans from those who'd bet on him.

Floyt, who'd looked up from his survival tool too late, gaped. Two officials, each stratoed on a different substance, brought out a measuring scanner and tried to meld their separate realities to establish how far the locker had been knocked.

"One and one-half meters," it was determined. Among those who'd backed the challenger there was more bellyaching, and hands were waved in the air.

Now Lugo toed the starting line, ready for his defending effort. "Heavy gravity type," Amarok concluded. Floyt paid attention this time.

The champ launched himself in a ponderous run that drummed the deck. But he gathered speed very quickly, catapulted himself headfirst, and bashed the locker with the din of a deepspace collision.

This time it flew like a frightened bird, as Lugo neatly caught himself on the deck. It landed nearly twice as far as it had for the challenger.

Onlookers were yeowling and sloshing drinks, cursing or exulting; fists were shaken on high and caps flung aloft. Bets were being paid even before the befuddled officials could confirm the winner.

Payoffs were in Spican Bank notes, ovals, ducats, personal markers, precious stones and metals, weapons, and other personal possessions. One very distinguished-looking woman appeared to be transferring ownership of her very handsome-looking young male companion to an even more distinguished-looking woman. The boy seemed pleased with the whole idea, embracing his new patron.

"We might as well be going," Amarok decided. "Something's wrong here, but This One can't tell what."

"That's fine with me, Rok. But before we go back to the *Pihoquiaq* or whatever, I want to double back and exchange this." Floyt held up the survival tool. "The compass is broken."

Amarok was about to shrug that off, but then became suddenly and predatorily interested. "You said what? What makes you think so?" He drew Floyt over to one side, shielding the conversation with his body.

Floyt said, "Uh, the damn thing went crazy a few moments ago, spinning around and around. It seems all right now, but since that merchant said it was guaranteed—"

Amarok was shushing him. The Innuit was looking around, eyeing in particular the foul line, where the locker had been positioned. He rubbed his jaw, muttering, "Could it be that simple?"

Then he laughed aloud, took Floyt by the elbow, and made for the hatch. The rest of the crowd was laughing and carrying on; Amarok and the trailing Floyt went unnoticed. Floyt tucked the tool in a pocket, along with the book he'd bought.

Reading frame markings, Amarok found the spot, one deck down, directly beneath the wall-locker-head-knocker hold and, more to the point, the foul line. From a nearby compartment a cable was routed up through the overhead, toward the deckplates beneath the lockers.

"Well, hole Someone and blow Him away!" Amarok breathed.

Floyt was beginning to understand. He followed as Amarok stole over to the compartment from which the cable emerged. The hatch had been left a little ajar, a common practice in the dilapidated *Rantipole*, with its aged environmental systems. They both hunkered down low, to peer within.

An old man seated at a small table, was drawing ecstatically on a smoke carburetor and failed to notice them. Before him several monitors showed the wall-locker competition area from various angles.

Amarok, glancing around, spied a tool locker in the passageway. He went to it and began sorting through the things he found there, returning with a clamplike device, making adjustments to its instrumentation, setting it.

"Surge breaker," Amarok explained in a whisper, thrusting

it into Floyt's hands and putting his back up against the bulkhead. Bending his knees and making a stirrup of his hands, he whispered, "Hurry!"

Floyt, still feeling the effects of the meltdowns, didn't even know where to begin demurring. So he put his foot in Amarok's big palms and stepped up onto his shoulders, a bit wobbly until the trader clamped strong hands around his calves. The cuff of the surge breaker adjusted itself to the cable, locking around it with a conspiratorial *click*.

When Floyt was back down, Amarok went back to the locker. He selected a flat length of some leathery synthetic stuff and trimmed it with the ultrasharp scissors of Floyt's survival tool. He shucked his top and somehow inserted the piece into his roll-top collar.

"Every little edge helps. Now, let's get back," he said in a hushed voice, "before someone beats us to it!"

Back at the scene of the outlandish contest, Lugo was having difficulty finding a new opponent. No one felt like collecting a concussion or injuring their spinal column in a match Lugo seemed destined to win. The champion showed surprise when Amarok swaggered up to him and casually inquired about having a bash at it.

Floyt found himself called upon to witness the setting up of the locker and the arrangement of the weights in its bottom. One of the reeling officials ran a quick detectorscan on Amarok, to be sure he didn't have an armored skull, reinforced skeleton, or other unfair advantage.

It wasn't hard at all to lay off five hundred ovals on Amarok at three-to-one odds; in fact, bettors were climbing over each other to try to get in on the action. Amarok was betting even more than Floyt. It was the first time Floyt had seen Amarok cough up any money. Soon fortune was in the offing.

Amarok handed Floyt his gunbelt, then toed the line. He raced off down the lane, moving like a young god.

Amarok launched himself cleanly, arms well back, When he struck the locker, it flew backward as if it had been yanked by a hawser, not landing in the dust at all but beyond it, sliding until it fetched up against the bulkhead.

Lugo stood slack-jawed. There were whistles and salutes

from the bystanders. Amarok rose, rubbing his head, smiling at Floyt. He hadn't been injured, due in part to the black hair padding his head, but one side of the locker was stove-in.

Lugo, faced with the alternatives of forfeiting or denouncing Amarok for having somehow sabotaged Lugo's own con, went on instead with the contest. Huffing and puffing, he took his mark, working his arms, pawing the deck like a bull. He was, Floyt admitted to himself, a human projectile. Those who'd wagered on him called encouragement.

"He appears to be getting ready to put it through the bulkhead," Floyt observed, despairing over his five hundred ovals.

Lugo lumbered off again with that same prompt gathering of momentum. But his coordination seemed a bit off, either because he'd been unnerved by Amarok's showing or due to the number of licks he'd already taken on the head.

Lugo threw everything he had into a ferocious take-off, smashing into the locker with a sound like a peal of sheet-metal thunder. It lofted in a long arc but crashed to the deck short of Amarok's feat, scraping an all-too-visible smear in the rearmost area of the white dust.

Lugo thundered to the deck and stayed there, out cold.

The crowd lost all control. Lugo's backers and shills were collared at once by those who'd taken a chance on Amarok. Bottles and jugs were passed as the winner was kissed and slapped on the back, punched on the arms and patted on the seat of the pants. Floyt hurried to collect his and Amarok's winnings. It took six people to haul Lugo from the scene.

Floyt and Amarok made a hasty departure, wished a fond farewell by those who'd bet with them, cursed and reviled by the Lugo contingent.

They agreed that the situation called for several more melt-downs, and made their way forward, following homemade arrows that exhibited a universal EXIT symbol underneath, off to meet Professor K'ek at the Oasis. Every so often Floyt, in an uncharacteristic display, kissed his winnings.

They went down stairwells and through passageways, causing Amarok to frown. "This somehow does not feel right; it can't be the correct route to the for'd airlock, no matter what the signs say."

They were halfway through an echoing cargo hold that was empty but for some huge crates. Its few lights cast more shadows than illumination.

Floyt heard no warning sound, sensed no movement. Something flicked his neck with cold lightning and he found himself paralyzed. Dropping, he was whirled around, the revolver whisked neatly from his belt, and discarded in a heap on the deck.

As Floyt slumped, conscious but helpless, Amarok spun, hand dipping for the hammergun on his hip. But a green, glassy stave struck his wrist as the pistol came clear; the gun whirled, clattering, across the deckplates.

Clasping his hand, Amarok backpedaled away from the expected followup, but none came. The pneuma-warrior, in a fighting stance, stave ready, waited until Amarok was well out of range.

Then he quickly picked up the hammergun and hurled it, along with Floyt's Webley, high atop a huge packing crate.

Amarok came forward a step, massaging his bicep; the stave whirled and came on the ready.

CHAPTER 9

IF WE SHOULD DIE
BEFORE WE WAKE

MERRYWELL AND ALACRITY WERE OBLIGED TO CHECK THEIR sidearms and leave their bodyguard behind at Bulkhead Twenty, far forward in *Caveat Emptor* toward the bridge and the living quarters of her owner and master, Costa.

The dividing line was heavily guarded. Nearly all other visitors, wanderers, or would-be deal makers were turned away. On the other side of Bulkhead Twenty a very different ambience prevailed. There was quiet and calm, in richly appointed compartments and elegantly decorated passageways. Even the security fixtures and defensive implacements were chic.

The enforcers who'd accompanied Alacrity and Merrywell that far were left behind too. Their new escort was a comely young woman with mounds of ringleted red hair, who went barefoot on the deck shag and wore an ensemble of something resembling scarlet cobweb. Alacrity spotted a number of other females and a few males dressed the same way.

"Costa's social directors," Merrywell commented. He seemed inclined to take his time, slouching along, dragging his feet. Their escort didn't appear to mind. Neither did Alacrity, who relished a chance to look around the Grapple's most exclusive neighborhood.

They walked slowly past a roomy compartment draped and curtained in lush copper velvet. In it was gathered a crowd of

Grapple attendees totally different from the rabble on the down-hill side of Bulkhead Twenty. Costa's special servitors circulated among them with trays. Sprightly, unobtrusive music played. In the center of the compartment was a low, plush, circular dais under a strong spotlight. On it was a naked woman, a healthy, wholesome-looking wheat-blonde, eighteen or so. Her cheeks were slick with tears she'd cried a short time before, but she looked cried out. To the sides, holographic displays gave pertinent data: medical exam results, skills and education, warranties.

Merrywell spied her too. Both men heard the bids as they passed by.

"Most likely she was abducted," Merrywell told Alacrity, puffing a red cigarette, more dour than ever. "Damnfool kids from some civilized place—Gemütlichkeit, maybe, or Éclat—they go off on their *wanderjahr* or Grand Tour or what the hell ever, without the first idea what can happen to them or what to watch out for. There's a little back-passageway trade in run-of-the-mill merchandise, back of Bulkhead Twenty, but the prime stuff gets the gold-gavel treatment."

Merrywell spoke softly; their escort didn't appear to take any notice. Alacrity tried to put the scene out of his mind. He could do nothing about it.

For now, he amended. He opened the trove of his hopes for a moment and looked at an image he'd held for a long time, of a time when, if he did everything just right, human history would change for the better. And he recalled the flaring of the causality harp.

Not for the security-minded Costa to sit in a winter garden out on the hull of his ship; their escort led them to a compartment below and forward of the bridge. The captain's quarters were in one of the best-armored, best-protected parts of the attack transport. They were lavishly decorated in iron-and-gold tech-deco.

Captain Jobold Costa sat in an airfloat conformer behind a landing-field desk of jet-black wood. He wore a tissuey green lounging jacquard. He had dense gray eyebrows that looked as though he combed them backward. He also had a direct gaze, but his eyes were pouchy and bloodshot. He wasn't much overweight, but had a lot of slack flesh. He struck Alacrity as a man whose business had gotten the upper hand on him.

And here's a guy who's got a piece of who-knows-how-many rejuvenation clinics, antigeronic centers, health spas, and whatever. Maybe he doesn't realize he looks like he's ready for planting? Alacrity thought.

Around the compartment were holographic projections, not of nebulae and the stars, but planetary scenes. That made a sort of sense; how often would such a man leave the only safety he trusted and walk the surface of a world? It looked like a pretty good bet that he didn't even trust his own doctors and clinicians.

Merrywell gave no hint of noticing the grandeur of Costa's personal domain. The captain of the *Magus* shuffled over tiredly to slump in a priceless Newlantean Empire chair. Alacrity took another next to it.

"We'll make this brief; I can't spare you two more than a moment," Costa told Merrywell curtly. To Alacrity he added, "What's your name, by the way? And don't waste my time with an alias."

"Cap'n Costa," Merrywell interrupted, before Alacrity could decide whether or not to challenge the question. Costa had offered nothing so far and demanded more than was polite at a Grapple.

"This man and his friend and Cap'n Amarok are here in the *Pihoquiaq*, grappled to the *Magus*. And so you'll be understanding my interest in this matter. They'd be very grateful for your aid and advice, but that doesn't entitle you to know what you just asked."

Costa's eyes burned on Merrywell, who didn't appear in the least discomfited and in fact gave a wide yawn.

"Who are you to tell me what I may and may not ask in *Caveat Emptor*, you bundle of frowns?"

Merrywell wore the expression of a particularly depressed blue-tick hound. He worked his words around in his mouth like a wad of chewing gum before he said them, pointing his long cigarette holder at the other.

"You 'n' me have managed not to cross courses so far, Costa. And you were the one who invited me to just say the word if there was ever anything you could do. D'you recall that? Listen: if you put one more warning bolt across my vector, I'll make you live up to it, and we'll see which vessel has the real goods, the *Magus* or this whorehouse of yours."

Costa wavered for a moment between anger and retreat, while Alacrity thought how bad his and Merrywell's tactical situation was. Merrywell didn't look concerned.

After a time that, for Alacrity, stretched out like two weeks in a fleabag hotel, Costa chuckled. "How can I help the boy if I don't know what it's all about? Let be, let be—we'll start again. Tell me your problem, son."

"My friend and I want to get to Blackguard."

"To—*hmm*." Costa drummed his fingers on the desk. "It can be arranged—I *believe* it can be arranged. Question is, how can it profit me?"

That he had a right to ask. Merrywell was somehow faster than Alacrity to field that one, in the most casual voice. "It would be in the form of a consultation fee, Cap'n, not a share of the enterprise."

"If you say so, Captain." Costa focused on the distance for a moment, concentrating. "It can be done. I know a vessel that will be stopping at Blackguard direct from here: the *Mountebank*."

"Never heard of her," Merrywell answered.

"An old scow, but new in these parts. I'll arrange for your friends to travel in her. Part of the fare will bounce back to me, a finder's fee. I'll make sure it's reasonable."

Alacrity was about to say thanks, knowing it was a small transaction, hardly worth Costa's notice. But Costa leaned toward him first, eyes alight.

"And in return there's something I want, if you can do it. I want to know about Blackguard; nobody seems to know what really goes on there, either at the preserve or the population center. You two get word to me, and I'll make it worth your while."

Alacrity didn't take long to think that one over. "Agreed, aye—if we can."

Costa pursed his lips, gauging Alacrity and the weight of his word.

"Done," he said at length. Then, decisively, slapping the desk: *"Done!"*

Amarok's wrist seemed to be coming around again; somehow, by some precise and instant control, the stave's effect on him had been much different from that of Floyt.

The pneuma-warrior twirled and whirled the weapon in a brilliant demonstration, too fast for the eye to follow, leaving afterimages of green glass and silver banding. Amarok settled into a ready position, showing no emotion. Floyt wanted to cry out, help Amarok, or flee, but could only lie there watching.

The little man in black suddenly rendered Amarok a salute with the stave, then lofted it up after the pistols. He assumed an odd, disjointed pose.

Amarok, radiating strength, dropped into a more rigid one. They closed slowly, circling, watching. Amarok's moves were all lithe power; his opponents' were eerie, marionnettelike, but flowing and very fast.

There was some feinting. Amarok threw a combination of snapping punches and kicks and was extremely quick to recover, offering no openings. The pneuma-warrior avoided them all by a good distance, so wary that he even dodged the feints, appearing to flinch. His prancing, sliding technique incorporated wide, rotary moves, elaborate posturings, a balletic aloofness. Where Amarok was a whirlwind, the silent man was a shadow skimming over rushing water.

The pneuma's eyes showed only the cold, cobra stare. Amarok's face was tense and grim, jaw muscles clenched and blood vessels pulsing like hoses in his neck, his fighting snarl in place.

Amarok pressed an attack. The pneuma seemed not so much to dodge or retreat as simply to be elsewhere. The slashing edges of Amarok's hands, the great stony knobs of his knuckles, sword-plane of his foot—all the fearsome striking surfaces of him—failed to make any contact.

Floyt dizzily recalled what Merrywell had said about pneuma-warriors being kinesics readers. Amarok's skintight suit and bared midsection were betraying him. For all his fine-honed ferocity, he was no more able to connect with the little man in black than sledgehammer a specter.

Then the pneuma began to hit back. Pirouetting aside from a fierce kick, he struck Amarok's knee a numbing blow with his elbow. When he might have followed up, he let the bigger man retreat, then minced and stalked after.

Amarok was bathed in sweat, and his leg was giving him trouble. With the cruel detachment of a cat with a mouse, the pneuma began disabling him bit by bit, striking almost at will at the brachial, solar plexus, carotid sinus, and larynx. Amarok made desperate counterattacks and defensive moves, only to be hurt again and again. His left eye was nearly swollen shut and he could barely breath through his damaged throat; he was weaving and staggering, a crippled giant.

At last he summoned from some depths the *kime* for a flying kick. The pneuma barely moved, drawing his head to one side and striking as Amarok went past. The *Pihoquiaq*'s master flopped to the deck and didn't rise.

The little man stood straddling him; Amarok was wide open for any death blow the pneuma might select.

Floyt had been trying desperately to cry out or move, either to help Amarok or escape. Using his proteus would be impossible; the Grapple was a communications sink hole, with too many hulls, bulkheads, fields, and other obstructions and interference sources between himself and Alacrity.

But he did manage, for the first time, to get out a strangled, unintelligible sound, then draw a deeper breath. With that he felt some power of movement returning in a slow trickle.

The pneuma's hand had been making slow debate over the fallen Amarok, going through permutations of Claw, Hammer, Needle, and Sword. Hearing Floyt, he left off his contemplations. He stepped over his opponent and went to the packing crate. Floyt watched, terrified and puzzled.

The pneuma went through some preparatory motions, then began climbing straight up one corner of the smooth plastic crating. In another moment he was back down with his stave, to hover over the reviving Floyt. He showed no sign of emotion, or exertion. Floyt could only cringe and wait, moving feebly, unable to look away from the dark, unblinking eyes; he couldn't imagine resisting or escaping this incredible man.

The pneuma-warrior made a quick adjustment to his stave, touching it to Floyt once more. Again there was the freezing electricity, and the Earther went limp.

The pneuma gathered him up easily in a fireman's carry; he stepped back to Amarok, making a last adjustment on the stave. Its ferrule went toward the nape of Amarok's neck; Floyt could only watch with lolling head.

The ferrule touched the collar over Amarok's neck; his body arched once, then subsided.

The pneuma looked aside abruptly, listening for something Floyt couldn't hear. Then he was out in the passageway again, Floyt still over his shoulder, dogging the hatch behind, Floyt's weight and mass hardly impeding him at all. As he retraced the route Floyt and Amarok had followed, he pulled down the directional signs and tossed them aside. He'd evidently scavenged them and used them to lure his prey into the hold.

When they emerged into one of *Rantipole*'s main passageways, the pneuma simply sashayed along as if nothing unusual were going on. Anyone who happened to notice would of course assume Floyt was just another casualty of the wall-locker-head-knocker game or one of the ship's other risky diversions.

Floyt's captor emerged into the smoky din of *Caveat Emptor*, and paused to be sure neither Merrywell's followers nor anyone else likely to interfere was on the scene. Floyt was feeling the first stirrings of neuromotor control again, but was at a loss as to what to do with it. If he moved or even tried to cry out he'd only get another shock treatment.

Then he spied, almost upside-down, the cafe called the Oasis, a modest little collection of nearly miniature chairs and tables clustered around a service counter, with an awning against the occasional condensation drips. There sat Professor K'ek, swinging his legs and gloating over his hardbound books and other purchases piled on the table.

K'ek chanced to look up just then, picking out Floyt; the eyes went wide in his tamarin face. The pneuma, having already dismissed the professor as insignificant, was looking elsewhere.

Floyt tried to gather his own *kime*. In one effort that was more than he'd have believed himself capable of, he dipped into the bellows pocket on his right thigh, seizing what he was after in one grab.

The pneuma felt the motion, of course, even though he couldn't see it. He brought his stave up in an all but disinterested tap; Floyt's survival tool dropped from his hand, hitting the deck with metallic racket. The sounds covered the fall of the other object Floyt had grabbed at the same time, the one he'd *meant* to leave behind.

The pneuma turned and started off once more, casually using the infernal stave as a walking staff.

Professor K'ek slid down off his seat, watching the pneuma wend off through the crowd with Floyt over his shoulder. He scampered over to where the survival tool lay, his tail rippling in the air. Floyt had dropped something else.

It was a book microfiche, one of the ones he'd purchased when he'd met the professor. K'ek read the title, and his eyes went even wider.

The pneuma-warrior strode down the deserted passageway leading to the boat lock where the *Lamia* had moored to *Caveat Emptor*. But he stopped dead and Floyt, managing to lift his head, saw that the lock was sealed and its indicators registered it as vacant. *Lamia* had departed.

Before Floyt's captor could absorb that, pulsed bolts of blue-white light began hosing back and forth across the passageway from behind, licking over bulkheads, deck, and overhead, all in a moment, catching the pneuma and his burden.

The little man in black reacted instantly, letting go of Floyt, leaping to one side, and dropping flat. But it was impossible to avoid the rays in that confined space.

Floyt had been numbed when the light first touched him; he hardly felt himself hit the deckplates. His vision went dark for an instant, then cleared momentarily.

The pneuma had been hit too, and landed awkwardly, dropping his stave. But then he was dodging and weaving, rolling dextrously and leaping to bounce off the bulkhead, trying to stay out of the pulses as he rushed toward the source of the beam, still without uttering a sound.

But the gunner could saturate the entire field of fire in split seconds with movements of his wrist, while the pneuma was obliged to dodge through meters of space; it was a losing proposition. The beam brushed the pneuma just as he dove to one side. His leg buckled under him. He landed in a tuck, went into a handspring. A random swing of the lightray scored on his forearm.

The handspring couldn't carry him clear of the danger; the narrow passageway was better than a shooting gallery for some-one splashing an energy weapon around. The pneuma rolled again, digging into a sleeve pocket. He wriggled around and hurled something that spun and threw off sparks, humming, but the blue-white bolts caught him fleetingly as he did. His aim was ruined and whatever he'd thrown glanced off the side of the passageway with a radiant burst and a shower of fire-flecks.

In the meantime, the beam pinned him squarely. It held him for an instant, then he flopped down, under and away from it. Impossibly, he was still moving, dragging himself in Floyt's direction. For the first time his eyes betrayed something: the effort it took to make his body respond when it should by all rights have failed him.

He groped stubbornly, clumsily, in a leg pouch, eyes fixed on the Earther. Floyt knew the little man meant to kill him.

The beam caught him again, though, and held to him. No nervous system, however conditioned and trained, could with-stand that. The pneuma blacked out, his head striking the deck. From his limp fingers rolled an autostyrette, to fetch up against Floyt's leg.

An indeterminate time went by, then Floyt heard a familiar voice say, "As the Perfesser puts it, 'We don't know the mean-ing of "*guts*"!'"

Floyt found that his voice was coming back. "Alacrity—" It came out "Arl-kee."

Alacrity held one of Merrywell's matched stunguns. He tucked it through his belt and assisted Floyt in sitting up. "Isn't that right, K'ek?"

Professor K'ek poked his head around Alacrity, to goggle at Floyt. His eyes were as big and bright as desert moons.

"Kreegah! Stand by to scuttle the schoolmarm! Take no prisoners!"

"He got your little message and came to get me just as Merrywell and me were coming to find you at the Oasis, Ho. K'ek tracked you and the masked marvel, here, by scent, at a dead run. You should've seen him."

Alacrity held up the book fiche Floyt had dropped for K'ek to find. It was *The Prisoner of Zenda*.

"This isn't supposed to be some kind of horrible pun, is it, Ho?" Alacrity glared accusingly. "And by the way, where's Rok?"

"Back in the *Rantipole*," Floyt said, trying to rise. "Let's get out of here. Away from"—indicating the pneuma—"*him!*"

"Ho, it'd take a kiss from Prince Charming and a three-day head start to wake *that* boy up. He's Cinderella for the time being."

"Cin—Oh!" Floyt struggled to his feet. "You mean Sleeping Beauty."

"Well, *one* of those cartoons." Alacrity shifted to kneel by the little man, picking up the fallen styrette. "Anyway, I just want to see if he's carrying anything that'll tell us what—"

"No! Now!" Floyt said, grabbing his arm.

"What's the matter with you, Ho? We've got to find out what's going on and whether Sile is in with somebody or—"

"Alacrity, you don't understand! This man isn't human! I *saw!*" Alacrity was trying to tug his arm free, but Floyt had it and wouldn't let go.

Alacrity jumped to his feet and yanked his arm loose. Professor K'ek skipped back out of the way, tail lashing and quivering.

"Now, dammit, Ho, *I'm gonna get mad in a second here!*"
"You blind idiot! You didn't see what I saw!"

They were both breathing hard, as close to a real falling out as they'd come in a long time. Alacrity saw fear and awe on Floyt's face, his pallor and fright. He got his temper under control and queried sweetly, "If the little scut's superhuman, how come he's off doing *kata* in dreamland?"

Floyt simply looked down at the pneuma. Just then there were hurried footfalls in the passageway, Merrywell and his party bringing up the rear, guns ready, having gotten sidetracked trying to keep up with Alacrity and K'ek.

"He's okay." Alacrity waved. Then: "Ho, look, you can't let it get to you. All he is, is another would-be-mystic chop-and-drop man from some zilchtech planet."

As he spoke, Alacrity lowered himself to one knee again to search the pneuma. Merrywell and others gathered about.

"They're not bad at sneaking around bopping people from behind," Alacrity grouched, "or doing the kung-fu hula. But you see who's up and who's down, don't you, Ho?"

"Where's Amarok?" Merrywell demanded. Floyt told him, and the gloomy captain led his party to find the big trader.

"We'll meet you in the *Magus*," Alacrity said, returning the stungun.

When they'd gone, Alacrity ripped open the black blouse. The pneuma wore padding and an arsenal of weapons and devices strapped to his surprisingly slight body and hidden in pockets and pouches: climbing spikes and adhesive pads that had let him scale the packing crate; throwing stars; rappelling equipment; styrettes; explosives; garrote and more.

"For which reason is it that he docs not bear a firearm?" K'ek wanted to know.

Alacrity shrugged. "Out to prove something; they usually are. It's probably part of the bylaws."

He was looking the styrette over. "But I'll tell you what: he's nothing but another goon. Probably had to pull stakes and run when the peasants found out what a little gunfire or coherent light does to pneuma magic."

He bent and took the pneuma's arms. "No point leaving him here for Sile. You feel well enough to help me get him on my shoulder, Ho?"

Floyt did, barely. As they went along, Professor K'ek keeping pace, Alacrity said, "We've got a lot to do in a hurry. Wouldn't want to miss our ship."

"No, of course we—what? Wait, *ship*?"

The *Magus*'s sickbay was better than many of the clinics at the Grapple. Amarok, arriving there, had his injuries pronounced serious but the prognosis excellent. The insert of syn-

thetic he'd slipped into his collar had spared him the pneuma
stave's full effect. Merrywell explained all that, while returning
the retrieved Webley to Floyt, at the *Pihoquiaq*'s lock.

"The kid'll be on his feet before the Grapple's over,"
Merrywell went on, the flattening of his frown signifying wild
jubilation. "If he needs a hand with *Pihoquiaq*, I can spare
somebody for a while; got too damn many people underfoot
anyhow. Alacrity, tell Hobart about the *Mountebank*."

Alacrity did. Costa had made arrangements for them to
travel with a dealer in new identities and fugitive placement
by the name of Urtho Skate, who owned a rather worse-for-
wear converted mail packet even older than *Pihoquiaq*, the
Mountebank. Skate had several fugitives already waiting inboard
his ship and was planning one brief stop at Blackguard for an
"insertion." He was certain he could get Alacrity and Floyt
down safely and set them up with a situation, but beyond that,
they'd be left to their own resources.

Best of all, because Blackguard was a port of call anyway,
the cost of passage for Floyt and Alacrity would be within their
means.

"What I don't understand is why Sile should send in his pet
pneuma and then leave him high and dry," Alacrity said.

"Cold feet?" Floyt hypothesized. "Or perhaps a foulup in
communication?"

"Either way, I've had it with Sile." Merrywell exhaled
wearily. "The next time I see him I'm doing the universe a
good turn and putting him out of it."

"Captain Merrywell, we don't want you getting embroiled
in a vendetta because of us," Floyt objected.

*"Will you please just let the man kill somebody if he feels
like it?"* Alacrity yelled.

"It needs doing anyhow," Merrywell contended. "Are you
lads ready to go? You've just got time to see Amarok before
Skate gets underway."

"Just one thing, Captain," Floyt began tentatively. "The
pneuma—don't give me that look, Alacrity; I'm all right!—
what did you do with him?"

"We took the autostyrette and gave him the shot he was
going to give you," Merrywell said, stolid and yet sad. "Funny;

it didn't kill him. It went right to work on his nervous system; he won't be any use in his old line of work, ever. I'm not sure what I'm going to do with him."

The Earther stroked his beard; whatever it was would no doubt have killed Floyt.

"Want to hear something sad?" asked tired old Merrywell. "Under that mask-hood thing, he was a kid, maybe sixteen, seventeen or so. Anyway, we figure we'll get some information out of him sooner or later."

Alacrity and Floyt had just fetched their gear. With no idea what they were getting into, the two companions had packed along most of the things Dorraine and Redlock had given them, but had agreed to bequeath a part of Alacrity's seasoning and spice hoard.

"We flagged some recipes that were in the *Pihoquiaq*'s data banks," Alacrity was telling Amarok a few minutes later. "Ho found them. Y'know, it's not a terribly hard thing to learn, cooking."

"Better than going back to mealtrays," Floyt added.

"True." Amarok smiled slowly. He was suspended in a flotation field, his knee and various other parts of him swathed and strapped. His throat was encased in an assist collar, to spare his damaged larynx.

"And we're both very, very sorry for the trouble, Amarok," Floyt said.

"Ah, well; One should expect surprises if He decides to be a breakabout, eh?" He didn't have the strength to laugh. "Keep This One in mind, if you two are ever looking for jobs."

Alacrity promised to do just that, but Floyt's conditioning gave him a twinge. As the two left, Professor K'ek scrambled up to perch in a high chair next to Amarok, holding a textscreen in his lap and preparing to read aloud from one of the professor's favorites, *Riders of the Purple Sage*.

The *Mountebank* was yet another step down in transportation, two thirds the size of *Pihoquiaq* and in an advanced state of neglect. But, because she carried little cargo, she had more living space than the monitor.

Urtho Skate turned out to be an effusive character about

Floyt's size but portly, his dressy outfit of glittering buttons and ruffled cuffs looking like he'd slept in it—several times. Gathered in the ship's tight little combination mess-lounge were Skate, Alacrity and Floyt, and the other two passengers who were making the trip.

It was difficult to tell anything about the last two, gender included. They were costumed as grotesques, their heads encased in monstrous casques that were contorted and painted in demonic expressions and fitted with red compound eyes. They wore burnooses with exaggerated shoulders and platform shoes. One wore dress gloves; the other had fingernails bitten down to the quick.

The masks contained devices that disguised their voices; their greetings came out eerie and synthetic. Word from Merrywell was that such disguises were common in Black-guard.

Alacrity and Floyt were wearing disguises too, improvised ones they'd scrounged up on the *Magus*. In place of casques they had crash helmets, visors adjusted to full reflectiveness. In response to the greeting, Floyt only nodded, while Alacrity gave a barely intelligible answer in crosstalk. The four seated themselves in a messbooth.

Skate went forward to cast off and begin the trip, without offering any blastoff cocktails. Alacrity wasn't surprised; people on the run could hardly expect Red Nova class service.

As *Mountebank* got underway, the passengers took a final look through the viewbleb. The Grapple was still a lightshow of strobing beacons and flashing holosignals, but fewer ships were moored than when the *Pihoquiaq* arrived.

Floyt thought with a little regret about rejuvenation and antigeronic clinics, and wondered if the temptation would present itself again, unsure whether he wanted it to or not.

Alacrity turned to their fellow passengers. "Either of you have any idea where we should stow our bags?"

"There'll be plenty of room for them in the hold," said one of the flat-voiced demon masks. "And for you, too." Empty handed, Alacrity half rose from his seat. At Skate's insistence, both he and Floyt had packed their guns in their bags.

Before Alacrity could do more, muzzles appeared from the

billowing reaches of the burnooses. One spat at Floyt, who only had time to yip and slap the spot where the dart hit him before his eyes rolled up in his head and he keeled over.

Alacrity froze as both guns trained on him. First one mask came off, then the other, with Alacrity covered the whole time. Sile and Constance smiled at him.

"We just wanted to welcome you inboard, dear, dear boy," Sile caroled. "Did you really think Captain Dincrist wouldn't find out that you and Floyt shipped with Amarok? And sourpuss Amarok—there was just one place *he* could be taking you!"

Merrywell said *these two crawlies have a secret patron,* Alacrity remembered. *When Dincrist jinxes somebody, he sure makes it stick.*

"We're going to have *such* fun!" Constance added, gnawing at a thumbnail, eyes practically bursting from her head with excitement.

"Do you know how much trouble you've caused me?" Sile asked. "First Amarok taunted Tah-Skass into coming after him on his own, without my orders, and almost spoiled everything. Then *you* beamed poor Tah-Skass down like an animal, didn't you? My most valuable man, my pneuma."

"But everything's right as rain now," Constance said brightly. "We've got you, and you're going to pay."

She shot Alacrity just as he was making a last-option lurch across the table, and he hit it hard, thinking, *There's just no justice!*

Alacrity began to come around again, realizing foggily that things were getting a little coherent, expecting gradual improvement. There was none.

Instead, he rose to a certain depth just above unconsciousness and below real thought. He drifted, drifted, registering distantly that he was still under something—a drug, maybe, or too much drink. But he couldn't recall what or how, and lacked the will to pursue the point.

Someone peeled back his right eyelid, letting in an unforgiveable light. Alacrity heard a half-recognized male voice.

"Can you hear me? You hear me? *Answer!*"

Alacrity achieved a sort of moaning slur, making no sense.

He wanted to swat the hand away but his arm wasn't working. His eyelid was permitted to fall back into place; he forgot his pique, lapsing into a comfortable void, looking around for images with his mind's eye, unable to make any appear.

Someone was unsatisfied with that. There was an insignificant sensation in his shoulder. After some time, he was again aware, but less able to think.

"Let's give it another try, go-blood," the voice said. "All right, *open your eyes!*"

It was easy to open his eyes; Alacrity found himself looking up at the underside of a ship's bunk. He could also see part of a grimy compartment. He didn't look around because nobody had told him to.

His body informed him that he was strapped into a lower bunk that was, like most, too short for him. A deeper sense let him know he was inside a starship in Hawking. Blank of thought, he registered that and nothing more.

Fixed above him was a compact piece of audiovisual gear. No mystery there, although he was too vacant to think about it much; he'd seen equipment like it before in teaching facilities and in the Earthservice's conditioning bailiwick.

Seated beside the bunk, just at the edge of Alacrity's vision, holding a pneumodermic injector, was Skate.

An arm was hanging down from the upper bunk, recognizable as Floyt's by the cheap proteus it wore. The Earther could've been asleep, unconscious, or dead. Alacrity absorbed that in a detached way; emotions seemed far off, and he wasn't even worried about his *own* well-being.

Skate took Alacrity's chin in his hand and shook it a little. "Pay attention now, eh, high-mover? We have to have a talk."

Skate's face was sweating and his breath smelled of Perkup; a random thought crossed Alacrity's mind, that the man had been at his backpack of travel accessories.

Skate drew his floatcushion closer, leaving Alacrity's face pointed toward the AV unit overhead. Without resentment or much curiosity, Alacrity obediently paid attention, as ordered, watching the thing.

Skate activated it, and it began projecting hypnotic light patterns, reinforcing them with subsonics. The unit scanned

Alacrity, carefully adapting itself. The subject slipped quickly and readily into a deeper trance state.

"Now, we start with your name," Skate said. "Tell me your real name."

"Alacrity Fitzhugh."

"Eh? Is that an alias?"

"Yes."

"I want you to tell me your real name, the one you were born under!"

Alacrity began to answer, but then something clicked in, deep inside. His mouth stayed shut; he just looked at the machine, at peace, with the command short-circuited.

"Tell me your real name," Skate ordered again patiently. He looked as if he was both angry at Alacrity and nervous about something. He glanced over his shoulder at the dogged and locked hatch. Alacrity watched the flashing gyrations of the lights, felt and listened to the pulsations.

"Your *real* name, son," Skate resumed. In spite of his harried expression, his voice was soothing and friendly, a sign that he'd had a lot of experience at that sort of thing.

That same short-circuit removed the question from Alacrity's train of thought again, before he could even bring the answer to mind. Skate saw, and didn't waste more time on that line of attack.

"Why can't you answer? Tell me what's stopping you."

But each such question brought Skate up against an impenetrable wall that protected Alacrity's past. He gnawed his lower lip, fuming, not realizing that it had nothing to do with why he was there or how he'd run afoul of Sile, or why Floyt was important to them.

But Skate knew when to abandon a fruitless line of inquiry. "Now I want you to tell me why you want to go to Blackguard, Alacrity. What's there?"

Again Skate ran into a blockage; this time it was the one put there by the Earthservice behavioral engineering team, part of the programming that bound him to Floyt and the *Astraea Imprimatur* mission. It wasn't nearly as deeply planted or all-embracing as what Skate had touched in probing Alacrity's deeper secrets.

Skate saw that Alacrity was near answering, the programming weakened by the traumas and stresses of the journey, and the effects of the drug, and the AV barrage.

The identity merchant bit his lip once more in indecision, then put the pneumodermic to Alacrity's shoulder again and gave him a megahit.

Alacrity could barely focus on the AV. His mouth was very dry and his skin acutely sensitive. Strangely, sound was a distant and not very important sensory input.

"Do you feel the blockage that's there, Alacrity? The one around you and your friend and what you're involved in?"

Alacrity did indeed, and nodded; it was the one Earthservice had implanted. He knew every twinge and twist, every train of thought that would set it off. He'd mapped his lost freedom against it, plotted and triangulated it laboriously over the past weeks, finding its shoreline in terms of spasms and sharp jolts to his free will.

"That's good, Alacrity," Skate said into his ear. "Hold the shape of it in your mind, because we're going to take it away. Now, I want you to think of the pain you feel when you try to go against this prohibition. Think of the very instant it hits you, but *don't feel it*!

"I'm not going to ask you any questions; I just want you to get that prohibition clearly in your mind. I'm going to take it away..."

It went on like that for a while. Skate was good; under his guidance, the whole structure of the conditioning simply began to fade. A part of Alacrity watched it approach the vanishing point.

Then, with a calculated prod, Skate diminished it to a mist. Alacrity, in stuporous amaze, felt as if he were looking over someone else's shoulder, watching what was going on within him.

Skate repeated the sequence. The conditioning dwindled to nothingness, gone altogether from Alacrity's cerebrum and gut. Along with it, it took the artificial underpinnings of his partnership with Floyt.

"Now, son," Skate crooned, hunkering forward, eagerness edging into his voice. "Back to the beginning again. We'll begin with Sile's patron, Captain Dincrist. Do you know Captain Dincrist?"

"Sure." Alacrity felt exactly as if someone else were speaking for him.

"Good! Tell me, why did Dincrist order Sile to—"

Skate stopped as the hatch controls were tried. When the person seeking entrance found out it had been secured, there was a hammering and railing from the other side.

Skate suddenly looked terrified. "Go to sleep!" he rasped at Alacrity. "Close your eyes!"

Alacrity did. But the drug had him parsecs from true sleep, so he simply lay there, an unfocused void. He heard the AV unit being whisked away. He heard Skate cross to the hatch and open it, heard the fury in Constance's voice as she charged into the compartment.

"What're you doing? Why was this hatch locked? *Answer me, you slimy toad!*"

"Just keeping an eye on these two," Skate explained smoothly. "I was just making sure they—"

"You can't open your mouth without lying, can you?"

Alacrity heard her cross to the bunk and felt her lift his arm to examine his shoulder. Again his eye was peeled back; he had a bleary glimpse of light, nothing he could fix on.

Constance let his eyelid fall. "Open your eyes. Open them!"

Alacrity complied. Constance was standing there, having shed the burnoose disguise, wearing a chiaroscuro fleshpeel. She turned to Skate without warning and fetched him an open-handed clout across the ear that sent him toppling against the bulkhead; she'd changed from a teasing sextoy into a homicidal maniac with mad eyes.

"You just get them ready for cachesleep. And if you try anything else, I'll kill you," she whispered.

Skate, rubbing his face and glowering at her, whined, "I was only trying to get some straight answers out of them—for Sile."

"*I'll kill you,*" she repeated tightly. "And you've never done anything for anyone except yourself in your life."

She looked to Alacrity. "In fact, we might as well put them both into cachesleep right now."

"What? Why?"

"So that you won't be able to get to them again. We'll have the extra space that much sooner and I'll have that much less to worry about. And you'd better not so much as cross my path these next few weeks. *Poustis!* I can't believe Sile stuck me with this job! With *you!*"

"It won't be so bad, Constance. *Mountebank*'s got plenty of entertainment, 'cause she's a little slow-going," Skate tried to placate. "And in any case, we'll get to Blackguard before Sile and Dincrist."

"It's not the trip; it's being cooped up with you." Reaching out of Alacrity's field of vision, she produced a pneumodermic kit. "Go aft and get the cachesleep wrappers ready," she ordered. "I'll prep them myself."

Another pneumodermic touched Alacrity's skin.

CHAPTER 10

FLEEING FROM THE WOLF
TO THE TIGER

THE IRONIC THING ABOUT THE SLAVE COLLARS WAS, YOU COULD take them off if they got uncomfortable.

They were several centimeters wide, like circlets of hammered strap-iron with rings and hinges, like something out of a history text. And they weren't welded, lasered, or riveted onto the necks of the recipient; they were *issued*. They were mainly for show and to give the Betters of Blackguard a thrill.

Blackguard had much more businesslike and effective means of keeping its chattels in line, and they'd been put into place during the long weeks of cachesleep in *Mountebank*. Alacrity and Floyt noted the collars from a distance, registering them along with other evidence of disaster.

Nauseous, stripped of every possession, desperately depleted from cachesleep and its attendant drugs and resuscitating equipment, Floyt and Alacrity blinked and winced stupidly under the mauve sky and amber sun of Blackguard. They'd come to, lying on a cargo skid not far from Skate's vessel, with mouths dry and caked, eyes filmed, feeling as though they'd been racked and knouted.

They had lost a great deal of weight—making Alacrity, in particular, look emaciated—an awful lot of which had been moisture.

Moreover, Skate hadn't been too particular about keeping

153

them clean. They stank, caked with filth, and both had bed-sores. Floyt realized dully that the dental space retainer was missing from his mouth, and his new teeth had grown markedly.

"Are you all right, Alacrity?" Floyt somehow compelled his leathery mouth to say.

"Ghurk."

People and machines were moving around the spaceport structures in the distance. The landing surface was a small one, a few dozen hectares or so. The nearest ship on the field, aside from the *Mountebank*, looked to Floyt like a chambered nautilus made of glazed ceramic. It was unloading itself with articulated metal tentacles, another oddity of the Third Breath. From the ship, four people had just emerged, two men and two women. They were pointedly nondescript, dressed in the drab denim worksuits and blue skullcaps of achievement coordinators from Egalitaria.

Around the field's perimeter were a variety of structures—hangars, offices, servicing facilities, and so forth, Floyt supposed—done up in elaborate rococo. Standard employee attire appeared to be maroon. Beyond the field was a ring of tall pylons maintaining the ghostly backdrop of an energy curtain.

The sky was busy with local traffic, as Frostpile's had been. But where there'd been variety in Frostpile's assorted vehicles, here there was something more like disparity: a glassy swanboat and a primered replica P-38 fighter; a flying chariot drawn through the air by stallions that Floyt took to be robotic; and a modern fast-attack patrol flier weighted with the latest in weaponry and detectors.

As Merrywell and others had mentioned, Blackguard was a place of masks, at least for the ruling class. A woman floated by overhead on a graceful vehicle that was a cross between a speakers' rostrum and an abstract sculpture, her face concealed behind a winged veil of gauze and sequins. The long, filmy train of her gown rippled and swayed ten meters behind her. Nearby, the occupant of a hovercoracle wore such a massive headdress that it was impossible to gauge sex, size, or anything else.

The two revivees labored to sit upright on the skid, trying to focus, looking around. Ground personnel and other members of the lower orders were for the most part unmasked. They were, as far as Alacrity could see, a cross-section of human types, some identifiable, some not. Except for one or two cargo vessels, starships grounded on the field ran to pricey private executive craft and luxury yachts.

Even in the midst of his suffering, his conditioning stirred Floyt and he tried to spot the *Astraea Imprimatur*. He could see no vessel with that marking.

Steadying his gaze and straining to focus, Alacrity studied the other captives—slaves, prisoners, whatever—moving around the spaceport. It was easy to tell who they were; they were unmasked and doing menial jobs and manual labor, some wearing those collars, none in maroon. And as Alacrity watched, one looked around, made sure nobody of any significance was watching, and opened his slave collar. He rubbed his neck and wiped the sweat away from beneath it, then clamped it shut again.

The typical local ran to Floyt's height or less and was inclined toward obesity. They were all well tanned from exposure to Invictus, Blackguard's primary, but looked to be of fair-skin stock, with light hair often bleached to yellow-white.

Some wore castoff outworld clothing, adapted as shorts or loincloths and halters. Others had on what had to be native attire, of pretty much the same in coarser fabric.

They heard footsteps and looked around dazedly. Skate was approaching, followed by two other men. One of these was also an offworlder; his maroon skinsuit had extravagantly padded shoulders and codpiece and he was tall, taller than Alacrity.

The other was a local, who wore shorts and eyeglasses that appeared to have been tinkered together from scavenged metal scraps and wire, the lenses mismatched.

The faces the three made as they approached told Alacrity and Floyt that they smelled just as bad as they felt. The fellow in maroon consulted a handheld unit. He was evidently satisfied with the readings.

"All right, Skate; both jots check out functional."

Alacrity closed his eyes, fighting to keep calm. At some point Skate had implanted almost microscopic actijots into Floyt and Alacrity. It was obvious why slave collars were super-fluous.

With actijots to control, track, I.D., or punish slaves, nothing more was required.

Alacrity knew there wasn't any point in inspecting his sore, encrusted, repugnant person trying to find where Skate—or had it been Constance?—had implanted the jot. When the procedure was done right, the minuscule puncture healed virtually at once.

Floyt had come around, sort of. Looking over the bespectacled local, he concluded that Blackguard saw little traffic with the galaxy at large. The man had pockmarks and subcutaneous cysts, a missing tooth and two missing toes on his right foot, a fracture of the femur that had healed badly, and a disfiguring scar across his cheek. A misalignment of his teeth had given him a severe malocclusion that any advanced medical treatment could've fixed quickly; obviously, native Blackguardians weren't indulged with that sort of care.

Thinking of the actijots brought a blurry, fragmented memory to Alacrity, of some poor woman he'd heard of, a POW with an escape plan. She'd been certain she'd located her jot and done a crude amputation of her own right hand.

But she'd gotten it wrong and was recaptured. *How'd the rest of it go*? his mind reeled. *She tried again, only this time she went digging and probing around an eyeball. Probably crazy by then; I can see how it'd happen . . .*

He gave his head a painful shake, forcing his thoughts back on track. "Water," he forced himself to croak.

The local had a collapsible water bottle slung over his shoulder. Soliciting permission from the man in maroon by eye, he poured sparingly; a kindness, given Alacrity's condition. The breakabout drank; nothing in life had ever been so good. Finally, though it felt like there was no slaking his thirst, Alacrity forced himself to move aside so that Floyt could take a turn at the bottle.

"So then, everything's in order, right, Zenyo?" Skate was saying to the official. "Well, then, I'll be getting these two over to Orion Compound—"

"Correction: they stay right here, in the central labor pool,"

Zenyo stated coldly. "Captain Dincrist can claim them when he arrives."

"Huh? No, no, that isn't—" Skate sputtered as Alacrity and Floyt looked to one another in utter defeat. "These two are a special consignment, Zenyo; orders from Captain Sile. They're to be held under close guard at Orion."

Zenyo shook his head. "I know nothing about that, but I have my orders. They go to Central Labor until Captain Dincrist vouches for the transfer."

"But he didn't know I was bringing them!"

Alacrity inconspicuously put a fingertip to his lips. Floyt kept mum. Anything that distanced them from Dincrist was to be accepted.

At that moment Constance appeared, turned out in her purple cavalier getup, piloting a small hovertruck. Manacles were bolted to the truck bed, actijots or no.

In seconds she was in the middle of the dispute, hands on the gold-and-horn butts of her dress pistols.

"Listen carefully, Zenyo. I'm Captain Sile's second-in-command. These two here go to Orion Compound and that's final." She showed her rather long canines in a challenging snarl, half pulling a pistol. "Or do you want to test me?"

Zenyo rolled his eyes, chuckling. "Are you insane? Woman, this is *Blackguard*! Pull that gun on me and you're scorched meat." He gestured to the guard towers that were located around the hardtop's perimeter.

"So now," Zenyo went on, "try it if you don't believe me. And when you're a pile of stinking ash, things will still go just the way I've said they will. That is Baron Mason's decision."

Constance's breath rushed out between clenched teeth. She stamped one foot; the rowls of her ridiculous spurs clashed. She rammed the pistol back down into its scabbard.

"I'll just see about this," she seethed. "In the meantime, nothing had better happen to these two, or I'll make sure Captain Dincrist gives you to me, sweet baby."

She turned to the addled, rank, and dejected Alacrity and Floyt. "As for you two, Shipwreck Mazuma and Delver Rootnose, keep your mouths shut and don't go starting trouble. I'm warning you."

Then she went legging back to the hovertruck, spurs clinking, leaving Skate to catch up at an ungainly lope. The hovertruck shot across the hardtop, headed for the spaceport gate. Alacrity wondered why she'd practically ordered them to use their Forager names.

Zenyo then addressed Alacrity and Floyt. "Do you two know what'll happen if you get out of line or try to escape? Or do you need proof?"

Alacrity waved an arm in abnegation. "No, no; we believe you."

"Good, because the first warning is agony. Neither of you wants to know what *real* punishment feels like." He signaled the local. "Gute, get 'em cleaned up and billeted." He strode off.

Gute considered the two, adjusting his improvised glasses, and gave them the water bottle again. "Feel bad, hmm?" Gute asked in tradeslang.

"Very," responded Alacrity. "But my friend here mostly talks Terranglish."

"Oh." Gute sniffed loftily, then shifted to that language. "Well, just behave and you'll be feeling better in no time."

He beetled his brows at them as they slugged water. "But you start trouble, and we're going to have some problems."

Alacrity traded evaluating looks with Gute. The local stood some 180 centimeters and was less given to corpulence than most of his fellows. His safari shorts had been expensive when new, possibly a donation from a patron, or perhaps something he'd lifted somewhere. Gute wore a pendant necklace, anklets, and headband of intricate metallic beadwork, and worn but serviceable shoes.

Gute looked to be in good shape, and aside from the fact that Alacrity felt like a wrung-out rag, he had the actijot somewhere within him, ruling out any meaningful resistance.

Alacrity gave Gute a slow nod, saying, "We understand." That seemed to satisfy him.

Floyt finished the last of the water and returned the bottle to Gute.

"Now we go get you two cleaned up," Gute announced. "Get you some more water and some food."

That got them both unsteadily to their feet. They shuffled off after Gute in the warmth of what felt like late midday.

"Central Labor's not so bad," Gute philosophized as they went along. "It could've been worse. Offworlders who come in like you, jotted and all, they usually go to Grand Guignol Compound, or Circus Maximus, or one of the other bad ones."

"What about Orion?" Alacrity asked, stepping along uncomfortably, the hot hardtop searing his bare feet.

Gute made a birdlike gesture of the head, canting it from side to side, apparently to indicate that he didn't know "Mostly games, lots of hunting. Dincrist sure loves that."

Floyt and Alacrity had already found that out. "Wait a second!" Alacrity paused, grabbing Gute's arm in excitement. Gute frowned at the hand until Alalcrity removed it.

"Is there a woman at Orion Compound?" Alacrity almost shouted. "Tall, almost as tall as me; white-blond hair; very, very fair skin? They call her Heart, or maybe the Nonpareil?"

Gute eyed him dubiously, then answered slowly. "Never heard of her. But a lot of the Betters have masks on just about all the time, at least when anybody's around to see them. Many use names that aren't their birth names, I think."

Alacrity was about to press the subject. Gute gave him a shove in the direction of the central labor pool. "No more questions, you! Get going!"

Alacrity tried to accept the manhandling with good grace; there wasn't much else he could do.

Every structure on the field, even meldslab hangars and squeezebond repair domes, had been prettied up with all sorts of baroque trimmings and gingerbread. The control tower was a neotech minaret, heavily decked with detector and communications equipment.

Beyond the field's energy curtain they could see a sizable complex of gleaming spires among elaborate, lacy buildings. All sorts of air traffic moved around it at various levels.

Elsewhere, farther away, the uppermost portions of what had to be satellite structures stuck up out of the thick forest cover that began just beyond the curtain. There was a place built on the style of the Acropolis, another like a monolithic stone fortress, and a third that was all froth and flying bridges.

Gute led them to a row of low buildings tucked in one corner of the spaceport. As they went, he made sure the two were aware of basic laws of existence for labor pool workers. Most of it boiled down to a warning that if they worked and behaved everything would be all right. Alacrity knew how an actijot could turn the human nervous system into a grill of unendurable pain; he made a mental note to impress that on Floyt, and solemnly acknowledged Gute's instructions.

To hear Gute tell it, the work wasn't usually all that bad. What was important was to keep the Betters—Blackguard's offworld overlords—happy, especially by acknowledging their superiority.

They came to the central labor pool, low blockhouses with a minimum of baroque decor. Gute took them into a hygiene station and hosed suds onto them, supervising from one side as they lathered with broad-spectrum disinfectant-vermicidal soap. Much as it stung, they both welcomed it. They used dental lavers as they dried before warm streams of forced air.

When they were dry, Gute gave each a pair of threadbare shorts and a set of soleskins. Then he took them to a mess hall large enough for a hundred or so people. No one was there but the cook staff and helpers. After a short argument with a sweating, fleshy cook, Gute got them two trays of cold leftovers.

They ate tiredly but enthusiastically. There was fish stew and a herb-and-vegetable mash, along with fried dough. The sullen cook, seeing the shape they were in, had given them plenty, more than they could finish.

Nearly out on their feet, they followed Gute into a barracks. It was set up in small cells. In each cell were two rows of nooks, one atop the other, to either side: twelve claustrophobic sleeping spaces to a row, lined up like open-ended coffins, less than fifty centimeters wide and high. That made forty-eight in a low-ceilinged room five meters wide and about as deep. There was no plumbing except for a small drain in the middle of the floor, no heating or cooling, no air circulation or light beyond what came from the door.

Gute threw each a light sleeping cover, then assigned them nooks. "Sleep for now," Gute told them gruffly. "But hear me!" He cuffed Alacrity's shoulder; Alacrity endured it silently.

"Tomorrow you both start work. Work hard; no complaints. Or else I may think of you next time they want someone for the Wild Hunt or a little fun in the cages, understand?"

They understood well enough to agree to do their best. When Gute was gone, the two hauled themselves exhaustedly onto the ledge that ran along the lower row of nooks. Floyt had been assigned a place in the bottom row, Alacrity the one directly above. The spaces smelled of disinfectant.

"Feet in? Head in?" Floyt wondered. His eyes were slits; his bottom lip hung slack, exposing his lower teeth.

Alacrity decided, "Might as well sleep feet in; get to know the neighbors when they come back."

They slid into their spaces slowly, aching and groaning. The material of the nooks was somewhat resiliant, more comfortable than it looked. It was usually Floyt's habit to curl up on his side, especially in his bunk in the *Pihoquiaq*. Here, that was uncomfortable for him—even worse for Alacrity.

"I don't know what's going to come now, Ho; I just don't know what we're going to do next."

"We'll think of something, Alacrity. Get some sleep."

They could've fallen asleep on gravel; the lassitude of the cachesleep hangover put them out with a vengeance.

Floyt drew his cover over him. He dreamed of Earth, and his wife and daughter, and a life of comforting uneventfulness as a functionary third class.

Their barracksmates, who began wandering in as Invictus lowered toward the horizon, were a mixed bag of locals.

The two companions roused enough to discover that the men stored their few possessions in hinged compartments under the bunk tiers' ledges. Alacrity didn't see any one chief bully, something he'd been worried about, the type he'd encountered in boxtowns and crew quarters before. He breathed a little easier; he was in no shape to go up against somebody like that, even with Floyt to help.

The Blackguardians looked the two over, talking among themselves in a local tongue that sounded like it might have Germanic roots. It was getting dark, and the only light came from area illumination banks and spotlights around the field.

Men began preparing to go to sleep. Alacrity saw that he and Floyt had missed supper.

Most of the locals wore clothing similar to what Gute had issued Alacrity and Floyt, but a few wore odd costumes, suggesting various historical periods and assorted cultures. Everyone began settling in for the night.

In spite of the snoring, the coughing, and the other sounds from all around, Floyt and Alacrity spent most of the night sleeping, their bodies famished for real rest after the prolonged cachesleep.

They were rousted around sunrise, by Gute and others hitting the doorframe with long, flexible sticks. A fog had settled over the spaceport; the sounds of automata and insects could be heard, mingled with strange sounds from the forest.

Men hawked and spat, blew their noses with their fingers, and went off to relieve themselves. They scratched, broke wind and yawned, complained and grunted.

"When I grow up," muttered Alacrity, hauling himself out of his nook, to Floyt, who was also emerging, "I want to live in a seraglio." Still, he felt much better, and Floyt did too.

They stowed their blankets, then filed out to the messhall. After a breakfast indistinguishable from yesterday's lunch, the other men left for their assignments. Floyt and Alacrity, chivvied out by the cook, were left shifting from foot to foot indecisively, wondering what they should do. Alacrity was thinking about the ships sitting on the hardtop and wondering how good local security was. But almost certainly, anybody with an actijot inside him was asking for trouble by going into restricted areas.

Before Alacrity's plans had advanced very far, Gute appeared, driving a surface-effect runabout. Hitched behind it was a jarringly incongruous two-wheeled cart made of roughcut wood. In the primitive cart were several tools and a large coarse sack.

Gute was smiling, which gave the two pause. At his instruction, they piled aboard. Alacrity took a whiff of the cart bed. "Barn duty, Ho."

The tools supported that; they were manual implements of wood and crudely forged metal, unearthly variations on the hoe, shovel, broom, and scoop.

"Oh, well; that's not *so* bad." Floyt shrugged. At least it sounded better than being remanded to a place with a name like School for Scandal. Then he recalled some of the savage creatures he'd seen being used as saddle beasts on Epiphany, and he wasn't so sure.

The runabout's controls were childishly simple, but Gute sat stiff and erect and handled them with the dignity of an admiral commanding a battlewagon. They swung out across the field for the main gates. Floyt elbowed Alacrity. "See if you can spot the *Astraea Imprimatur*."

The *Mountebank* was still present, as well as a number of other craft, but none had the markings they were looking for. Floyt was tempted to ask Gute, but thought better of it. There was no telling who might then get wind of their interest in the ship.

They went through the gate and down a wide road of well-kept squeezebond. Blackguard's foliage was rank and high, with an odd yellow-blue tint to it, looking vaguely Jurassic. They could see numerous trails and what looked like bridle paths. Once a glassy white swan-boat passed by overhead, music and laughter trailing from it; apparently the partying and carousing went on at all hours of the day and night on Blackguard. They met no other ground traffic.

As they came over one rise, Floyt thought he smelled an oceanic, salty aroma. Gute passed by the turnoff for the large complex, which shone like a mirrored beacon, and wound down toward the big, forbidding castle keep they'd noticed the day before. The place looked authentic, if unweathered, and a strange architecture showed what seemed to be Moorish and Asian influences. Some features baffled them, like the enormous polyhedron at the summit of the central tower. Shrine or command center? Observatory or hangar?

Gute stopped in a clearing to one side of the road, just at the edge of the forest, and shut off the engine. Digging into the sack, he began throwing items of clothing at Alacrity and Floyt, saying, "From here we go afoot. Put these on and get the cart unhitched."

There were baggy diapers of lumpy, loosely woven homespun the color of oatmeal. Their intricate knotting had been fastened into place with hidden stitches; convenient stat-hesive closures, also concealed, were provided for use by the novice. There were, in addition, floppy knee waders made of some synthetic that looked like natural gum.

"The garb of Waldenian manuremen," Gute informed them, removing his spectacles and leaving them in the runabout.

"Very much in vogue these days," Alacrity noted. But he and Floyt had already agreed that there was no future in antagonizing Gute. Gute handed each of them an unbelievably archaic slave collar. They dutifully clicked them on; the silly things didn't even lock. The collars were only required costume, Gute had explained, at some of the compounds, where certain of the Betters obtained their pleasure from seeing fellow humans debased.

Under the Blackguardian's supervision, the two unhitched the cart and began pulling and pushing it up the long incline to the castle. In moments they were sweating heavily, the collars vexing them. The diapers began chafing at once.

For the most part, the place was built of gargantuan stones, not much of a feat given modern equipment and transport, but it plainly replicated the traditional keep of some lapsed, nontech culture. Floyt and Alacrity both spared a moment's uneasy thought over what a job building one of the originals must have been.

On the battlements stood figures in long outdated war-dress, armor, and the fighting regalia of a half-dozen worlds and a few of Terra's historical periods. Gute signaled, and the portcullis was raised. With Gute in the lead they passed over the drop-away drawbridge and under murder-holes and other defenses.

The place was only lightly tenanted, by people living out roles as nontech warriors and other romantic stronghold residents. Most of them affected a single glove tucked through belt or sash: embroidered, gilt, and jeweled ones for the unarmored; heavy gauntlets for the ironclads.

Traditional, for giving or accepting challenges, Alacrity concluded. *Mark of nobility—they're playing it to the hilt, all right*.

Only a few servants were in evidence, and none of the workforce of serfs or slaves it must've taken to run such a place for real. That made sense; many of the compounds were probably only occupied part time. It was only logical to keep the in-house staff as small as possible, with augmentation as necessary from Central Labor.

"I guess none of the paying customers are anxious to take part in the authentic dung detail," Alacrity groused as he and Floyt shouldered the cart over a courtyard of big, square cobblestones.

"Shut up!" Gute whispered harshly. "Spoiling their illusion is the surest way of getting them angry!" Then he began tugging his forelock in all directions, going through strange, gyrating genuflections.

Ersatz warriors and courtesan looked down on them, lording it. Floyt noticed more than one pair of Betters joining hands or embracing. *Being jaded sure leads to some odd ways of getting your newtons loose*, he decided.

The citadel compound was rather austere, with no contemporary conveniences that they could see, except that the unglazed windows on the higher levels—the Betters' domain—seemed unwisely large for a bow-and-catapult society. The three passed through the inner curtain and followed a dim passageway lit by occasional slit windows.

The place was cool and a bit stuffy, but without the indefinable smells of age. Gute halted them by a low, thick stone slab door framed in iron. He took big swaths of cloth from the sack, giving one each to his unwilling helpers and keeping one for himself. Both were puzzled; there didn't seem to be anything like a stable nearby. But when Gute tied the cloth around his nose and mouth they were quick to imitate him.

Gute turned the rotor of the door's peculiar disc-lock and shouldered it open. The smell that wafted out made it easy to tell that they were peering into an open sewer.

"Cesspit," explained Gute, taking a pair of torches from the sack and glancing around to make sure nobody was watching. He lit them with a thermonode he'd hidden in the folds of his diaper. The two friends shied away at once, certain that there'd be a methane explosion, but none came.

"There's no drainage for the Betters' garderobes because they're between the inner and outer curtains—just like the originals," Gute continued, handing each man a torch. "So you two clean it out."

He lit a third torch from Alacrity's and ducked into the cesspit. They followed. The place was two meters or so wide and perhaps twenty long. Far overhead, the darkness was broken only by faint light coming through a string of ominous round holes.

"Actually, you are lucky," Gute asserted. "This place wasn't due for cleanout for another month. But they're getting ready for some kind of big fest, so you get to do the job in knee boots instead of hip waders."

The contents of the place had accumulated in little hillocks and splattered the walks. Holding his torch high, Alacrity saw that minute lifeforms had created a city of their own. They squirmed and scuttled away from the light; he sighed inconsolably.

Under Gute's supervision, they backed the cart in and chocked it, the bed tilted for more convenient shoveling. "Why don't they just put in plumbing?" Floyt barked, scandalized. "Is this supposed to be a resort, or not?" His voice sounded strange, muffled by the cloth.

Gute shrugged. His muffled answer was "The Betters don't want anything modern in the citadel. Damned uncomfortable, if you ask me. Candles, praying cells, halls of feasting and watchtowers . . . garderobes. There's lots of trysting around here."

He too sighed. "Myself, I'd give anything to do it up there where the stars are, and you don't weigh anything—or so they say. Or on a luxury compound."

But Gute didn't come from some overgroomed world, or a sealed environment on a hostile planet where every last part of the environment was closely monitored, or where social pressures made any sort of role playing impossible. Alacrity shook his head, thinking about it, limbering up his shovel. Perhaps the most important thing to the Betters was that they had absolute power on Blackguard—at least over their offworld captives.

Besides which, they don't have to deal with these cesspits, Alacrity reflected.

He craned to look at the holes high above, garderobes of the inner curtain. "What about those, Gute? Can't you block them off?"

"Or at least give us umbrellas?" Floyt suggested.

"The garderobes have been marked out of service," Gute explained with rising impatience. "So now, be about your work. Work hard; behave; do not be nuisances. It isn't too late for you to be assigned to the Wild Hunt."

"Dig in, Ho," Alacrity urged. "It'll put hair on your chest."

Floyt gave in. "Right-o; just pretend they're daisies."

Saying he'd be back soon, Gute left, closing the door behind him. Rank odors might be part of castle life, but the attitude around the citadel seemed to be one of realism in moderation.

The air was thick, and their eyes stung a bit at first, but aside from that the job wasn't all that bad. Still, Floyt cast occasional apprehensive glances at the holes overhead. They wedged their torches into sockets drilled into the stone and set to work.

"Could be worse," Alacrity commented after a while.

"And how would you know?"

"Worked on a honeywagon once when I was a kid. When we were hard up."

"What's next?" Floyt said.

"When we get it all shoveled, we sweep the place out, I guess."

"No, no! I mean us! And Astraea Imprimatur, and especially about Dincrist. Alacrity, I'm not doing a very good job of not thinking what he's going to do with us when he gets his hands on us."

"Me either. Well, it sounds like we have a little breathing space, anyway. Just be glad Constance and Skate aren't keeping us entertained."

"Granted, but that could change any time."

"All we can do is keep our ears open, find out how things work. There are always angles."

"Alacrity! Do you think there might be another Inheritor here? Besides Dincrist, I mean? I could appeal for help—" Floyt was suddenly crestfallen. "But then, we don't even know where my Inheritor's belt is."

"Shh!" Alacrity hissed quietly, having heard voices floating down through the holes in one of the garderobes. They were the processed voices of Betters.

"Empty, right enough," one said. "Just the place."

"Fine, fine," said a second. "Damned fine idea, m'lord, to get away from that uproar for a while."

"I must say, much as I cherish tradition, the Nightwatch Fete makes one realize there's such a thing as too much ceremony. Care for a lick or two of synaptiflake?"

"Don't mind if I do, even if the purists wouldn't approve. Nobody here but us, eh, baron?"

There was a moment's silence. An unmasked man's voice said, "Ah, that's better! Kind of you to offer, m'lord!"

Alacrity and Floyt were leaning on their shovels. Alacrity motioned Floyt to be still; Gute had warned them not to be nuisances. *And*, he told himself, *intelligence info is where you find it*. He stuck out his tongue and pointed to its tip, where a synaptiflake would be placed to melt. Floyt nodded comprehension.

They heard gasps as the flake-surge hit the two Betters; Alacrity felt a twinge of envy.

"Phew! Not bad, eh?"

"Oh, premiere stuff, Baron, premiere. Would you care for a cigar? They're from Ascensión."

"Thank you, no. It's a wee bit rank in here for me, but do go ahead."

The baron's voice sound like that of an older and quite cultured man, Alacrity decided; his companion's, indeterminate. A few seconds later, a spent match—a real, primeval, wooden lucifer—came arcing down through a hole, leaving a thin thread of smoke, to hiss out nearby in layered aristocrat poop.

"Will you be racing, Matterse?" the man called the baron asked casually.

"Wouldn't dream of missing a regatta," Matterse answered stoutly.

"As I was saying, that fellow Dincrist, the one from the Orion Compound, will be the one to beat this time. I can't see how Praxis even permitted him to enter; a damned upstart from the word go."

"Ah, well then, blood will no doubt tell," Matterse posited. "Can't say I care much for that Sile person of his, though," he added thoughtfully.

"Quite. While I've got you here for a moment, Matterse, there's something I wanted to ask you. It's in the nature of what might be called a clarification. I hope you won't think I'm speaking out of turn . . ."

The other hastened to fill the meaningful pause. "No such thing, sir! Please do go on."

"It's just that rumors have reached me that you plan to petition for a Royal Charter of House when we get back to Styx."

Matterse's answer was very stiff. "With all deference, m'lord—that is a private matter. May I ask how you heard such a thing? Has Marita perhaps been speaking out of turn?"

"What Marita did or didn't say is hardly the issue, young man! We of the High Seat have to be extremely careful about who we admit to our ranks. And there are more applicants clamoring after charters all the time."

"Er, yes, that's true, but in my case—"

"Splendid; I'm glad you understand. Now, about this claim of yours to the old Blood Royal: your lineage is Matterse out of Morstrube, from the Second Ship, is it not? That makes you a peer, m'boy, but never Blood Royal."

"Ah, yes, but," Matterse hastened, "I've recently had a genealogy done, of my family tree and ancestors *before* the ship left the Solar system."

Alacrity looked to Floyt; this was his specialty. Floyt simply raised his eyebrows in the wavering torchlight, the cloth hiding the rest of his face.

"My ancestor resettled on Luna," Matterse was saying, sounding well rehearsed. "He was originally of the Rose line, but was forced to divest himself of his title in the Lunar Abjuration of 2534." He hesitated, then said, "Er, do you mind if I . . ."

"Eh? Ah, I suppose not."

"That's what the place is for, eh, m'lord?" More briskly,

Matterse went on, "So, with this new information—I have certified copies of the original documents—I should think I would qualify—"

As Alacrity was wondering what all the doubletalk meant, hoping the two would start talking about Dincrist again, he and Floyt found out what the lesser subject had been. A yellow stream of urine poured down from above, splattering in the dung, splashing their gumboots.

They jumped back with a curse. Floyt, unable to endure any more, ripped down his cloth and, coughing once, screamed up hoarsely, "You cheap, contemptible, unthinking, incontinent bastard! And not only that, *there was no such thing as the Abjuration of twenty-five-goddamn thirty-four!*"

Alacrity looked at his friend glumly. "As if the shit wasn't deep enough . . ."

CHAPTER 11

WIT'S END

IT TURNED OUT THAT THERE WERE CERTAIN MODERN CONVEN-iences available to denizens of the citadel. Prominent among these was one that summoned other castle denizens dressed as warriors—and Gute. All the Betters of the citadel seemed to be products of selective breeding, nutritional programs, and genetic manipulation, standing a half head and more taller than Alacrity.

The two unwilling manuremen found themselves gazing up through the early-morning sunlight, with Gute off to one side.

On a low-railed pergola a few meters above them, two Betters peered down upon them from within massive war casques decked with exotic plumage. Each had one of the beautifully made gauntlets tucked in his belt.

"Which is the one who dared raise his voice to us?" demanded the mask that resembled a hissing serpent, in Terranglish. There was no identifying the voice, but Alacrity assumed that Matterse would defer to the baron. While the breakabout was speculating on possible ways to get out of this one—without much hope— Floyt settled the matter.

"Ah, that would be me. You see, I was just startled, that's all. *Heh.* I'm really very, very sorry and it won't happen again, I assure you. Sirs."

The other Better, in a mask modeled on a snarling feline of

some sort, broke in, shouting, "What was that you had the audacity to yell?"

"Nothing!" Alacrity blurted. "We just said, 'Hey, what's going on?' or words to that effect!"

"'Words to that effect,'" mused the baron somewhere behind his mask, a contemplative god. The two captives held their breath, waiting for the worst.

"Very well," the baron decided. "We cannot in all fairness punish you for being surprised, can we?"

Matterse choked outraged nonwords. The baron turned to him—turning his entire upper body, since his bulky mask wasn't jointed. "You may go, sir. I will deal with these."

"But I—they insulted me. Are we to be obliged to accept that here? In the very citadel?" His long fingers clenched on the railing and he looked down on them through mirrored eyepieces.

The baron raised a hand rather lazily. "My dear young friend, I doubt very much these lowmen even know where they are. And it ill behooves us to be wasteful of strong young serviles, eh? I'll just make it a point that the central labor pool be more thorough in instructing its crews."

Matterse still seemed undecided.

"Go see to the guests," the baron said. "They'll be wondering what's happened to us."

The two Betters moved out of sight. Disappointed onlookers drifted back to whatever they'd been doing, deprived of some good old-fashioned, medieval-style fun at the expense of the lower orders. Floyt dared hope the incident was over, and he'd come through unscathed. Even Gute seemed unsure.

But a moment later, the baron reappeared at the courtyard door, having removed his towering headgear. His imposing height aside, he wasn't much different from a Terran of middle age.

The baron's head of thick, curly black hair was touched with white—not gray—at the temples, and there were streaks of it in his beard, which projected in two menacing spikes, the middle of his chin being clean shaven. His black eyes were direct and piercing, but his lashes incongruously long and curled, almost girlish. His ceremonial gauntlet, of scarlet mesh and scale armor, had long, glittering, hooked silver claws. He might be a decadent nobleman or oligarch, but the big body looked to be in excellent shape.

He'd stopped some distance away, having caught their scent. He motioned negligently to Gute. "Wait over there by the gate."

Gute, surprised, clearly knew better than to argue. Ducking his head obediently, he trotted off. The baron looked the two over.

"Now, which of you mentioned the abjuration? Speak up; I've no time for nonsense."

"I did. Sir," Floyt confessed.

"Ah; I thought so. And how do you know so much about history and genealogy? Or were you just ranting?"

"It was a sort of a hobby of mine, Baron, back on—back where I came from."

"I see." The baron regarded him closely. "Can you prove what you said? Can you disprove that young upstart's claim to nobility?"

Floyt spread his hands. "Not without my reference materials, my books—"

"A detail," snapped the baron, distracted now as he thought through others. "There are large data banks at the Central Complex. But can you retrieve the information I require?"

Floyt thought about it, where Alacrity, in his place, would've said yes immediately whether it was a lie or not.

"If the data's in there, sir, I don't see why not," Floyt decided at length.

"That's the spirit," the baron said with a kind of patronizing robustness. "And while you're at it, lowman, you can look into a few other matters for me. Matterse isn't the only pleb running about with pretensions to gentle blood."

He beckoned to Gute and, when the local arrived, indicated Floyt. "Have this man cleaned up and suitably attired, then delivered to me at the main entrance of the Central Complex at the tenth hour, tomorrow morning."

Alacrity cleared his throat loudly. The baron lifted an eyebrow toward him.

"Uh, what about me?" the breakabout plunged in. "I'm his, uh, helper."

Floyt nodded. Gute's expression was blank.

"And you would describe yourself as an apt, hard-working fellow?" the baron asked. Alacrity nodded for all he was worth.

"In that case, you'll be able to perform cesspit details by yourself, won't you?"

The next morning Floyt went through another cleansing and deverminizing process, though he and Alacrity had taken a long one only the evening before. His lowman outfit was replaced with a nondescript coverall of yellow and brown and stiff, uncomfortable slippers.

He rode beside Gute in the little runabout while Alacrity, riding a flatbed trailer behind, glared sourly at them both. They stopped in front of the Central Complex. Floyt was ushered in, the maroon-clad guard having instructions from the baron on the matter.

Then Gute headed back for the spaceport. "Lucky, your friend Delver," he told Alacrity, who'd moved up to the passenger seat once Floyt had left. Gute didn't seem to mind. "Good, easy work, I'll bet. Safe."

"Who is the baron, anyway?"

Gute spared Alacrity a rare sidelong glance, then went back to the prestigious business of driving. "It's not a very good idea to ask too many questions, Shipwreck. Make sure your friend knows that."

The next job of the day involved transporting two big plastic vats of succulent-looking salted hams from their holding point at the spaceport to the kitchens at the complex. The vats comprised the complex's share of a joint purchase.

Alacrity did all the work, of course, but it wasn't too hard, since they had a powerjack along. At least the job didn't require a slave collar and a funny costume.

As the runabout eased away from the loading dock, Alacrity commented offhandedly, "Gute, I've been thinking."

"That is not permitted without written permission from the Betters."

"No, really; I'm just wondering how come a bright fella like you isn't doing just a little better for himself."

Gute kept his eyes on the lofty task of driving. "I will not forbid you to talk, within reason, at this time. But do not expect me to answer or agree to any disloyal or dishonest proposal."

"Of course not! You bet. Well, I'm just sitting here saying to myself, 'There must be something Gute would like to have for himself.' A luxury—some clothing, or a bottle of something offworld, maybe? Or a gift for somebody you'd like to be nice to?"

Gute didn't comment; Alacrity pressed his luck. "There's a lot you could get for yourself if you instituted a few creative management procedures around here."

"Creative—that has a very impressive ring to it."

"Pull over there—right behind that shed—and I'll show you what I mean."

Gute thought for a moment, then complied.

Alacrity dismounted and took up a water hose attached to a spigot at the rear of the shed. "Name something you wish you had. Within reason, that is."

Gute looked around carefully. Seeing no one, he answered uneasily, "A Spican Atlas."

"Seriously? Huh!" Alacrity blinked, surprised. He'd expected Gute to have his heart set on a flashy loincloth, liquor, or maybe a particular partner for some slap-and-tickle.

The Spican Atlas was a magnificent book, showing all the beauties of that populous system and its unparalleled Precursor wonders.

"Yes," Gute said excitedly. "Denzio, the master of hounds at the Hellfire Compound, has two copies."

"Here's a simple solution." Alacrity held up an index finger. "One: Gute would like one of those atlases—so he can see the places he'd like to visit."

Gute shrugged irritably but didn't deny it.

Alacrity turned on the hose, splattering an irregular, tepid trickle onto the hardtop. He held up a second finger of his free hand.

"Two: what's Gute got to swap?"

Alacrity looked around, scavenged a discarded plastic liter bottle from a waste bin, and began filling it. Gute finally lost his temper.

"What are you getting at? We'll be missed; we should go!"

"I'm just timing the flow, the weight of the water. Be through in a sec." He counted off the time to himself under his breath.

"But what has this to do with an atlas?"

The bladder had filled; Alacrity tossed it aside carelessly, doing conversions in his head. "You need something to swap. If you just look back there in the vats, you'll see a small mountain of trade goods, courtesy of Gresham's World."

Alacrity put his finger over the hose's nozzle and began experimenting, trying for a fine spray.

"Put that from your mind!" Gute yelped, round-eyed with shock. "The hams have been counted. I would be nerve-flogged and cast out! You would be put under the flensing beams, or have your actijot energized, full force!"

"The hams haven't been counted, dammit," Alacrity corrected. "They've been *weighed*. By the *vat*. It's stenciled right here on the sides of the vats, in Panlang." He was keeping careful lookout, to make sure no one was watching.

Gute, who could puzzle out a little Terranglish and trade-slang but plainly couldn't read anything else, furrowed his brows.

"But what of that? They will weigh the vats at the complex, surely."

"Uh-huh. And the weight'll come out just right, making allowances for the difference in gravity."

So saying, Alacrity turned the fine mist of the hose and began wetting down the meat, keeping count of the time so that he had a pretty fair idea of the weight of water he was transferring.

"Or maybe just a little more, to be safe," he pondered. "Would you do me a favor, please? Check and see how much is leaking through?"

Gute was familiar with the way salted meat absorbed water. He went through a moment's torment of doubt, then, thinking of the wonderful Spican Atlas, did as Alacrity requested.

"Nothing yet." He, too, looked around. "And the vats will weigh the same? There will be no trouble?"

Alacrity was shifting some of the hams around as he hosed them down. "They will once we take out two or three for you to trade to Denzio. There'll still be plenty left for the Betters;

they bring in twice as much as they can stuff into their faces anyway, isn't that what you told me? It's just that you're getting the leftovers off the top, instead of the kitchen staff hogging them later."

"You still have not told me how *you* profit from this," Gute pointed out dubiously. But he was already shifting the meat around so that Alacrity could get at it with a hose, picking out two hams for himself.

"You keep me and my friend off heavy labor duty—if he doesn't have a solid berth already, that is. Keep us off the dirty jobs and the dangerous ones. I'll show you a lot of other things we can do for you. Gute, I've been around starports most of my life."

When Gute looked hesitant, Alacrity added, "You can always change your mind later. You can also blame everything on me; what more can they do to me?"

"And what happens when Captain Dincrist shows up?" Gute objected.

"Then the deal's over." *Only, I plan to be long gone by then! Because I'm a free operator again!*

It bothered him and yet he exulted in it, the one thing he hadn't brought himself to tell Floyt. Since awakening, he'd been free of the torment of the conditioning. Whatever Skate had done to him in the *Mountebank*, he'd inadvertently freed Alacrity of his bondage to Floyt and the mission. He was his own man once more.

"There's a little water trickling down here and there," Gute reported, "but only a bit."

"Well? What d'you say, Gute?"

Gute hefted one of the hams, feeling its weight. "Teach me more about science."

The baron's mask that day was a conservative visor of thin, dove-gray leather trimmed in red-orange flame of metallic thread, his forked beard projecting from the bottom.

He came alone, in coral body swathings, meeting the Earther at the guard post where Gute and Alacrity had dropped him off. The guard sealed around Floyt's wrist a short-term color-coded pass bracelet that would dissolve when no longer valid.

The Earther was also given an unremarkable, yellow, half face-mask, a loaner.

The baron motioned for Floyt to follow him. Floyt hastened to take up position one pace behind and to the right, where he'd seen other servants station themselves.

The megastructure of the complex was soaring, prismatic, letting in light and broad sky-vistas, vaulting high and open to the air.

It's not Frostpile, Floyt thought, *but it's damned impressive. Gorgeous, for such an evil place.*

They crossed a vast rotunda under a splendid bowl of sky-light into a spacious high-ceilinged promenade. The motif was sybaritic-cathedral; the area was devoted to very decorous shops and spas, cabarets and galleries. Mason led Floyt past sensory cloisters, rejuv clinics, and debauchery agencies. Most of them had discreet metal or holo placards offering goods and services "By Appointment Only" or to "Members Only."

Mason led him off along a grand esplanade as Floyt saw for the first time that the complex fronted a wide, rainbow-sanded beach and a serene red sea.

The gaudy and boisterous Betters of Blackguard strolled or frolicked through the place under the watchful but very tolerant gaze of big, businesslike offworld guards—male and female both—in the maroon outfits with grotesquely padded shoulders and codpieces. There were sometimes exchanges of nods or passing pleasantries between groups, but the masks kept things on a very reserved and standoffish basis.

For all the opulence of the place, and the Betters' pretensions to sin and depravity, the complex—and the Blackguard itself, for that matter—seemed tame to Floyt in comparison to the Grapple.

The baron appeared to be strolling along contentedly, in no hurry and paying little attention. Floyt ventured, "You refer to this place as a kleptocracy, isn't that right? Government by, um, theft?"

The Better considered that for a few paces, then stopped to face Floyt. "Are you a discreet man? Do you know what happens to indiscreet people here on Blackguard? Take the interrogation chambers at my own Citadel Compound, for example;

that's where indiscretions have led a good many people. One of the first things my interrogators do is pull all the subject's teeth, so he can't bite off his tongue or gnaw through the arteries in his wrists or some such, to escape his situation. Were you aware of that?"

"N-no..."

"Ah. Now, as to kleptocracy—yes. But in Blackguard's case, a government by *thieves*, not by theft. And many of us are descendants of long, long lines of successful thieves—rulers, not cutpurses. Our diverse governments function by the age-old forces of supply and demand, and function to our profit at every turn. Are you still with me?"

"Yes, I think so."

"So. Master thieves are very proprietary of their prerogatives. Their plunder, if you will. They resent *arrivistes* and upstarts. I think you're a man who knows about upstarts. I think you're a man who can root them out for me."

"You're Baron *Mason*, aren't you?" Floyt said. "You're the one who ordered my friend and me be held at Central Labor instead of Orion Compound. And you drew Matterse into that conversation in the garderobe because you had us put on cesspit detail, and you knew we'd overhear."

Baron Mason nodded, eyes narrowing. "I count myself very fortunate you came my way. Yes, it served Matterse right for not knowing his history; the citadel is built precisely to old specifications, and spies eavesdropping on the garderobes was a classic ploy during Styx's dark age."

"But how did you know I knew about genealogy and history?"

"I'd already had word from others who were there, of the difficulties Dincrist had with you and your friend on Epiphany. And after all, you *have* had a monograph picked up for offworld publication . . . Citizen Floyt."

Floyt wet his lips but said nothing.

"And you have my word you'll be much better off with me than you would if Dincrist fed you to Sile and Constance."

"And when Dincrist comes back?"

"Problematic, of course. It might even turn out that you've died, and there'll be a body to prove it—though it won't be your body. But in the meantime, let's see what you can do for me, eh?"

They continued. Fountains blossomed; joyslaves followed or led their patrons along. Music and subsonics played, to encourage passion and excitement; they were as wasted on Mason as they were on Floyt.

"Your name will continue to be—what is it?—Delver Rootnose?" the baron said offhandedly. "Yes; to *everyone* but for myself, is that clear? Confidentiality, you understand." Floyt nodded vigorously.

"There are things I wish you to know," Mason went on. "For example, have you ever heard of a man named Praxis? Head of the Church of Human Potential? 'Saint of the Irreducible I,' and all that? No? No matter; you will."

A party of revelers came the other way, laughing and shouting, waving drinking vessels and big, filigreed inhalers. One, trailing, staggering a little, was being helped along by two giggling adolescents—a slim boy and a coltish girl, both of them wearing filmy chlamys. The children were very merry, very forward with him; actijots made for conscientious joyslaves.

The man had taken off his bull-mask and was puffing on a long black cigar. He wore an extravagant suit of shirred and ruffled black silk and dancing shoes covered with gold sequins. Floyt recognized him, one of the dour, drab achievement coordinators from Egalitaria from the spaceport.

They left the public-access corridors behind, entering a restricted zone of blank walls and security fixtures. The numerous doors needed only Baron Mason's least gesture to move aside. Floyt dogged his heels.

"Most of that back there—it's a pitiful excuse for iniquity," Floyt said.

"The point behind Blackguard is that the kleptocrats—and some few of our friends—are better off not letting the subject populations know what we do, or how we enjoy ourselves."

"Couldn't you do that at home and just keep it quiet?"

"Well now, in a repressive society, the ruling class can get away with anything. But most of us come from places where public opinion—and public outrage and public prosecutors—count for something.

"And what does that leave us? Isolated playrooms? Moldy basements? No, no; you miss the point, Citizen Floyt. The point is to live high, wide, and handsome—to set ourselves apart from the sheep. To prove what we are, in a place that is all ours."

A descent to a subsurface corridor and a short trip on a railbench brought them past several checkpoints to a heavy vault door. It occurred to Floyt that all the baron's talk of torture might be leading up to something. But this was hardly the route to the citadel's dungeon, and the Better didn't seem the type to indulge in a lot of unnecessary deceit.

The baron debarked the railbench; Floyt followed suit. They were admitted to a command center staffed by a dozen or so nonhumans.

The Earther flanked Mason past rows of monitors and data banks, displays and commo panels. Those on duty showed some surprise, noting Floyt's bracelet; no one dared question the baron.

"Is Pollolo active just at the moment?" the baron asked the empty air at random. A little, stick-thin humanoid—who put Floyt in mind of a cricket—dashed to fall in at attention before the Better.

"Yes, Lord. But he is, ah—Superintendent Pollolo is in ablutive submersion right now. He's due for a molt very soon, and—"

"He won't be otherwise occupied, then." Baron Mason approved with a fey smile. He started for an armored hatch set in the far wall of the command center.

The humanoid started to object, thought better of it, and retreated, bowing.

Floyt trotted after the Better, avoiding eye contact with anybody but taking in as much as he could. Much of the equipment mystified him; technologies had diverged after the First Breath and were only slowly reconverging in the opening laps of the Third.

With only a limited amount of off-Terra experience behind him, he nevertheless thought he recognized a lot of the equipment, at least in a vague way—enough, that is, to make him envious. It was very advanced stuff, far beyond anything available on insular, xenophobic Earth.

The tall hatch rolled aside, admitting them to a corridor lit only by free-standing lightshapes glowing a dim red. At the opposite end another hatch was marked with a universal warning symbol indicating an area of altered gravity—in this case 86 percent Standard, as opposed to Blackguard's 98 percent. Passing through, they came into a chamber nearly as large as the main control room. Floyt suddenly felt light on his feet.

This one had a minimum of apparatus, a few stations for live operators widely separated, partitioned off from one another by their placement. All, that is, except for one position at the center of the place, the most remarkable. There, human-style controls had been replaced by smaller, more complex, almost miniature ones. There was also what looked like electromagnetic induction and receiving gear, but not shaped for a human skull.

The walls of the chamber were covered with projections and excrescences that poked and protruded, clotted and bulged, seemingly assembled bit by bit, like a coral reef. Floyt noticed that the facility was equipped with a small swimming pool or large bathing tank set at floor level. It was filled with murky, gray-brown water.

Where the main operator's chair or lounger ought to be, there was instead a big platform or dais with—Floyt double-checked to be sure he was seeing right—*drains* in its surface.

Baron Mason held his hand up to a pulsing green polyhedron, one of a number of free-floating geometric shapes, an ancillary of some sort. The polyhedron rang; the pool's dark waters stirred, then heaved.

Floyt felt an instinctive fear as the waters surged, and stationed himself well behind Mason. Something large came to the surface, the water rolling off it. Floyt asked himself what sense it would make for Mason to bring him all this way just to feed him to a big, brown-green exoskeletal thing with a fondness for computers.

He couldn't identify the being, but then he hadn't had time to study the sentient species of the galaxy to any great extent.

Getting his first clear look at the claws, the clashing mandibles, and whipping antennae, he shivered.

"Good of you to receive us, Pollolo," Mason said with mild insincerity. The creature didn't answer, but reached for an object like a cross between an electronic horsecollar and a highly instrumented . . .

Lobster bib, thought Floyt the history buff.

Once that was in place Pollolo responded, his voice synthesized with surprising clarity and humanness.

"Baron Mason," he said in a tone without much warmth. He didn't appear to manipulate controls; probably control pulses were fed into the collar by antennules located down near the creature's mouth.

"Things going well, are they?" Mason inquired politely.

"Everything under my authority is functioning at peak efficiency; I do not tolerate less," the thing answered. Floyt couldn't decide if it more resembled a seal with a shell or a lobster pretending to be a sea otter.

The joints of Pollolo's armor bulged, exposing patches of purple-white tissue. Floyt recalled what the humanoid had said about molting. Pollolo studied Floyt with long eyestalks.

"This lowman here is going to be doing a spot of research for me," the baron said.

The eyestalks and antennae appeared to start a bit, a very interesting sight. The sound matrices in the collar gave a few erroneous sounds before producing, "Research? Where, may I ask, Baron?"

Mason said coldly, "Here, of course."

This time the collar squawked before Pollolo got out, "That is quite impossible! Within limits I shall be happy to feed any data you request to an outside terminal, but it's out of the question for an outsider—and a lowman at that!—to have access to—"

"The terminals in this room are the only ones with no info filters or AI governors. I wish this man to use them," Mason broke in sharply. "And don't ever tell me again what is and isn't possible on Blackguard, do you understand?"

The creature bridled, rearing up on his hind legs. He was

several times the human's mass. The baron didn't flinch, but his thumb rested on a decorative boss on his belt.

Whether Pollolo knew that as a threat or simply reconsidered, Floyt couldn't tell. The being quieted and squatted on the floor again. "As you say."

"That's very good of you." Mason conducted Floyt over to a terminal that was set up for a human accessor, behind stacks of peripherals and other equipment. Near it, more of the light shapes were drifting and throbbing softly.

Pollolo trundled heavily to the dais, shedding the last of the water as he went.

The baron sat Floyt down in the operator's airchair. Mason began explaining a few basics, then he called up a program of his own, a powerful AI named Balthazaar. Floyt was astounded at Balthazaar's speed and sweep. Mason had Balthazaar set up a subordinate program for Floyt to use in his research.

"What will be the designation, Citizen?"

"Um . . ." Floyt looked around at the intimidating array of equipment, the matter and energy peripherals, with the uneasy feeling that he was in an enemy camp, or 'nighted in hostile territory. "Diogenes, I guess."

The baron's voice spoke his amusement. "Diogenes it shall be." He gave Balthazaar the necessary orders.

For Floyt, an Earthservice accessor of the grade functionary third class, it was all quite intoxicating. He'd never had so much sheer computer power and limitless data at his beck.

He put aside preoccupations with captivity and the actijot, Dincrist's impending return, the *Astraea Imprimatur*—after all, there wasn't much he could do about those now—homesickness, and worries about Alacrity.

Diogenes put himself at Floyt's disposal. It was a little like being offered a ride on Pegasus.

"Thanks," he said warily to Baron Mason, who nodded punctiliously. "Where do I begin, Baron? Matterse?"

"Matterse, yes. But do not neglect Praxis. Balthazaar will tell you who interests me and what it is I'm after. There are things that will be very difficult to ferret out, even here. You *have* divined why you'll be doing your work here, haven't you?"

Floyt waved at the room in general. "You've accessed all the other compounds' systems, the restricted parts, either by physical tap or SIGINT, right? What else would be the point?"

"Not bad. It may have been better luck than you think that brought you to me. You have potential."

Floyt nearly laughed in Mason's face, having been held from promotion to func-two, in part, for lack of proper motivation. But this was the sort of digging and casting about, prying, noodling, and connection making he loved. On Terra it had gone out of style along with the professional librarian and career archivist. Floyt still thought it was more fun than grinding for a promo.

Mason went to the hatch and paused, looking back to Pollolo, who poised on his dais surrounded by machinery and ancillaries. The hobgoblin stopped what he was doing and rotated eyestalks and antennae toward the baron dutifully.

Mason waited a beat, then said, "Extreme tact."

Antennae waved. "As you say, Lord."

Once the hatch had swung to, Floyt went to work. As a get-acquainted project with Diogenes, he began to correlate all available data on Praxis.

Caught up in his task, Floyt took a few moments to realize he wasn't alone. He nearly vaulted, yammering, from the airchair as the strangely agile bulk of Pollolo sidled closer, claws held high.

With nowhere to run, he sat where he was, fingers gripping the arms of his seat causing it to wheel slightly. He blanked the displays so the creature couldn't see what he'd been doing.

"A word of caution," Pollolo's synthetic voice warned. "You're still a lowman down here, as above. And from now on, you're to wear a collar, understand?"

Floyt, fighting for breath, husked, "Yes I do. And I also understand 'extreme tact.'"

That gave the thing pause. Pollolo's serrated claws opened and closed once as his antennae waved and his eyestalks drew close to Floyt. Floyt couldn't stop himself from shrinking back in his armchair.

The collar uttered something like a rasping chuckle; Pollolo withdrew. Floyt wilted with relief, shaking, as the thing clambered back onto its dais, resuming its work.

Floyt brought Diogenes back up, trying to collect himself. He paused, looking thoughtfully at the displays. It might've had something to do with Alacrity's influence, but he found himself getting angry. He set his jaw and commanded Diogenes to add a new item to his research:

POLLOLO.

CHAPTER 12

FLEXIBLE RESPONSES

IT WAS UNTHINKABLE THAT ANY UNDERLING WOULD DARE ENTER the office of an Earthservice Alpha-Bureaucrat without very deferentially asking permission, and there was an inflexible rule in Alpha-Bureaucrat Stemp's domain that all visitors be announced. And so when his door slid open without overture, he resolved to crush whoever it was who'd violated his seclusion. A moment later, though, he swallowed his anger.

Citizen Ash, the Earth's executioner, strolled unhurriedly across the huge office. Stemp slipped chameleonlike into reserved good humor and informality as he stepped around the several square meters of desktop to press flesh with the man in black. Stemp was a tall, portly, imposing individual with a high forehead and thick salt-and-pepper hair; Ash, smaller, mustached, had a dark intensity that might have made him dashing, except that in him it was coupled with a distant, brooding quality.

Theoretically, Ash was as subject to Earthservice heirarchical etiquette as any other citizen and as subject to cooling his shoes in outeroffice buffer zones. But in practice, it came as no surprise that no one, guard or receptionist, had risked barring his way or detaining him. The powers of his office were rather intimidating, and he'd been known to deal harshly with people who obstructed him.

187

"Good day, Citizen Stemp," the executioner greeted him blandly.

Citizen. While virtually any Terran was free to address any other that way—with very few exceptions, all were part of the all-embracing, all-controlling Earthservice—few had presumed to do so with Stemp in recent memory. Alphas addressed one another informally, as proof of their preeminent rank; all others spoke to them in subservient terms.

The whole visit had an air of effrontery, but Stemp had no inclination to waste time and energy skirmishing with Terra's headsman over minor points of decorum. He knew he'd been put on notice: Ash hadn't come to play the game Stemp's way.

"Citizen Ash," he answered, faintly jovial, "yes. A very good day indeed." The Alpha showed the executioner to a plush sofa, offering refreshments.

Ash had started his Earthservice career as a criminal investigator, Stemp knew, and later become a member of the Earthservice Barrister Pool, defending or prosecuting as random draft decreed. It was an extraordinary person who would accept the job Ash held, the obligations and personal modifications that went with it.

A classified psychoprop profile suggested that Ash's deepest motivations could be traced to his boyhood. He'd been raised in the primitive and remorseless subculture of the undercrofts and outer perimeters of a North African coastal urbanplex, losing two family members to criminal violence and three more in vendettas. It was amazing a human being could come through such an upbringing to emerge a secure, even-tempered, and dispassionate seeker of the truth, renowned for his absolute devotion to justice.

Or perhaps not so surprising at that, Stemp mused. "What can I do for you, Citizen?" He sipped delicately at a tulip glass of real orange juice.

Ash, declining refreshments, said, "I've come to inquire about the progress of your Project Shepherd. You remember: the young offworlder who was convicted of homicide—the one I remanded to serve as escort under the alternative sentencing program? It's been quite some time now; I thought you might have some word on them, Alacrity Fitzhugh and—what was that functionary's name? Hobart Floyt?"

Stemp set his glass down precisely in the center of the marquetry on his coffee table. "I don't believe I understand," he parried. "Why come to me? That project is under the guidance of Supervisor Bear."

"But she's answerable to you; the project ultimately comes under your authority, and I know you pride yourself on keeping abreast of such things."

"May I ask why you're interested? The case is no longer a matter for your office, after all." Ash's position gave him vast powers of review and investigation of the cases sent to him, since he was the one who must carry out the death penalty. He showed no hesitation in exercising them, which was one of the things that made him so dangerous. Still and all, the Fitzhugh matter should by all rights stand safely and permanently closed.

"Oh, simple curiosity, for one thing. Professional interest as well; I'm always eager to weigh alternative sentencing. I do not enjoy discharging my primary responsibility, I assure you."

Stemp was grateful that Ash showed no misgivings about Fitzhugh's conviction. The hasty frameup improvised by Supervisor Bear and the coverup she'd organized in its wake still gave Stemp worried moments.

"But this is in no way an official visit," Ash clarified. "In certain ways the limits of my office are rather rigidly defined, you know."

Stemp did; it was one of the few comforting things about Ash, the reassurance that he couldn't become a loose cannon on the deck. He was required to observe the boundaries of his office, such requirements reinforced with deep and powerful behavioral conditioning. Earth's executioner was not, himself, capable of willfully breaking the law or abusing his powers.

"Quite," Stemp replied. "But let me ask, what makes you think there's been any news?"

"I had it that a starship from the area of Epiphany made planetfall on Luna. Rumors have a way of filtering down, on shuttle runs and so forth; the psychprop bureau and peace-guardian intel people keep track of such things, to be doubly vigilant when offworld cant and canards and disinformation present their greatest threat. My own intelligence conduits are of course modest in comparison to yours. I thought you might have had news."

Ash was being modest about his informational pipelines. Stemp had not yet been apprised of the starship's arrival; it would have been regarded as a routine matter by some, but not by the Alphas, who'd taken a worried interest, a little too late, in the Floyt-Fitzhugh business.

"I have no news of any recent developments," Stemp answered with unusual honesty.

"Ah. Then I've wasted your valuable time, I'm afraid, Citizen."

After the executioner left, Stemp dove to make an encrypted, max-classified commo connection with another Alpha.

The image of Cynthia Chin, rival and adversary in the councils of the Alphas, stared at him with venomous satisfaction. "Why, yes, we've had word," she confirmed innocently. "I was just about to call you."

Liar! "Well? Out with it!"

"Endwraithe's dead. Apparently Floyt and Fitzhugh killed him. They were subsequently sighted at some sort of underworld rendezvous, something called a 'grapple,' but they disappeared somehow. We still have no idea what the Weir bequest was, or where they've gone. That adorable little Bear woman of yours has brought on a crisis situation. Congratulations."

He fought to keep his temper. "The Custodians on Blackguard should be contacted and warned, just in case. It's just possible the Weir legacy is connected to the Repository."

"That's being done, and Camarilla agents are hunting for Floyt and Fitzhugh. I think we really must have a full Alpha conference on this issue."

He broke the connection rather than give her the satisfaction of seeing him lose control. In moments he had Supervisor Bear on his screen in a similarly shielded call. Despite Chin's characterization of her as "little," she was tall and epicene, a woman of forty or so, her most attractive feature being her longish auburn hair.

"Have you any idea what you've done? You and your bloody Project Shepherd?" he practically shrieked.

"B-but it was such a cost-effective, propagandistically sound project."

"Stop babbling and pay attention. I want you to double-check and make sure there are no leaks or exploitables in your coverup of the Machu Picchu incident. If there are, I'll see to it that *you* are the one thrown to Citizen Ash. Do I make myself clear? And begin dismantling whatever remains of Shepherd at once. Blank all incriminating data. You will not surrender any of it to anyone, particularly other Alphas, do you understand? By this evening it's to be as if Project Shepherd never existed."

"But—but it was so *cost-effective*!" She was still blubbering as he cut the connection. Then he stood gazing out at wandering clouds, wondering how the devil that imbecile Endwraithe could've let himself be beaten by a bumbling functionary and a shiftless piece of space trash. He calmed himself with the thought that other, more capable agents were moving against the two now and that they couldn't hide for long.

Besides, in the final analysis, the two were still subject to the conditioning given them by Earthservice. They would be drawn, sooner or later, back to Terra, to be dealt with.

The thought of the conditioning filled Stemp with relief. All was well.

CHAPTER 13

THE COMPANY WE KEEP

"ALL RIGHT, PAY ATTENTION NOW, GUTE," ALACRITY SAID, settling the deck of cards into a modified mechanic's grip. He shooed away some circling bloodgnats with his free hand and brushed a snail-slow, stupidly curious dustball spider off his leg. "I'm gonna show you how to deal seconds and win at blackjack."

Gute, sun-dappled by the shade of the whiffer bushes, sitting cross-legged in the little clearing waiting for the summons of the Wild Hunt, beetled his brows. "Is this legal, what you're teaching me?"

"Huh? Hell, no, it's not *legal*. I'm not trying to teach you how to enjoy the game, dammit; I'm trying to teach you how to *win*."

They were conversing in tradeslang, which Gute spoke rather well. "Ah," he said enthusiastically, resettling himself and paying greater attention. *"Winning*. Fine!"

Alacrity was about to continue this lesson, but from nervous habit they both checked the sky again. They were part of the big, supposedly safe—though dreary and gruesome—body-tagging detail, theoretically immune from attack; but it payed to be careful. Members of the hunt were capable of anything when their blood was up, and the fact that Gute had no actijot and Alacrity's wouldn't trigger a quarry-tracer was no guarantee.

They went back to the cards. "I hope this is of more use than the dice, Shipwreck."

Alacrity had gaffed a pair of dice for Gute, six-ace flats, rather artfully done considering the limited resources available. The problem was that the locals didn't shoot craps, and Gute didn't have much luck instituting the game. Cards would take a lot longer to teach, and Alacrity himself was no expert cheat—he was much more used to spotting cheats—but there was time. *At least until Dincrist gets here*, Alacrity thought. By then he would either have something worked out or . . . he had a depressing fallback plan.

"Yeah, yeah; *much* more useful than the dice, Gute. Now watch this."

Alacrity's sniffing and prying around hadn't come to very much except that he'd become passable friends with Gute. Gute had indeed kept him out of the compounds' more dangerous and objectional jobs. Now that he knew more about the compounds of Blackguard, Alacrity appreciated just how fortunate that was.

Plenty of offworld captives had come there only to end up strapped to a surgical unimech or locked in an iron maiden over at Grand Guignol Compound, or been served up as one of the long-pig repasts at Hellfire Club. Alacrity had been on cleanup crew after one of those feats and hadn't been able to eat or sleep very well since.

He'd decided he would give Blackguard no satisfaction beyond his death, if it came to that; he'd already scouted out a cliff, two bodies of deep water and an unguarded maintenance machine, besides a number of toxic substances. In a pinch, any would do for a little improvised suicide.

Having profited modestly from Alacrity's various schemes and cons, Gute seemed content. He'd kept Alacrity's advice in mind, never being too greedy, and also kept his end of the bargain. His joy at owning a Spican atlas was funny and a bit sad. Gute's people, a few small tribes of them, were the only native inhabitants of that part of Blackguard when the Betters expropriated it, and were the only ones tolerated in that hemisphere. Almost all worked for the Betters.

Alacrity still saw no escape from Blackguard, and his luck couldn't hold out much longer. More and more ships were arriving for the Wild Hunt; with each arrival Alacrity's dread grew that *this* would be the starship from which Dincrist would disembark.

Security at the spacefield was just too thorough for anything like a hijack and getaway. As the nerve-fire from the permanent actijot fields there doubled with every step, one attempt to approach the off-limits areas had convinced him of that.

Simply ankling off into the bush was no good either; the jots could be activated through comsats that were part of the all-embracing Mark-X Talos Worldshield defensive system the compounds used to control their planet. The Betters could locate, disable, or kill him anywhere on Blackguard.

He still held out hope that Floyt could do or find out something of use, but that was fading fast. Nine days had passed since the incident at the Citadel Compound, and Alacrity had heard nothing from the Earther. There was only word that he was working in some capacity or other at the Central Complex, under the aegis of Baron Mason. Alacrity had seesawed between desperate hope and deep despair, praying to see Floyt show up with a pilfered ship, some way of deactivating the jots, a gun or the keys to the complex, but tormented that it would instead be Dincrist, with Sile and Constance, to take him away to a compound room with restraints, nerve rays, and flensing beams, all the obscene paraphernalia to which so many of the Betters seemed drawn.

Still, a part of him maintained, *the harp, the harp* . . . He tried to hold tightly to that memory, that affirmation of his life's most important question. He shook himself now, bringing his attention back to matters at hand.

"Okay now, Gute: watch close. Here goes—"

He was interrupted as clumps of palette-ferns parted at the edge of the clearing.

Both men jumped up in alarm, Gute bringing up the frightlight prod, the only weapon they had. At the edge of the clearing stood a young human male, maybe sixteen on the Standard scale. He was weaving a little, and blood seeped from the cuts and scrapes he'd gotten slithering and crawling, running and crouching in the undergrowth.

The kid was marked as a quarry, in a dermal stain that made him look like some kind of animal, a blotchy rust and green with a dotted white midsection. Alacrity supposed it was meant to imitate prey from some Better's homeworld and wondered whether the kid was someone's personal enemy or just unlucky.

The quarry's flimsy indoor soleskins were in shreds and his feet were in bad shape. He panted for breath, eyes starting from a face with sunken cheeks. He looked at them as if he'd never seen a human being before.

"Hide me?" He said it with the hopelessness of someone who'd suffered Blackguard's cruelties to the end of prayer and endurance.

"Psyche's sake, kid," Alacrity grated, pocketing the cards, "how'd you get here?" The hunt had swept the area earlier, supposedly driving before it or capturing all quarry.

"I hid in a nook in the rocks . . . doubled back . . ." The boy panted, shaking so badly he could hardly stand. "You've got to help me."

He took a quavering step forward; Gute swung up the frightlight and gave it a quick burst. It flared, its brightness and heat driving the boy back.

"You did not elude them," Gute said. "They only let you live a little longer, to play with you. They do that sometimes. Go on, run! You can't stay here."

The look in the kid's eyes was unbearable. Alacrity pleaded, "Gute, my god, we can't just—"

"*He can't stay here!*" Gute yelled into Alacrity's face. "The Betters will find him. The Betters always find their quarry. Always! Is that what you want, to bring them down on *us*?"

Alacrity couldn't answer. Finally he slowly rippled his hand to Gute, almost a waving motion, a negative gesture—the local equivalent of a shake of the head.

"Please help me," the boy said, but defeatedly, in his oddly accented tradeslang.

"We can't even help ourselves," Alacrity told him, his voice cracking, knowing it really wasn't an answer at all. A nervous tic moved the corner of his mouth; he was helpless to control it.

"I'm not going to let them take me. I won't let them do those things to me again," the boy said, taking another step toward them. This time even the blare of the fright-light couldn't make him back away.

He was in tears now. "I won't let them . . . *do* . . . those things to me ever again!"

With a curse Gute threw down the fright-light and whipped his actijot unit out of his raggedy loincloth. Setting it, he swept its invisible beam at the boy. Alacrity shied away; the unit would affect any jot it hit.

The boy made a forlorn sound of pain and fell back, sobbing.

"You want us to die too?" Gute was yelling, half mad himself. He gave the kid another jolt. "Go! Run! Get away from here!"

"Stop it!" Alacrity knocked down the jot unit and went to the kid's side. Gute brought it up again, centering on Alacrity, hand wavering. In the end he held his fire, looking anxiously into the sky.

Alacrity knelt by the quarry. The kid was wailing like a lost soul. He threw his arms around Alacrity's leg.

"Don't let them . . . don't let them . . ."

"Listen to me. I said *listen to me, god damn you!*" Alacrity shook the kid until his teeth rattled, held his chin so their eyes met. The quarry was gulping, hyperventilating, saliva and tears and snot mixing on his face.

Alacrity said slowly, "A hundred meters or so over that way there, there's a cliff. The drop's maybe sixty, seventy meters. Take it head first, to be sure."

At first the boy's face clouded up with incomprehension. Then he understood, and an awful emptiness came into his eyes. He looked to Gute, whose face was like a graven image's.

"Listen!" Gute snapped. They heard it far off: banshee horn, piercing and discordant.

The quarry gave a strangled cry and pulled himself up by Alacrity's shoulder, drawing him off balance and leaving him on all fours in the dirt. The boy staggered off in the direction of the cliff, weeping and moaning but moving as fast as he could.

Gute stood over Alacrity. "Is that why you make sure you know the lay of the land? To know what cliffs are near? What else have you spied out? Rivers? The mires?"

Alacrity pushed himself up. "Among other things."

Gute looked him in the eye. "Don't think too much, Shipwreck. You might make me decide you're too dangerous to know."

They broke off glaring at one another as a rush of air came over the low treetops. Down swooped a single-passenger flier, a rostrum crafted of nielloed metal with a facade in the form of a Niflheim sphinx-face. The man flying it stood upright, hands on the controls.

He was well built, wearing spiked wristbands and a sheath of skinfilm that made his hide look like oily blue snake hide. His mask was the mythical Second Breath villain, the evil, mocking Knave of Knives.

Alacrity and Gute stood rooted, as they'd been taught, hands out from their bodies, chins high to show their collars. The hunter waved his actijot baton at them, a big, elaborate Better's model, all gemset, polished nightquartz. The rostrum came to a hover as they looked up into the ravening knave-mask. The eyes they saw belonged there. In his other hand the hunter took up a nervefire lash.

He knew they weren't quarry but hesitated over them anyway, the lash sizzling and coiling in the air. This had been a big hunt; he'd drawn blood and slain quarry that day. There was no counting on his sanity.

Alacrity stared up at him. Like all Betters, this one had another life on another planet that must be kept absolutely separate from Blackguard. *And when you're there you think a lot about here, don't you?* Alacrity thought. *You wish life could be like this all the time. You headcase.*

The hunter seemed to reach a decision. Seeing the narrowed eyes behind the mask, Gute and Alacrity got ready to run from the lash.

Just then another aircraft arrived, a lepidopter, a jeweled marvel built in the shape of a luminous butterfly. In its saddle of carved jade were two more hunters, a woman dressed as a braided, metal-sheathed dagger-dancer from Synod, and behind her a man in costume as a slavetaker from Friends' World, his bone armor chased with strange whorls, snapping a razorwhip.

"Where did he go?" the woman called. "Are those quarry down there?" At her knee was a quiver of neurobandilleras. The hovering lepidopter beat its radiant wings, stirring the leaves.

The Knave of Knives left off his contemplation of Alacrity and Gute, letting his lash dangle by its wrist thong. He consulted some instrument on the sphinx-face rostrum, then pointed toward the cliff. "That way!"

With a wild hunting call he soared off in that direction, cracking and crashing the nervefire lash right and left. The 'dopter went after.

Then more of the Wild Hunt passed overhead: a winged war god in antigrav harness; an antlered forest spirit on a phallic jetstick; an imitation warlock on a surface-effect flying carpet; a shouting Grim Reaper on a robotic horse that galloped across the sky. They carried lariats, catchpoles, nets and bolos, snarleyballs and tangle-flails.

Demonic music came from somewhere. They winded horns, gulped from wineskins and skull-cups, brandished ancient weapons and modern ones, howling frenzy.

More came, fanning out overhead: ghouls, fire elementals, overample mother-goddesses, hooded inquisitors and witches in flowing, transparent veilsmokes, each using a unique small flier or lifting device. Some had quarry draped over a saddle bow or cowling, or hung by the heels from a rail or bowsprit. The quarry all bore tags identifying the hunter who'd taken them. A few were still alive.

Alacrity and Gute held their pose, watching the fly-over, not daring to move for fear of attracting a dart or beam.

Then the night band was past. The two slowly lowered their arms. They could see the Wild Hunt circling, not too far away, and hear the sputter and crackle of the whips. The laughter sounded demented.

Alacrity hefted his sling of tagging equipment and started

for the circling hunt. Gute caught his arm. "Have you lost your mind? They won't pass you by twice!"

"They will if I don't get in their way. Just doing my job, remember?"

"Part of your job is to stay clear of them." Gute's hand rested on his jot unit. "I'm not getting myself punished just because you feel sorry for some other offworlder. What makes this one any different?"

"I don't know. Just that I saw him, I suppose." Alacrity turned and went on, gambling that a man who'd coveted a Spican atlas and longed to visit the stars wouldn't lay him out in agony with an actijot control unit.

In another moment Gute was by his side. "At least keep down, you idiot! There—through the bushes along there."

They ended up creeping forward, hearing the quarry at bay before they could see. Parting the spinnaker grass, they looked across the forty meters or so of open land leading to the cliff.

The quarry was crouched in a heap. Every time he moved or tried for the edge one or another of the Wild Hunters would drive him back with a fiery lash or a thrusting catchpole. A neurobandillera hung from the kid's back; Alacrity couldn't see why he was still conscious.

The man in the knave mask floated near the brink, looking down on his prey, his lash swirling sparks and discharges around his head. A woman dressed like a robed angel, face hidden by misty veils, riding a hovercraft shaped like a flaming chariot, dove in. She was shaking out a biocling net, preparing to end the game. A two-faced merman shot coruscating darts here and there, to keep the quarry in his spot.

The kid was more dead than alive, wanting only the mean clemency of the cliff. The hunters weren't about to grant it; there were still the special entertainments of the compounds. The kid got to his knees. Alacrity was amazed. The angel circled, her net spread, and the knave grabbed one corner to help.

"Gimme that," Alacrity whispered to Gute, snatching the jot unit. Before Gute could stop him, he fired the silent, invisible beam into the quarry's back.

The kid found one last instant of life in that wash of pain, lurching forward. Alacrity ran the charge to the top; the quarry fought forward through lashes and flails, the bandillera bobbing in his back, ignoring the lesser pain, disregarding their cries.

He plunged off the cliff head first. A chorus of cries and outraged howls went up from the creatures of the pack. Gute and Alacrity couldn't follow the kid's fall, but watched as the masks and veiled faces did.

The knave looked around. Gute and Alacrity stayed stock-still, hunched down among tufts of spinnaker grass and palette-fern. The mad eyes passed their way, and Alacrity couldn't tell for the life of him if he and Gute had been spotted.

Hunters were winding their horns now, some of them diving out of sight for a closer look at the remains. The knave floated his rostrum over to the lepidopter, taking a drink from a flask the slavetaker offered him.

Gute drew Alacrity into deeper brush and shadow. Alacrity handed back the jot unit. They took a brief breather, both of them shaking, sitting with heads down. Then they rose and circled around a thick stand of coral trees, coming to the cliff from another direction, trotting in answer to the summons of the horns. Neither had said a word since Alacrity fired the unit.

The Wild Hunt had been going on since the previous night. It was midafternoon; most of the participants were getting tired. They were already climbing higher, making a last, halfhearted scan for prey but already thinking of the divertissements that had begun back in the compounds by then.

As Alacrity and Gute doubletimed out into the clearing, even the lovely butterfly-chopper was rising gracefully, winging home. Only the original hunter was left. He descended to hover near the two taggers, who waited with heads lowered.

"Look at me."

He bobbed gently in his sphinx-facade flier, his skin showing oily, well-cut highlights. They shifted nervously.

"You there; you're not a local."

Alacrity made a quick twitch of the shoulders, tilt of the head. "That's right, Lord. I'm offworld."

"You, the other one; go tag my catch. Be quick about it."

Gute swallowed. "But, Lord—there won't be anything worth—"

"Don't you question *me*!" The nervefire whip spat and flared, throwing off sparks. Gute scurried away, familiar with the layout of the area, to make a roundabout descent.

When the two were alone, the knave-mask asked Alacrity, "What made you think you could spoil my kill and get away with it?"

Alacrity only got out, "I don't know what you're—" The torture of the jot stole the rest of his words from him and turned his nervous system into a webwork of pain. He found himself flat on his back, fighting to suck in air

"You're not a local; what are you doing in the central labor pool? Answer me!"

Alacrity couldn't, because at that moment the Better hit him with another charge, sending suffering into every part of him.

"Well, it doesn't matter," the hunter decided. "I told my friends I'd bag my last quarry live, and you'll do."

A definite violation of the operating rules of the compound, to kill a Central Labor worker or take one as prey, but not too troublesome.

The knave eased his rostrum a little closer, muscles rolling under the oily skinfilm as he centered the jot baton on Alacrity. A sudden hiss and a cracking explosion sent smoke, steam, and burning specks spurting up out of the hunter's back. He let go his controls and the baton, and started screaming a second later. Alacrity thought for a moment that the jot unit had shorted out or the flier had malfunctioned.

The sphinx rostrum tilted, settling toward the ground as the Hunter ignored his controls, collapsing against them in pain. Alacrity realized then that the man had been shot. The knave sagged, barely conscious, as the flier grounded at the edge of the cliff.

Alacrity's head was clearing. The hunter was moaning weakly, pawing clumsily at a wound he couldn't reach.

Alacrity scrabbled and slid forward on his back, digging with his fingers, hauling, drawing his feet up close. When he was near enough he kicked out flat-footed, slamming the soles of his feet square into the Niflheim sphinx. The light flier bounced back off the cliff.

He had a last view of the knave flailing helplessly, losing

his grip on the rostrum's rail, already half out of it. A long shriek trailed away.

Alacrity, up on one elbow, gazed around. Blinking up into the sky of Blackguard, he saw a splendid female figure in a gorgeous white-on-white combat costume, like some Third Breath valkyrie. In one hand she held aloft a white battle rifle with a scope the size of a top hat. She descended in a triumphant swoop, standing on a chrome-bright, contoured, skeletal flight frame.

Her helmet had sweeping, aerodynamic vanes, and its reflective visor was cast in the cold beauty of a Diana. Rifle held high, she swept down at him with an exultant war cry. He decided groggily that his troubles might not be over yet.

Whoever she was, she was good. She braked and set down like a snowflake in the winter garden, alighting from the minimal flier with an agile leap, the rifle held level.

Alacrity was back on his feet by then. "Um, I didn't get to see; did you happen to notice if that son of a bitch splattered when he hit?"

The voice was muffled by the visor. "I wasn't watching. I couldn't take my eyes off your lanky body." She stowed the rifle in a boot attached to the flight frame, then pushed up the visor.

It was Heart. The Nonpareil. "Nevertheless, Fitzhugh, would you very much mind moving around downwind? *Phew*!"

He laughed out her name a little hysterically and rushed to take her up in his arms, lifting her off the ground even though she was nearly as tall as he. Her full breasts flattened against him a bit; her corselet pinched the skin of his midsection and her shinguards banged his kneecaps. He also bumped his forehead on the side of her helmet as he kissed her. They lost track of time until they had to come up for air.

"How did you get here? Is your father here? How'd you find me?" Alacrity suddenly felt a clenching in his gut, and he was trembling, thinking of Dincrist, Sile, and Constance, and the diversions of the compounds.

"Look, Ho's here too, but I don't know where they've got him. D'you have a way out of this place? Those hunters could come back looking for their buddy. Oh, yeah, and by the way, thanks a lot for saving my life."

He took her up and kissed her again, until she protested a little, trying to push them apart.

"Hobart's being sought, Alacrity. Father's not here yet, but he's due at any moment. We're working on a way to get you off Blackguard."

"'We'?"

She gave him a sly grin. "I'll tell you later."

"But I mean, how'd you know I'd be right *here*?" He suddenly went deathly pale. "Don't tell me you—"

"I what?"

"Never mind."

She gave him a chilly look. "Was I really part of the Wild Hunt, you were going to ask?"

"Forget I said it!" He threw his hands up, indicating Blackguard and all it entailed. "You can see why I'm not thinking right, can't you? You found me with a jot tracer, isn't that it?"

She mussed his thick mane of silver-shot gray hair. "Yes. And I think it's time we were gone from here."

"Hold on." Alacrity ran to the edge of the cliff and looked down. The broken figure in dark skinfilm lay draped on the rocks not far from the shattered remains of the quarry. Twisted wreckage of the sphinx rostrum was strewn all over the place. Gute was nowhere to be seen.

Good analysis, Gute, Alacrity approved; the furor this would raise would be no place for a local. Chances were, Gute was halfway back to his runabout by then, planning an alibi.

Heart had come up behind him, taking his hand. "We have to leave. Do you think you're up to riding tailgate on that thing?"

He looked the flight frame over. It wasn't much more than a small, prettied-up pod containing a power pack, with an instrument panel attached. Styled to suggest exotic pinions, gracefully contoured handlebars and footrest posts swept from it. The shallow bowl of fairing was just enough to protect the pilot's face. Definitely a one-rider craft.

"Up to it? How come we're not gone yet?"

There was just enough room for his feet to crowd next to

hers under the loops of the footrest plates; none for him to squeeze inside the waist bar. Heart put her hands inside the cupping control guards at the handlebars' ends. The flight frame rose unsteadily. Alacrity clung to her. "Couldn't you afford an air-brougham?"

"You don't know how lucky I was to get this clotheshorse, or you wouldn't complain."

"At least it goes with your outfit."

She laughed as they made a shaky ascent, then accelerated. The frame answered sluggishly. Heart cut a course away from the main grouping of compounds, bound for a peak some twenty kilometers distant.

The wind made it impossible to talk, but Alacrity's elation grew even while he thought over the practical aspects of the situation.

There were probably only hours before knave-face was missed, and not much chance that Gute wouldn't crack and spill what had happened. By that time, Alacrity would have to be offworld, or the Control Complex would send out a signal that would jot him silly. Then they'd find him with a tracer and hand him over to a Torquemada aficionado.

Hours. With the right luck, he and Heart and Floyt would be in Hawking by then.

Heart nursed from the flight frame all the speed it had to give. They soared up the slopes leading to the summit. The semiwilderness was deserted except for a few distant craft making their late way back to the compounds. Nested in a midway glen was a chalet set aside for use by the Betters for trysts, seclusion, and such. It was technically the property of Orion Compound, Alacrity knew, just as various other compounds had their hermitages and lovenests. In practice, the places were commonly loaned and shared; there was supposed to be a certain lofty cordiality among the Betters.

Not dressed for the higher altitude, he was shivering as they landed. The chalet was a frothy cluster of onion domes and flanged turrets and reticulations in the style called Arabian Nights Dymaxion.

They came to rest on a high-gloss green deck outside the main entrance. Heart dismounted after Alacrity and went to the doors, removing her white gauntlet, saying, "I've never seen this place, but it's supposed to be a plush little hideaway."

She held a big ring she was wearing up to a decorative curleycue in the wall pattern. The doors swung open. Alacrity, holding the battle rifle, made ready to enter.

Heart saw it and made a sour face. "The place is empty; don't you think I asked? We have to stay hidden for a little while."

"I can bear that, but you just can't be too careful. I've had all the surprises I want for a lifetime."

But she was right. The controls to the place were somehow keyed to the ringwearer's hands; Heart wandered around the overdone birdcage-harem of a chalet, making grand gestures like a symphonic conductor. Curtains closed and lights came up; alcoves slid open and hospitality modules appeared as service automata came forth. Something vaguely light-classical began playing in the background.

Alacrity sank into a pillowlift sofa, looking nonplussed, the rifle across his knees. A cyberwaiter drifted past, all salvers, trays, platters, and lazy susans. He grabbed a plate of tea cakes, the first thing that came his way, and a big tumbler of something fizzy and blue that tasted like lemonade.

Heart pulled off the helm, tossing it aside, shaking out the wavy chalk-blond hair, running her long fingers through it until it hung around her shoulders. She watched Alacrity watching her as he wolfed down the cakes and drank deeply.

"You look like you missed lunch, Alacrity. Also breakfast and dinner. Damn! You were skinny enough as it was!"

"I had it better than most around here, but they don't go out of their way to fatten us up. Besides, they keep us busy. I must say I prefer this place of yours. Look, do we have to listen to that racket? Isn't there something a little more appropriate for you and me?"

She went to a control plate and started making finger motions. He finished the cakes and drained the tumbler. Ballroom music came over the sound system, making it seem like they were standing in the middle of the band. He put the rifle and bandolier of tagging equipment aside and went to her, snapping off his slave collar and hanging it around the neck of a passing robot domestic.

She arched one eyebrow. "You're not dressing for the dance?"

"They told me informal would be all right."

He took her in his arms and they began to dance, easily and very well, as they had on the first night they'd met one another. He inhaled her and held her and closed his eyes, trying to force the memory of the hunt out of his mind.

They swayed and circled; they'd been good together, matched to each other's rhythms and movements and grace, right from the start. The elegant enchantment of it took hold of him after a bit—a rapture, he reflected, that he didn't seem to bring to anything else in his life.

Well, almost nothing, he amended.

They moved and glided together, holding each other close. "That's a ravishing outfit," he said after a time. "How does it come off?"

"What's the matter, an adventurous high-mover's afraid to experiment?"

"Step into my laboratory." He steered them toward a long, wide chaise, figuring out the side seam first. Her broad, ornate cincher-belt went, and her mantlet. The beautiful blouse unwrapped and fell open. He helped her with the sleeves and they left it behind them.

She'd been busy too. "Da-*dahh!*"

"So what? The tough thing about loincloths isn't taking them off; it's keeping them on."

"It is around here."

She helped with the kneeboots and reinforced tights. Underneath she wore only a winding creeper of black fleshpeel, which meandered from the instep of her left foot to the lithe curve of her right shoulder, stark against the incredible whiteness of her skin.

He bent to kiss it. Suddenly the quarry's hopeless eyes came back to him and he felt everything go still and dead inside him. But she pulled him close, caressed him, and brought him back to her again.

She trailed fingertips along his rib cage. "I'm going to have to fatten you up."

"I'm all for that. Only let's do it far away." His head lay on the taut, pallid lowlands of her stomach. She had one knee raised and he was admiring a faint blue vein under the alabaster skin of her inner thigh.

"Yes, yes. Very soon now."

"Will your father come after us?"

"I hope not. Alacrity, I don't want a confrontation with my father. I mean for us to be gone before he gets here."

"I know. I put you in a bad spot with him at Frostpile, wooing and pursuing you, I understand that, but—"

"You *don't* understand."

She propped herself up on one elbow, so he rolled around to look deep into her hazel eyes. And she could see his big, sloe topaz ones, eyes that might, she thought, almost be some animal's.

"Alacrity, it mustn't come to a head-on with my father. Not yet. So I obeyed him on Epiphany, and if everything goes the way I have it planned here, I'll still be able to claim I'm innocent. The thing is, there's a lot more involved than just Heart the Nonpareil getting out from under her daddy's thumb."

"Such as what?"

"Such as the family business. I'm not the only one who's unhappy with . . . with some of the things he's doing. But I have to be very careful."

He nodded slowly. "There's a medium-size mountain of money involved, hm?"

"It isn't the money, at least not primarily. There are some parts of the family empire—holdings, businesses, controlling interests—that are vitally important to me. Even more important than money."

He whistled softly. "Pretty important." He licked her hip.

"Yes. I'll tell you about it later, if you want to hear."

"So you took an awful chance, coming here."

"Well, he always left me the option of visiting Orion Compound if I wanted, although he never dreamed I'd come here without him. He knows how I loathe this place."

"You've been here before?"

"Once, when I was little. I didn't see much of it then; I don't think my father meant for me to see much of it now, just his guided tour. But his personal servants at Orion know me; they were afraid to confine me, so I commandeered a disguise and some transportation and came after you just as soon as I could."

"When did you get here?"

"A few hours ago. I have a ship at the field. As soon as Hobart's been sprung, we're leaving."

"How are you going to explain this to your old man?"

Those lips that aroused him so easily curved upward a little. "You're going to kidnap me."

"Great idea. Are you going to enjoy the ransom! But who's looking for Ho? It's a big place, and if whoever it is doesn't know their way around, we'll all be—"

She put a finger to his lips. "It's an experienced operator. You're not going to believe *how* experi—"

A soft alert-tone sounded from somewhere among her clothing— her proteus. Heart slid past Alacrity and went searching for it.

He watched her avidly. She had the most smashing derrière he'd ever seen; the most mouth-watering haunches; she was so fragrant and lithe . . .

Squatting, she poked through the stuff and found her proteus, a *ne-plus-ultra* Impéria Opitech disguised as a gyve of natural wavestones, ardors, and satan's tears, and precious metals. She spoke a word or two, then listened for a moment.

The Nonpareil jumped to her feet, switching off the prote and clapping it onto her wrist. "My father's arrived!"

He was already grabbing for his loincloth. "Does he know you're here? Or me?"

"I don't think so; not yet." She threw a heavy white lock back from her eyes with a toss of her head as she pulled on her tights.

"Who was that you were talking to?"

"Can't you guess, 'Bright eyes'?"

He got it then, recalling who'd given him the name back in Riffraff Alley. "Here, you'd better take this," Heart said, picking up her corselet and the cincher belt. She handed him a glittery little device that reminded him of a bos'n's pipe. "Short range and limited power—nothing like that dinosaur gun of yours, so if you have to use it, take careful aim."

He looked it over, then concealed it in a fold of his loincloth, smoothed on his ratty soleskins, and went to check the battle rifle. Two servant robos startled him from behind with their irritating *ping*ing and beeping for attention. He impatiently touched a control in the armrest of the sofa and sent them back to their places in the kitchen.

He picked up the rifle again. "We have to try your plan now: you get your ship from the spacefield and—"

"*Alacrity!*"

He pivoted, hearing the alarm in her voice and starting to raise the rifle, even as he heard a faint *tff*! and felt something sting him hard over his left shoulder blade. He began to fall, getting a glimpse of Heart leaping toward him and human figures in the doorway.

Something made the *tff*! sound again and Heart's breath hissed from her in pain. He felt very disoriented and couldn't move, staring at the ceiling.

After a while somebody came into his line of vision. It was the male Better who'd been riding the 'dopter, the one dressed as a slavetaker from Friends' World. He waved a jot tracer at Alacrity.

"Like I told you: this one's jot doesn't register," he called. "He isn't the one Mason wants."

"Well, this one is," a woman's voice answered. She was the one who'd piloted the butterfly aircraft, the ersatz dagger-dancer. "She's the one he wants, all right; help me get her on the 'dopter, and you can pilot her flight frame back."

"But what about him?"

"Who cares? The tracer says he's not the one. Kill him if you feel like; we can't carry him. Only hurry. I want to get back to Grand Guignol before we run into trouble with Dincrist."

The slavetaker picked up the white battle rifle as he thought it over, the muzzle pointed right between Alacrity's glassy eyes.

"Shame to mess the place up," he said.

"Then just give him a max jotting."

"But he might even be one of ours. What the hell; we can always send somebody out for him. He won't be going far."

"Then come here and give me a hand with this white sow; she weighs a ton."

The slavetaker shouldered the rifle and passed out of Alacrity's vision.

CHAPTER 14

FAST MOVES ON BLACKGUARD

POLLOLO HAD COMMANDED FLOYT TO RETURN TO THE INNER sanctum within an hour, so the Earther dawdled a bit, walking back through the main corridors of the Central Complex. He only dared defy the creature enough to irritate without making it worth Pollolo's bothering Baron Mason with a complaint.

Not that Mason had any right to be vexed. Floyt had been drawing information out of the various computer systems, raiding and collating, with increasing skill. Mason's game was blackmail, or at least pressure politics; Floyt was making himself as useful as possible.

As he strolled, he kept his tunic collar up straight, hiding the iron slave collar Pollolo insisted he wear. It wasn't that Floyt could keep the guards or Betters from realizing his status; his bracelet gave that away when it slid down his wrist, and so did his plain clothing, although he was still wearing the mask Mason had gotten him that first day. But now staff members in the outer rooms of the computer facility were used to his upturned collar, so that they never noticed when he entered wearing a neck shackle and left without one.

He browsed along displays in the shops of the main concourse. At one infocenter he scanned the Whereabouts. Among the images there was a face he recognized from the Grapple.

This time Janusz, the Rasputin lookalike outlaw, appeared

211

in a forthright Wanted blurb. The blurb had been sponsored by the Langstretch Detective Agency, which in turn started Floyt fretting over Alacrity and wondering what was happening to him.

Preoccupied, he wandered past the display case of the infoemporium a few steps before registering what he'd just seen. He paused literally in midstep, one foot in the air, then backed up.

There were piles of them in a mountain range display: hardback books, info-wafers, and a half-dozen other formats. The mountain range was flanked and fronted by holopromos and subliminal pulsers, pyrotechnic flashers and computer-generated dramatizations of selected passages.

The window was just about filled with *Hobart Floyt and Alacrity Fitzhugh in the Castle of the Death Addicts* and *Hobart Floyt and Alacrity Fitzhugh Challenge the Amazon Slave Women of the Supernova*.

Oddly enough, Floyt's first coherent reaction was, *Great and Holy Spirit of Terra! Didn't Sintilla even tell them what we really look like? That's not me; it's some triathalon champion with eye makeup!* The Alacrity figure was an even more perfect specimen, slightly younger, and had nicer hair.

The illustrators had pulled out the chocks. Floyt, mesmerized by one of the promo loops, had to admit he didn't recall attacking a fangster with his bare hands and teeth. And if Alacrity really *had* participated in something called the Ecstasy Ritual of the Vortex Viragos, he'd neglected to invite Floyt along.

The ads proclaimed the books instant smash hits. As Floyt watched, the proprietor of the shop retrieved a microfiche edition from the window display for a masked Better.

Floyt gawped, wondering what Sintilla was going to do with all her money. He was speculating idly on where she might be and what she might be doing when he felt a tap at his shoulder.

He knew instant dread. He whirled, prepared to look up into the face of one of the outsize guards, stuttering an excuse for his loitering. But he was looking into empty space. He panned downward past a mop of brown curls, two of the merriest eyes he knew, and a sunburst smile on a round-cheeked face.

"That collar just does not become you, Hobart. I don't think iron's your look. Have you thought about a twillsilk ascot?"

"*Tilla!*" Looking around apprehensively, he recovered from the outburst. Few guards were around right then; most of the Betters were either at the compounds or out on the Wild Hunt. He'd gone unnoticed.

He contained himself, his questions and relief and joy, and drew her over into the half concealment of a spa doorway, making sure no one was watching.

"How did you get here? How did you find me? What—" He had all the same questions Alacrity had.

Sintilla grinned smugly, smoothing the material of her frilly, daringly translucent dress rompers. Floyt couldn't help noticing that she wasn't as chunky as he'd always thought, was actually rather shapely, in a compact kind of way.

"I got here because I followed you two." She inclined her head in the direction of the infoemporium. "Sales are jumping; you're both gonna be famous and make me rich! I can't afford to lose you now."

"Heh!" They'd fled her without so much as a good-bye, he recalled guiltily. He'd never been so happy to see anybody in his life. "But how did you find me?"

She showed him a jot tracer. "Some horrible woman named Constance left her jot implanting unit around and one of the servants at Orion Compound noticed the settings—yours and Alacrity's. We don't know where Constance is, but we think she took a ship called the *Mountebank* up into orbit for some reason or other. There're eighteen kinds of hell waiting to break loose around here. Dincrist is due in."

"Tilla, have you seen Alacrity? Can we get out of this place?"

"Heart's here too, that's how I got in. She's out looking for Alacrity now. And, sweetie, we're going to get the both of you out of here just as soon as we can. An hour or two, if we can pull it off."

A pair of the tall guards, a male and a female, in their wide-shouldered maroon suits and pouter-pigeon codpieces, stepped around a distant corner. Sintilla whipped up the smoky green mask she'd been carrying. With the proprietary air of a Better, she took him by the wrist and led him across the broad corridor past a fountain, right by the guards, Sintilla tottering a bit on platform sandals.

She drew Floyt over to an oriental robotíque-style settee under a bubbly steeple of skylight tori. Lively brown eyes sparkled at him through a serene giaconda face. "Just let me fill you in, Hobart, because we haven't got much time."

"Less than you think. I should be working. I'm expected."

"All right, but first I have to tell you, I, um, I sort of pulled a dirty trick on you—when you guys gave me your proteuses to hold during the airbike race, remember? Well, I rigged yours."

"Come again?"

"That cheapie model Earthservice gave you—well, it wasn't too tough."

"But—you didn't gain access to any of my protected data files. I made sure of that."

"Of course not, dopey! I put something *in*, so whenever you queried Frostpile's data network, the query would also be routed to my proteus. Get my drift?"

"Whew!" And he and Alacrity had been trying to find out about Blackguard at the terminal on the landing roof at Frostpile while they were waiting for the *Blue Pearl* to pick them up.

"It was devious, I know. D'you hate me?"

"Only if you leave me here, Tilla."

She patted his knee. "Not a chance. Anyway, I knew Dincrist had some kind of connection with Blackguard; found that out back when Weir was still alive and I was snooping around Frostpile. So I figured Alacrity was off to find Heart and you were tagging along. Only Heart wasn't going to Blackguard. I discovered that just before you two left in the *Pearl*. The obvious conclusion was, you guys were off on a wrong trail.

"I'd heard this and that about Blackguard, but I didn't have the first idea how to get here. So I did the next best thing and tracked down the Nonpareil. *That* took a little doing! When Heart heard what was going on she requisitioned one of her family's ships and we came here. Y'know, I never had a starship at my disposal before. I must say, it's the only way to travel."

Floyt was trying to absorb the newsflood. Sintilla had jumped to completely the wrong conclusion about why Alacrity and Floyt had come to Blackguard, but it wouldn't be smart to correct her now, especially here. Floyt was listening with one ear, calculating variables like Pollolo, Baron Mason, and most of all the actijots.

"We're going to have to time this just right," Sintilla cautioned, "otherwise you two could have a bad time with those actijackti's you're carrying."

"What's your plan?"

"When we're ready, Heart's going to bring Alacrity in from where they're hiding. Then she goes to the spacefield and gets ready for lift-off, and I bring you two along at the last second.

"It'll be a legitimate take-off, and we'll be out of jot range and into Hawking before planetary defenses can— what's the matter?"

Floyt had been shaking his head. "Listen, it's more complicated than you think. Alacrity and I can't get close to a spaceship; our jots would fry us."

"What? But there's got to be some way around that! Hobart, if we're still around when Heart's father shows, we're all in the plopper!"

"It wouldn't be anything new for me." As he had in the vault of the causality harp, Floyt exerted all his will, getting a grip on himself. "We may be able to do this yet. There's a Baron Mason who's trying to gain control around here, and he's interdicted control of the actijot system. I think I can do something in the facility where he put me to work."

"That's it then! You've got to!"

"Not that simple. There's also an XT there—a creature called Pollolo; he's on watch all the time. I've been working on a scheme, but—I'm dubious about its chances at this point. It may be too soon to—"

"Hobart, it's practically too late! Whatever it is, you've got to do it!"

Floyt took a deep breath. Being torn limb from limb by Pollolo could hardly be worse than whatever Dincrist would have in store for him.

Sintilla was still wearing her proteus. "Give me your contact index and wait for my call," he said. "I'll just have to try my idea. I'll try to meet you here within, say, two hours. If you don't hear from me . . . good luck. Tell Alacrity I'm sorry for everything he's been through because of this Weir thing—because of me."

She lifted her mask for a moment, pulling him close, and gave him a sound buss on the mouth. There were tears on her cheek. "Get going, and don't bobble it!"

"I haven't even thanked you yet, Tilla."

"There'll be time for that later. Now, go!"

As usual, the inner sanctum was dim, making the strange projections and corallike decorations on the wall eerie and threatening.

Floyt entered Pollolo's domain warily; the creature liked to take him by surprise just to watch him jump. But he could see stirring waters in the tank and could by now judge the waterline by eye. Pollolo was still immersed.

Floyt brought his terminal to life and called up Diogenes, so it would look as if he'd been working. He adjusted the worklamp to a fairly low glow then sent it to hover high on its magnetic field, near the ceiling-mounted baseplate. It was a small, adaptable lightshape, a modest miniature version of the grandiose ones in the corridors and esplanade. Right now it had taken on the form of a pale-blue dodecahedron.

Pollolo had been against Floyt's bringing in more illumination, preferring his little kingdom gloomy and quiet. But the creature grudgingly relented rather than bother Baron Mason with the matter. Pollolo warned Floyt to keep the light well over in his corner though, behind the partitioning data banks and stacked modules. That was just perfect with Floyt. The lamp was an important victory, critical to his plan.

Floyt checked an access plate in one of the upper components of a control stack, where it would be awkward for Pollolo to reach without leaning against the sacrosanct systemry. The hair he'd spit-glued across it, a melodramatic precaution, was still in place.

Floyt quickly opened it and drew out a slave collar he'd hidden in there. Anxiously checking the waters again for the preliminary roiling that usually preceded Pollolo's emergence, he darted to the room's Classified Materials Disposal device.

Wonderful little gadget, when you stop to think about it, Floyt reflected as he fed the collar into it. Installed for routine and/or emergency destruction of documents, code matrices, commo and crypto equipment, and so forth, the CMD device also did a first-rate job turning iron slave collars into a pile of filings.

He was grateful to whatever powers there were that Pollolo hadn't noticed that Floyt always entered with a slave collar on—Pollolo's mandate—but often left without one, tunic collar pulled up. Sometimes more than once a day. The collars were easy to come by around the Central Complex, and nobody bothered to keep track of them.

In fact—Floyt pulled off the one he was wearing and ground it up too. He also threw in the odds and ends he'd collected in his wanderings: a few scraps of this and that, the metal working end of a small utensil, a few decorative studs furtively pried loose from a door. Floyt had recently become a hawkeyed scavenger of iron.

As he worked he cast wistful glances at the Most Secure Module. Thanks to the staff members Mason had co-opted, the jot control system could be reached and manipulated through that ordinary-looking hunk of apparatus, along with spacefield operations and some security ops. Unfortunately, only Pollolo could unlock the Most Secure Module.

Floyt hastily filled his pockets with the filings, wiping and blowing away the remains. There was a slow churning of the waters. He dashed for his place, sliding into his glide-chair just as he heard the surface of the pool break around Pollolo's form.

There were familiar noises as the creature clambered out, shedding water, and donned his interface collar. "Delver Root-nose!" came the synthesized voice, using the alias Floyt had given. "Get over here!"

Floyt hurried to show his face, carrying a roll of info-wafers and a case of tapes.

"Why are you late, Rootnose? And where is your collar?"

Pollolo's new shell was just about complete. His great chelae ground ominously as he spoke—or, rather, transmitted. Floyt stayed clear and showed the fear Pollolo liked to see.

"Heavens!" Floyt clutched at his throat. "I took it off to eat, and I guess— I'm so sorry; shall I go get it?"

"No! You've wasted enough time as it is! Baron Mason called for a progress report. He still wants to know about Praxis, and the Regatta for the Purple."

One of Mason's obsessions was the regatta and how his foe Dincrist, a nouveau-riche social climber, had managed to get himself accepted for it. Mason suspected it had something to do with Praxis, who was also chairman of the race committee.

"I'm working on it, but I haven't had much luck."

"Well, work harder! And I don't want to see you without a collar again! This is the last time I warn you!"

With any luck. Floyt hid the thought with the finesse of an Earthservice functionary.

"Get busy!" Pollolo snapped his huge claws close to Floyt's snout; Floyt backpedaled hastily to his workplace and brought up Diogenes.

He very nearly forgot his troubles as the powerful AI routine lit screens and holo displays, projected images, made light dance, and turned readouts into mosaics of information. Signals and sound pulses crowded over one another. It was like standing inside a kaleidoscope or, he supposed, a causality harp of information. Floyt didn't see how, as he'd heard alleged, contact could be any more intense for a headboarded accessor, directly wired to the AI or not. Diogenes had even come up with some very interesting information about *Astraea Imprimatur.*

"Hello, user Delver," came Diogenes' voice. He sounded like a cultured, wise, and simpático Terran male a good deal older than Floyt.

"Hi, Diogenes."

"I have the data and correlations you requested, Delver. I've also compiled new avenues of investigation."

"That's fine; thanks. Dupe them for Pollolo and, uh, keep a record for yourself. And Diogenes?"

"Yes, Delver?"

Floyt hesitated; he hated the thought of leaving Diogenes behind. The AI was so much less wooden to work with, so much more cordial and capable than the deliberately limited and lumpish Earthservice constructs he was accustomed to that Floyt couldn't help wishing.

Then he told himself to stop. There wasn't time, there probably wasn't a way, but more to the point, Earthservice would only confiscate Diogenes. Functionary thirds—particularly ones in bad odor for having been offworld—did not get to keep brilliant, virtually alive AIs for their own use and companionship.

"Nothing, Diogenes. Dim it down a bit, if you will, and just keep the overview displays up."

The fountain of light and data died away. Floyt tiptoed cautiously through the labyrinth of equipment to peek around a corner.

Pollolo was working system status checks in a far corner of the spacious room. Floyt lightfooted back to the pool and speedily dumped handsful of iron filings into it.

He had only a rough idea how many kilos he'd dumped into the tank so far, but thought it was quite a few. He'd ground up scavenged struts and shelving supports and cable clips—anything that wasn't nailed down. He'd been haunted by the fear that Pollolo would notice the missing items, or a strange taste to his water.

Finished, Floyt knelt to brush and blow a few spilled filings into the water to avoid leaving any trace of his work, then sneaked back to his chair. Diogenes was still working. Between them, the two had already exhumed and pieced together enough blackmail information to keep Mason fairly content. Most of it was the sort of stuff that would be of use only to the baron or someone in his circles, nothing criminal or illegal, but matters of record that would be embarrassing or demeaning, and threaten status or bring ostracism. Floyt's background in genealogy had been especially useful there, as he tracked down spurious family trees.

Mason made no effort to conceal from Floyt what he was doing or why he was doing it. Floyt found that ominous. The Earther, agonizing over his plan and the many things that could go wrong with it, brought up the critical passage of the information he'd gathered about Pollolo's species.

He scanned it again. Statocyst lining divestiture; sensory tendrils; statolithes. It talked about sediment, but not in specifics. Sediment was attached to sensory tendrils inside the statocysts and the pull of gravity gave Pollolo's kind their sense of equilibrium. But there was simply no precise information.

Floyt shook his head. The whole scheme was insane.

"Rootnose! Get yourself over here, worm!"

Floyt ran. Pollolo's collar was switched to what Floyt now knew to be commo mode. He was saying to it, "Yes, Baron. I understand. You may depend on me, my lord." The creature ended the call, then its eyestalks swung to Floyt.

"Delver Rootnose? Your master and owner-of-record, Captain Dincrist, has just come out of Hawking. He'll be here shortly."

Floyt swallowed. "And?"

"Why, he'll raise a fuss about you and the other one, no doubt. No doubt." The cruel claws opened and closed. "You're an embarrassment to the baron now. You're to be held for disposition."

Floyt's heartbeat was fast as a hummingbird's. "But—but I've found something new," he lied. "I've uncovered something about . . . about Praxis! The baron needs it."

"He shall have it." Pollolo sidled a little closer. "I will give it to him. We no longer require your services."

Floyt ducked away from a clashing pincer and retreated toward his work area.

He'd been lucky Pollolo hadn't used a jot unit on him; that would have been the end of everything. The creature came after him slowly, claws spread wide, certain it had him cornered.

Floyt kicked his glide-chair in Pollolo's direction and it scooted freely that way. Pollolo batted it away. In the meantime Floyt palmed the control unit for his worklight.

Pollolo came on almost mincingly, claws held at waist level; Floyt backed into the corner, a horrible gulf in his chest and stomach.

"I'm glad you bolted, glad for this sport. Didn't you know I had this in mind for you all along? Now it's over; come to—"

Floyt ran the magnetic control all the way up to max. Pollolo was directly beneath the ceiling baseplate. Small metal objects—stylus, tape-clip, bits of debris—leapt up to adhere to it. The lightshape was flattened overhead.

Pollolo's collar gargled. From the creature himself came a noise totally unprecedented, a shrill, almost hypersonic bleat of terror.

Pollolo abandoned his attempts to seize Floyt and clutched desperately at nearby machinery, at console legs, and even tried to get a grip on the floor, his eyestalks squeezed shut, quaking in fear.

"Well, what do you know," Floyt said, open-mouthed. "It *worked*!"

Eventually Pollolo's antennules regained some control of his collar, but not much. "Please-please-stop-oh-please-ah!" was about all he could produce, and he seemed incapable of going through the more complex procedures of opening commo connections. With extreme caution Floyt moved a little closer.

But Pollolo really was pasted to the deck, unable to let go. His intellect told him gravity hadn't changed, that he'd been tricked. But he was a creature of strong instinct and reflex; the metal filings that had entered his statocysts were being pulled upward by the baseplate's magnetic field, and that told his body that he was clinging to the ceiling, in danger of falling, triggering a very strong reflex. He could no more disregard it than a human being could thrust an arm into a nervefire field.

Floyt tossed a few objects at the thing, in case it was a trick. Then the Earther circled round, got his glide-chair, and beat Pollolo on the anterior surface a few times, experimentally. Pollolo, eyestalks squeezed shut, could only make the pleading sounds and his own shrill keening, immobilized.

Floyt inhaled a resolute breath, then scrambled up onto Pollolo's back. The thing made a tentative effort to swipe him off, but couldn't bring himself to let go any of the clawholds he'd gotten. He vibrated and rocked a little, but was fairly stable.

Kneeling on Pollolo's back, Floyt tried to work the releases for the commo collar. It wouldn't do for Pollolo to pull himself together long enough to send in an alarm.

Losing patience with the alien fastenings, Floyt gave them

a couple of hearty kicks with the heel of his foot. They clacked open; he pulled the collar loose.

He stamped his foot on Pollolo's shell a few times to make absolutely sure the monster wasn't faking. He then indulged himself in a bit of revenge, tap dancing a few steps over the thing's braincase while Pollolo vibrated and chittered. Having done so, Floyt leapt down.

Now the creature could only make inarticulate sounds. Floyt looked the collar over; he'd been quite attentive, these past nine days or so. He located the commo feature and jabbed a laze-probe in where it would do the most good. There was a sput, discharge, and smoke.

He toed the collar over beneath Pollolo's antennules, which flipped and flopped on it. The claws stirred the merest bit; Floyt was back well out of reach with one frightened bound.

He backed off the magnetic field just a tick, trying not to picture what would happen if the light-duty field in the little baseplate burned out from the demands he was placing on it. Pollolo's antennules moved a little.

"You're not going anywhere," Floyt told him; Pollolo froze. "Just access the Most Secure Module for me *and don't do anything else*! I'll know if you do."

Pollolo didn't comply. Floyt ran the field all the way to the top again and held the tip of the laze-probe under the thing's sensors.

"One more chance, then I burn you smooth as a curling stone and plug this into your excretory passage!"

Floyt wasn't sure how much he was bluffing. Commo displays were already showing inquiries and contact signals addressed to Pollolo. How long could it be before somebody from the outer staff worked up the nerve to see what was wrong?

But when Floyt eased up on the field again, Pollolo's antennules flew feverishly to the collar. The Most Secure Module blipped, ready and accessed. Floyt increased the field again and took the collar back, sliding it aside and leaving the creature immobilized again.

Floyt's head was spinning and he felt faint. He fought the impulse to hyperventilate and brought up Diogenes on the MSM.

"Delver, this feels wonderful," Diogenes said. "What do you want me to do?"

"Um, you don't detect any fail-safes? Any booby-traps?"

"Not over the MSM, Delver."

If Diogenes was being forced to lie to him, Floyt would find out soon enough, he decided. "First, I want to make changes in the actijot system."

He switched his own code signal, then Alacrity's, burying them in the system, giving them both, in effect, unlisted numbers. A direct shot from a jot unit would still clean their clocks, but it could no longer be done by remote, nor could they be traced.

That left the problem of the spacefield defenses. But even Diogenes could only show the system to him; Mason hadn't managed to tap into it yet. As he was doing that, Diogenes reported an incoming command over the jot system—lethal charges to both Floyt's jot and Alacrity's, a little too late.

Floyt stared soberly at the Most Secure Module, wondering about the baron's timing. Mason had apparently decided to minimize his liabilities, like witnesses, right away, what with Dincrist coming—"

"Holy First Light! *Diogenes!*" Floyt hollered. A quick inquiry told him that Dincrist had already set down in the *Lamia* and left it, in the company of Sile and Constance, in Sile's spaceboat, the *Harpy*.

Floyt patched through to a commo channel and got Sintilla. "Tilla! Can you get through to Heart?"

"Yes. What's keeping you?"

Floyt explained. "Tell her to meet us—ahh, at the central labor pool. Warn her that Dincrist has arrived on Blackguard."

"I'll do that right now, Hobart. Get out here; I'm waiting for you."

"I'm on my way. And tell them to hurry!"

Floyt broke the connection and got back to Diogenes. "Look, I don't want to leave you behind."

"That would sadden me, Delver—or shall I address you as Hobart?"

"Either. Is there any way to transfer you, or is there perhaps some form of storage?"

"I can transfer all that I am, through the MSM, into a storage cube, Hobart, circumventing Baron Mason's safeguards." A storage locker door controlled by the MSM popped open. In it were several blank memory cubes.

"Great. Is there any way you can arrange for this place to seal up when I—when we leave? Keep anybody from getting in or getting through to the MSM?"

"Oh, certainly, for a while at least. Shall I?"

"Not just yes, but *hell* yes!"

It took Floyt three tries to get a cube in right. While Diogenes was making the high-speed transfer, the Earther took a last look around.

He grabbed Pollolo's collar and, opening its seals and access panels, heaved it into the tank. There it produced sparks, discharges, and steamy minor explosions that made him feel good.

He thought about kicking Pollolo farewell, but that would only hurt his foot. Instead he took a stick of indelible stain marker from the storage locker. As Pollolo quivered helplessly, he scrawled HOBART FLOYT WAS HERE and TERRA FOREVER!! across the creature's back.

"Think of me next time you molt, Pollolo," Floyt said proudly, chucking the marker aside.

Diogenes' transfer was by then complete. Floyt ejected the memory cube and slipped it into his pocket, then pulled up his tunic collar to cover his naked neck and sauntered from the room.

CHAPTER 15

CHANCE, KINGS,
AND DESPERATE MEN

"I'M NOT GETTING FITZHUGH'S SIGNAL. MAYBE HE'S NOT there?"

Constance frowned over the scope imager as Sile arrowed the *Harpy* toward the chalet. They were dressed in their regatta costumes again.

"He's there," Sile said, "and she's with him. That dimwit housemaid said Heart took the ring-key to the place." He trimmed the choice little spaceboat and dove for the landing oval outside the chalet's doors. "And besides, you don't pick him up anyplace else, do you?"

"No. Maybe Dincrist burned out Fitzhugh's jot with that long-range jolt he sent him?"

"Mm. Not likely." Sile kept the boat's chin gunpod trained on the chalet but saw no targets. "Maybe somebody's removed the jot."

"You mean that ice-bitch?" Constance smiled her dreamy, slit-eyed smile. "What Dincrist should do is give her to us."

Sile shot her a quick look. "Don't even joke like that; you're talking life-and-death trouble with Dincrist."

He came to an abrupt stop on the green-gloss oval. There was no sign of life.

"Well then, you must let me have Fitzhugh." She pouted,

giving Sile's shoulder a caress. "And poor old dippy Hobart
Floyt too. Promise."

"That's up to Dincrist, I'm afraid, my treasure." He checked
the charge of a heavy-duty stungun. "After the jolt Dincrist
sent through Fitzhugh's jot, he may not be able to feel much.
I hope he's as strong as he looks; a shot like that could've
killed him, and Dincrist doesn't want a corpse."

"Fitzhugh's strong," Constance purred, rising to follow him.
She was wearing her long dueling pistols and, like Sile, had a
jot unit on her belt. "Oh, yes; strong enough for lots of sweet
education."

They carefully walked to the chalet's doors. Keeping to
cover, peering in from either side, they saw Alacrity's body
sprawled on the floor. There was no sign of Heart.

"Let's get him out of here," Sile said. "I don't like being
so far from the *Lamia* with Dincrist and Mason due to go at
it."

"What about dear, dear Heartsy?"

"If she's here, let me handle it. We don't want her hurt."
He checked the doors. "The place isn't locked. You go around
back. And take your spurs off."

Constance went, her fingernail sheaths making her hold her
matched pistols a little oddly. Sile eased his spurs off, laying
them aside, then waited, watching. Alacrity continued to lie
motionless.

Sile went in, searching and pointing the stungun every which
way as he moved to Alacrity. The rooms and alcoves and service
nooks were all open, but there were hangings and draperies
and a lot of other places for an ambusher to hide.

Alacrity still hadn't stirred; Sile debated hitting him with a
stungun bolt or jotting him again before venturing to check
him. If the young sod died, Sile could always blame it on the
massive jotting Dincrist had transmitted just minutes after arriving on the planet.

As Sile came a step nearer, weighing gun and jot unit, still
deciding, Alacrity opened his eyes and shot him with the bos'n's
pipe pistol Heart had given him. It had been difficult to judge
the angles. Still, Sile took a pinbeam in the hip, leather breeches

charring and burning, flesh boiled and steam-ruptured, and went off balance with a wailed obscenity.

He was bringing the stungun to bear, more used to it than the jot unit, when Alacrity fired twice more. Sile crumpled, pistol and jot unit falling from his hands.

Alacrity eased himself up, edging forward, getting a hand on the stungun. A sudden noise from the kitchen made him look around. Constance was just coming into the doorway, a presentation pistol in each hand.

He pegged a quick shot at her with the bos'n's pipe, but it was way off and she could see that even though she ducked away from it. Alacrity threw himself behind the cover of the pillowlift sofa. There was a whamming flash as Constance let fly at him, and a lance of flame shot clear through the sofa. It passed over Alacrity's back.

He started to creep forward, to shoot around the end of the sofa, but she outguessed him and blasted away at the spot, sending him shrinking away from the white heat and setting the rug afire.

"Come out, baby," she crooned.

He took a hasty look under the sofa—a very narrow space— and saw by her boots that she was still in the kitchen doorway, prepared to take cover if she had to. He reached up to pass his hand over a control in the sofa armrest.

"Show that pretty face," Constance sang, "and take it standing up." She put another beam through the sofa back. He hunkered, watching under the sofa.

Suddenly an insistent *ding*ing sounded behind her, and Constance spun around, spitting in fright, letting go with both pistols, blowing to smithereens the cyberwaiter that was trying to come in answer to Alacrity's summons.

Alacrity was up by then, shooting repeatedly with the stungun. The bolts were weird, writhing patterns of green electricity. Constance screamed, her short hair standing straight up, and fell into the kitchen, rolling over the machine's ruins and coming to rest a little beyond.

Sile was dead and Constance was well and truly out. After checking them and beating out the several small fires started by Constance, Alacrity sank onto the smoldering sofa, trying to pull his thoughts together, reflecting on what would've happened if he hadn't recovered from the dart in time to realize the *Harpy* was landing.

He recalled a little of what the slavetaker and the dagger-dancer had said—enough to figure that Heart was at Grand Guignol by then. He was still a bit lightheaded from whatever they'd shot him with, but adrenaline had brought him around quite a bit, and he forced himself to concentrate.

He knew he wouldn't get very far wearing labor pool worker's attire; he looked around the chalet for something else to wear, but didn't have the Nonpareil's electronic access to closets and storage areas. The purple comic-opera outfits of Sile and Constance were both far too small.

What he did find in Sile's inner jacket pocket, though, was a lock transceiver. It was a beautiful instrument, solid and set with polished sunstreamers and glitterwheels. Alacrity stared out to where the *Harpy* sat.

He yanked a cloth off a serving table, sending its centerpiece flying. He bundled up guns, proteuses, purses, and jot units, took the transceiver, and hurried out to the landing deck.

The *Harpy* was an elegant craft designed like nothing he'd seen before, but reminding him of Aeroflow Neoclassic. She opened for him without ado.

Sile's idea of comfort was sumptuousness to a fault, decor in the idiom known as *Narcíssissimo Industríale*. But a quick recon told Alacrity the *Harpy* mounted a healthy arsenal and was fast and well equipped.

He located a medical kit and gave himself a half dose of Engine, to help counteract the effects of the dart, and did some pondering. Even with a buccaneer boat like *Harpy*, he doubted his chances of simply blasting his way in and grabbing Heart. Besides, the very capable Blackguard defense system would probably take unkindly to his shooting up Grand Guignol Compound.

The commo rig was blinking, having recorded a message after Constance and Sile disembarked. It took Alacrity a few moments to figure out how to replay it.

He was looking at the sweating face of Urtho Skate. "Sile, where are you? The security people are giving me a hard time about keeping the *Mountebank* up here in orbit. They had me shift to a new one and said that I might have to land or leave soon."

Orbital data flashed for a few seconds, then Skate's face reappeared. "What should I do? Contact me as soon as you can!" The message ended and Alacrity did some more thinking.

Recalling the Nonpareil's "Bright Eyes" hint, he tried Sintilla's proteus contact index, she having given him the nick name.

Sintilla answered in a quiet voice. "Bombastico here."

The connection probably wasn't being monitored—but then, he wasn't sure what the Blackguard security people were capable of doing, or how distracted they were. He addressed Sintilla by her pen name.

"Bombastico, this is some other Riffraff," he said, referring to Riffraff Alley, their housing area at Frostpile. "Listen, my sweet*Heart's* gone. I think she's at a party at Grand Guignol Compound."

"Oh! Well, I've got the Inheritor with me; shall we try to come get you?"

"No; I'll meet you there."

"Good. Don't worry, Bright Eyes; we know how to find you."

"Fine," Alacrity said, not quite understanding. "Um, do you have any idea where my date's father is?"

"No, but something big seems to be coming up."

"It's starting now. See you soon."

He scavenged around the spaceboat, trying to work out a plan as he went. He found clothing, but nothing he could squeeze into except a bedroom wrap.

Then he discovered a small locker containing costumes, masks, and other accessories, Blackguard stuff. Most of that was useless too, but he finally came across a suit-of-thongs, an asymmetrical one-size-fits-all network that glittered like black ice. He rummaged some more and turned up a matching gargoyle cod-cup of molded duraglaze, and a black kabuki-style demon mask with a crown of white plumage. There were also soleskins.

Single-size notwithstanding, the suit-of-thongs was a tight

fit, especially where it stretched across his back and chest, but he could live with it. One of his worries was that the *Harpy* definitely wasn't the usual sort of Wild Hunt transportation and might attract the wrong kind of attention.

He had a sinister inspiration and moved quickly to the airlock. A few minutes later he was back in the pilot's poz, warming up the engines.

The ship had a control layout strange to him, with far more than the usual countermeasures and antidetection gear. The weapons systems were reasonably straightforward, though. Sile had landed in a high state of readiness, and Alacrity left things so.

He lifted off carefully, and got underway at a modest fraction of the speed Sile had used. It was a well-proven fact of the technological ferment of the Third Breath that presuming too much of an unfamiliar piece of machinery was a good way, as Alacrity himself put it, "to flunk out of life and get expelled."

He kept to low altitude, flew inexpertly and swore, all the while expecting the *coup de grâce* from his jot. There had to be some reason Dincrist or Mason hadn't fried his follicles by now. The Slavetaker/Better had said his jot didn't register. *What's going on?*

He came into view of Grand Guignol Compound, an Omnidynamic-*Sauvage* pagoda lit up like the scene of an accident.

As Alacrity began his laborious approach, other fliers appeared and converged in a loose formation around the spaceboat, like escorts.

At first he thought he was being challenged; he licked his lips, ready to yell fire commands at the weapons systems. Then he realized his new wingmen were only carousing Wild Hunters, perhaps returned late from a distant hunting ground or arriving at Grand Guignol after visiting other compounds.

He swore again and lurched to pull on the kabuki demon mask even though it made flying more difficult. Its biocling microfield held the mask in position; the gargoyle cod-cup was already in place and even less comfortable.

There was again the nightmare mix of airborne fiends, animal figures, and threatening archetypes. They'd been doing some power-celebrating already; many were having trouble flying.

A crimson she-devil mailed in flecks of crucible-amber, her barbed tail coiling and lashing, swooped closer to the spaceboat on a jetstick with a goat's-head fairing. She showed long white fangs as she moved in for a curious look through the cockpit canopy, then noticed what was strapped across *Harpy*'s nose. Giving Alacrity a high sign, she rocketed on ahead.

He leaned forward a bit to make sure Sile's naked body was still secure across the spaceboat's downswept nose. It wouldn't do to lose his membership badge just then. Sile was still there, and so was the hunter's tag fastened to his heel by Alacrity. Alacrity's second shot had made it unlikely that anybody would recognize Sile.

Alacrity painstakingly brought the *Harpy* down on an open lawn just beyond the compound's walls. There was already a jumble of jetsticks and flight frames, hoverchairs and antigrav harnesses there.

Once down, Alacrity hid the bos'n's pipe gun behind a cushion on the couch in the main cabin. He left one of Constance's dueling pistols under the *Harpy*'s chippendale control console, tucking its twin into a hunter's game bag. Along with that went Sile's stunner and his jot unit.

The dusk had become a cool, starry, full dark. Sounds of revelry drifted over the walls. There were no exterior guards. Alacrity took the game bag and secreted Constance's other pistol by the convoluted, warty base of a thornbower tree. As he neared the incandescent arch that rode, free-floating, over the gate, a figure stepped from shadows into the half light and said to him in tradeslang, "You're a fool for coming here."

Alacrity grabbed for the remaining gun in his bag, then stopped. *"Gute!"*

Gute came a step closer, the lenses of his makeshift glasses reflecting the light. "There's nothing you can do in there, only die."

Alacrity had been about to let go of the stunner. Now he held on instead, keeping it out of sight. "What're you here for?"

"They brought that woman here—the one in white, who

saved you from the Hunter. Someone said she's Dincrist's daughter. The rest is not so hard to piece together. Just seeing her, I knew you'd be coming for her. I heard that your real name is Alacrity."

Gute had his jot unit in his waistband and a shoulder bag weighted with something that might be a weapon. But he didn't appear to want a fight; Alacrity relaxed just a little. "Where is she, Gute?"

Gute motioned to Grand Guignol. "The main hall, I guess. Baron Mason will have her before the compound Holders in a mass gathering. They know she shot that hunter today."

"How?"

"Now from me! I've kept clear of it. And so should you! They say her father, Dincrist, will be coming to defend her, or perhaps take her by force if he can. It's the confrontation between him and Mason."

"Then I'm here in time?"

"This isn't for the likes of us! Little men like you and me get crushed between when the Betters collide! Now, come away."

"Sorry, Gute. But thanks for the warning."

"Ah, I didn't think it would do any good. Pay attention to me: the baron was very confident up to a little while ago, but something's wrong, I think, something down at the Central Complex. I heard some things from a slave I know on his household staff. It's got to do with Delver Rootnose—if his name is really Floyt—only they can't find him."

"I know."

"I thought you might. The baron, it looks like he's got a lot of the Betters on his side, especially the Holders. That Dincrist has a lot of people mad at him."

"That's what he's good at. Look, I'm going in, but thanks again, Gute. Any advice?"

Gute scratched his groin ruminatively, adjusting his spectacles with his other hand. "My best is for you not to do this. Next best is, do not be rash. Dincrist should be here any time. And don't try to take a gun inside; they're detectos everywhere."

"I figured. Thanks again."

Gute looked the *Harpy* over. "What a lovely bird landed in

your hand." He backed for the shadows. "I should be back at
Central Labor. Just one thing more: I heard from my friend on
Mason's staff—well, she's more than a friend, really—that
Mason jotted your woman."

"Actijotted?"

"The thing is, my friend happened to be watching when
they did it, only nobody knows that."

"Gute, where? You know how important this is. *Where did
they implant it?"*

He could barely see the man now, scarcely hear the voice.
The madness in the compound was louder."Alacrity, I want to
know something. Are all the other worlds as bad as this one?
Do the Betters and the rest of you take this kind of life everywhere you go in your starships?"

"What are you talking about?"

"Just answer me!"

"Some places are like this. Hell, a lot of them are even
worse, I suppose. But most are better, at least the way I see
it. Gute! Are you still there?"

"Her left leg." The voice was low but clear. "Behind the
knee, in her left leg is where they put the jot."

Alacrity called again, but Gute was no longer there.

Sile's stungun wound up behind a decorative icon prism just
outside the gate. Alacrity undid the clingstrap lashings from
the *Harpy*'s nose and slung Sile's body across his shoulder.
The jot unit was clipped to one of the braided thong loops
banding his upper left arm; he hoped he looked the part of a
Wild Hunter. Holding his breath, he passed under the glowing
arch.

None of the maroon guards were on the scene, and at Grand
Guignol all slaves were collared. Compound guards—most of
them slaves dressed as menacing imps—were taking advantage
of their masters' distraction and the general confusion to sneak
drinks, whiffs of Perkup and Voltage, puffs of weedstick and
styrettes of Engine, along with hugs and kisses from the serving
slaves.

Slaves everywhere meant that most of the household jot
barriers were down. Still, just about every Better carried some
kind of jot unit: bracelet or swaggerstick, magic wand or cane.

Most of the household automata, fuddled by the comings and goings of so many Betters and slaves, were operating at their lowest levels or shut down altogether.

Alacrity swaggered into Grand Guignol.

CHAPTER 16

DURANCE VILE

THE PLACE WAS DECORATED IN REPELLENT POST-TECH SER-
aglio *Fantastique*. The huge, organic-looking lamp sculptures
and light integrants shone and beamed.

Many of the serving slaves had been altered to suit the mood
of the place by the Betters who owned it, turned into freaks
and grotesques. Alacrity passed a beautiful woman who was
wending among the guests with a tray of drinks. Carefully
tended blossoms grew through apertures in her skin, bobbing
and waving languidly as she moved. Her feet had been altered
to give her hooves. There was a man circulating to offer tobacco,
opium, guillotine, marijuana, and other smokables. His nose
had been docked flat and his ears made enormous, fanlike
things that swung slowly as he went. He kept his eyes lowered
to the floor.

At the outer fringes of the sabbat, Blackguard's overlords
laughed and courted, boasted and roared in twos, threes, or a
few more. None were armed. Alacrity stepped around a pair
of satyrs who were coupling on the floor and continued on.

Carrying proof of identity over his shoulder, he was greeted
with an occasional raised goblet, congratulatory slap, or smile.
But by and large he attracted little notice; a lot of other Wild
Hunters had already appeared with their catches.

He passed into the main hall of Grand Guignol. It was the

235

size of several indoor sallyball courts, with a balcony three meters or so above the main floor, running completely around the room. The celebration was a madhouse.

Displayed along the side walls were some of Blackguard's other fauna: bunches of game flyers, a great-antlered beast burned nearly in two, sinewy predators now almost comically elongated in limp death, and a thing like a wheel of scaled muscle.

But the entire far wall was lined with tagged human bodies, quarry hung by their heels or from hooks. Some were marked by energy shots, others by pellet weapons. Many carried marks of energy scourgings.

In the crowd were Betters he recognized from various labor details, but he couldn't see Baron Mason or Heart. A lot of the more important Holders and other Betters were gathered near the fireplace at the far end, by the ranked quarry. They stood on a transept a half meter above the rest of the crowd.

Around the room large screens, projectors, and image tanks played scenes from the hunt, which most of the guests ignored unless they had been involved in the particular kill or chase being shown.

Alacrity moved off along the balcony, above the main bedlam. To his left a servant was jostled, spilling a drink. A drunken Better cursed when the liquor splashed his bare leg. He whipped out a jot unit and fired a powerful jolt. The edge of the beam caught Alacrity.

He missed a step, almost fell, grabbing a lamp sculpture for balance, and bit his lip hard behind the kabuki mask to keep from yelling out. There was laughter and jeering.

"Stea-*deee*!"

"Stop off on the way, did you?"

"Need a little rest, honey? *I'll* show you where to lie down!"

Two servants ran to lift Sile's body and hustled it down to be hung with the others. Alacrity reached to take a drink from a passing tray then opted not to; the dart and the Engine had been more than enough chemical trouble for the time being.

Seconds later he forgot about that completely. A side entrance opened, an enormous circular stone slab that rolled aside, and

Mason strode out onto the transept, dressed in formal robes rather than hunt clothes.

Behind Mason followed two of the maroon-suited guards, male and female, both unarmed. Between them they held Heart. She looked as if she was groggy but seemed otherwise unhurt. She was still in her white-on-white valkyrie getup.

Alacrity shouldered around a Better who was yelling details of his catch, and was about to work his way down a short, broad stairway thronging with drugged and drunken Betters, when he found his path blocked by a short, solid-looking Better in a suit of copper wire. He looked like a wound armature, his mask a sequined casque with a mime face. At his side was a small woman with a sturdy grace to her and an ethereal face-mask. Alacrity was about to edge around them when the woman spoke to him. "Buy you a drink, Bright Eyes?"

"Over this way," Floyt said from his mime mask. He led them around the balcony to a little alcove from which they could see Baron Mason and Heart. In a niche there was a household systems terminal.

Mason was standing with the other Holders and Betters, chatting calmly but not drinking or laughing. Heart had been seated on a chair with a maroon on either side of her.

"Don't tell me you traced me," Alacrity said. "I don't show up on the tracers any more, or something."

"You don't show up under your *old* code," Floyt corrected. "We've both got new ones. I'll tell you about it later."

"Do either of you know what Dincrist's doing, or where he is?" Alacrity said.

"From what we could find out, he's been working on damage control since he got here," Sintilla said.

"It's all coming to a boil between him and Mason," Floyt added.

"They deserve each other," Alacrity snarled, rapping his knuckles harder and harder against a stone corbel.

"Hobart's done some sabotage," Sintilla said. "Mason and Dincrist both know it by now, but they're too busy with the main event to worry about us."

"The maroon guards and the other free staff will probably stay neutral in the power struggle," Floyt predicted. "But if the Betters all side with one of the two, the other's going down in flames."

"I've got Sile's spaceboat outside," Alacrity said. "I don't know how long it will be before somebody figures out what's going on. We've got to get Heart somehow and get to the spacefield—"

"Hobart's got a plan," Sintilla announced, "a pretty cute one."

Floyt nodded. "But we have to wait," he said.

"For what, Ho?"

"Dincrist."

"No-no-no! That might be too late! They've implanted an actijot in Heart."

Floyt drew a deep breath, light glittering across his copper windings. "I know the timing is tight. Hell, they might break into the Inner Sanctum any time now."

"I don't know what that means, Ho, but it sounds bad."

"It could be. Still, we have to have both Dincrist and Mason here together for this thing to work."

"For what to work? What've you got—"

He shut up as the volume of noise in the room dropped. Dincrist had appeared. He was backed by a cluster of other Betters and Holders. They were all turned out in formal dress, all masked except for Heart's father.

The merrymakers parted before Dincrist and his supporters, who came down the very center of the hall. Mason looked steady, but his contingent closed in behind him. He put one hand on the Nonpareil's shoulder, the other on the jot unit hooked on his belt.

When Heart recognized her father, hope came into her features. She started to rise. Mason pushed her back down in her seat and whispered something to her. She stayed put.

Dincrist came up to the transept, halting a few paces from his daughter. The two factions measured one another silently for a few moments.

"I'm here for my daughter," Dincrist finally said. He turned to take in the crowd with a swing of his hand. "And I'm here to say something to all of you as well!" The crowd was interested and eager, still filled with bloodlust.

"You speak when I permit you to speak," Mason said.

"Your Citadel Compound is controlled by my people right now," Dincrist informed him. "And there are others here who'll stand with me when they hear what I have to say."

Mason smiled coldly and filled the room with his voice. "An *arriviste* like you is always shocked when he learns how wrong he can be."

"I want my daughter back."

"You may take her when you leave, Captain Dincrist, as I promised you. But first I'd like the Betters of Blackguard to see something."

He gestured. Scenes from the hunt disappeared from the screens and projectors, replaced by other images.

Data began running, showing Dincrist's attempts to bribe and intrigue his way into control, to secure financial and black-mail leverage against the Betters. People in the audience who saw their corporations or governments or confidants mentioned—who understood then what Dincrist had been trying to do to them—hollered or bellowed as though they'd been gored. Others caught the fear and anger like a plague, taking up the outcry.

Dincrist glanced around impassively at the shaking fists and concealing masks. He didn't answer.

It would only make them madder, Alacrity saw. Floyt watched with a certain professional detachment; some of the material was stuff he'd gathered for Mason, and he'd wondered how the baron was going to use it.

Mason didn't have to defeat Dincrist physically now. Dincrist would be lucky to get off Blackguard in one piece. In any case, his influence among the Betters was broken; even his own supporters were drawing away from him.

"I hate to see Mason win, but I'd've hated to see Dincrist win even worse," Sintilla said.

"They're gonna tear him apart in a second," Alacrity yelled to Floyt over the uproar. "They might go for Heart too! Do something!"

Floyt was making putting-off motions to him, fiddling with the systems terminal, into which he'd inserted an AI memory cube. After an interminable wait, the familiar voice came like a miracle. "Are you safe, Hobart?"

"Yes, yes, Diogenes, for the moment. Can you run that information for me?"

"Beginning now."

The incriminating evidence against Dincrist stopped flowing and everything went blank as Diogenes assumed control of the household systems. The AI began displaying the information Mason had had Floyt digging up.

The assembled Betters were treated to an overdub of Mason's instructions to Pollolo and Floyt, while they scanned the damning exhibits. Mason was quite simply dumbfounded.

"What have you been up to?" somebody howled.

"They're in it together!"

"Traitors!"

The mob started closing in on the two factions, pointing fingers, waving fists and riding crops, cigar holders and ashtray stands. Punches were exchanged. The slave guards were forced aside or downed by jot charges. Alacrity and Floyt ducked back, to avoid stray jolts.

"Look alive!" Sintilla yelped. "This is it!" She was off at a run, the two friends right behind her, around the balcony to a spot above the commotion. With all that was going on, few people noticed or cared when the three climbed over the rail and dropped onto the transept.

"Get her and stay close behind me!" Alacrity shouted. He wormed his way through the crowd in Mason's direction.

The baron and Dincrist were immobilized by the vengeful Betters, while their followers tried to reason with the mob. Information was still flashing, even though Floyt had recovered and pocketed Diogenes; the AI had dumped enough data into the household system to keep the screens and displays lit for some time to come. Every so often a man or woman in hunt disguise would wail as some personal matter or secret was illuminated. The crowd milled and struggled.

No one was watching Heart as Floyt and Sintilla barged their way to her and pulled her out of the chair. Even stronger and more agile than she looked, Sintilla did her share of the blocking. Floyt saw a hefty male Better back up against her;

she sent him tumbling with a leg trip. With Heart half in tow, half on her own, Sintilla and Floyt began fighting their way through the press.

Alacrity, capitalizing on height and strength, made good headway through the thronging Betters. Many of them were taller and far heavier, but the breakabout was well trained, in good shape, and highly motivated.

He reached Mason, who was turned toward another Better, exchanging loud accusations. The other had removed his mask; it was Matterse, who'd used the garderobe when Alacrity and Floyt were down below.

"You Judas!" Matterse was bellowing. "You treacherous old bugger!"

"Shut up, you ignorant young parvenue! *Shut up! And take your hands off me!*"

Alacrity eased up behind Mason and grabbed his right arm. Plenty of people were accosting the baron and jabbing fingers at him, but Alacrity's move opened the floodgate, unleashing real violence and determined layings-on of hands.

Alacrity worked fast, unclasping Mason's proteus and dragging it off his wrist. Mason's indignant protest was lost in the melée, but he managed to swing his head around, seeing the silver-in-gray banner of hair waving behind the black kabuki mask. *"Fitzhugh!"*

Mason went after him but was held fast by the press of his accosters. Alacrity, disappearing into the crowd, waving the proteus tantalizingly, called, "See you in the garderobe!"

Mason was excoriating everyone around him, pointing to Alacrity, crying, "Stop him! He's the one behind all of this! He and his friends! *Stop them, you fools!*"

But at that moment a new image came on all the visual units. It was the logo and lead-in music of the New Pathé News Service, with its crowing rooster.

The mob of Betters, terrified before all else of *expos   *, stood rooted for slow seconds, still holding Dincrist and Mason.

"Oh, suffering *Shiva!*"

"The newsspews! It's on the newsspews!"

"I'm ruined! *Ruined!*"

Mason took advantage of the confusion to shake loose the

clutching hands and leap up, hauling himself over the balcony railing. Betters swarmed after in pursuit. Dincrist tried to emulate the baron but didn't get far.

Alacrity caught up with Sintilla and Floyt, moving in under the Nonpareil's arm to bear part of her weight.

She smiled at him wanly. "Hi, handsome. I think we're even now."

"Had to look after you; I think you might be an heiress soon."

Alacrity showed the proteus. "I took this away from Mason; he's gonna have trouble borrowing a spare or using the house commo. But we've gotta be away from here fast."

"Then let's. I can make it." She pushed free and took his hand. He drew her along as he followed Floyt and Sintilla through a side door and into the night.

Sintilla was for grabbing the first decent-size craft they came to, but Alacrity insisted on the *Harpy*. He was trying frantically to think what he should do about the jot behind the Nonpareil's knee.

Alacrity recovered Constance's pistol from the thornbower tree.

At his order, Sintilla detoured to fetch Sile's stungun from behind the prism icon, with Floyt guarding her back. There was no one around, but a terrific furor was coming from Grand Guignol.

It was that much more of a surprise when a jot unit downed Alacrity, Heart, and Floyt like a scythe.

Mason bounded out of the darkness, a hammergun pistol covering Sintilla and a jot unit in the other hand. "Don't be foolish, little lady. Throw your gun aside. I'm really rather vexed at the moment."

Sintilla, caught off guard, obeyed. The other three were writhing, just getting their breath back.

"Now, where's the lock transceiver for that boat? Quickly!" Mason cast a fast, nervous glance over his shoulder. The three who'd been jotted were trying to get to their feet now, Alacrity helping Heart, Sintilla assisting Floyt.

"Come, come, who has it? Fitzhugh, I'll kill them all if you don't give it to me."

Mason's vast stores of calm were just about gone. He'd broken into a sweat and the hammergun shook. "I should kill *you* anyway!" He brought up the jot unit, aiming it at Heart. "This is your last chance."

Alacrity was in an agony of indecision, but he didn't think he could bear to see Heart hurt any more. "The ship isn't locked; I didn't want to have to waste time getting clear of here."

Mason kept the pistol on him, moving to pull Heart to him and get her to the boat. Alacrity prepared to move. But before he could, the baron was struck from behind by a short, hard club. He fell without another sound.

Sintilla started for Mason but froze as Gute, waving the cosh, squatted next to the baron and snagged the pistol.

"I thought you were headed home," Alacrity got out.

Gute motioned to the spacefield. "All holy hades has been loosed, Alacrity. Everyone gives a different order. This is what happens when many know-it-alls rule a place jointly."

Alacrity recovered Constance's handgun. "What next, Gute?"

"You say it's not like this on all worlds?"

Alacrity answered slowly. "Like I was telling you, some are better, some way worse. On the average, better, I'd say. Why?"

Gute shifted his burdens, dropping the club and tucking the gun under his left arm, dipping into his laden game bag. He drew forth his treasured Spican atlas just enough for Alacrity to recognize it. They both smiled. "I think I shall find out for myself," Gute said.

"Well, don't drag your feet; we're in a rush." Alacrity and Heart went to the *Harpy*'s lock. Floyt picked up the baron's jot unit and Gute, after a moment's thought, offered him the hammergun grip first. Then Gute trotted to the lock too, Sintilla following.

"Whup! What about him?" Floyt toed Mason, who was beginning to come around.

The boat lock was open. "I don't care," Alacrity said. "Do whatever you feel like, only do it now; the timer's running out." He disappeared inside.

Mason stared up at Floyt, who was less than two meters away. The baron swallowed. Floyt thought for a moment, then brought the hammergun up and took dead aim, letting Mason look into the barrel. Mason opened his mouth to speak, couldn't, and waited open-mouthed, hypnotized.

"Gives you a new perspective, doesn't it?" Floyt lowered the gun and walked away.

Sintilla was waiting at the lock. "Hobart Floyt, do you mean to tell me that's all, after what he did to you?"

"What do you want me to do, execute him? I couldn't find it in my heart."

"Then maybe you oughta start looking in your *head*!" She turned and fired for effect. The bright tanglevine of energy bowled the baron over flat, just as he was struggling to get up.

"Tilla!"

"Settle down, lovie." She held up her weapon. "Stungun, see? You don't want him getting through to Heart's jot anytime soon, do you?"

"No. Good thinking."

"Now get in! Alacrity says company's coming."

The *Harpy* lifted as the hatch was closing. Floyt and Sintilla passed through the boat's hedonistic main cabin. Gute sat on a couch, transfixed, staring out a viewbay.

The cockpit wasn't much roomier than the bridge of the *Pihoquiaq*. Floyt and Sintilla wedged themselves in behind the pilot and copilot pozzes. Alacrity yielded the controls to Heart, who was more familiar with them.

"We had to head away from the spacefield," Alacrity said. "The defenses are on alert."

"I want to get a little farther from the compounds area before we start taking on altitude," Heart explained.

"Altitude?" Sintilla repeated. "What for? This crate doesn't have a Hawking, right? So the only way we're going to get out of this system is to get your ship, Heart. The best time to do that's now, while everything's all stirred up. Maybe we can get in on the ground somehow."

The Nonpareil was shaking her head. "The whole area's sealed off, and they'll be searching everywhere soon, no matter whether Mason wins or my father. But Alacrity's thought of something."

"Constance and Skate took the *Mountebank* up; it's still in orbit," he explained. "With him aboard, I suppose. Now, the *Harpy*'s got a lot of countermeasures equipment, stealth stuff. Ho, I wouldn't be surprised if Sile and Dincrist were tied in with the intruder ship we ran into at the Precursor site on Epiphany."

"That may be," Heart put in. "My father is very interested in the Precursors. Obsessed, you might say."

"So I say we try a rendezvous with the *Mountebank*," Alacrity went on, "and take her."

Heart was beginning a long climb, playing with some of the controls among the stealth systemry. "I can take us right off their screens," she said.

"No," Floyt said. "Security doesn't know we've taken the *Harpy*, and they won't fire on a vessel your father uses. Let them see the *Harpy* leaving Blackguard."

Alacrity gave Floyt a troubled glance.

"Taking *Mountebank*'s the best idea for Heart and Tilla," Floyt said. "Heart has to get out of Blackguard's vicinity before Mason can activate her jot. But Alacrity, you and I—we'll have to remain behind."

"Are you serious?"

"Very. You see, I've got a lead on *Astraea Imprimatur*. I came across the information in the computers using Diogenes. She made a visit to Parish, the population center on the other side of this planet, about a year ago."

Sintilla was looking them both over; it was the first time she'd heard the ship's name. Heart was occupied piloting, but spared a quick sideward glance for Alacrity.

Alacrity just gazed, straightfaced, out the canopy. Finally he said, "Let's take it one subroutine at a time here."

"Of course; what else do we know how to do?" Floyt tried to sound jovial, but he could imagine what his friend was feeling. After all, Alacrity had been through so much already, been reunited with Heart at last, only to have circumstances drive them apart again.

But none of the others knew one of the things that had Alacrity withdrawn: the location of Heart's actijot. He sat with Constance's pistol cradled in his lap and stared vacantly.

If there was a warning jolt or spasm, he might, just *might*, have one chance to save her, and that was destroying the jot. He'd adjusted the long dueling pistol down for close range work at high power. He felt a tightness in his chest.

Detectors quickly found *Mountebank*'s location, and Heart closed with the antiquated heap. The *Harpy*'s visual signals blazed away in patterns for *emergency—commo systems not functioning*. They had some tense moments as they listened to Skate try to find out what was going on, then threaten to go into evasive action.

But, as Alacrity had expected, Skate didn't dare think on his own, especially if it risked angering Sile and Constance.

Harpy made fast to *Mountebank*'s lock. When Skate cycled it open he took one look at their guns and collapsed in a near-faint. Gute rushed inboard with the other four as they made sure Skate was the only one there. Sintilla stood guard over Skate with the hammergun; Alacrity stayed close to Heart, the dueling pistol unobtrusively ready.

"Well, she's old, but this tub should still take you to safety without any real trouble," Floyt was telling Heart and Sintilla a few moments later. "I'm really sorry we got you two into all this, and I truly do thank you both, more than I can say. And I wish there was some way I could pay you back."

Alacrity stared at the deck, having trouble getting started. "The thing of it is, Ho, I won't be going back with you."

"Alacrity, you're only making it harder."

"I *mean* it. After Sile and Constance tricked us—before they put us into cachesleep—Skate, over there, tried to pump me for information. He dug out the Earthservice conditioning instead. It's gone. I'm a free man again, Ho."

Floyt felt his very life coming apart. Alacrity had been his only ally, the single thing he could depend on. That had held Floyt's sanity together and kept his morale from withering away.

"You—that is, congratulations, Alacrity. I'm glad for you, I really mean that."

Alacrity held the dueling pistol in one hand. He brought the other out from behind his back. It held Sile's stunner.

"I thought about laying you out flat, Ho. I thought about *making* you give up on the inheritance, taking you someplace where we could get your conditioning wiped too. I thought about that since I woke up on Blackguard. Wouldn't work, would it?"

Floyt shook his head sadly. Sintilla's eyes were brimming. The Nonpareil hung her head, one hand on Alacrity's shoulder, one on Floyt's.

"There's only one way home for me," Floyt agreed. "That's tracking down *Astraea Imprimatur.* Can you set the *Harpy's* controls to land me somewhere near Parish?"

"I think so. Let's see what you can use from *Mountebank,*" Alacrity said. The jot still waited behind the Nonpareil's knee, and his mind was on haste.

There should have been a frenzy of preparation and leave-taking. Instead there was a long, agonized silence, none of them moving from their spots, while they shifted uneasily and avoided each other's eyes.

Finally Gute stepped forward. He took Sile's stungun from Alacrity, turned, shot Skate at close range. Skate came partway off the couch as the green lightning crashed around him, beginning a shriek, then fell to the deck.

"Gute, what'd you do that for?" Alacrity shouted.

Gute adjusted his makeshift specs and regarded them all calmly. "Didn't I hear correctly? There isn't much time left, isn't that right?"

"Yes, Gute, that's right," Heart confirmed quietly.

Gute nodded to Floyt. "And you have to go to Parish, isn't that so? It's something a little like a jot, hey? No choice?"

"Something like that."

"Then you'll go with him, Alacrity." Gute held up his hand when Alacrity would have objected. "You've already decided; you just won't admit it. Look at you: this isn't how you usually operate; I *know.* You're not thinking ahead or moving fast like you always do. You dither and vacillate.

"Where are the snap decisions that come so quickly from you? It's because you already know, inside, you're not leaving."

Gute turned to Heart. "And you and he are—" He hooked his forefingers together emphatically. "Hah?"

The Nonpareil's lips turned up; a glint came into her eye. "That's close, I would say."

Gute nodded shrewdly. He pointed to Sintilla. "You came along too, to save them, except that I don't understand why, if it's not because you're a friend. I think you are."

"I do *not* do things for personal reasons," she corrected primly. "I have press credentials to prove it. But you're right about the first part; I'm not walking out on a juicy story."

"Yes," Gute said, digging a device from his game bag. "So, offworlders who use up so much of my valuable time, please don't bother me any further with your protests. *Someone* must leave here with this fellow and let the Betters' security detectors see him do it, otherwise the Betters will know to look for you in Blackguard's system, likely in Parish, and may even think to use their jot system. Don't worry; I will send your good-byes down to them as I leave, and they will be satisfied that you are gone."

Gute had lifted Skate's sleeve back, and held the nozzle of his gadget against the unconscious man's forearm. It didn't make a sound, but after a moment a red light went on at its tip.

"Actijot?"

Gute looked up at Sintilla. "You're smart. Yes; after all, this fellow may not go along with having a new master. At first."

"Aw, Gute, I don't know . . ." Alacrity began. "No offense, y'understand, but Skate's really slippery, and you haven't been around much—"

But Gute had gone on to lift Skate's trouser cuff, implanting another actijot in the man's calf.

"—even though you do know a couple of angles yourself," Alacrity finished.

"Yes, yes; the naive little barbarian learned one or two things while working for the gods from the stars," Gute said a little heatedly as he looked around the compartment. He took Baron Mason's jot unit and set its timer. If Gute didn't deactivate it before the timer went off, it would cripple Skate with intolerable pain. Gute looked around and concealed the unit in the folds of a recliner.

"Y'know, I think he can do it," Sintilla said.

"I am *not* going back to Blackguard," Gute assured her.

"Well, you've got yourself a private starship and a very loyal personal servant and pilot," Floyt observed. "That's more than Alacrity and I started off with. It's more than we've got now."

Alacrity passed Gute the jot unit he'd taken from Sile. Gute still had his own clipped to his loincloth. *If that doesn't give him the edge, nothing ever will,* Alacrity concluded. And when *Mountebank* left Blackguard's vicinity, that would certainly register. Mason and everybody else would think the fugitives were gone, out of jot range. Heart would be safe.

"Gute," Alacrity said, "d'you think maybe one more jot . . ." Floyt, with a pensive frown, headed forward to the bridge.

"Definitely, Alacrity," Gute replied. "I was thinking just behind Skate's jaw, inserted from beneath?"

"You're in charge. We'll run a fast check on the ship, then set up the next leg for you while you're waiting for Skate to come around. By the way, where were you planning on going?"

Gute was turning Skate's head this way and that, deciding on the procedure. He blinked at Alacrity in surprise. "Why, Spica! Where else?"

"But is this wise?" Heart persisted as they went forward. "After all, *Spica*? And what if Skate turns the tables on Gute somehow?"

"I figure Gute has a pretty fair idea what to expect. By the time these two get to Spica, Gute'll probably have his name on the ownership pinks. He's got a fair chance, which is more than he would've had back at the compounds. Everything worth doing involves risks, and—"

She nudged him with a hip that was level with his; he toppled off balance for a second. "Next time you preach to me I'll *really* rough you up, Fitzhugh. Let's go; we're running late as it is."

"Aye aye, sis."

However, as they were making their way to the bridge, they ran into Floyt coming the other way.

"You don't have to bother," he said, meaning the bridge.

"We have to set up the jump," Heart said. "What's that mean, 'Don't bother'?"

"Well, come along and I'll show you."

In the main cabin, they found Gute standing over a very frightened and groggy Skate.

"You know what's happened, don't you?" Alacrity asked.

Skate licked his lips. "Fitzhugh, you can't let him do this to me. He'll get us both killed."

"No, he won't," Floyt piped up, "because he's going to have a little help." He looked at the ship around him and said loudly, "Isn't that right, Diogenes?"

"As you say, Hobart," the *Mountebank* answered in Diogenes' voice. All the others jumped.

"Gute, I want you to say hello to a good friend of mine named Diogenes."

"Hello, Diogenes," Gute ventured.

"Very nice to meet you, Gute," Diogenes responded. "It will be my job and my pleasure to watch over you and serve you."

"Ho, are you sure this is such a good idea?" Alacrity said dubiously.

"Yes, I am." Floyt jerked a thumb toward the bridge. "Diogenes was designed for a lot bigger jobs than this; he already has all the ship's systems and information at his disposal."

"Hey! Fine!" Gute slapped his stomach and studied the blank bulkheads. "Very fine, Diogenes!" he called.

"Thank you, Gute."

"We're just about done sweeping your ship," Alacrity told Skate. "I think we got most of your stash-weapons; I *know* we got your own jot unit, and Gute has more besides. You already know what'll happen if you try anything stupid, because you've done it to other people."

"I can pay you—"

"Gute's hanging on to the money we found inboard. We're keeping whatever Sile left in the *Harpy*. You better hear me good, m'friend: Gute's taken all kinds of precautions with those jot units, tricks I bet even *you* never heard of, read me? So even if you did somehow get around him and Diogenes, you'll spend a few days dying in this crate, wishing it was over."

Skate, face the color of yogurt, sank down in his chair without another word.

Alacrity put his fingers in his mouth and whistled. "Tilla! Let's get gone!"

There were footsteps in the passageway. Alacrity was about to add something when he yelled out *"Malákas!"* instead.

Tilla had come in with Floyt's Inheritor's belt over one shoulder and the Captain's Sidearm, in its gunbelt, over the other, dragging Alacrity's warbag and Floyt's luggage. The two ran to her and started ransacking through their belongings, pausing occasionally to kiss her, as Heart looked on.

"I almost missed it," Sintilla said. "Skate's good at hiding things."

"Everything's here," Floyt was rejoicing. "Our proteuses, my Letter of Free Import, your brolly, Alacrity . . . Look!"

He held up his Wonderment, the souvenir gift the Sockwallet Outfit had given him on Luna, a commemorative coin marking Terra's first five hundred years in space. It had Yuri Gagarin's profile on it.

Alacrity scooped up his share of the pillage. "Gute, time's up."

Gute nodded. He tapped Skate on the head lightly two or three times with a jot unit. "Bridge! Diogenes, we're on our way."

"I'm ready when you are, Gute," Diogenes replied.

Skate rose without protest and slumped off for the bridge.

"I would like to know how I can find you again later," Gute told the others. "I would like very much to see you all again."

Sintilla grabbed a qwikgraf and scrawled something on the arm of the couch. "You read tradeslang, Gute? Great; this is my editor's name and address at First Burst Publications. He'll know how to find me. Leave word how to get in touch with you."

The four had gathered their things. Heart and Sintilla kissed Gute's cheek and Alacrity swapped hugs with him at the lock. Floyt exchanged handclasps.

"Farewell, Diogenes," Floyt said to the bulkheads.

"And you, Hobart. I look forward to what is to come with great anticipation."

"Make sure they deal all your cards from the top, Gute," Alacrity said. "See you around, one of these days." He cycled the lock.

"I will, Alacrity. Thanks for everything." As the hatch closed, Gute, his Spican atlas under his left arm and jot unit in that hand, waved with his right.

Inboard *Harpy*, Heart took the pilot's poz again. She deactivated all systems except stealth gear, cut loose from the *Mountebank* and drifted toward Blackguard.

"Are you sure they won't pick us up down there?" Sintilla asked anxiously from her jumpseat.

"Sile's got stuff I've never seen before," Alacrity said. "I don't see how anybody can pick us up except maybe on visual."

"In *Mountebank*, I was monitoring transmissions at the compounds before," Heart said. "They don't have time to worry about us."

"What about your father?"

"He was trying to get in touch with *Mountebank*, Hobart. But the transmissions were coming from *Lamia*, so I think he's all right."

"It sounds like it's turned into a four- or five-way whatchamacallit—a Siamese standoff," Alacrity put in. "The way I have it scanned, they'll all slowly disengage, try to get the hell away before anything else happens."

"And that leaves Parish," Sintilla said, "where you ask after this starship of yours, Hobart? Terrific; maybe there'll even be a way to undo your conditioning. I've been worried about that since the first day I met you two duds."

"The hell you say!" Alacrity hooted at her.

She smiled sweetly. "It must've been a fast course of treatment, hmm? You get that kind of dose and you know what happens? You can't make overt admissions, but you're likely to let it slip without thinking about it. Like you did, Alacrity."

"I never! When?"

Sintilla leaned forward, saying to Heart, "Hobart was warning him that a romantic entanglement with *you* was not part of their mission; I was standing right there, at Frostpile. And do you want to know what the soul of discretion here said? He said there just wasn't enough conditioning to keep him away from you, that's what he said."

Heart kept an eye on her instruments but blew Alacrity a kiss. "It's mutual."

"Like I always say," Alacrity claimed, "it pays to have witnesses."

CHAPTER 17

LIVING IN INTERESTING TIMES

"ALL THIS SWAG—WHAT WAS WITH SILE? DIDN'T HE TRUST anybody?"

Sintilla was picking through the loot they'd amassed from hiding places throughout the *Harpy*. She was wearing great ropes of warm, luminous lava pearls from Amadla, all of them flawless "eight-way-rollers," studying one through a cyberscan jeweler's loupe.

"Manifestly not," Floyt replied, "and it was mutual." He had resumed the bush fatigues he'd gotten on Epiphany and now wore the Webley in a shoulder holster discovered among the plunder. His all-purpose survival tool was on his belt.

They were sitting in the deep pile of the main cabin deck carpeting, sipping cups of Irish coffee. Around them were stacks and cannisters and accordion-folded blisterpacks, heaps of bottles and vials, hermetic cartons, tubes, rolls, and bags of drugs and other recreational substances. Sile and Constance had eccentric taste in music, but Floyt had located some glass harmonica recordings, and those were playing.

Spread on the carpet were sets of encrypted memory wafers and locked data packets, keys to unspecified safe deposit boxes, articles of jewelry, bundles and purses of assorted currencies in large denominations, and sheafs of Spican banknotes. The fugitives had turned up weapons and a lot of epicurean food and drink.

They'd also found all sorts of rigged gambling equipment and fake identification.

"I didn't get a real good look when we were at the Grapple," Alacrity said, coming back from a search of the power section. "But I think Sile had a special boatlock for the *Harpy*, away from the regular ship's boats in *Lamia*. That way he could make a fast getaway if he ever had to, with the pick of his loot."

He was wearing his faded shipsuit, blue bandanna and pathfinder boots again. He sank down into an adjust-lounger. "But at least he didn't booby-trap this tub. As far as I can tell, that is."

Heart came aft from the bridge. She looked like a jetskate racer in Alacrity's dress skinsuit of high-sheen ice blue, with silver trim. She wore her own boots; no other footgear in *Harpy* fit her right.

"My gods! More stuff?" The Nonpareil toed through containers of opium pellets and love philters, pressure cartridges of blisswhiff and packs of orgasmitropine chewing gum; disguise kits; drugged pomanders and a humidor of hand-rolled narcogel-and-megaweed cigarillos; matched anklets of large, glowing phoenix eggs set in platinum; and a pair of weighted slapgloves with retractable, envenomed claws.

"He even had one of these, Alacrity. I was telling you about it, remember?" Floyt held up an Ouroboros ring, like the one the trader at the Grapple had tried to sell him, and demonstrated how to open the hidden compartments.

"Whoo! Yeah." Alacrity took it and looked it over. "Sile probably loved it; that's how his mind worked."

He handed the ring to Heart, asking, "What's it like outside?"

She slipped the Ouroboros ring on her finger, admiring it. "The rain's letting up. It'll be dark in a few hours, though. If you're going today you'd better do it soon. Are the two bold explorers ready?"

"*They* think so," Sintilla said, studying herself in a vanity imager. She'd tried on a pair of plasmanode earrings that grazed her shoulders. She'd put aside her diaphanous rompers for a red velvet dressing gown and matching houseboots from Sile's closet, all of them a bit large on her. Sile's elaborate monogram was picked out on the robe in fire-fancies trimmed with shimmerettes.

All four were feeling better after a night's rest and taking turns at a relaxing cleanup in the spaceboat's compact spa/head. "No sign of pursuit from the compounds?" Floyt asked.

The Nonpareil shook her head. "Detectors picked up three more ships going into Hawking. They're too busy running for cover to worry about us, I guess. And I didn't pick up any locals sniffing around us, or anybody from Parish. I think we got away clean."

"Perfect," said Floyt, trying the heft of a haversack improvised from a large tool bag. It would do, he supposed; they weren't carrying very much. Alacrity would use the big game bag.

"Not *perfect*," Heart said archly. "Perfect would be if Alacrity came to his senses and admitted that Sintilla and I should come along."

"Hear, hear!" Sintilla chirped. "This splitting up of forces is a bad idea, Bright Eyes."

Alacrity shook his head, pulling on the Captain's Sidearm. "The only lead we have is the Parish Spaceport. Ho has to go because he's the Inheritor. I have to because I know spaceport towns and besides, I'm the one who's supposed to. Look how well it worked last time, you two coming in as reinforcements."

"Look how much better you'd have made out if you'd shown up on Blackguard with us in the first place, instead of in *Mountebank*'s bilge," Sintilla riposted.

"*Duh!* Score one for you. But still, we can't just leave the *Harpy* sitting out here in the mud, even camouflaged. And if all four of us get in trouble in Parish there's no one to bail us out. But with this crate's weapons as emergency backup—what's that do, d'you think? Double our chances? Triple 'em?"

"All right, all right!" Heart conceded, crossing to his adjust-lounger. She lowered herself to straddle his lap, facing him, caressing his face as she had now and again through the night, giving him a beguiling look. Her waist felt so good between his hands, she smelled so wonderful and looked so devastatingly good to him—a melting fondness welled up in him, taking his breath away.

"Just don't get your idiot self hurt out there, Alacrity. Now, I'm serious here. And for Fate's sake, listen to Hobart when he's trying to talk sense to you."

"Don't get hurt. Listen to Ho. Could you write all that down?"

She poked him in the ribs. "Time to go; you don't want to hit town in the middle of the night."

The interior hatches were secured and all lights doused when Floyt and Alacrity stepped down from the lock. The sky was a sullen teal color and Blackguard's sun was hidden.

The *Harpy* was grounded in a little dell under some high, thickly leaved spumetrees. To avoid detection they were relying on the fact that the local population was small and scattered, and that the vessel wouldn't be there long.

The two friends eased through the underbrush resting against the ship. Floyt was still apprehensive about the unfamiliar local flora and fauna; suppose those corkscrew things took a notion to drop off their branches and try to bore into his skull? And what if there was something a wee bit peckish lurking in that spongy clump of whatever-it-was? But Alacrity claimed to have learned a lot about the planet's life forms from Gute. Floyt could only hope, trust, and stay ready.

They made their way out through splintweed that was still wringing wet with rainwater. Floyt shivered a little, though he wore heavy underwear beneath his fatigues. Alacrity, wearing the thermal insert for his shipsuit, was comfortable. Neither had a jacket; there weren't any in *Harpy*. So they wore the shawls Dorraine and Redlock had given them.

They passed along between sharkthickets and up a treacherous wash of mud and shallow puddles. In the end Floyt was soggy to the knee; the pathfinders had handled the walk with ease. Floyt had begun to understand why breakabouts, who spent so much time in nice, warm, dry starships, made it a point to own gear that would keep them comfortable in inclement weather.

The road was a two-lane gluefused relic of an earlier era. It hadn't seen a real repair crew in decades; cracks and deep ruts had been filled with rocks, deadwood, hardened flickwasp comb, and other debris that had come to hand. They footed off for Parish. Floyt pulled out two bars of chocolate from Sile's snack supplies and they ate as they walked, washing it down with swigs from a water bottle. The overcast was beginning to break up.

"I guess we'd better start looking the part," Alacrity decided. He and Floyt put on the wound-scarf headdresses Sintilla and Alacrity had whipped up, the best they could do in imitating a local garment neither of them had ever seen in real life. The two men wound the dangling ends around their faces, as was the practice. Alacrity concealed his big offworlder eyes behind a reflective wraparound visor he'd found in the *Harpy*; it was cheap and nondescript, nothing that would look out of place in Parish.

The two knew, from what Floyt had managed to find in the data banks, that Parish was the center of a complicated tribal coalition. Lots of different dialects were spoken, although almost everyone spoke the *lingua franca*, which was basically trade-slang with a lot of Terranglish cognates and loanwords and a little neighborhood topspin.

Alacrity was relieved to learn that the natives were peaceable. Nevertheless, he carried the Captain's Sidearm and the bos'un's pipegun, hoping he wouldn't have to use them on anybody.

Parish had once been a city of some prestige, but Blackguard—known in the local tongue as Finders-Keepers, the other being the Betters' name for the place—was one of the many worlds that had fallen out of touch with mainstream humanity in the disruptions after the Second Breath. Large tracts of the town were in disrepair and dilapidation. The population was only two thirds what it had been in the city's heyday and the quality of life was, for most, lower than it had been for their ancestors centuries ago. The benefits of the Third Breath had for the most part passed the planet by, since the

Betters sharply limited offworld trade and forbade territorial expansion.

Tribal warfare had done its damage as well, though a fretful peace had been in effect for the last generation or so. Parish was really several separate communities: Parish proper, with its tribal precincts, industrial, and commercial zones; the space-field with its boxtown; and Parish Above, a colony of guarded estates and private enclaves in the foothills beyond.

Parish carried on limited offworld commerce. Different tribes maintained separate landing facilities, the ancient, moldering spacefield having been in effect carved up like a pie. Ships came and went via rigidly defined corridors. Straying risked being classified as hostile by the compounds' Talos Worldshield and blasted out of the air. Adding in the fact that Blackguard/Finders-Keepers had nothing truly outstanding or unique to lure profit takers, offworld contact with the place was kept to a minimum, usually no more than a ship every month or two, rotating among the tribal port facilities.

They passed the miserable hovels, huts, and lean-tos at the town's outskirts, then entered Parish itself. The buildings in the best condition were usually the least ornate; decorative cornices and corbels crumbled and stone facades and ginger-bread went dingy and rotted from age and city fumes. Wooden buildings had fallen prey to fire, insects, and weather. The most durable structures were the factories, warehouses, and so forth, plain slabforms, geodesics, and such.

The streets, built to last with Second Breath technology, were still in good condition. There were some wide, well-kept boulevards, but side streets were often nearly impassable with junk and rusting vehicles and wreckage. In many places organic garbage was heaped along the middle of the streets, where scavenger animals and a few desperate-looking people rooted through it.

The two offworlders immediately noticed places where the underground sewer system had succumbed, and sewage was stagnating in open channels. Traffic was a roughly equal mix: crude, artificially driven vehicles of local manufacture, animal-drawn and human-powered. A pall lay over the town; a lot of heating was done with coal, peat, and wood.

Sky traffic was limited: a few lighter-than-air cargo lifters and some grav barges, and what looked like a private hoverlimo bound for Parish Above, along with several tribal scout ultralights. At the top of the tallest remaining building, one transmitting tower was left. People looked reasonably well fed and clothed, but good medical care didn't seem widely available.

Alacrity and Floyt ambled along together, not standing out much except, to some extent, for Alacrity's height. The headscarves were a circumstance very much in their favor, and quite a few natives mixed offworld clothing styles with the very varied tribal costumes.

They kept to the well-marked common zones, avoiding the tribal borders with their guards and checkpoints. Every intersection of the winding hill-and-dale streets had its tribal militia observation post or sentry. Every traffic circle had its fortified bunker or watchtower. In the precincts, they saw, there were sandbagged sniper pozzes on the roofs and basement pillboxes. Even children playing in the street and old women hanging out of windows—which usually had barred or armored shutters— were on watch, often with vision enhancers or binoculars. Weapons ranged from reasonably modern to obsolescent.

There were shops and stores, bistros and cabarets whose clientele were strictly restricted along tribal lines; mingling went on only in the common zones. The original squabble that had so divided the tribes had to do, Alacrity was given to understand, not with religion or politics or economics, but with the traditions of tribal arts. Irreconcilable esthetics.

Late in the afternoon they finally came to the spacefield. It was typically Second Breath, covering a huge amount of ground, but the tribes had permitted most of it to fall into disuse and ruin. The locals jealously guarded their territories here too, though; the fences had been kept in repair and there was vigilant surveillance, including patrols with attack animals of some kind.

Alacrity and Floyt approached a stretch of shimmery metalgauze fence that hummed softly and carried skull-and-crossbones warning signs. They gazed across the field to the crumbling main terminal area, the broken-down hangars, warehouses, and customs complex.

"Would they know about *Astraea Imprimatur*, d'you think, Alacrity?"

"I haven't a clue. If we just walk in and ask, we might give ourselves away. The first thing we should do is find a place to hole up for the night; it's getting dark fast and it looks like it's going to come down heavy again soon. Maybe we can find out something tonight. In any case, we can take a stroll around the field perimeter tomorrow."

"Where do we stay? The tribes are awfully particular who they let into their precincts, especially after curfew."

"Right over there." Alacrity pointed to a district that began at the perimeter, off to their left. It was jammed with irregular structures and slapdash forms with an improvised look to them.

"What is it?"

"Only one thing looks like that, Ho. At least, near a spaceport. That's the local boxtown."

The light was going fast by the time they got there, and silver diagonals of rain were falling. They walked together under Alacrity's big brolly.

Boxtowns accumulated on most spacefaring planets at some point or other. The one at Parish spacefield was long past its prime, sixty hectares of corroded hulls, acid-eaten scrap, cracked plastipaneling remnants, and wormeaten wood. It had a desolate, underinhabited, haunted feel to it, different from any boxtown Alacrity had ever been in. The natives called it Tombville.

Tombville lay across a moat of rotting garbage and stinking sewage spanned by a rickety footbridge. As they crossed, Floyt gazed down and noticed a little six-footed animal, a scavenger of some sort, about the size of a small dog or a big rat. It was at the edge of the scummy drainage, extending its long neck to feed delicately on a discarded fetus that had floated to rest against a mound of decaying filth.

"Keep your eyes open, Ho. Boxtown's dangerous the way a place can be only when there's not enough of anything to go around."

There was no streetlighting in the dusky maze of Tombville, of course. Intermittent holo signs, flash panels, and neon lights were starting to come on. Floyt read signs advertising "KARMIC

REPAIR," "MEDICAL CONSULTATION," "LUCK COUNSELING," and "REHAB SERVICES." Small insect things were burrowing and scuttling everywhere, and larger vermin that barely took the trouble to get out of their way.

They passed people hurrying to find shelter for the night. There were goitered ragmen and dissipated bar dogs moribund with drugs and drink; leprous beggars; palsied and scabrous fortune-tellers and children with stick legs and bellies swollen by intestinal parasites. All gave the two a wide berth.

Most Tombville dwellings showed no light at all, either abandoned or thoroughly barred and curtained by occupants who rightly feared the night. Alacrity reflected sourly on the fact that Sile's hoard of toys and tidbits hadn't included a simple handlight.

"Alacrity, I'm not so sure about this place," Hobart said as they turned into an alley. "Do any of these shacks look trustworthy to you?" It was getting late; they couldn't even make out one another's face in the gloom. Alacrity flipped up his visor.

"I've got one idea." Alacrity slipped off his proteus and moved off to one side, leaving Floyt in the rain. The Earther stepped back into the shelter of a boarded-up doorway, keeping his hand on the gun under the shawl.

Alacrity went to a nearby wall, the sort of wall he'd been looking for. He could barely make it out, but it was big and smooth and seemed to have peeling handbills on it.

He adjusted his proteus quickly. Unlike Floyt's it had a miniature projection feature for data display. By turning the contrast up to max, he used it as a weak but serviceable light. Holding it, he bent close to the wall.

It was a mural of faded stencils, layered deposits of grafitti, spit and sputum, pockmarks that might have been bullet holes, ominous stains suggesting old blood, childish attempts at art and pornography, primitive scrawls and messages, occult symbols and arcana, unreadable political slogans, and what looked like lovers' initials.

Holding his proteus close to the wall, he examined the markings and indentations, particularly around the edges. He passed a spot, stopped, and went back to it, bending close.

Floyt, getting uneasier by the second, swiveled his head, searching the shadows. He could see no one, but from what Alacrity had said about boxtowns, he was sure they were being watched.

Alacrity doused the light and came back, replacing his proteus. "There's a reasonably safe place to stay on the next street over. I saw some Forager cues."

"How's that again?"

"Cryptoglyphs. The Foragers use 'em to leave each other word about the local setup. Whether it's dangerous or how the pickings are, and so forth. But these ones weren't new; I'm surprised there've been Foragers through here at all. Let's go see how we do."

Alacrity closed his umbrella and tucked it through his game bag straps, leaving his hands free. They were well into the alley before they heard the footsteps. Floyt spun. Alacrity stole a quick glance behind—three men were blocking that end of the alley—then immediately swung to cover the way ahead. Sure enough, two more footpads were just edging their heads around the corner for a peek.

"Get your back up against that wall," Alacrity said, doing the same on his side. That way, a net dropped from above would have less chance of getting them both, and each had a field of fire over the other's head.

Floyt took out the Webley, the lanyard ring jingling, and cocked it. The sound seemed very loud. He plastered himself flat against the wall.

The three men who'd come into the alley after them had stopped. Now the two at the other end edged into silhouette, sliding along the walls on either side.

"No warning shots!" Alacrity declared in *lingua franca*. "We've got two alley-hoses here; get out or we'll throw a barbecue!"

"Get ready, but don't fire unless I tell you," he whispered. Then, dimly, Floyt saw him turn, move to the middle of the alley, and bring the heavy sidearm up with both hands. The footpads kept coming.

Floyt, knowing what to expect, looked away toward the trio, bringing up his free arm to shield the ear closest to the pistol. The Captain's Sidearm went off with an explosion that seemed too much for the alley to contain. The flash gave Floyt a brief glimpse of three very surprised, disheveled men with beards and tangled hair. Each held something; one had what Floyt was pretty sure was only a knife, but there wasn't enough time to see what the others carried. He cringed, waiting for them to fire back, but no shots came.

Someone was screaming from the direction in which Alacrity had fired. In the other, the trio had frozen. Alacrity was already flattened against the wall again, gun in one hand, the other cupped to his mouth. "Last chance!" Floyt saw that Alacrity's hand was shaking. There was a silent instant as the universe seemed to sit still and listen.

Then there was shuffling. The three made darker shapes against the mouth of the alley. Alacrity moved away from the wall, gun up and pointing, its muzzle twitching and trembling. Floyt caught a look at his friend's face in a stray beam of light. It was a face of unspeakable hatred.

It's not fear that's making him shake, it came to Floyt then. *It's the effort* not *to fire*. It was an old, cold wrath from Alacrity's past.

In a moment the trio was gone. "What about the other two?" Floyt whispered.

"I sparked one of them," Alacrity murmured. "The other might've gotten away by now, or he might be there—"

He broke off, staring up wildly, at the sound of loud clapping. It came from above them, one person's applause. They pointed their barrels here and there overhead, but saw no one.

"Not bad, outies," a disembodied voice called, a young male. It spoke Terranglish, not *lingua franca*.

"*Boosh!* Nice gun! Real strong! But why didn't you finish the gag?"

"On your way, before we finish *you*, juviezits," Alacrity warned.

A smiling face leaned into view above them, just barely, lit by a handlight held out of sight. "Whatever you say, skipper." It was a round, sullen face, a kid somewhere past adolescence but short of manhood. He wore a dark beret; his hair, escaping from it, bobbed in loose curls that glittered strangely; so did his smile.

Three other faces crowded into view, two boys and a girl in early- to mid-teens. "It was a pleasure watching," the applauder said. Drawing his companions with him, he pulled back out of sight.

"Stay ready," Alacrity warned. He and Floyt sweated out another full minute, guns trained at the rooftop. Nothing else happened. They resumed their way, sliding along the walls, checking refuse piles carefully before going near them, trying to look in every direction at once.

They found the corpse of the man Alacrity had shot, its cratered flesh still smoking. No one else was around. They splashed through a foul pool and out onto a narrow street covered with decaying garbage, castoffs, and odd hunks of refuse, as softly yielding and treacherous as the floor of a rain forest.

"That must be the place."

Alacrity meant a thirty-meter-long, rusting hulk that had once been a reusable booster rocket. It lay on its side, fitted in workmanlike fashion with a heavy metal door and windows, on its second story, that were covered with stout gratings. It had been sandblasted, soniscoured, and wire-brushed to something like presentability; the street in front of it was clear and clean. It was a rambunctious island of light and noise in the middle of Tombville.

A ciphercrawl panel over the heavy-gauge door radiated the name of the place, THE DIS HILL CARAVANSARY.

The two kept hands on their guns as they came to it. A prowling pack of dog-things hissed at them, then fled as Alacrity stamped his foot.

In an alley off to their left, an old man or woman in layered rags lay slumped against a wall, passed out or dead. Several emaciated, tubercular-looking children were rifling for what pathetic pickings there might be. They gave Alacrity and Floyt feral looks not so different from the dog-things', and went on with what they were doing.

Alacrity flipped down his visor again and rapped on the door of the Dis Hill Caravansary with the improvised door knocker, a detonator cap off an old fusion missile. An enormous fat man with an antique pepperbox laser in his waistband opened up, looked them over, then stepped aside for them.

The interior was lit with weak glow-globes and furnished in a potpourri of whatever the proprietor had been able to salvage, scrounge, or throw together.

In booths and at tables and the long bar were toothless bunco steerers, addict-pushers, and devious pimps; one or two cashiered breakabouts trapped in a terminal nightmare; failed con artists; prostitutes of all description except handsome; thugs and cutthroats, informers and bottom-rung racketeers.

The odors of strange food and strong drink competed with vomit, sweat, unwashed bodies, incense, feces, urine, and blood, all overlaid with a disinfectant strong enough to open Floyt's nasal passages to full max.

Alacrity had his brolly back in his hand. He and Floyt paused at the door, glancing around. Everyone in the place was looking them over in return. Half a dozen people were already moving on them, not threateningly but to make some solicitation.

The first to reach them was a pimp, a beringed, white-bearded little man wearing a soiled mirrorflash suit.

Alacrity waited until the man was close enough, then brought the brolly up like a fencer executing the stop-thrust. He'd taken the ferrule cap off its tip; the pimp barely halted in time to avoid impaling himself on its wicked point. The others stopped short, standing where they were or sliding back toward their places. Alacrity advanced, pinking the pimp lightly until he fell backward over a chair.

Floyt and Alacrity looked around. No one else wanted any. Alacrity picked out a booth at the far end of the room. They piled their bags on Floyt's side, between the Earther and the wall. Alacrity turned down the booth's cone-spot, preferring darkness.

The waitress was a light-heavyweight at least, one of the more intimidating people in the place, with a big neurosap tucked in her apron pocket.

Alacrity held up two fingers and said, "Beer." She went away.

He stared distractedly at the door.

"If you're thinking about the man you shot, you shouldn't be blaming yourself, Alacrity."

"You have it wrong, Ho. I was just thinking: those others we chased off will go out and drag down some poor feeb who can't defend himself. Or herself. They'll kill somebody tonight if they get the chance. When I was a kid I swore I'd slaughter 'em all if the opportunity ever came my way. Things never work out the way you picture 'em."

"Amen."

The waitress brought the beers in big, mismatched plastic schooners, keeping them in hand until Alacrity passed over a square silver-alloy piece. She gave them the drinks but no change.

As she turned away a youngster slipped around her and practically into the booth, except that Alacrity was showing the muzzle of his pistol. Floyt's hand, concealed by his shawl, went back to the Webley. It was the kid from the rooftop.

Close up, in better light, they could see his thin fuzz of mustache, the barely there down of beard. The kid's hair was iced in metallic gold and his teeth had been replaced with gold ones set with nova buttons, shimmerettes, and plasmabeads. He held his hands up, all smirking innocence and good intentions.

"Easy, Overmen! Refrain! I'm on your side!" he said in Terranglish.

"We don't need anybody," Alacrity said stiffly. "Keep cruising."

"What're you gonna do, conduct business with the people you meet in here? They'll cheat you just on the principle of the thing and then kill you for fun."

"But you're a good guy, is that it?"

The kid gestured to a nearby table. About a dozen kids, mostly teenagers, were pulling chairs up to it. Other patrons studiously ignored them. They wore an assortment of clothes, mixed and matched and layered indiscriminately. They didn't look at all like anybody's victims or sexual playthings.

"You're in town to do business. You need somebody who knows where the wires are attached," the leader said. "That's me. My name is Notch."

Alacrity said casually. "Now, I'll tell you, Notch: why don't you just find yourself somebody else to crimp? There's nothing you can do for us."

"There is if you want to get on the spacefield grounds," Notch said. "Why don't we talk? A free audition, no charge."

"Sit down," Alacrity said. "But you buy your own drink." He eased over to make room, holstering his gun but sitting so that he could get at it. Floyt held his revolver in his lap.

Notch signaled the waitress, then sat. "I saw you looking through the perimeter fence before. No one knows who you are or where you come from. I figure, you broke off a deal with one of the tribes and you're looking for a way to do your business, right?"

"Just say what you dropped by to say, Notch. One more question and I'm kicking your skinny little rear out the door. And I'll braise your youth group over there if they give me any trouble about it."

"Settle down! Refrain!" Notch protested quickly as the waitress returned with his drink. "All right; I compute that you're looking for a spacefield connection. I've got lots of them, but they cost money."

"Prove to us you know something," Alacrity shot back. "What kind of ships are in port? What vessels call here? What about a rundown on all the action for the last year or so? We might have something special in mind." He unwound the scarf tail from his face and took a drink of the beer.

Floyt hesitated, then did the same. The beer was watered and flat.

"Oo, ooo." Notch smirked, cupping his hands around a shotglass of blended whiskey. "That will cost you. How about something on account?"

"So far you've said just enough for me to pay for your drink, dung-brain," Alacrity snapped. "And if you don't tell me more, I'm gonna kneel on your neck and pour it down your nose."

Notch, still smirking, gave Alacrity a gimlet look. "Don't threaten me anymore, go-blood. It's unhealthy. Check with anybody in Tombville."

"Your time's up, runtbug." Alacrity yawned. His hand was on his pistol again. "I said talk or walk."

"I can tell you whatever you want to know about any ship that's in port or that's been here or that's expected soon," Notch drawled. "Just tell me what it is you're looking for. Say, a hundred ducats now and two hundred more when I get back to you."

Alacrity regarded the smiling Notch for a moment, then reached into an inner pocket. He pulled out a single ten-unit Spican banknote, worth perhaps half what Notch was asking. He carefully tore it in two and tendered one half to Notch.

"You get the other half when you come to us with a complete list of everything that's going on, especially all the shipping that's gone on in the last year. *Everything*, understand? You're getting twice what the job's worth, so I want to know everything about every ship. Read me?"

"Roger that," Notch said, flashing them his jeweled smile again, but his eyes threatening. "You two staying here? It's as good a place as any." Notch stood up.

"We'll be around," Alacrity said.

"Oh, I'm not worrying about finding you, old poppa. Don't bother yourselves about that."

The kids rose and fell in behind him. They marched out, still ignored by the hardened boxtowners. "They've got everybody scared," Floyt said. "I never saw anything like it, even in the roaming troupe."

Alacrity stared after them. "You get kids that age, place like this, they don't care if they live or die, don't even really understand what death is. They don't know anything but their alley gang. They're quick and fearless and they haven't got one atom of conscience in 'em." He shook his head. "You can't have worse enemies in boxtown."

He looked Floyt in the eye. "You ran with a roaming troop on Earth. You know. If anything happens, don't waste your time feeling sorry. Shoot. Shoot right away. Because what you saw there were people with most of the human being leeched out of 'em."

"I do know. I'll keep it in mind."

"Let's see what they've got in the way of a room. Did we bring any antivermin spray?"

Accommodations in the Dis Hill Caravansary varied according to guests' requirements and wherewithal, of course. They passed on the boblines; sleeping space on the floor was too cramped; conditions among bunks close-stacked in a big flop area would have left them too vulnerable.

The two decided that they could afford to splurge, and negotiated the best the Dis had to offer, a big reefer cargo box that had had its cooling equipment and insulation stripped out of it and been spot-welded into place on the second floor. By that time twelve ovals seemed cheap.

Floyt, studying the grimy mattress—a bubblefoam futon on the floor—sighed deeply. At least the single blanket given them by the owner seemed reasonably clean. Floyt suddenly thought of something, got Alacrity's attention with gestures, and mouthed, *Do you think this place is bugged?*

Alacrity shrugged, putting aside his visor, then nodded that it might well be, and went back to checking the place, making sure the door wasn't gimmicked. He inspected the bars on the windows and spotted possible escape routes.

They lay down still clothed, boots on, heads pillowed on their bags. Alacrity kept his pistol under his right hand; Floyt laid the revolver next to his haversack. Alacrity took first watch and turned down the filament ball.

Floyt woke to Alacrity's touch against his shoulder and took up the revolver. Very light footsteps could be heard on the sheet metal of the hallway. They stopped at the door to the reefer box.

The two friends moved as quietly as they could, off the futon to either side, giving themselves clear fields of fire. Alacrity made sure he could cover the window as well. They were both sweating.

Floyt expected some sort of burst-in or long eavesdropping to begin. Instead there was a light rapping at the door. Floyt could see it took Alacrity somewhat by surprise too.

Alacrity eased over, keeping to one side of the door, and flicked up the latch lever, then moved back fast, bringing up the Captain's Sidearm.

"It's open."

The door opened wide. A man stepped in, framed in the

weak light of the hallway. He was empty-handed, squinting into the darkness. "I hope I didn't disturb you and your friend, Citizen Floyt," he said. "Or rather, since you're *Astraea Imprimatur*'s new owner, perhaps I should have said *Master* Floyt?"

Alacrity turned up the light a little. Floyt gasped. It was the man he'd seen in the Whereabouts at the Grapple, and later at the Newsspew at the Complex, the famous outlaw and fugitive from justice, Janusz.

CHAPTER 18

THE TERRAN INHERITANCE

"I'M SURE YOU'LL FIND IT A LOT MORE COMFORTABLE STAYING with us," Janusz was telling them a few minutes later as a roomy old airsedan bore the three men through the night to Parish Above. The hills were lighted with the mansions and villas of the large estates.

Alacrity noticed that Janusz scrupulously avoided flying over any of the residences and concluded that, as usual, the wealthy had the means to keep out intruders, even airborne ones.

Janusz's craft was a classic with wood paneling, indigo veneer, nickeled pipes, and blue crimson interior. He handled it very well.

"Although," he added, "the Dis Hill Caravansary is a scenic place."

"Especially the way *you* come and go," Floyt said.

"People up on Dis Hill are used to watching the streets, but not the sky," Janusz said. He had a soft, cultured voice that commanded attention even though he spoke with an almost stiff propriety. He was dressed in soft ankle boots, flowing trousers and blouse, and puffy vest, his sleeves held back from his hands by what looked like old-fashioned sleeve garters around his upper arms.

Alacrity noticed that Floyt had his finger close to the emergency button on his proteus, just in case, and nodded approval when Janusz wasn't looking.

They barreled in low over a high, spikey blue vitristeel wall that radiated an antipersonnel field. The estate was a sizable piece of property, three hectares or so in what appeared to be a most exclusive area of Parish Above. There were trees and flower beds and several small ponds.

The stately old sedan touched down on a circular landing pad in front of a large chateau resembling a regal, burnished epergne, rising in tiers and levels of elegance and beauty surrounded by splendid trellises, arbors, a lovely belvedere, and a guest house like a jeweled music box.

As they climbed out, something lazed by overhead. Alacrity looked up and saw a very modern, lethal security drone, an Azrael model.

"Welcome to Old Raffles," Janusz bade them. Floyt smiled.

Alacrity saw another of the dolphin-shaped Azraels as they entered the foyer.

Old Raffles wasn't anywhere near as grand as Frostpile or even the compounds, but it was genteel and stately in unisystem polyglot.

Household robots, offworld products, approached to take their luggage. Janusz did not suggest that they disarm.

In a society like that of Parish, domestics and staff ought to be cheap and plentiful, a glut on the market, Alacrity knew. But Old Raffles' looked completely automated. There was even an expensive system of whisk-platforms like flying coasters, to zip occupants around the rambling chateau. Alacrity was beginning to be concerned about what he and Floyt had gotten into, and was very alert. A starship was worth an upright fortune—enough, perhaps, to tempt someone into eliminating a troublesome Inheritor who happened to pop up and wouldn't be missed much.

They passed through a spacious receiving hall furnished with monolithic furniture and lit by polychrome glow-cages. "Why'd you smile before?" Alacrity asked Floyt out of the corner of his mouth. "What's 'Old Raffles' mean?"

"Cracksman, Old Earth style."

"Oh. What's a cracksman?"

"Later."

Janusz, in the lead, showed the way to a smaller—but not very much—room, a lavish library. A real fire burned in a free-standing fireplace shaped like a Buddha. Soft music played from the sound system, medieval Terran stuff.

"Welcome, Citizen Floyt."

Janusz had been enough of a surprise; in her own way, the woman who greeted him was even more so. She was warming her hands by the fire, a woman closer to Floyt's age than Alacrity's, dressed in a mauve househabit that showed an almost painfully slender figure, and a belt of polished, rough-cut calefacts set in woven copper filaments. She had regular, unremarkable features, a pleasing plainness, pale and freckled, except for the biggest, most astute brown eyes Floyt could remember seeing, under heavy brows. Those eyes were snares, hard to look away from. Her close-cropped sorrel hair shone with highlights from the wavering fire.

"I hope the music's to your taste," she added.

"Eh? Oh, it's very fine, very fine," Floyt hastened, realizing that Alacrity was simply staring and waiting.

Janusz moved in her direction, then changed course to end up at the other side of the fireplace. He still had a clear field of fire, Alacrity saw nervously.

Calm down, he told himself. *They could've killed you anywhere along the line. Why do it here?* It was difficult not to think of the ugly surprise of being ambushed inboard the *Mountebank*, though.

"And you would be Alacrity Fitzhugh," she said.

"Yes, that's me."

"My name is Victoria Roper. We're glad you two are finally here."

Which you could mean a couple of different ways, Alacrity mulled.

Floyt said, "That's very kind of you. There are certain things we have to discuss, I suppose."

"That's correct," Janusz said, turning to warm his hands by the fire. "But first—"

He turned back with a snubby little scatterbeam pistol in

either hand. Victoria had brought a slim sonic tube from her sleeve, leveling it at them.

Alacrity ground out, "Damn, perverse, *sonuvabitch*!" but he didn't move; he had no chance against them. He was no gunslinger, and Janusz was way too fast. Floyt's finger pressed the emergency button on his proteus.

"Hold still, Citizen Floyt," Janusz barked. "I almost shot your hand off just now."

Floyt spread his hands. Alacrity knew with a sinking feeling that Heart and Sintilla couldn't get to them in time to do any good. It was just the way the breaks went. He braced for the sonic blast or the white-hot wash of the scatterbeams.

Instead, Victoria reached among the things lying on the Buddha's mantelpiece stomach and took down a baton, an exquisite thing of nacreous icestone, glittering black Lilith's Touch, and plaited red leather. Its cap was a figurine shape like Winged Victory.

She moved in on Floyt with it—from the side, leaving Janusz and herself clear shooting angles. "I regret having to do this, Citizen Floyt; I apologize. I'll ask you to show me your Inheritor's belt now."

Floyt didn't see any alternative. His hands went to his fatigue jacket. "*Very* carefully," Janusz advised. "Please let us have no unfortunate misunderstandings."

Floyt opened his jacket to show the belt. Victoria verified it somehow with the baton, just as the major of Celestials had when Floyt and Alacrity first boarded the *King's Ransom*.

Victoria put aside the baton with her sonic tube. "Welcome, Citizen Floyt. And please forgive us for all of that." She came to him with her hand extended and he automatically took it. Her fingers were short and square-nailed, cool and strong.

"How about you?" Alacrity said to Janusz, whose guns had vanished. "You sorry too?"

Janusz bored into Alacrity for a moment with that plasmadrill stare. Then he said, "If you like, yes. My most abject apologies to you both. For taking entirely sensible, necessary precautions, Master Fitzhugh."

"Y'know, we almost lost the belt along the way."

"That would have been unfortunate, but probably not lethal, for you," Janusz responded calmly.

"Yeah? Oh, well, that's okay, then."

Victoria said to the empty air, "Corva, I believe you should join us now." To Alacrity and Floyt she added, "And that will complete our roster."

"Three, huh?" Alacrity said, trying to puzzle out just what he and Floyt had stumbled into. He heard the sound of the door behind him.

"Yes," a voice said. *"Ning-ning-a-ning!* Swiftly and boldly come Floyt and Fitzhugh! Heroes of the spaceways! (I'll believe it if you will!) *Ning-ning!"*

The young Srillan was thinner and shorter than Lord Admiral Maska. His pelt still had some of the tawny highlights of adolescence. He nevertheless reminded Floyt of a sleepy aardvark shambling around on its hind legs.

Floyt felt an instant aversion to a creature whose kind had devastated Earth, despite the fact that the Earther had reached an accord of sorts with Maska—or at least a tolerance for him.

Alacrity, who'd spent quite a bit of time among the shaggy humanoids, said, "Woo! Whatever next?"

"Next," answered Victoria, "we discuss the Terran Inheritance."

"Do we really need to go through a big discussion?" Alacrity asked a few minutes later, as they made themselves at home and domestic robos circulated around the library offering all sorts of delights. Floyt was having trouble convincing himself that Tombville had been real.

"All we really need to know is where *Astraea Imprimatur* is and what kind of shape she's in. We want to get out of here as soon as we can." One robo had tankards of ale with frost on the sides; Alacrity took one gratefully.

"The ship is in perfect condition. She's at the spacefield, hidden in a hanger," Corva said. "Nobody knows she's here but us."

"Pretty fair trick," Alacrity said.

"Not so difficult. We got an old hulk spaceworthy and tricked it out as the *Stray*, in secret. Landed *Astraea Imprimatur* and hid her in the hangar, and conned the hulk out pretending she was the *Stray*. Anyhow, that's not the Terran Inheritance Victoria meant."

"Retro back," Alacrity said, making a long arm and catching the robo before it got away. He held up the tankard. "How long is this story going to take? Should I grab a backup?"

"Perhaps if you'd simply listen, it would turn out to be less time-consuming," Janusz suggested mildly. Alacrity let the robo go and it floated away.

"Just a moment," Floyt said. "Before we go into this, I think I'd like to use the, er, washchamber."

Victoria smiled. "To call whoever you were signaling before, Hobart Floyt? That's not necessary; Old Raffles is shielded. Nothing got out. But you're free to get in touch with whomever you want, of course, and you're welcome to use our equipment. You might care to know more about your situation first, however."

Floyt relaxed again, sipping a praiseworthy cup of demitasse. "You're right, of course. Please go on."

Victoria had returned to warm herself by the fire, though the library wasn't very cold. Corva was perched on a low floatstool and Janusz was leaning over the back of a Fifth Empire chair.

"Perhaps Corva ought to start it," Victoria said. "But let me assure you first, Hobart: that what we say, we can prove. It means you'll have to change your mind about some of the most fundamental beliefs you have. Do you think you can do that?"

"Maybe if you quit badgering him and get started, we can find out," Alacrity interposed.

"Fair enough," Corva said. He shifted into a more comfortable position, a typically Srillan one, something like a squatting monkey.

"What you Terrans have inherited—what's been foisted off on your whole race and mine as well—is the end product of two hundred years of lying, deceit, *brutal* power politics and manipulation. The center of it is a Conspiracy—the Camarilla—that's kept Earth isolationist and xenophobic for two centuries."

Alacrity glanced over to check Floyt's reaction. The Inheritor was listening, sipping at his demitasse.

"The Human-Srillan War never should have taken place," Corva said. "We later began calling it The Bungle War, did you know that?

"But I'll tell you something: there were humans who welcomed it. Srillans as well. As it drew to an end, there were people on humanity's side who decided to insure that the outcome was in their favor—their *personal* favor."

"You have to remember," Victoria said, "up until then it was Earth, always Earth, and the Solar system, running things. Earth dominated and she wasn't always kind, and every other political sphere—even Spica—was subordinate. That's simply the way it had always been. The potential profit and power to be realized by changing that were beyond calculation, almost beyond imagination. And there were a lot of people who had nothing to lose."

"So the Camarilla was formed," Corva resumed. "Hidden agreements reached, deals struck. High-risk power players; you understand, Hobart? They were used to big gambles. They lived for them.

"The Srillan High Command was encouraged to make that last strike at Earth—the one the Terrans call the Big Smear—even though a lot of them disagreed with it and thought Srilla ought to sue for peace. The High Command thought it had a chance to deal the human race a knockout blow because Earth was vulnerable. *Because it was meant to be vulnerable*."

Alacrity tried to digest that. He wasn't much of a historian, but he knew the Smear had always generated arguments and speculation. A lot of conspiracy buffs talked just the way Corva was talking. Of course, they never had proof, and the ones who got press seemed always to be the ones who needed major attic repairs.

"And it was a double cross," Corva went on. "Because the Spican fleet showed up too late to save Terra but just in time to wipe out Srillan military power."

"Whoa; are you saying there were Srillans in on it?" Alacrity interrupted.

"I am. They were, like their Terran counterparts, ambitious

underlings and former top-rank leaders who'd fallen from grace. Most of them died in the final strike and others were eliminated subsequently, even before the surrender; there were triple crosses, and we are as ruthless a species as you."

"The overview, you already have," Victoria said. "The focus of human civilization shifted to the Spican system. What else, but for the wealth and power of the human race to begin accumulating there?"

Corva nodded, scratching his long snout. "But the Camarilla had to make sure Earth wouldn't reemerge. The Spicans, especially, would've been happier to see the planet eliminated altogether. But that was impossible; the Terran Camarillans were in power there, and they'd have revealed everything to humanity at large if the Spicans tried it.

"Anyway, that's how Earthservice got started. Its main function has always been to see to it that Terra stays isolated."

"Yeah, yeah," Alacrity objected, "but for two hundred *years*?" Floyt didn't seem inclined to comment or even ask questions.

"For two hundred years. This Camarilla is a set of mutually opposed forces—or maybe 'competing' is a better word—that nonetheless have common interests. It's a delicately balanced system with its own stabalizing forces built in. The main one is that all the damning evidence of the Camarilla and what it did is still in existence."

Alacrity almost leapt at her. "What? *Where?*"

"About four kilometers from where you're standing, Master Fitzhugh," Janusz said with the bare hint of a smile.

"Hah? Now, wait. You mean to tell me they didn't destroy it? That can't be."

"Yes, it can; look at it from their point of view, Alacrity." Victoria took up the tale again. "The Bank of Spica and the other cartels who were in on it didn't trust the Alpha-Bureaucrats, and the Alphas didn't trust the Spican government leaders. And the outsystem plotters—they don't trust anybody, and so on."

"But then . . . who's in charge?"

"A group of men called the Joint Custodians," Janusz said. "They're what amounts to a priesthood, mind-engineered clones, neuters. They've hung on to the secrets of the Camarilla and adjudicated the balance of power almost since the beginning."

"Four klicks from here. Why Blackguard?"

"It wasn't Blackguard originally, Alacrity." That was Corva. "As far as we can figure out, the original site of their Repository was in the Solar system. Then for a while it was in the Spican system. One faction or another tried to get control of it every so often, but the Custodians managed to thwart them. In response, these last twenty-odd years, the Custodians have shown signs of becoming a power unto themselves. The more so, as Hawkings get faster."

Victoria moved away from the fire to take up the thread of the story again, eyes bright and huge, the great wing-brows lifted. *Not conventionally beautiful, but absolutely striking*, Alacrity found himself thinking.

"About eight years ago, the Repository was moved to Blackguard. It was an obvious choice, when you stop to think about it, something both the Camarilla and the Custodians agree on. They knew about the compounds, so they knew Blackguard— or Finders-Keepers, if you prefer—is well defended and seldom visited. And there are a lot of powerful people who have a stake in seeing to it that no one comes snooping around or lets word of the place get out."

"Nobody ever got wind of it until now? That's impossible."

Victoria was nodding. "You're right, Alacrity. People found out, one way or another. But you're talking about a coalition of some of the most powerful people in human space. How hard d'you think it is for them to silence somebody who sounds like a paranoid in the first place?"

"Not very, hm?"

"Not very. They kill them or brainblank them or whatever seems appropriate. Let me tell you something: there's a Camarilla member in the top level at the Langstretch Agency."

Alacrity stood frozen. For the first time, Floyt glanced up from his demitasse to his friend.

"*Langstretch*," Alacrity whispered. Then, "Are you sure? How could you know a thing like that?"

"Because that's where I found out about the Camarilla,"

Victoria answered with a wolfish smile, "back when I was a Langstretch Field Operative, Class One."

Alacrity shifted his face back into neutral the way Floyt had seen him do before. "A class one."

"I found out about it by mistake; nearly got myself shot for that. Now the Langstretch is after *me*; I should think that I'm just about at the top of the rat-'stat by now. Of course, I have a few advantages most targets don't. I know the whole operation from the inside."

Janusz was staring into the fire. There was an almost palpable tension in the air, something between Victoria and the outlaw. But Alacrity didn't want to get bogged down at that point, and certainly not on the subject of Langstretch.

"As I recall, this was all supposed to be leading up to the subject of Weir, no? And me and Ho and *Astraea Imprimatur*?"

"Weir was really the turning point," Janusz said, coming away from the fire. "While he was looking into the Earthservice for reasons of his own, he found out about the Camarilla. He was the first one with a power base and resources enough to protect himself . . . up to a point. He put together an apparatus of people, a counter-Camarilla. One by one—or in twos or whatever—we gravitated to it. Weir couldn't save everybody; a lot died. And more when this shadow war started."

"How long? How long has this program been running?"

"For Weir? We don't know, Alacrity. A very long time, I think. Victoria and I have been involved in it for almost three years now; Corva for about two. We're the last, you see, the last of this apparatus."

Alacrity found that very distressing news. "And us? How come we're here?"

"Weir funded us, helped us all he could. He insulated us even from his sister and top advisors. We have no real avenue of approach to Redlock and Tiajo now. There are some emergency procedures, but quite frankly we're not inclined to use them. Even in Weir's Domain, and especially in Frostpile, I think, the Camarilla has its plants."

Alacrity said, "It does if the Bank of Spica's in on it. One of their board members tried to kill us at Frostpile. Didn't make a grain of sense to me until tonight."

"Yes, that sounds reasonable. At any rate, Weir helped us set up several different scenarios for what we should do with the Repository information once we get it. After all, we can't simply start taking out advertisements or hand it over to the governments involved; that's how all this started in the first place. We'd just disappear like all the others. One of Weir's scenarios had to do with getting word to Earth as a start."

Floyt's brows knotted. Alacrity said, "Earth? Ha, some chance! How?"

"Well, one way to get the word there is in a starship, but starships are prohibited there, have been for centuries."

"I know," Alacrity said impatiently. "I read all about those early experiment disasters."

"The only way a starship can land on Terra," Victoria said, "the only way it could get past the Solar Defense Forces and land even if the Alpha-Bureaucrats don't want it to, is—"

"Is with a Letter of Free Import," Floyt said calmly. "That's what this finally boils down to, isn't it?"

"That's what it finally boils down to," Corva agreed softly. "Weir got word to us; he'd found out about Project Shepherd and the Letter of Free Import that was involved."

"And all of this was just to get a letter."

"And to get an Earther, just one, to know the truth," Victoria insisted. "To put the facts before him. I think Weir was very impressed with what you'd done—your histories and genealogies. I think he wanted you in particular to serve as representative for your planet. There seemed to be something about you, something he didn't go into."

Floyt found himself thinking about the causality harp and Strange Attractors.

"It could work," Alacrity said, fingering his chin, looking up at the swirling glow-worm arabesques patterning the ceiling. "Besides, think how surprised Supervisor Bear would be, Ho, and all those Alphas."

"I'd rather not." Floyt's conditioning was giving him the whimmies as it was.

"There are rather more immediate things to consider anyway," Corva said. "Such as the uproar we detected at the compounds. Ships have been departing in great numbers, and intercompound commo traffic is fast and furious. We detected some heavy-weapons activity too. We'd like to know what's happened, if you can tell us."

"We got diverted for a while," Alacrity said. "They held us there for a bit, but we got away. I guess we left them in a flap, but that's not really relevent right now."

"It is to the Camarilla," Victoria corrected. "Over at the Repository they've taken notice too, and we think it's got them nervous. We think they may be planning another move, off Blackguard, very soon now."

"But you folks have a plan, am I right?" Alacrity said.

"We have one on schedule," Corva answered, "a carefully worked out schedule. That schedule will have to be discarded now. We will have to make our attempt within a matter of days."

"I—I . . ." Floyt was having trouble getting started. He'd seen nothing to prove the terrible things they'd been telling him, and yet he found them credible. But he turned his mind away from the snarled evil of the Conspiracy.

"I'm not involved in this." He brought forth the words at last. "I'm here for my Inheritance, the *Astraea Imprimatur*; I can't become part of—of this other matter. I *can't*! I have to return to Earth."

Díos, I was so involved with this crazy story I forgot! Alacrity realized with a start. *He's still under the conditioning!*

"And if we do not choose to give her over to you?" Janusz asked.

Alacrity was very wary in answering; Janusz was no one to provoke. "Is that the way Weir wanted it?"

Victoria answered before Janusz could. "No. It was hoped that Citizen Floyt would help us. Quite frankly, Director Weir seemed to think that hearing about our situation would persuade him to come over to our side."

"I wish I could be of help to you. But I cannot."

"What're your plans, Ho?" Alacrity inquired mildly.

Floyt squared his shoulders, unconsciously fingering the Inheritor's belt. "What they've been all along. I have to take *Astraea Imprimatur* back to Terra."

"The Earthservice'll put you through a debriefing and wring

you out like a rag," Alacrity shot back. "The Alphas'll put you under, find out what you know, and never let you wake up again."

"I can't help that, Alacrity." Floyt sighed.

"I know; I just wanted to be sure."

So saying, Alacrity brought forth the jot unit he'd taken from Constance and, nearly getting himself shot by hair-trigger Janusz, jotted the astounded Floyt into unconsciousness.

CHAPTER 19

NOW IN REHEARSAL
FOR REAL LIFE

"ACTIJOT?" JANUSZ ASKED INTERESTEDLY, PUTTING HIS GUNS away as Floyt's paroxysms stopped and he slumped in his chair.

"Yeah," Alacrity said, putting the jot unit back in his pocket. "Rough, but I had to do something before his conditioning *really* kicked in and he started thinking ahead. He's a pretty capable guy. You'd be surprised."

"Would you like to explain yourself? Other than the fact that you want to save your friend's life?" Victoria invited.

Alacrity knelt by Floyt, peeling back his eyelids. "Life is right." He filled them in quickly on the conditioning and how his own had been accidentally removed. "If I let him go now, he'll be walking right into the Camarilla's hands."

"Ah! You believe us!" Corva explained.

Alacrity nodded. "I always had the feeling Ho and me had at least two sets of enemies. Three, counting Inst."

Inst had been killed, and Endwraithe. That supposedly left only Dincrist as their avowed foe. But the feeling hadn't gone away. The existence of the Camarilla would explain everything that had happened to Floyt and Alacrity.

"And so you've saved Citizen Floyt from himself," Janusz observed. "But what will you do now? Or hadn't you thought about that?"

Alacrity turned to Victoria. "You were a Langstretch Field Op One. I was sort of hoping you'd be able to help."

She looked him over with heavy-lidded reserve, the dark, thick brows poised high. "You know quite a bit about Langstretch, don't you, Master Fitzhugh? Well, you're right; I've been through the advanced training."

"Can you do it? Deprogram him?"

"I think so. I'm not the best there is, but I'm the best you're liable to find around here. How long was the conditioning regimen?"

"Oh, maybe two, two and a half Standard days. Earthservice was up against a deadline."

"That's very good for us. My equipment is up on the third tier. If you gentlemen will take Citizen Floyt's arms and legs?"

Alacrity and Janusz hauled Floyt into the foyer and loaded him aboard a whisk-platform. Victoria gave a verbal command to the empty air, and they were all wafted up to a vacant room, bypassing ramps and staircases.

Floyt was deposited on a sleep dais. Alacrity wanted to stick around, but Victoria said no. She was setting out devices resembling the things Skate had used on Alacrity, except that they were newer and more elaborate. "This will be difficult enough without interruptions or distractions. You're just going to have to trust me, Alacrity."

Corva put a paw-hand on Alacrity's shoulder, and Alacrity relaxed to the inevitable. He took Victoria's hand and gave it a squeeze. "Thank you."

He noticed that that drew an instant's glare from Janusz.

The whisk-platform carried the two men and the Srillan back down to the study smoothly and quickly. "Janusz and I have to see to a few details, make sure Old Raffles is secure for the night and whatnot," Corva told Alacrity. "If you wish, you can contact your other friends and make arrangements to meet with them tomorrow. They're welcome here at the chateau, of course."

Alacrity thought that over. "Maybe. But when you come back, I'd like to hear a little more about *Astraea Imprimatur*. I also wouldn't mind knowing how you're planning to take this Repository."

Corva made the snuffling sound his kind used for laughter.

"Yes, I think you'll find that intriguing. You see, they have a total-destruct mechanism in place. Rather than lose the Camarilla evidence to outsiders, they would eliminate it."

"But, hold on now," Alacrity objected. "There's got to be some sort of catch, or else why hasn't one Camarilla faction, or two, or all of 'em, tackled the Repository long since? I mean, the evidence goes up, *poof!*, and they're out from under the Custodians, no?"

"That's very astute, Alacrity," Corva said, "except that there's a deep backup in place. If the Repository's put out of commission, certain dead-man precautions cut in, and duplicates of the evidence are delivered to all the Camarilla factions. It's what you might call the Sampson Option; it would trigger an all-out power struggle, and none of them want that.

"Oh, and as regards the *Astraea Imprimatur*, you and Hobart can inspect her whenever you choose. I think you'll be impressed. As for the Repository—the key to everything, you see, was in our gaining a controlling interest in the Parish Ink and Paper Company."

"The which? But what's that got to do with—never mind. I'll be in the library."

He opened a commo connection and broadcast a sketchy situation report in a prearranged message code he'd worked out with Heart and Sintilla, naming a time for his return to the *Harpy*. The *Harpy* didn't acknowledge, but he didn't expect her to; they didn't want anyone happening to get a DF fix on her.

When Janusz and Corva came back, all three settled into comfortable chairs. Corva cued displays of Parish city maps, the floor plan of the Repository, timetables, and flow charts. As Alacrity began to understand the significance of the Parish Ink and Paper Company, his smile grew wider and wider.

In return, he told them about the Grapple and the Blackguard compounds.

"Which brings up something else," Alacrity said. "We've still got those actijots in us. Can you arrange for us to visit a medicenter, or bring someone out here?"

Corva looked distressed, but Janusz barked a laugh. "To

remove actijots? We'd have to kill or confine everyone concerned after it was over."

"He's right," Corva said somberly. "One or two fugitives from the compounds have reached here over the years. The people of Parish don't know much about what goes on on the other side of their planet; they don't wish to. But they know enough to stay well clear of anybody escaped from there. There were some dreadful object lessons from the Betters, in the beginning."

"Aw, *fancula!*" Alacrity snarled, slouched in his chair. Then: "Oh, well; there'll be time for it later—and no chance we'll be traced. I guess we can live with the jots until we're off-world."

"Yes, to be sure; we'll find help for you at the earliest possible opportunity," Corva said.

The door opened just then and Victoria came in, looking weary. She sat down, refusing refreshments, massaging her neck.

"The Earthservice isn't as thorough as it might be," she said. "I suppose that was because they wanted Hobart socially functional, not robotized. In any case, I've countered the conditioning. I got it all, I'm fairly certain."

Alacrity almost kissed her until he remembered the dirty look he'd gotten from Janusz just for squeezing her fingers. Instead, he proposed they have a round to celebrate.

Victoria declined. "I'm all in, and we have a lot to do in the next few days. I'll see you all in the morning."

She left. The other three raised their glasses in a toast to what lay ahead. Alacrity felt on top of the world. *This Camarilla's gonna wish they never heard of a couple of hard-luck riffraff named Floyt and Fitzhugh!*

Janusz excused himself and left a few minutes later. Alacrity began yawning as Corva directed the autoservants to straighten up.

"Look, it's none of my business," Alacrity said tentatively, "but if Jaunsz and Victoria are—together, you know—they don't have to play innocent for my sake. After all, you three are taking us in, and all of that."

Corva's droopy-lidded eyes looked him over for a second. "It's rather more complicated than that. You know who he is?"

"Heard of him, yes."

"Well, once all of this Repository business is over, I'm afraid, Victoria plans to arrest him and turn him over to the authorities. Unless he kills or disables her first, or gets away. I, unfortunately, am sworn not to intervene; it's part of our compact."

Alacrity's mouth had fallen open. "He . . . she . . ."

"She was about to do that back when they first became aware of the Camarilla. They formed an alliance of necessity, or they'd both be dead now. It's a very complicated situation, Alacrity; I'm telling you this so that you and your friends don't get involved. It's something strictly between them."

"Thanks. You won't get any arguments from me. As long as they hold off until the Repository's taken care of, that is."

"They will. Of that much I'm certain."

Corva took one whisk-platform to his second-tier room; Alacrity boarded another programmed for the third-tier bedroom he'd been assigned. As he floated up through the great epergne of Old Raffles, he changed course to check on Floyt.

The Earther was sleeping soundly. As Alacrity left Floyt's bedroom, he heard low voices around a turn in the curving hallway. He eased in that direction, listening. Being a courteous guest had its place, but he preferred knowing what was going on and where he stood.

He peeked around the turn. Farther along, Victoria stood with her back to her bedroom door, Janusz standing very close and looking down into her eyes. Whatever the conversation had been about, it was over. Victoria reached up and put her arms around Janusz's neck. He embraced her, putting his lips to hers.

Oh, yes, they've got themselves a ceasefire, all right, Alacrity thought, watching Victoria draw Janusz into her bedroom.

Alacrity drew back around the corner and started for the whisk-platform. As it wafted him upward, he tried to figure out why things never got simpler, but only more and more complicated.

"But I still feel like I want to go back to Earth. In fact, I know I do."

"Well, naturally you do, Ho," Alacrity said patiently. "It's where you live and where your family is. That hasn't changed."

Floyt, propped up on the sleeping dais, sipped at tea flavored with local herbs and spices.

"See here, Alacrity: I appreciate what you thought you were doing for me, but the deconditioning didn't work, period. The tension's still there—in my gut and in my head—over getting the ship and all of that."

"Of course, because those are real problems, Ho, and you'd be crazy not to be worried about them, but—okay; watch."

Alacrity gesture opened the door to Floyt's bedroom and he beckoned in Corva, Janusz, and Victoria.

"Now, Ho," he said. "Tell them who Chief Clinician Skinner is."

"What? Why, he's the one who—who—who conditioned us." He looked at them wonderingly. "Then it's true," he said slowly. "Oh, this is . . . Victoria, I'm forever grateful to you."

"Uh-huh, even though you're still going to insist on taking the damn ship back to the Earthservice, aren't you?" Alacrity said in mock disgust.

"You're very welcome, Hobart," Victoria said. "Did you rest well?"

Floyt nodded.

"Good," Alacrity said, "because there's lots to do."

"Things are getting active over at the Repository," Corva explained. "We think the Custodians are preparing to move their operation. We will move against them just as soon as we can, about eight days from now."

"So there're all kinds of things to see to," Alacrity said. "Look, Ho, I've been thinking: how would you like to learn to fly?"

The chateau's spacious hangar-garage had a half-dozen ground vehicles, everything from a beat-up old power rickshaw to a stretch touring car, and four aircraft, including a spaceboat slightly larger and somewhat older than the *Harpy*.

"How did you people come to be so well set up?" Floyt

asked as he, Alacrity, and Victoria walked the row of vehicles. "The chateau and all this—it must have taken a great deal of money," Floyt added.

"Weir funded us generously," Victoria explained. "And—money came our way, from time to time. It's like that when you have your own starship."

Alacrity nudged Floyt on that one, fluttering his eyebrows. Floyt pointedly ignored him.

"Plus," she went on, "every so often we saw our chance to take off people tied in to the Camarilla, or underworld types, or whomever. I mean, between what Janusz and I know and things Corva picked up before he became a contrition-knight, we mounted some pretty good takes, if I do say so myself."

Alacrity had halted. "Corva's a Srillan contrition-knight?"

"Yes. He doesn't mention it very often."

"No reason he should, I guess. Thanks for telling me, before I went and shot my mouth off or something."

"Think nothing of it."

Still panicked by the thought of flying an aircraft, Floyt decided he didn't care what they were talking about. The three passed the airsedan and stopped by a larger craft, a skytruck with flat battleship-gray hull and no trim.

Alacrity started to climb into the pilot's poz, but Victoria stopped him. "Friends shouldn't teach friends; it puts too much of a strain on things."

She buckled herself in and Floyt, after some hesitation, took the copilot's seat. Alacrity fastened himself into a rear seat.

To Floyt's enormous relief, Victoria said, "You just watch for now." She ran through a preflight check, explaining things as she went, then brought the power up and signaled the hangar door open. She guided the skytruck out with a deft touch and made a smooth ascent. Floyt calmed a bit; it didn't look all that hard. As Janusz had the previous night, she followed the ground-access roads to avoid provoking the residents of Parish Above.

"Aren't people curious about you three?" Floyt asked.

"Nobody knows Corva's here; a Srillan would attract too much attention. Poor thing, except for one or two times he's been offworld in the last year or so, he's had to be pretty much a shut-in."

There was some traffic below, animal-drawn and motor-powered mostly, tradespeople and others servicing the great houses. Few other aircraft were up, all of them over Parish Below. For privacy, Victoria kept the cockpit windows at full tint.

Alacrity gave her her course. She banked for open country and cut back speed, gesturing to Floyt's controls. "Take 'er, Hobart."

Of course he was too tense at first, overreacting then over-correcting. But the old skytruck was a steady flier and Victoria was patient, taking back control only once or twice, long enough to straighten things out, instructing but never criticizing. Floyt quickly calmed down and began doing rather well.

Alacrity stuffed his knuckles in his mouth to keep from butting in, convinced that the two of them were doing everything all wrong. To distract himself, Alacrity asked, "What's with that kid Notch and his gutter babies?"

"He runs errands for us. He's well connected in Parish Below, and he knows how to keep his mouth shut and make sure his troops do, too. He had a standing order to be on the lookout for anybody like you two—he thinks you're all part of a medium-small interstellar contraband operation."

Victoria debated with herself for a moment, then added, "Notch likes to taunt Janusz and he's getting bolder and bolder with me. He's decided he wants me and convinced himself I want him back."

"He's a lifelong boxtowner, right? It's a good bet he's not right in the head."

"Well, soon we'll be shut of him, Alacrity, but we need him for the raid against the Repository. Once that's over, we leave the house, the businesses, everything, and jump in the *Stray*—in *Astraea Imprimatur*."

"Businesses? What businesses?" That was Floyt, who was gaining confidence in his slow maneuvers, fighting down a sublime giddiness.

"Fronts we acquired so it would look like we were properly crooked, if you see what I mean. We own a couple of warehouses, a fencing operation, and control a hangar at the space-field through one of the tribes. And there's a salvage yard out on Scrap Metal Hill; oh, and *we* actually own the Dis Hill Caravansary . . . You're doing very well there, Hobart; I think you're the one to make our landing approach."

Floyt did a creditable job on the approach but Victoria took over for the last part, setting them down neatly near the camouflaged *Harpy*. Blackguard's primary was just reaching its zenith.

When the spaceboat's hatch opened Heart was pointing a stungun and Sintilla was backing her up with Constance's pistols.

Heart greeted Victoria with unfeigned warmth, but then gave Alacrity a long, very moving welcome-home kiss and hugged Floyt. Sintilla was a whirlwind of hugs, kisses, handshakes, and more hugs, Victoria included. All the while she was bombarding them with questions.

Alacrity held up his hands. "Answers galore in town, Tilla! We'll be there in no time. Ho and Victoria are going to fly the skytruck back; you can go with them if your life insurance is paid up. We'll bring the *Harpy* along as soon as it's dark. Corva has a landing beacon set for us."

"Who's Corva? What's all this about, damn you?"

"You'll find out all about it, I swear," he said.

Sintilla, eager to see everything, decided to go back in the skytruck. After a final admonition from Alacrity to be careful, it lifted away unsteadily, Floyt making his first take-off.

"If we have to wait it out, we might as well get this place cleaned up," Heart said, looking around the boat. "You can answer a few hundred questions for me."

A number of Sile's info-wafers and memory lozenges were lying around, along with various readers and adaptors. When Alacrity asked what had been going on, she explained, "We spent some time seeing what we could find out from Sile's records, Tilla and I. It turned out some of his codes and scrambles were based on my father's commercial ones. Here; brace yourself, and look at this."

She loaded one lozenge. Alacrity found himself looking at a somehow familiar old man, white-haired and very distinguished. The setting seemed to be an underground room or dungeon, and the old man had neuroprobes, flensing beams, and so forth. And he had a live victim . . .

Alacrity averted his eyes, the breath hissing from him. "There's more, even worse," Heart said, freezing a closeup. "Recognize him?"

"Wait . . . yeah. That's Praxis, isn't it? The guy Baron Mason had Ho trying to find out about?"

"The one and only. So now we know why Sile had influence with my father, and why my father was permitted to enter the Regatta for the Purple."

Praxis was chairman of the race committee, Alacrity recalled Floyt's having told him. And Sile had this kind of thing on him. Alacrity let the scenes flow again. "God . . ."

"It's even worse than it looks at first," she said. "Don't you see his victim's face? The resemblance?"

A son? No. "A clone of himself."

"Yes; and there were others. The Avatar of the Spirit of the Irreducible *I*; the holyman of self-understanding and forgiveness. He's insane, Alacrity, or at least part of him is."

Alacrity shut off the reader. "And so your father gets to sail in his race."

"If he's still alive and the Blackguard trouble blows over. But I'll tell you something: if I had any doubts about what I'm doing, they're gone. My father knows about that, what you saw, and all he can think to do is take advantage from it. Well, I'm going to stop him doing that kind of thing."

She started tidying aimlessly. "There are—things that have to be protected from him."

He heard her sniffing, thought of leaving her be for a while, but took her wrist instead. "You're not alone. I love you, and I'll back you."

Later, they lay on the deck carpeting and their clothes. She toyed with the deep V of slate-gray hair that burgeoned like a mane down his spine.

He rolled over, laying one hand on her white hip. "Let's mate for life, like swans."

CHAPTER 20

COMMANDING LEAD

"WHAT YOU INHERITED HERE," ALACRITY SAID, FLASHING Floyt a grin as he caught up with the Earther in *Astraea Imprimatur*'s control room, "is a starship that can't do any one thing preeminently well, but *can* do just about anything you can think of, at least half-assed."

"Which means you approve?" Janusz asked from the pilot's poz—Floyt near his shoulder, Sintilla poised on the arm of his chair—where he had been explaining the instrumentation.

"It means I'm envious as hell." Alacrity beamed. "A starship with lots of guts and guns and ears *and* decorated in Bordello *Robotique*?"

"I think you mean Shangri-La Ultramax, Alacrity," Sintilla corrected.

"Whatever. Anyway, she's too damn good for those cutworms at Earthservice, that's for sure. Doesn't this just take the bark off your bole?"

The trio from Old Raffles had shown them specs, 3-D displays, and original blueprints, but those were nothing compared to the real thing. She'd originally been raised off the ways as a *Jaguar*-class corvette, the *Copperhead*, during the Calendar Wars out by Crossroads. She'd been through various incarnations as patrol craft, rescue/survey vessel, and other things, including being rigged out as a privateer by a lesser son of a

Grand Presidium member, for the Agoran Turmoils. The kid had spent even more money on luxuries and decor than on her new Hawking, weapons, and computers; and that was a lot.

She'd been adapted, retrofitted, and reretrofitted, and her hull altered. The *Stray* had an archaic yet backswept and fleet look to her. Alacrity pronounced her splendid; Floyt took his word.

"Well, if things go right, Earthservice won't get its hands on her," Sintilla said. She didn't seem too troubled by the point, though. She didn't seem too troubled by anything. Her eyes had begun glazing over from time to time, her face going blank as she worked out details of the story of the century, or perhaps the millennium.

"You're not just chopping your grinders, they won't," Alacrity agreed. "Ho, d'you know what she's packing port and starboard? Two missile tubes with a pair of Animus Vs in 'em, in perfect condition and ready to fire."

"Oh. Is that good?"

"Annie Vs? They built them for use by capital ships and O'Neills. That pair's probably worth almost as much as the *Stray*. They're damn near as big."

"According to the log, the tubes were fitted when *Copperhead* was part of the Last Ditch Armada," Janusz explained. "But she never got to fire them. That young Grand Presidium noble liked the idea of having them, so he incorporated the tubes in the revised design when she was being refurbished as a privateer."

"With two Annie Vs in his pocket, how'd he lose?" Alacrity asked.

Janusz gave him a fey smile. "He was surrounded by three ships, and he loved his life too much. He surrendered."

"Mmph. Probably didn't want the decor messed up either."

Alacrity had a point. *Stray* had lipstick-red runners in the passageways, Persian carpets in the cabins, and rather fanciful erotic frescoes on the curved overhead of the main compartment-salon.

Control levers had been replaced with great, scrimshawed tusks, handgrips plated with rare horn and ivory; gemstone chess pieces had been substituted for mere switches, touchpad buttons discarded in favor of crystals intagliated with technical symbols.

Tasseled crimson damask and silk abounded. The heads boasted the latest word in creature comforts. There were delicate porcelain figurines and stippled gold trim; there were brocaded draperies that cost more than the average breakout made in a month's work. *Astraea Imprimatur*'s supplies of food, drink, and other consumables made Sile's provisions in the *Harpy* look like bread and water. There was a sensedep tank and a multimedia sensorium.

"With this tub you could dust crops or survey a planet, Ho, including taking core samples. Or you could get a fast-hop postal franchise, I bet."

"Or throw one helluva fund-raiser," Sintilla put in.

"The only drawback is that she's got a real small payload," Alacrity said. "But she's all yours, and I'm very impressed."

"I'd give her to you if I could," Floyt said.

"I know; thanks. Maybe some other time."

"I'm just wondering," Sintilla went on. "Are we sure nobody else knows this Cleopatra's barge is here?"

"We're more than careful about that," Janusz told her. "No one aside from us knows, be assured. We have been very cautious; you saw the sensors and security drones yourself."

"But where do we go? After the raid, I mean?" Sintilla asked.

"To Srilla, and Corva's uncle," Janusz said. "Lord Admiral Maska."

"Maska?" Floyt and Alacrity yelled at once. *"Maska?"*

"Their favorite humanoid," Sintilla commented tartly.

Just then Heart and Victoria came forward from running a systems check. "Everything proofs out okay at the weather bridge and the tech pozzes," Heart said, smoothing out her utility coveralls. The midships control station, known as the weather bridge, was for conning the *Stray* if she sustained damage to her main control room.

"And we contacted Corva; everything's quiet at the chateau," Victoria added. "She's as ready as she can be." Saying this, she took in the starship with a sweep of her hand.

"That's it, then," Janusz said, rising. "Corva will be expecting us."

Floyt almost spoke but didn't. Alacrity piped up for him. "Do we have to go so soon? I'd sort of like to spend a little more time here and, uh, so would some of the rest of us, I think."

Floyt shrugged and nodded, blushing. Every time he touched the ship's brightwork or learned something new about her he fell a little more in love with her. It had started the moment he'd set eyes on her and increased drastically when Janusz officially noted his ownership in the vessel's log.

"If it wouldn't be putting anyone out, I'd like to stay here for a while longer at least," Floyt said.

Victoria brightened. "Why not? I think that would be fun."

Janusz yielded indifferently; the others grew festive. They turned the evening into a last respite; it was less than seven days' time to the scheduled raid on the Repository.

Alacrity insisted on cooking, while Sintilla tended bar. They played loud music and programmed all the salon's screens and projectors to flash planetary and celestial scenes. They ate and drank, swapped stories and recollections, laughed and worried a bit.

Alacrity and Heart danced, then Sintilla got Floyt to his feet. Victoria cut in on Sintilla, so Sintilla cajoled Janusz into dancing; he gave in with staid good humor. When he took Victoria in his arms to waltz, Alacrity looked for the tension between the two to crackle or even discharge. But it didn't, and he couldn't read what was passing in those fierce, probing gazes.

Floyt enjoyed himself more than he had since the Foragers' party on Luna. He couldn't pin down whether that was in spite of the fact that the raid was coming up or, in some strange way, because of it.

Alacrity and Heart were the first to disappear, diplomatically passing by the master's cabin and availing themselves of the first officer's quarters. Alacrity suspected that deep down, Victoria and Janusz still regarded *Astraea Imprimatur* as theirs.

Janusz and Victoria stayed awhile longer, chatting with Floyt and Sintilla and dancing a few more numbers. They were all a little drunk when Sintilla took the outlaw's hand and solemnly promised him that she would never, no, never betray his confidence by writing anything about him.

Then she thought a moment and added, "Unless I cut a *really* good deal."

Victoria burst out laughing, spraying part of her drink. Floyt roared and even Janusz cracked a smile. Victoria gave his hand a caress. The two soon retired to the master's cabin.

The music was lower now, and slower. Floyt decided blearily that he'd had enough tonsil oil and other treats. "There are—what—two crew compartments left? Which one d'you prefer, Tilla?"

She looked at him rather soberly for someone who'd put away so much vodka. "D'you think we ought to pick one out together, Hobart?" She put an arm around his neck, kissing his cheek before he could get over his surprise, keeping her lips close by his ear. "Do you think we ought to do that?"

He was astonished and a little dismayed, but he was also recalling how she'd looked in the costume at the Central Complex and realizing how much he delighted in her smile, how fond he was of her. He owed her his life, too, and, more to the point, found himself wanting her very much.

But the moment that went by before he answered was too long. "Tilla, I, I'm—"

She covered his lips with her fingers. "Don't. Don't say anything. Hobart, please forget I brought it up. Wrong time. It's just that everybody else—I was feeling a bit scared, and low, and lonely."

He would have put his arms around her, but she tousled his hair instead and slipped away. "See you in the morning, Hobart. That wife of yours—she's a lucky dame."

And her husband's an insensitive clod. Floyt sighed as he went to lay him down for the night.

Alacrity woke to the minute sounds of the *Stray*'s life-support systems and power units, and the pleasant smells of a spacegoing vessel that even the expensive systems couldn't mask or remove completely.

His mouth was dry and brackish from the alcohol; he was

halfway between tipsiness and a light hangover. Heart was lying with her spun-snow hair pillowed on one bent arm, the curve of her breast showing above the cover, the nipple alluring and rosy against flesh so pale. He got up as quietly as he could.

The cabin had a minilarder, but it was unstocked. As he crossed to the hatch, she said softly, "Bring back something for me to drink too, darling? And put something on; I don't want Victoria or Tilla tying a blue ribbon around it."

He found a wrap of some sort, couldn't figure it out, and ended up winding it around his middle like a towel. "Will some ice water do?"

"You're a love."

"Let's mate for life, like swans."

"Mmmm . . ."

He found a cold squeezebag of fruit juice in the pantry just aft the salon, opened it and drank deeply. The lights were low. Someone had straightened up a bit before retiring.

He padded to the main lock, opening the inner and outer hatches, using the code phrases Janusz had divulged to them all. The hangar was quiet and still except for floating security drones and traversing surveillance pickups on the hangar walls and *Astraea Imprimatur*'s hull.

He was troubled; he'd never intended to take a lifetime mate. There were still things he had to do, even if the *Astraea Imprimatur* business worked out all right, things that were grave and dangerous. He found it all worrisome, and yet when he thought of Heart he found himself chuckling and sighing, shaking his head.

He went back inboard for a moment, taking up Constance's pistol and putting on some slippers. Then he strolled across the hangar, the drones and security pickups tracking and recording him but refraining from putting in an alarm or opening fire. He found a small people-hatch in the giant roller-door and opened it.

The spacefield was fairly quiet most of the time, even more so now. He listened to the cicada song of a tame tractor beam being used to move some heavy burden. Yelling and laughter carried faintly across the flight surface from another tribal enclave. Somewhere an engine was tested briefly, booming for a few moments then falling silent. He thought back over other ports and other years, other boxtowns and planets. Other companions and loved ones; another life.

Footsteps sounded behind him and he turned, the pistol hanging in his hand. Victoria came toward him, a man's bathrobe held tight around her, its hem blowing a little in the breeze. Her hair fanned out like gossamer. "Aren't you freezing out here?"

"No. I knew we'd have to talk sooner or later, but I didn't mean to wake anyone up or drag you out here. Sorry."

"That's all right. I'm a light sleeper, especially inboard the *Stray*."

They looked out at the night. Alacrity gazed up at constellations he'd begun memorizing during night work details with Gute.

"It never occurred to me who you are," Victoria said. "I mean, who you really are. Until Tilla started cadging information on the flight back from the *Harpy*."

"I sort of thought something like that might happen. I was hoping maybe people wouldn't be interested in me anymore."

"Langstretch is always interested when someone will pay, Alacrity. I don't think you want to know how much you're worth to them."

"You, ah, you have a kind of truce with Janusz. I thought we could declare one too."

She raked back strands of her windblown hair. "What's between Janusz and me is different; it doesn't have anything to do with Langstretch anymore. It has to do with seeing that a debt is paid, because it has to be paid."

"And me?"

"With you it's rather different. I don't think I'd target you for Langstretch even if I still worked for them, much less now. Friends?"

"Uh-huh." They clasped wrists.

"Let's go back in, Alacrity; you're shivering and I'm icing over."

"All right."

As they walked back, she said, "There were some reports that you were dead, you know."

"I started a few of them myself."

"Well, you can forget about that, now that you've gotten yourself involved in this Inheritance affair. My guess is you're not too many jumps ahead of a gang of field ops. In a way, this getting shanghaied to the compounds was a stroke of luck; your tail's cold, cold. But only for a little while."

"I read you. But once this is over—who knows?" He looked the starship over. "I might have some first-class transportation. That'd change the odds."

"That's so. My advice to you is a new identity, not just a new alias. How did you pick such an unlikely name, anyway?"

"Oh, some go-bloods were taking care of me when I was younger. They gave it to me. It's a Terranglish pun: Alacrity Fitzhugh."

"Well, you'd better think up another."

"I'm used to it; it's been so long now. But—no arguments. I'm just finding it a little hard to think beyond this Repository operation. I'm worred about us all, and it's hard to keep my mind on what I have to do afterward."

"Very hard," she said, hugging the bathrobe around herself, head lowered. "Oh, very hard."

"Which Custodian is it, Alacrity?"

Alacrity focused the tripod-mounted vision enhancers tightly, coming in close on the front door of the rundown mansions that served as a front for the Repository. "It's the oldish one with the white vane hairdo. Number, uh, twelve, isn't it? No identifying marks or scars. *Managgia!* How d'you tell clones apart?"

"I recommend we corral them all and brand them," Floyt said as he noted the sighting. "His codename in the surveillance book is Nicodemas. Anything to put under 'remarks'?"

Alacrity backed away from the enhancers and the mirrored viewpane. "Tall, slender, esthetic, like all of 'em. Same Pinkish complexion. Prominent nose and Adam's apple; fine hair balding in the back. He was wearing a working smock, like a lab jacket or whatever, brown. There was a guard with him."

"Did you happen to see which guard?"

"Just like every other guard: two hundred-kilo sumo wrestler. They just receipted for the packet from the armed couriers and closed the door again."

Notch, sprawled on the single desk in the cluttered little office, phlegmatically fast-forwarding through a porn-spool, paused. He said in a monumentally bored voice, "Did they look healthy? Worried? Tired? Could you get a look inside the door? Were they carrying any tools or weapons? Was there anything new or different visible in or through the entranceway? Which courier team was it? That's the kind of stuff Janusz wants logged."

Alacrity settled back on his adjust-stool, resuming his watch. "I recorded it. Janusz told us what he wants, kid."

Notch yawned, showing the bedizened gold teeth, shoving the reader aside. It slid off the table to bounce on the floor. He didn't bother to pick it up. Alacrity's upper lip thinned to a line in anger reflex.

"That's more than he tells me," Notch said, rummaging among the thermatrays to see if anything appetizing was left. "So you two are getting along good with your hosts, huh?" He smiled. "That's fine. It must be quite a change for the others with seven of you sharing the chateau now."

Floyt turned to Notch before Alacrity had a chance to make a slip. "What makes you say that?"

Notch licked bits of frosting off an empty sweetroll wrapper. "That's the way I have it figured, is why. Even though you two are the only new ones I met. The way I see it, two more came with you and there's the other one who's been in Raffles all along, the one nobody ever sees."

"I got a hot tip for you, smiley," Alacrity said with his back still to Notch. "You better spend more time worrying about yourself and your cribmates doing your jobs right and less time snorkling around. There's a lot riding on this deal, and if you screw up you won't know what landed on you."

Notch got to his feet. "Don't panic, Slats. You either, Old-timer. We're ready. We been ready for something like this for a long time."

Alacrity swung his stool around. "Not something *like* this, you silly little fart. *This*, precisely, to the split second. If you mess up, just leave word where I should ship the body. I mean that."

Notch looked at Alacrity for a second, then raised a middle finger to him. "Know what I mean, Slats? If I ain't afraid of Janusz, I sure ain't afraid of you."

"You little scumwad—"

"Alacrity—"

The old commo relay tower's asthmatic liftshaft was making sounds. The three forgot the skirmish and listened. Floyt punched up the view from a shaft pickup. It showed Victoria being floated up on a lift platform, coming to a stop at the top-level landing. The three relaxed.

She was wearing a subdued, all-concealing travel robe in a style favored by some of the Parish tribeswomen, but her lean, graceful sway set her apart from the natives.

"Hello, Victoria," Notch said, moving to intercept her at the door, looking up at her with a gems-and-hardware smile much more earnest than his usual simper.

"Oh, get back," Alacrity growled. "Can't you see you make her skin crawl, kid?"

Notch whirled on him, furious. "That did it. I just made up my mind about you, Slats."

Alacrity came off the stool. "What mind, Chromosome Damage?" Floyt grabbed Alacrity's elbow and Victoria put herself between the two.

"That's enough!" she snapped. "Alacrity, Hobart: we're closing down here. Please make sure the remotes are working properly. Notch, I want you to be certain your group is ready."

"We are, we are! When are you going to let us in on the details, Victoria?"

"Soon. Please listen carefully. I left a surface lorry parked outside. When you leave here, take it and bring your group— *all* of them—to Old Raffles at one-niner-point-five-oh tonight. Don't tell any of them where you're bringing them. Don't let any of them contact anyone. Don't warn any of them ahead of time and don't let any of them out of your sight once you give the marching orders, do you hear me? Do not draw any attention to yourselves; and be there on time, will you please do that for me?"

He was nodding, eager and receptive, a completely different person. Alacrity made a sour face.

"I'll see you then." Notch leaned forward all at once and gave her a kiss on the cheek she couldn't quite avoid. He paused in the doorway for a last jeering look at Alacrity, then he was out of sight.

Alacrity started to help Floyt square the place away, stuffing empty food cartons in the disposal, gathering their things, making sure the automatics were picking up the Repository. He waited until the pickup showed Notch driving off in the surface lorry. "Jeez, Vic; that little bubo worships you."

She let her breath out all at once as she sank into a chair. "I know. I don't like to, but I use that sometimes. Otherwise he'd have fallen out with Janusz and tried to sell us out, I think, and then I'd have had to kill him."

Victoria seemed to be feeling a sudden chill. "Come; we should be going."

Alacrity dumped a last cluster of trash down the disposal. "I hope you brought your crash helmet. Vapor Trail Floyt here, never settles for the copilot's poz these days."

"Care to see a perfect Immelmann?" Floyt inquired proudly.

"Lynx rufus," Janusz said, dropping the bullets onto Floyt's palm. They were on a firing range in Old Raffles' first sub-surface level, a small one laid out for short-range work. "I told you the arms dealers of Parish Below could duplicate anything."

Lynx rufus—wildcat ammunition. Floyd looked one over. He couldn't tell it from the dum-dums he'd acquired along with the Webley; they had the same look and feel.

"I fired a few when I accepted the order," Janusz was saying. "They are reliable. And they do damage."

"Yes, they do that." Floyt nodded soberly. He broke the revolver and emptied the old rounds into a tray, the lanyard fixture ringing.

Janusz was watching him. "You know, you don't have to come along on this op, Hobart. Neither does Alacrity, for that matter, nor Heart, nor Tilla. Victoria, Corva, and I have this thing well set up; it's not necessary that you put yourself through this."

Floyt, fitting new rounds into the chambers, half grimaced. "You mean, you would have had everything perfect if Alacrity and I hadn't come along and gotten matters all stirred up; that's not a new feeling for us. Anyway, thank you, Janusz, but when I get back to Terra there'll be a lot of questions, no matter what. I'll have to bear witness. I have to be able to tell what happened." He closed the pistol.

"In that case, make sure you keep one thing in mind," Janusz told him. "We are going in shooting, Citizen Floyt. I'm not sure you understand what that means, not really. But it means that everyone at the Repository, except for our group, will be the enemy. *Everyone!* I'm warning you, don't hesitate or dither. If you spot anybody, light his fuse before he lights yours. To be candid, you're the least proficient one among us."

"I see," Floyt said thoughtfully.

"I hope you do, but I despair of it. Bear in mind what I've said."

"I will. Shall we try a few rounds?"

Janusz activated the target sequence.

Lights came up out in the target zone. Floyt hadn't felt ready for anything ambitious like moving holoimages or a "funhouse" situation walk. Simu-soma targets popped up. He blazed away at a distance of about fifteen paces.

Alacrity had said the Webley had surprisingly little kick for an old-fashioned bullet firearm, but Floyt still found it disconcerting as the pistol recoiled in his hand, spewing flame, throwing out acrid smoke, with a cracking report. The simu-soma targets contained flesh-and-bone analogs structured something like a human head and torso, marked for hit value. When hit, they reacted somewhat as a human body would.

Floyt's round hit the first pop-up dead center. The jellied, translucent flesh, quivering mock-up organs, and dark, linear bone structure jarred with the impact, splintering and splashing, driven backward, creating a wound channel shaped something like a beehive. For a moment Floyt thought he could see light through the target.

But the recoil and report brought back his flinching reflex, and he closed his eyes as he fired the second time, missing completely. He fired even before aiming on the third, another miss. He let the next pop-up rise and fall without firing, calming himself.

He only partially overcame the reflex, but caught a piece of the next target, in the region of the collarbone. His fifth shot would've made a fatal belly wound; the final one went high.

Janusz brought the lights back up. "Great Gehenna! What a mess! How can you concentrate with all that pop and belch?"

"It's not easy." Floyt broke the pistol again, ejecting the spent shells.

"I should think not. Hobart, we'll all be carrying other firearms, but take my advice: let me give you an energy weapon to carry as your backup. If you need one, it will be more accurate, easier to handle, less prone to stoppage, and quicker to use."

"That's very kind of you. I've practiced enough to use a shockgun if I have to, but trying to pull a beam pistol in a hurry I'd probably end up burning my own foot off. I think I should stick to what I know."

"Mmmm, just the way Alacrity feels about that precious field piece he carts about. Well, how did the ammunition feel?"

"If there's any difference, I can't tell."

"Good. We've got plenty; I would deem it wise that you get in more practice."

"You're quite right; I haven't done this very much."

"I'll reload for you; you can check your targets."

Floyt went out to the target zone. The carnage was less than it might have been, because the simu-soma was designed not to resemble human blood, organs, and bones too closely, to avoid traumatizing shooters. "It's a lot prettier than the real thing," he muttered, looking over his hits and noting where his misses had struck.

"That is exactly what I think to myself whenever I come down here," Janusz said.

Floyt returned, accepting the Webley. Janusz hit the lights; the pop-up started.

Floyt squeezed one off, trying not to flinch. High. The next one was another hit, but it was pure luck. On the third round he squeezed the trigger and the hammer fell on an empty chamber with a *ping*ing click. Floyt had his eyes nearly shut, against a report that didn't come.

Janusz grabbed his arm with one hand, bringing up the lights with the other. "You see, Hobart? *You see?* By the Benign! Don't you think it's impolite to kill someone without at least looking at him?"

"You did that to me on purpose!"

"An old, old trick. Now, do you want to learn how to use that blunderbuss properly? Because your life will depend upon it, and others' lives as well."

"Yes." He looked at the pistol in his hand. "I'd be very grateful if you'd help me."

"Right. Keep your eyes on your target. Concentrate."

He restarted the target sequence. Floyt brought the Webley up in both hands, cocking it. A target popped up and he squeezed the trigger.

The hammer fell on another empty chamber. This time his eyes were wide open.

"Pay attention," Victoria ordered. The two youngest kids in Notch's gang stopped grab-assing, menaced into silence by the others. The whole bunch, two dozen in all, shifted and looked around uncomfortably, fascinated but intimidated by the formal holoviewing amphitheater on the chateau's first surface level.

Victoria and Notch had made them sit down front and center in direct contradiction to the kids' habits and instincts. As it was, the alley runners hunkered their heads down between their shoulders and glanced around every few seconds.

"You ought to change the name from Old Raffles to Fagin's," Alacrity observed, sitting in the last row with Janusz to his right and Floyt to his left.

"These are children who feel they've lost control over their situation if they aren't stealing, intimidating, terrorizing, or otherwise proving their hostility," Janusz replied. "They're just fine for our purposes, as good as any tribal militiamen—better than most, in fact. Stronger killer instincts."

Alacrity and Floyt both nodded knowingly.

"Again," Victoria said firmly. She was standing in a speaker's pulpit off to the left of the proscenium, controlling the displays, conducting the briefing. She was above the kids and dressed in severe, majestic robes, and her lighting had been carefully arranged. She was creating just the impression to keep the boxtowners at least minimally attentive and quiet. The kids had already seen and—after some dangerous experimentation—accepted the chateau's security restrictions, and a form of house arrest.

"Eanna's team here," Victoria went on, "with the other smarts launcher." An arrow-cursor darted through the ghostly projection of the Repository's grounds and structure, to the reverse side of a nearby hilltop.

"Smarts teams fire their missions on my say-so. The smart rounds will be targeted here, here, here, and here." The arrow-cursor flew to show them. The kids watched sullenly, having heard it all before, but didn't dare heckle or act-up. They knew how Notch felt about her; nobody wanted to be slapped down.

"Questions? All right then, that's the last run through; you all know what you have to do. Double-check all weapons and supplies; tomorrow we pull the take. You will get half your money before we move out, the remainder upon completion. Upon returning to your quarters you'll all get a full night's forced sleep and imprinting treatments to make sure no one forgets or fouls up."

Unkempt heads turned toward Notch, who stood behind them, impassive. A few of the kids were shifting in their seats, but they held their places, even more frightened of Notch than of being subjected to sleep programming.

"Why should we?" someone managed to yell without being identified, at least as far as Floyt was concerned.

"Because I say so," Notch decreed, materializing behind one girl and whacking her on the back of her head with his knuckles. None of the others had anything to say. Notch got them all on their feet, Gippo and one or two other young lieutenants taking over, and moving for the secure quarters in the chateau's first subsurface level.

Notch went in Victoria's direction. Janusz was no longer in his seat. Scowling, the outlaw interposed himself, moving into the middle of an aisle. Notch was indecisive for a moment, then flashed his most infuriating smirk and moved off after the rest of his gang. "Sleep tight, Victoria," he called. "See you later."

Alacrity watched him go. "We'll give them a few minutes, then go in and make sure they're bedded down, Alacrity," Janusz said. "Would you mind giving us a hand?"

"Not at all." To Floyt, Alacrity added, "Victoria dosed their last round of coffee and whatnot; they're all gonna be tired in a few minutes. I wonder what'll happen to them after the raid. They'll have money, but—I dunno; what do you do with kids like that? Will they change?"

"I'll tell you what Earthservice did," Floyt said. "They had a thing called Operation Vidocq. Rounded up the roaming troupe that ran the urbanplex corridors. I just missed being picked up myself; I'd dropped out of one."

"What did Earthservice do?"

"Most of them were dispersed, put into labor programs with very carefully indoctrinated peer leaders. The important part was to keep them from forming a children's subculture. Most of them, that is."

"What about the others?" Alacrity asked.

"There are always two or three tough characters like Notch— the incorrigibles. They were culled out, given a shot at rehab. If it didn't work they were brain-changed or put to death. And I'm talking about thousands and thousands of people."

Floyt was looking off where the alley-gangsters had gone. "I can't help thinking if it wasn't for Notch, though, those kids would probably be selling themselves, or dying slowly in a sweatmill, or wasting away in the gutters."

"Well, stop feeling sorry for them. And watch your back."

Alacrity went to help Janusz and Victoria. Floyt went through a meticulously monitored and defended isolation zone and back into the chateau proper. He heard strange sounds that alarmed him at first, the swooping of a whisk-platform, inhuman snorting laughter, and giddy *hoo*-ing.

He stepped into the vast foyer and looked up in amazement. Corva was zooming up, over and around, uttering his Srillan laugh. Floyt gaped up at him as the alien looped over a staircase then dove around beneath it.

When Corva noticed Floyt the antics stopped with comical suddenness. "Oh! Er, hello, Hobart," he said, flustered, letting the whisk-platform descend slowly to the foyer floor. The fur along his snout and between his shaggy ears stood up a little; Floyt wondered if that was the Srillan equivalent of a blush.

"I, ah—I just give way to senseless boisterousness sometimes," Corva explained as the platform touched down. "I don't get to leave the chateau. Sometimes I can't help getting . . . getting . . ." He made tight, furious motions with his hands, searching for the Terranglish word.

"Apt-happy," Floyt supplied, still staring at him. "Shack-wacky. Alacrity calls it bulkhead fever."

"Just so. But don't be alarmed; there's no reason for you to fear for my—my mental equipoise, I assure you."

"Oh, I know; don't worry." Floyt actually wanted to get away, feeling uncomfortable in the creature's presence, especially without Alacrity or any of the others around. He found himself starting to edge away, then realized how rude he must look. "You've, ah, you've only been out of the chateau once or twice since you got here?"

"Offworld, to make some arrangements, yes," Corva said eagerly. It came to Floyt with an inner start that the Srillan was eager to talk.

"It's a tricky business, my getting offworld and back without being seen," Corva went on, "but there are certain connections that only I have. The rest of the time—Old Raffles is my world."

"It must be very wearing."

The Srillan huffed the peculiar laughter. *"Ning-ning-a ning!* Oh, cool and collected is Corva (When can we coax him down from the ceiling!) *A-ning!"*

"Does your uncle know you're here?"

"I think he suspects I'm engaged in work Director Weir began, but Weir was a very private, very security-conscious man, so I doubt my uncle knows anything specific. Weir; I commemorate Weir in my meditations every day. He contacted me and gave me a chance to make this fight against the Camarilla my atonement."

"Atonement—oh, yes; you're a contrition-knight, isn't that the term?"

"Yes. I did a great misdeed—well, failure, really, the kind the young are prone to. But it led to several deaths and a lot of suffering. I'm not so sure I agree with the Doctrines; I'm not so sure any kind of sacrifice or service atones for what's gone before. But I thought at least there would be relief from obsessive memories, and less chance of erring again, which is a fear of mine.

"But this Camarilla situation has me rethinking, Hobart. Perhaps there *is* some cosmic credit and debit system. At any rate, we have a chance to set right a wrong that passes understanding. It will be good for your people and good for mine."

"Then will you be free to go on with your life?"

"I will have to think that out when the time comes. It may be that I have other things yet to do. Many stay contrition-knights their whole lives once they've taken up the relic and sworn."

"I'm sure that all Terrans will be very grateful to you, Corva."
I'm sure that most Terrans would run screaming from the very sight of you, Corva.

"You're most kind, Hobart."

Floyt discovered he hadn't gotten any closer to breaking away. "Well, I'm sorry I interrupted your—your recreation."

"Think nothing of it. It's lonely sport, not much fun after a while."

"Oh." Floyt studied the whisk-platform. "How do you control those things manually?"

"You simply adjust this, like so, you see? Then it will respond to shifts in your body weight and pressure on the handrail, like so, and this control. Would you care to try?"

Now that he'd begun flying, Floyt wanted to pilot anything that came his way. He wanted to try everything. He longed to fly *Astraea Imprimatur* upside down under a bridge span. He got a whisk-platform and followed Corva on a brief training flight, then, with more confidence, soloed around the foyer and up into the epergne's curving corridors.

"That's very good!" Corva snuffled, soaring after him like a mother bird.

Floyt doubled around and dove back into the foyer, orbiting the chandelier. "This is wonderful!"

"Would you care to try something a little more ambitious?"

"Such as?"

"I have a course laid out, up and around through the chateau and back here. My best time so far is just over a minute. Shall we try for fifty-nine seconds?"

"Lead on!"

Off they swooped through Old Raffles like a pair of great bats, laughing and darting.

CHAPTER 21

AND, BY OPPOSING, END THEM

"Okay, Ho, run."

"Where?"

"Through the side of the truck, if you think you're up to it." Alacrity gave one of the straps on Floyt's wargear an extra tug to snug it up. "But I would advise you do it in place."

Floyt began to jog in place; Alacrity listened closely for stray sounds. "Come on, put some life into it. It won't be good for our health if we end up in a blackout situation and you start clanking, drawing fire."

Floyt pumped his knees higher. Alacrity heard nothing, but double-checked an adhesive buckle on the Earther's harness anyway. The Webley's lanyard ring had been silenced with tape.

Floyt stopped. "If we find ourselves in a blackout, shouldn't we be using vision enhancers? Won't the Custodians and their guards?"

"I don't know; nobody's sure how well equipped they are." Alacrity began running in place vigorously. "And Janusz doesn't have an extra pair of enhancers for us; half the ones he's got are malfunctioning. Hear anything?" His pathfinders made very little noise on the truck bed.

"Not from your equipment." Alacrity stopped running.

"Anyway, Alacrity, we won't be in the first attack contingent, so it shouldn't matter, isn't that right?"

"We weren't exactly walking point in the causality harp vault either, remember?"

"You had to bring that up." Floyt sighed and picked up his shockgun, making sure that it, too, was muffled against accidental sounds, its sling silenced, the metal of its slides and buckles taped. It was set for lethal, high-energy fire. It was a two-hander, short and easy to maneuver, with a horizontal U of elbow-crook brace for a butt.

Floyt had the Webley for backup, and Alacrity the Captain's Sidearm; they'd divvied up other ominous equipment as well. The explosives and battlefield medical kits were especially sobering. Floyt had had time for only minimal training, and Alacrity wasn't all that much more experienced.

The dashboard commo beeped and they hurried from the back of the hovertruck to the cab. On the visual link Janusz looked calm, almost casual, with the cab of the ground lorry in the background and Notch's elbow showing at the edge of the picture.

"The smarts fireteams are in place and ready," Janusz said. "Everything is on track."

"Same here," Alacrity replied. "We're monitoring you with the automatics. Let us know when you need us. Good luck, Janusz."

Janusz nearly smiled. "Luck? Yes, that would be nice." He broke the connection. *It's just not right for anybody to have that much sang-froid*, Floyt mused. Alacrity switched over to the remotes still focused on the Repository from the relay tower office.

The Repository was a rambling villa done in the blocky First Breath style known as Bauhaus-NASA. It was a functional, solid sort of place, not really in keeping with the elevated esthetics of the Custodians. The appeal of the place, for them, lay not in the building or grounds, but what was beneath.

As Floyt and Alacrity watched the screen, Janusz's ground lorry moved into view, down the winding driveway. Alacrity felt himself tensing up. "I hope they haven't bitten off more then we can chew.

Floyt nodded. The plan was based on a number of established facts, all having to do with Repository defenses and procedures for destroying Camarilla and other material. What Floyt worried about were the *un*established facts.

"We've got the primary advantage, surprise," Floyt answered. "We'll never have a better chance and, let's face it, it's now or never." Alacrity inclined his head minutely, shifting the shockgun in his lap, eyes fixed on the screen.

Janusz's voice came up over the commo net, this time without visual. "We are approaching the entrance portico. Last check: is everyone prepared?"

Corva and Alacrity acknowledged from their different locations, then Victoria. Heart and Sintilla did the same, and the teams of kids guarding their smarts launchers. Notch's lieutenant, Gippo, chimed in last, from where his van of alley runners waited.

"We carry on, then; it's in the mill." Janusz signed off. His lorry, which had been repainted, trimmed, and decaled to look like a courier vehicle, pulled up by the portico.

"You know, I really don't see how Janusz was planning to pull this off before we came along," Alacrity commented, watching the screen intently. "He would've been going in awfully shorthanded, at least in terms of people he could trust. Here they go; cross your fingers, Ho."

Instead Floyt rubbed the Yuri Gagarin coin, his Wonderment, for luck. Alacrity zoomed the visual pickup in tight as the villa's doors opened and one of the guards stumped out. Confusion made a brief visit to the suety face. Another guard stepped out behind him, and the doors shut tightly after.

They were of a type, like all the guards, just as the Custodians were of a type, clones born and raised to a single purpose, unchanging men from unchanging plasm. The mountainous guards shared thick, stolid, stoic faces, eyes like holes in pink plastic, and a high finish to their skin. They wore charcoal-gray uniforms, shoulder boards that made them seem even wider, and big disruptors in belt holsters. Their long, fine red hair was caught up in convolutions, pinned and wound in braids under glossy, flat-brimmed, electric-blue helmets. Their hands were broad, sausage-fingered.

The guards waited impassively. Notch and Janusz, wearing uniforms of the courier service, swung their doors open all the way. The lorry had pulled up with rear doors to the portico, as if to discharge cargo. Notch and Janusz paused in the cab, as though gathering forms, receipts, or whatever.

Alacrity drew a resolute breath. "Here goes." His hand went to the remote firing controls mounted in the middle of the dashboard. Secondary screens and displays were showing firing data.

The two guards had stepped around the end of the lorry and were waiting for Janusz, the driver, to emerge. He did, but immediately aimed down on them with his shockgun and let the two sumo wrestler types have deadly blasts full in the face. Impossibly, they stayed on their feet, reeling. Notch, who'd slipped around the nose of the lorry, opened fire too.

"Unbelievable!" Floyt breathed. The guards were still on their feet. But under that kind of fire, even creatures like the guards had to go down. They toppled against each other as they fell, like some sort of fleshy landslide. Floyt described it to Alacrity, who was too busy to watch.

He'd activated weapons mounted on the relay tower. They opened up at preselected targets on the villa's grounds. Heavy guns, disguised as antennae and pickups and other equipment until that moment, blazed and belched even as Notch and Janusz scrambled back to the cover of the armored lorry.

A belvedere went up in flames, and the observatory at an upper corner of the Repository as well, both of them camouflaged weapons emplacements. Alacrity remote-aimed at a cabana and decorative features of the villa, as they in turn salvoed at the tower. For people who'd been through no real emergency or battle in the course of their two hundred years in business, the Custodians and their guards had an awfully good response time.

For a few moments it was all crash and wham, villa and tower hammering away at each other. Then, from the lorry, Notch and Janusz touched off their surprise package. It was something Janusz had worked up, combination shaped charge and breaching cannon.

The back doors of the lorry disappeared, disintegrated. A

spearhead of pure light shot through and through the villa's front doors, annihilating everything in its way. It lasted only a second or two, leaving a two-meter-high hole in the armored entranceway, its edges dripping and molten, and peripheral fires that smoked and flickered.

"Hurdle number one," Floyt murmured.

Alacrity, with the advantage of surprise, had wiped out quite a few of the villa's armaments. But the counterfire began to tell; the tower, not heavily fortified to begin with, was being blown to fragments. Still, by the time Alacrity's instruments went dim only two of the Repository's gun positions were still firing.

"Victoria, are you reading this? And Heart? We've got them softened up, at least."

"We all saw," Heart said. "Not bad, boyo."

"Janusz's group is on the move," Corva reported, from the airborne *Astraea Imprimatur*. "I've got them on the lorry's rear pickup; it's still working. They're using shields and they're in the entranceway."

An even dozen of Notch's gang, an assault team armed with riprays, plasma rifles, and other heavy weapons, had been concealed in the compartment behind the cab. Alacrity wasn't patched through to the lorry; he was occupied trying to link to the *Stray*'s own long-range pickups, as the Srillan swung away from his station over the spacefield, creating confusion all around. "What else can you see, Corva? Firefight?"

"Nothing clear, Alacrity, and there's no sound, but there must be, yes. Janusz should be all right for now, though; the front-door guard station was right in the path of the breaching beam. All the assault team has to do is dig in and hold for a while."

"And pray for smoke signals," Floyt muttered.

"Pray hard, for green smoke signals," Alacrity agreed.

"Are all crews ready at the smart ordnance?" Victoria sang out.

"You want us to fire, you say so. No trouble," Gippo responded. Notch's lieutenant sounded like he didn't really care one way or the other.

Alacrity raised his voice over the commo net. "Come on,

come on! Doesn't anybody see smoke yet? Keep your eyes on the chimneys!"

Janusz's voice came up just then. "We're well deployed; we control the whole entranceway. No resistance yet, but we're staying at phase-point one. Any smoke yet?"

"We're waiting," Victoria said.

The Repository's underground areas were thoroughly sealed off from its upper structures. Those below, where the primary information cache was, would be debating the question of destroying sensitive material, but only tentatively; the encroachment wasn't critical yet. The destruction of lesser materials might begin, as a precautionary measure, but not obliteration of the Camarilla evidence.

Exactly when the Custodians would make their decisions, no one knew. The raiders wanted to push things to the point where the clones would begin destroying lesser data without forcing them to destroy everything. Janusz and his group had spent several years analyzing the attack. Their big piece of luck had been in obtaining an old Custodian destruct manual. Their main worry was that it would lead them into error; if it had been superceded by something very different, the plan was ruined.

"Corva, Heart—d'you have those last emplacements marked?"

"Ready to go, Alacrity."

"Affirmative, Bright Eyes!"

Alacrity spent a sweaty fifteen seconds glaring into screens and readouts. "We're getting counterattack activity," Janusz said. "Our crew-served weapons are well in place, but we will eventually have to either fall back or advance. Is there still no smoke?"

"Don't you think we'd have told you?" Alacrity countered. "Listen, this is no good. We're coming to get you out. You'll have guard reinforcements swarming on you soon."

"Remain where you are!" Janusz snapped. "We're all right for now." There was a loud explosion in the near background. Alacrity looked at Floyt, who looked back.

"We can't just leave him in there, Ho."

"No, I don't suppose we can." Floyt brought his shockgun around; Alacrity fired up the truck.

Just then they heard Corva's voice. "There! Smoke! I mark smoke from one, two—all four chimneys!"

"What color?" Sintilla demanded. "Corva, *what color*?"

"It's green! It's ours! Into motion, everyone! Green smoke!"

Alacrity was already moving. He yanked the hovertruck through a tight turn and bore down on a hillock nearby. Two of Notch's kids were there, a boy and girl, maybe fifteen or so, poised by a multibarreled launcher, making final adjustments. Floyt hit the release for the truck's side door, which slid open.

The truck threw up dirt and debris as it slid to a halt side-on. "Start the timer and get in!" Floyt hollered. The kids were into the truck like squirrels, clinging to their flopping bandoliers and equipment. Alacrity wristed the accelerator, twisting the steering grips. The hovertruck whined off over the hillock in a storm of dust.

"Time for you to come down to lower altitude, where you're less of a target, Corva," Floyt was saying. The Srillan rogered.

Alacrity tore along an accessway road and nearly hit a hoghoss-drawn wagon that was racing for Parish Below. There weren't many disturbances in Parish Above, but when there was one, the lower orders knew it was time to get out of the way.

Floyt hadn't had time to worry about any of the other estates becoming involved. Now he thought to, as Alacrity careened along at neck level, staying off the Repository's detectors. "What about the other mansions? What about the tribes?"

"Nothing yet, true to form," Victoria reported from the *Stray*'s spaceboat, stationed between Parish Above and Parish Below. "Now, if things will only stay that way." As long as the conflict didn't spill into the other estates or the much more distant tribal zones, theoretically, it remained a private affair.

"No sign of problems," Corva confirmed. "Shall I blow out the accessways?"

"No need," Alacrity decided. "Besides, it might start trouble." He slewed through a small grove, and halted next to the other smarts team. They hopped in too. Floyt closed the side door and the truck howled away.

"Our rounds are firing," the girl from the first team said twenty-five seconds after the smoke had first been reported. Alacrity poured on speed, not wanting to be caught anywhere near the launchers.

"Heart, where are you? Hit those last two gun positions, can you? Soften the place up just a little more, not too much. I think I got all the villa's external pickups, so they won't know where it's coming from."

"I read. I'll be in right after the airbursts."

The second launchers' smart ordnance started flying overhead just then. The truck swooped along, as Alacrity and Floyt waited to hear the report.

"Who are those other people on the net?" one of the alley runners in the back wanted to know. "You didn't tell us about them."

"*Shh!*" Alacrity said. "Let me drive, will you? Just a little change of plans, that's all."

"Airbursts, on target," Victoria reported from the *Stray*'s spaceboat. "Counterfire coming from the villa, hidden launch tubes. Keep low!"

Alacrity was doing just that as incoming rounds shrieked overhead, bound for the smarts launchers—too late. The special ordnance was already either at target or in the air. To the raiders' great relief, there'd been no midair intercept.

Heart reported, "The sealant blankets are deploying and settling, on target. All chimneys are well layered."

Alacrity heeled the truck around a corner at near ground level and saw it was true. The special rounds had dispersed airburst aerosols that congealed into vast translucent sheets. They settled in layer upon layer over the Repository, centered on four big chimneys from which the green smoke plumed.

The most chancey part of the operation had paid off. The Custodians were destroying their lesser materials—in-house records and codes, routine traffic copies, personal data and private files, and so forth. Now, if they would hold off on doing away with the Camarilla evidence, for even a little while . . .

"Still nothing from the other estates, except that they're on alert," Victoria said. That would be in keeping with the etiquette of Parish Above; the place was an enclave of independent fortresses, not a mutual defense community.

"Same at the spacefield and the tribal zones," Corva added. "No one's sure what's happening, so they're all keeping out of it."

"Terrific town; sensible people," Alacrity proclaimed.

"We're getting a strong counterattack here," Janusz said. "We could use some assistance."

"Almost there," Floyt replied as Alacrity rounded the last corner to stop near the villa's main gates. They were closed, and an energy curtain rose from the top of the fence. The raiders had expected it. "Victoria!" Floyt yelled.

"First attack run coming now," she answered at once. The spaceboat came flashing down, releasing missles at the two undamaged household emplacements, pounding away at the gates. The gates flew straight up in the air, amid secondary explosions from the villa's last gun turrets. Green smoke could be seen backing up under the draped and clinging chemical sheets.

Alacrity was through the fence, weaving across the rust-red lawn, decelerating. "Janusz, what's your situation?" Corva asked. "Should I bring in the *Stray* now?"

"No!" The others could hear yells and tumult and an intense firefight in the background. "We don't want them panicking down below and going to total destruct mode. Stand off until I give the word, but come quickly then. Alacrity, where are you? Things are becoming rather brisk here."

"Right with you," Alacrity said as the truck slowed to a halt. He'd heard just the slightest tinge of apprehension in Janusz's voice; it put him even further on edge. *Brisk!*

"Be careful dealing with the guards," Janusz warned. "They're hard to knock down and harder to keep that way."

"Everybody got that?" Alacrity asked. Floyt nodded; Notch's kids simply stared at him. "That's it, then. Don't forget that special equipment. Pile out."

The group came tumbling out of the truck and headed for the portico, laying down covering fire, coordinating their shots with their steps, aiming for the windows and around the grounds.

They, too, were armed with heavy assault weapons. The kids moved very well and kept out of one another's line of fire, doing as well as most infantry Alacrity had ever seen at work. They carried equipment for the next phase of the raid.

At the portico, the group discovered the bodies of the two guards Janusz and Notch had originally downed. They were slumped over three of the alley runners in the silent aftermath of savage hand-to-hand and a close-quarters firefight. The kids had been nearly dismembered, the guards shot to ribbons.

Alacrity kept his team moving through the smoke and dust, into the gloaming within the entranceway. They kept to cover and moved in frantic dashes. The villa's main lighting system had been knocked out; emergency glow-plates lit the place dimly.

Janusz, Notch, and the surviving members of their team were holding the entranceway area with heavy weapons, hosing their guns back and forth, going through ammunition and power packs prodigally. The four kids who'd come with Alacrity and Floyt moved to reinforce their fellows, breaking out more ammunition. Their firing positions commanded the various stairways and hallways leading into the big entrance area. The bodies of ten guards were in sight, all of them as ruthlessly blasted apart as the ones outside.

"They've dug in just out of range; their last counterattack almost made it," Janusz said, reloading his scatterbeam pistol. "Problem is, shockguns knock them down, but don't always keep them there. They take incredible damage and still keep coming at you. I don't think they're entirely human."

Alacrity looked around thoughtfully, then tossed his shockgun aside, bringing out the Captain's Sidearm. Janusz was looking at a comint device of some kind that he carried in an armored case attached to a lanyard around his neck.

"I was reading a lot of traffic from the underground levels a short while ago," he said, "between the Custodians and the guards. Encrypted, of course. Now there's nothing from underground and the surface units can't make contact. I think it's time."

Alacrity nodded emphatically. "Very well," Janusz said over

his comset. "*Astraea Imprimatur*, we're ready for you. Corva, get to it!"

"What's '*Straya 'Primatur*'?" Notch piped up suspiciously. "And who's Corva? And those others I heard before?"

"Not to get excited, kid," Alacrity said. "Minor change in plans. But everything goes just the way we practiced."

Notch looked from one to another of the three men. "This better not be a double cross."

"You've got a clear field, *Stray*," Heart reported.

"Coming in now," Corva said tersely.

"Everyone into your protective masks," Janusz ordered. "And get down. We're not sure what we'll be facing once that subsurface area is breached—watch out!"

Then he was shooting and shooting with pistols in both hands. Alacrity dragged Floyt to cover, booming away with his father's gun as a knot of guards, crouched behind a portable vortex cannon mounted on a big, thick splash shield, charged at them from a side corridor.

The raiders' shots bounced off the splash shield, even fire from the heavy weapons. The advance continued, slowed only by the weight of the cannon. Alacrity expected to be killed until he saw that the gun itself had been damaged and couldn't fire. Their bulk and their burden notwithstanding, the guards ran with impressive speed.

"Get down!" Notch yelled, and everyone ducked for shelter, covering their heads. Notch pitched something into the corridor, then hit the floor too, hands over his ears. Whatever he'd thrown bounced under the feet of the running guards, and behind them.

Seconds later the corridor was an infernal whirlwind of flying bodies and parts of bodies, twisted metal and explosive forces that threatened to crush them all, implode eardrums, and drive them back through the entrance breach like leaves.

Corva's voice brought them around. "Instruments say I'm right over the target point. Activating the drill now."

"Everyone stay down and get your masks on," Janusz called.

He didn't have to say it a third time. *Astraea Imprimatur* hovered over the Repository for the next critical step in the raid.

The *Stray* had been lent to Janusz's group not only because she was fast, well armed, and versatile, but because she'd done planetary survey: she mounted core-drilling equipment.

From a bay in the starship's underbelly, a multiaperture beam array descended, then activated. Mingled beams pulsed and strobed, or circled as individual projectors in the array whirled. The rays bored and cut.

Abruptly the corridor ceiling was holed by a spiraling cascade of light, unendurably bright. The energy drillbit descended on its tractor beam. At max aperture, it made a hole just over a meter in diameter through anything it encountered.

Corva's attention was all on the drilling operation, the *Stray* holding her place exactly. Heart and Sintilla, in the *Harpy*, and Victoria, in the other spaceboat, flew cover. Incandescent gases and debris gushed and belched as the boring bit into the sandwiched layers of special armor that protected the villa's subsurface levels—the ones that opened into abandoned sections of old-time Parish Within.

With a final blast of light and pressure release, the coredrill was through. Corva shut it off at once and retracted the drillbit. Half the villa was in flames.

"Bring the hoisting tackle. Kindly forget nothing!" Janusz called. They gathered up the stuff they'd brought and struggled off after him. Household units were attacking the flames, and Corva dropped four pods of firefighting chemicals on the villa's burning roof, extinguishing it.

The raiders ran along the corridor past the bodies of several guards. Floyt became watchful; more of the behemoths might lurk in the smoke and ruin. *Feel sorry for them later.*

The raiders found the drillhole, where molten flooring was quickly hardening under the steady rain from the extinguishing system. A little green smoke briefly curled above the hole, then stopped. While several of the alley runners set up a new perimeter, Alacrity, Janusz, and Notch assembled the hoisting tackle and set up its frame over the hole.

There was thunder from outside: *Astraea Imprimatur* landing on the lawn, ready to take on the evidence as soon as it was found. Gippo showed up with the last team of alley runners.

Harpy and the *Stray*'s boat made passes overhead. Notch glanced at the *Stray* every so often, looking troubled.

Alacrity checked his proteus. They were well ahead of schedule, but no one could tell what the timetable would be from then on. "We must move vigorously," Janusz announced, a little hard to understand through his protective mask. "A delay now might be disastrous."

He made sure his equipment was secure, then swung himself out onto the hoisting line, to rappel down. A moment later he called up, "Come ahead; it's perhaps ten meters' descent. Make sure your masks are in place; the gas is very thick down here."

Alacrity lowered himself away. Floyt was next, down into the swirling green smoke. He wondered why almost none of it escaped to the upper levels. *Thermocline factor? Sealing field?*

Floyt went down awkwardly and inexpertly, almost as badly as his very first practice drill off a staircase in Old Raffles. At last his feet touched down, and he found himself standing in an eerie but breathtaking underground world.

The Repository incorporated a part of Parish Within, the old subsurface district formerly used by the aristocracy. The three stood in a groined corridor that, despite the drifting knock-out smoke, had the feel of a chapel. There were marbilized walls in colors Floyt had never seen in stone before, and every sort of texture. Decorative flourishes were mounted with gems few of whose names he knew: moon roundels; Athena's Eyes; ice lenses. Floyt half expected to hear organ music or Gregorian chants.

"Notch, make certain your people keep guard on the line, and have one or two more come down to watch at this end," Janusz said. After Notch did that, he and the three men set off, shining handspots this way and that, keeping spread out, guns leveled. The passageways were filled with alcoves and niches; it didn't take Floyt long to see that those were furnished with artworks from Terra, things long thought destroyed in the Human-Srillan War.

He shined his spot into a little meditation grotto where fountains trickled and soft lights played in the gloom. He halted dead, and Alacrity almost bumped into him.

The sculpture was as Michelangelo had shaped it centuries before, Mary seeming almost out of proportion, as big as her crucified son.

"They said the Pietà was destroyed when Rome was," Floyt said, unable to look away or move. *Oh, the painful, painful beauty.*

Alacrity gave him a gentle push. "We can't stop."

They went on, around corners and bends, Alacrity marking the way with a sprayer loaded with luminescent dye. Floyt saw Flemish masterpieces, Etruscan terra-cotta figures, Tut's burial mask, and much more. "No wonder they never felt any need to go outside."

Alacrity tried a commo check. "No good; something down here's interfering. I can't even get the guards at the hoist."

They passed recesses and alcoves intended for solitude; all around them was the pick of Earth's greatest treasures, and works from a lot of other planets beside. Why the very sight of those things hadn't turned the Custodians against the Camarilla, Floyt couldn't imagine.

They began encountering the bodies of Custodians, stretched out on the floor and over furniture. Many were near fireplaces and burn drums and incendiary bays. There were batches of lesser classified materials that the Custodians had been destroying after the initial invasion of the villa.

Most such documents had been generated on Blackguard/Finders-Keepers, using paper or paper analogs, and with supplies of ink, dye, and such from Parish Ink and Paper. Pieces were still smoldering in the burn drums under backed-up vent tubes . . . giving off green smoke and the gas that had knocked out the Custodians.

"You weren't kidding about that stuff, Janusz; just look: you can see how fast it worked," Alacrity said.

"It would likely have been effective even without our blocking the chimneys; it disperses almost instantly. But let's keep going; we have to get to the main cache before—"

There was an immense rumbling, a quaking of the ground; they danced for footing. "Sounded like a big explosion, or heavy weapons," Alacrity said. They looked at one another.

"Whatever it is, the others can handle it," Janusz decided. "We'll carry on."

They doubletimed then, past more of the side ways and nooks, the stolen masterpieces, and more of the unconscious Custodians.

They came to a T at the end of the corridor. "Could the place we're looking for be on a lower level or something?" Floyt asked. Janusz shook his head, reading another instrument.

"Then it's one way or the other," Notch said. "Why don't we—"

Alacrity yelled, "Look out!" at the same moment Janusz cried, "Stand aside!" Both shoved Floyt out of their way; Notch brought his gun up.

The guard loomed slowly out of the dimness, tottering, sausage-fingers clawing and curling in the air. He didn't seem to know where he was or what he was doing, so disoriented that he'd come at his enemies barehanded.

Floyt brought his shockgun up too, bracing the U in the crook of his elbow. The guard bucked and blackened to the shots from Notch's plasma chopper, Janusz's scatterbeams, and Alacrity's pistol. Floyt couldn't tell if the shockgun had any effect or not.

The guard was jarred and twirled around, legs and arms crumbling. But when the obscene pirouette was done and he was on the corridor floor, when they'd stopped firing, the guard tried to come on again, scrambling at the floor with burnt stumps of fingers. Alacrity shouldered the others aside, took careful aim with both hands, and delivered the *coup de grâce*.

"Great Creator, what does it take to stop them?" Floyt whispered.

"He was probably the last," Alacrity said. "He was so wheezed up, he didn't even know where he was or what he was doing."

"He knew enough to want to get his paws on us," Janusz countered. "We must be cautious. There isn't much time, and so we'll have to divide forces. Alacrity, you and Hobart down that way if you will; Notch, you'll accompany me, please."

As they went off together, Alacrity said, "Uh, Ho . . ." and motioned to the shockgun. Floyt shouldered it and drew the Webley, thumbing the hammer back.

"If you see anybody—*anybody*—spark 'im," Alacrity said. "If it helps, remember what these people have helped do to your world."

Floyt said nothing. They proceeded through the gloom, shining spots around them. That went on for what Floyt's proteus reported to be only a short time, but it felt like eternity. Then they came to a pair of doors.

They were high and reticulated, double doors with carved meanders. There were heavy locks on them, and marks on the locks. Alacrity looked around uneasily but saw no one.

"Get back." He slapped charges onto it and stroked the timers. Floyt scurried into the shelter of a side grotto and Alacrity followed him. They both ducked and covered their ears.

The concussion almost knocked them silly even so, and the corridor was like an oven. They shook their ringing heads and went to see what they'd come up with.

The doors were hanging from their hinges. They went into the room beyond with weapons up and heeled to a stop, back to back, pointing all around, angling guns and handspots everywhere. They were shaken and spooked, and just beginning to realize they'd found what they'd come for.

"Well, I'll be—"

"Holy—"

There were ordered shelves and rotating racks of data, every shape and size and format Floyt could think of, in a chamber perhaps four times the size of Floyt's apt living room. Floyt stood up straight, reached out to a rack, and extracted a folder. He tucked the Webley under his arm and flipped through it.

"Alacrity, do you see this? Terran fiber paper. And two-dee photographs. And old-style molecular memory strands."

Alacrity began rummaging too. He held up a couple of spools. "Induction-copy records, old ones. Whatever's on them, somebody got his brain sucked out like through a straw and had it set down. And headboarder testimony. I don't think there's any way to fake these things. This is it, m'friend: your Terran Inheritance."

Floyt started pouring through more of the stuff while Alacrity tried his comset. Floyt scanned 3-Ds and notarized documents authenticated by complex chemical coding, and official depositions and oaths of allegiance that the Custodians had required of each new member of the Camarilla who'd come into it over the years.

"I'm not getting anything," Alacrity said. "I'm gonna run get Janusz and Notch, and leave signs for the kids when they follow along. You start figuring out which of this mess is the most important, okay?" He glanced at his proteus again. "We're right up against the deadline; we're over it. And I didn't like that explosion before." He stopped as he was about to leave. "Oh, and don't shoot me by mistake when I come back, all right? Thanks."

He left, and Floyt went back to the evidence, examining it worriedly. But his misgivings began to fall away. Any one or even several of the pieces of evidence might be subject to dispute, but taken as a whole, the cache was overwhelming, as close to conclusive as it was possible to come. Floyt disencumbered himself of his shockgun and began culling out the best.

He discovered one more Custodian, collapsed beside a burn drum, out cold. Near him was a complicated instrument panel. Floyt examined it for a few moments, using knowledge acquired at the complex, and concluded that he'd found the Custodians' main destruct mechanism. He dragged the Custodian away from it just to be safe. It was then he heard the scrape of a shoe behind him.

He wasn't the same man who'd left Earth, and even that Hobart Floyt hadn't been a slug. He lunged sideways and the butt of the shockgun only struck him a grazing blow; his attacker couldn't figure out how to release its safety, or Floyt would've been down for good. The weapon swung again; Floyt, rolling from it, trying to protect his head, avoided most of the impact but still saw whirling lights. He hunched into the shelter of a shelf stack, bringing his feet and free hand up to protect himself, trying for his revolver at the same time.

The boy was another, younger version of the Custodians, not even of age yet, by most reckonings. IIis lower face was swathed in layers of some shiny fabric, taped tight, a make-do filter mask of some kind that obviously sufficed. Floyt wondered for an instant if the boy was in some sealed-off area of the catacombs when the burning started. Obviously he didn't know the entry code to the cache; he'd tried to force the lock and it didn't work, then Floyt and Alacrity showed up to blow the doors.

The boy plainly knew the destruct code, though; he'd dropped the shockgun and was working away at the panel. It was alive with flashing symbols.

Floyt sat up, wobbling, drawing back the hammer of the Webley, trying to focus his eyes. "Stop . . . stop . . ."

The boy ignored him; he aimed, using both hands. "Son, don't make me shoot you."

The boy gave him a quick, hating glare, and mocked him with the muffled word "*Son.*" Then he was back at work, racing to blow the evidence and the cache and the whole underground area to nothingness.

Floyt thought hard, almost pulling the trigger. But the boy was only ten or so, younger than the youngest of the alley runners.

Floyt threw the pistol at the boy, hard, then dove for his shockgun, yanking back the charge level from lethal to stun. The instrument panel was glowing and beeping, ready for an ultimate command. The revolver missed the boy but cracked the panel and made him flinch from it. Floyt had the shockgun up, but the last Custodian's finger was going for a touchpad . . .

The second tremor-detonation shook the corridors just as Alacrity reached the other end of the T's crossarm, this time a more violent quaking, though the tunnel corridor showed no cracks. He agonized for a moment, then went on with what he was doing.

At the other extreme of the cross corridor there was no cache. Instead Alacrity came out onto a balcony looking down into a domed treasure chamber.

The dome, a meter thick, was of some transparent stuff. The treasure was more art from many worlds, set out for viewing and enjoying, and piratical heaps of conventional riches:

gemstones and ingots and bars, crafted pieces, bolts of exotic fabrics. Down on the dome's floor, Alacrity saw without being able to hear, Janusz and Notch were in a hostile tableau, yelling at one another. Victoria was with them. All three wore protective masks.

Alacrity tried the door of the place, a big servo-operated valve of the same transparent stuff, but it wouldn't open. He pounded on it with his fist, barely evoking a sound from it. He was about to search around for the lock signal when the tableau broke.

Janusz and Notch had been squared off, hands close to their weapons. Victoria reached out and grabbed Janusz's shoulder, swinging him toward her, apparently hollering at him. Notch seemed about to pull a weapon, but hesitated; Alacrity could see that Victoria was right in his line of fire.

Alacrity had pulled his own gun, but dismissed the idea of trying to shoot through the dome. Whatever the transparent substance was, it would very likely send the blast back into his face.

Though they were masked, Alacrity thought Janusz and Victoria were arguing bitterly. She yanked his arm, seeming to shout something, and he lost that icy control of his. Janusz pulled free, pushing her away. Victoria went off balance and fell against a pedastel, overturning a statuette that crashed to the floor and shattered.

Notch leapt like an angry devil, swinging his doubled fists down across the back of Janusz's head and neck. Janusz went down and Notch kicked him, drawing a pistol and bringing it to bear.

Alacrity was howling, pounding on the dome with the butt of his pistol, making no sound that penetrated. He expected to see Janusz shot to bits. But Notch stopped instead and looked to Victoria, who was gesturing weakly from where she lay on the floor. The way Alacrity read the dumb-show, she'd been injured—her head, likely.

Notch wavered for second. Victoria said something else, and the alley runner let Janusz be, ran to kneel by her.

As Alacrity looked on, she stroked Notch's cheek—then moved the barrel of his weapon aside as he froze, the muzzle of her pistol under his chin. Janusz was coming back to his senses, shaking his head. He saw Victoria gently disarming Notch, apparently talking calmingly to him. The gang leader was slowly, unwillingly giving up his hold on the gun.

Janusz gathered himself. Alacrity saw Victoria take notice and snap an aside at him, probably an order to stay out of it. But Janusz, eyes wild behind his eyepieces, launched himself, moving very fast. Notch sensed it, ignored Victoria's pistol and began to turn, bringing up his own.

Janusz hit him with a body block, knocking them both away from the woman. As Notch went down he was trying to draw a bead on Janusz, but Janusz drew as he fell, hitting Notch once while he was in the air and again from a semiprone position. The scatterbeams charred Notch's body and set his clothing aflame in hideous swaths. Notch's pistol discharged into the air.

Janusz scrambled up to regard his kill. By then Victoria was ranting at him, her sights fixed on his back. Janusz pivoted on her with his own weapon raised; their eyes met over gun barrels.

Alacrity had backed away from the door of the dome, to shoot at it at an angle. It was dangerously close range; he held the Captain's sidearm extended as far as he could, turning away a little and shielding his face with his left forearm and hand. He fired twice, the pistol's handshield protecting his gunhand, his clothing and hair warming, exposed skin seared by the backwash. The sounds battered him.

He hadn't even singed the dome.

He gaped, disbelieving, then looked inside. Victoria and Janusz had noticed him. They looked back to one another and slowly lowered their weapons.

Fortunately, Alacrity hadn't damaged the door mechanism. When the two opened it from inside, he said, "What happened? What's wrong with you two?"

"Notch wanted it all," Janusz said in monotone.

"Never mind that now," Victoria said. "Alacrity, did you find the evidence?"

"Oh, did we! Ho's pulling it together now. Did you feel those tremors? What's going on?" As the words tumbled out of him, he was chewing over what he'd seen, debating whether is was safe to put his own gun away. The truce between Janusz and Victoria had been pushed to the breaking point.

"A spaceship showed up outside after you went below," Victoria told him. "It came juicing over the hills and attacked my boat, made a hit on the first pass."

"What ship? From where?"

She shook her head. "We don't know. Whoever it was had overlooked the *Harpy* and the *Stray*, though, at least on that first run. Corva and Heart and Tilla gave it a couple of good volleys and went off after it. I managed to land on the grounds, but the spaceboat's useless now. The others were going to come back once they've made sure there's no more danger. We have to wrap things up quickly."

"It is my belief that Notch was in on this somehow," Janusz added. "He seemed to be expecting something, and he was upset by the appearance of *Astraea Imprimatur* and the *Harpy*. But he made his play nonetheless."

Victoria glowered at him, but didn't contradict him. Alacrity shook himself. "Victoria, Ho's in the evidence cache, at the opposite end of this corridor. Janusz, I think we'd better hide what's left of Notch." The body was still sending up clouds of smoke; he was glad he was wearing a mask.

Janusz nodded. "I'm sorry for what happened," he told Victoria. "The boy left me no choice."

She inspected him coldly. "You brought it on. You welcomed it. I was right about you from the start."

Notch's alley gangsters bought the story of their leader's having been killed by fire from a dying guard. They'd already learned how tough the clones were to kill. More, they were tense and anxious to be away, shaken by the battle. Loyalty to Notch suddenly ran a distant third behind getting the wealth they'd been promised and escaping the combat zone before something else happened. The raid was only thirty-two minutes old.

The alley runners had assembled cargo-moving equipment, loading boxes, and cases onto surface-effect handtrucks and pallet jacks. Floyt set aside his preoccupation and turned from the body of the young Custodian who'd almost entered the destruct code. There was a numb satisfaction that he'd managed to stop the boy with the shockgun rather than a bullet. But it had been so close, so close. Floyt was still sweating at the gamble he'd taken, wondering if he'd ever have the nerve to do a thing like that again.

He sorted through material that had kept the Camarilla in uneasy equilibrium for two centuries. "This appears to be an original compact or agreement of the first Camarillans," he said, showing Alacrity a document. "It's printed on natural Spican tissue-parchment; aged in a way that, I think, it would be impossible to fake."

Teams of alley runners were hauling the strange booty back to the drillhole. The adults pitched in, to hasten things. Floyt showed Alacrity a tube of memory rolls. "There's more, see? Centuries' worth. We've got all the evidence we need."

"But not all the time," Janusz interrupted, throwing another case of data onto a pallet. They'd stripped the room in a matter of minutes; the cache of primary data was smaller than many personal libraries Alacrity had seen. "Move quickly!" Janusz finished.

Jumpily eager kids took that as the signal to get going to the drillhole with the pallet jack. Off they rushed, leaving Floyt, Alacrity, Janusz, and Victoria alone in the denuded room. Only a few boxes were left, and some odds and ends, along with the unconscious Custodian boy and his elder.

"We should make a last sweep through the place," Floyt said dubiously. "There might be other caches."

"We've got what we came for," Alacrity stated. "This *had* to be it. If we don't get moving right now those kids are liable to take off for the skyline without us, or heist the evidence with the notion they can sell it off or something."

They took up the few remaining containers and loaded them with the last of the evidence. Alacrity found some current read-files, folders of Parish Ink and Paper material rather than primary evidence, but he tucked them into a box anyway, on general principles. They set off, lugging the boxes.

At the intersection of the T, they came across two abandoned pallet hacks, the one that had just left the cache and another, empty one that had been returning for a last load. All four adults had their weapons out, alert to danger, but saw and heard no signs of violence.

There was a sound to one side, in the direction of the treasure room. Gun barrels swung that way and one of Notch's kids, one of the ones who'd rushed off with the last load, came at them out of the drifting knockout smoke. She was holding gems and small bars of natural gold. Her eyes were huge behind the eyepieces of her mask.

"Look! Look at what Gippo found! There's a whole room of it back there!"

Janusz said, "We have no time for that now. You can all come back later if you wish, but you have a job to do first."

He went to take the plunder away from her, but she skittered back, dropping finger-size gold bars to produce her gun. "Not likely, old meat! Your highbreeds do what you want with your bloody trashpaper; we're working for ourselves now. And we're taking the moving rigs."

Janusz's posture said he was considering summary action but, perhaps with Notch's death in mind, he relaxed. "You may take the empty one. The other is ours."

She grabbed the control handle and steered it off to the treasure room, the pallet jack floating along behind her easily. Alacrity picked up one of the little gold bars, looked it over thoughtfully, and put it in his pocket. The four crowded everything onto the other jack. "You just can't find reliable help anymore," Alacrity observed.

"We really have no more need of them, if it comes to that," Victoria said. "What I'm worried about is that other ship."

"And the other estates getting involved, and the tribes, and who knows who else," Floyt extended the list.

They barged along, holding the precariously balanced material in place, Alacrity and Janusz doing the main pushing and pulling. Floyt and Victoria assisted, doing convoy duty and doubling back every now and again to shag some item or other that had fallen off the pile.

When they reached the drillhole, no one else was around. Handtrucks and other pallet jacks had been abandoned in the preliminary unloading stages. It was quiet, and the smoke seemed to be thinning.

"Gold rush madness," Alacrity said. "They're probably all back scrabbling around in the treasure room. This is a good time to exfiltrate. Those kids'll have more money than they can use anyway; it's not like we're stiffing them."

He went to the power lift the alley runners had set up. It was a circular platform, narrow diameter, attached to the hoist cable. Taking a box of evidence with him, he got on.

"I'll make sure everything's okay, then you can send up the rest. I'll tap the hole three times with this." He unlimbered his gun then hit a switch on a cable fitting and was hauled upward, passing through the green smoke, up into clear air. He still wondered why the smoke was not escaping through the drill-hole.

The upper level was empty too. He shoved the box of data aside onto the floor as soon as he came chest-level with it, scanning quickly in all directions. Outside a nearby window he could see that the blankets of sealant had been burned and rent by blasts, so that the remains were only shreds in the wind. The upper level was free of the gas.

He holstered his gun and dipped his head as he stripped off the sweaty, smelly mask, wondering if he'd be able to contact the *Harpy* or *Stray* now. He no sooner shucked the mask than he felt a gun at his temple, another at his back, and hands grabbing his shoulders, tangling in his hair to hold him immobile, clapping over his mouth to silence him. He was disarmed.

Something sharp and cold traced along his cheek, drawing blood, as he was held fast. "Hello, baby." It moved into his angle of vision, a jeweled metal fingernail sheath.

Oh, fuck! he tried to say, but it came out muffled.

There were *Lamia* crewpeople around the drillhole, and Constance had a thermobeam handgun close by his head. She was wearing her regatta outfit. "Who else is down there?"

The hands came away from his face, a little. "Snow White and the Brotherhood of Mineworkers," he said. So, the *Lamia* had been a diversion, to draw away the *Harpy* and *Stray* while this landing party sneaked in.

She tapped him hard on the bridge of the nose with her gun barrel, while other hands rifled his pockets. "What are you after, down there?"

"I'm telling you, there's enough here for everybody. Stay calm, Constance; you can have as much as you want."

"There *isn't* that much." Someone had found the finger-bar of gold and handed it to her. "So, this is it? How much more is there? Who else is down there?"

"If you'd be reasonable for a second, we can make a deal here."

One of her goons gave him a clout on the ear. "I knew you and the others hadn't left. Those cowards at the compounds— all they wanted to do was save their precious skins. I want your ass, and that little worm Floyt's," she said with a delicate *frisson* of anticipation. "It would take plenty to buy you out now, cutie."

There was still no activity below, Alacrity not yet having given the all's-clear. *Lamia* crewmembers covered the drillhole. Alacrity doubted those below had heard anything going on above through the narrow hole.

Constance gave his box of evidence a kick, sending it sliding. "And I don't mean a pile of memorabilia!" She flicked the thermobeam at it offhandedly. A reel of tape ran molten.

Alacrity drew a deep breath, looking at the box, thinking most vividly about one of Floyt's Earth stories. *Don't throw me in that briar patch!*

"Hey, watch it!" he yelped, trying to break loose. "Leave that stuff alone; it's important! You don't underst—"

Somebody hit him hard on the side of the neck and he rocked. "I can do whatever I want," she warned archly. "Now tell me what I want to know, or I'll do this—" She lit up a roll of memory lozenges with the beamer. "Or this—" A folder flared up, the wrong one, curling into ash and sending up gray flakes. Alacrity wondered if honest people had this kind of problem.

"Or this," said Constance as she fired at a current read-file. The file went *woof*! and green smoke billowed. Alacrity struggled—to distract them, not because he thought he could break free. Someone threatened to crush his windpipe with a forearm. He quieted.

The gas spread even faster than he'd hoped. Constance had a peculiar look on her face as she tried to keep her pistol aimed at him. The grips on him were already loosening, and he felt his head spin.

"This is your last chance to . . . to . . ." she said, trying to recall what she'd started to say. "Your last chance . . ."

Her eyes grew enormous as it came to her that she'd been popped. She tried to press her thumb down on the firing stud of her gun, its muzzle wavering off target so that her groggy crewpeople yowled and ducked, letting go of Alacrity. He heard bodies thumping to the floor as the smoke thickened and could himself barely stay on his feet.

Constance never got off a round. He had the satisfaction of seeing her go down first; head emptied of thought, he dropped.

After a long, drifty time, Alacrity came around for a moment. His head was banging, his stomach was rebelling, and even his eyeballs hurt. He was looking up at the frescoes in *Astraea Imprimatur*'s salon. "*Uhch!* Did we win?"

His head was in the Nonpareil's lap. "We did what we set out to do," she said. "I think that qualifies as a win."

Sintilla bent close. "We've got all the evidence, except for what Constance destroyed. Janusz and Corva and Victoria are getting us into Hawking now."

Floyt moved into his line of vision too. The Earther had handfuls of documents and data. "I think we also finalized accounts with Constance, Alacrity. When we left, Notch's gang was in control of things. The *Lamia*'s gone for good. I wouldn't be surprised if Constance ends up scrubbing floors for the kids. Oh, and you'd be surprised how fast word gets around in Parish; when we took our leave, there were mobs from Tombville looting Old Raffles and breaking into the Repository."

"Well, nobody needs a little plunder worse than they do."

He tried to move, then inhaled with a sharp hiss of pain. Whatever the knockout smoke was, it was *nasty*.

"Relax for a while, Bright Eyes," Sintilla said. "You'll need your strength."

"Uh-oh. I don't think I like the sound of that."

Sintilla grinned. "After all, we've got the evidence to crack the Camarilla wide open, but now we've got to *do* something with it. Are we gonna have fun now!"

CHAPTER 22

WITH THE RICH AND THE MIGHTY

"ALACRITY, I NEVER WOULD'VE GUESSED IT OF YOU: YOU'RE innocent. It says so right here." Sintilla held up the message wafer.

"Maybe the Custodians' intel wasn't so great after all," Heart said as she applied a dressing to Floyt's wound. She gave Alacrity a sweet leer. "Innocent, *ha!*"

"No, no, it says so right here in this report," Sintilla insisted.

Everyone but Janusz was assembled in the *Stray*'s salon, going through the captured materials. They found that along with the load of Camarilla evidence, they'd also seized the most recent packet of communiques from various Camarilla sources, including the Alpha-Bureaucrats of Earth.

"Let's see that," Alacrity said, putting his own reader aside. "'Background data' . . . 'Weir Inheritance' . . . 'Project Shepherd'—huh! 'Misexecution of the original plan to recruit Fitzhugh for Project Shepherd by arranging for him to be convicted of encouraging public disorder and incitement to riot'—I guess they didn't know how to spell 'frame'—'resulted in commission of accidental manslaughter by crowd member, for which Fitzhugh was subsequently charged and convicted. Indications of official involvement were suppressed and neutralized by Earthservice supervisor Bear.' Oh, if I ever see her again . . ."

"Time for that later," Heart said. "For now, it's time to not push our luck anymore and to get into Hawking. Janusz! When will we be ready?"

Janusz, returning aft from the bridge, said, "Whenever we want. I've put the last mathematical model into the guidance suite. The ship wasn't damaged, so we can start for Srilla whenever we want."

"Which would be fine," Corva said, "except that we can't go to Srilla or Spica either. We're in much worse trouble than we thought." He held up another reader. "This is the most recent message among the commo file the Custodians kept.

"It seems the Camarilla members are uneasy. They were aware that Endwraithe didn't finish you and Hobart, and they lost track of you at the Grapple.

"They've issued warrants under Spican and Srillan law— what you would call 'John Does.' The charges specify a terrorist conspiracy aimed at destroying interstellar unity and fomenting revolution. They're throwing everything they have into finding and eliminating you."

Janusz, leaning over Corva's shoulder to read, nodded slowly. "They're risking a great deal; they're betting they can discredit anyone who tries to move against them. I doubt even your Uncle Maska could help us now, Corva—even if we could get to him."

"I don't see anything to do but get back to Epiphany and open up to Dame Tiajo and Redlock," Alacrity said.

"That wouldn't be wise, according to this," Janusz said. "There's a Spican fleet poised to move against anybody who starts whistleblowing. Even Weir's Domain couldn't hope to stand against the Spicans. Besides, this message indicates that there is still at least one and possibly several active Camarilla contacts at Frostpile. Among the Invincibles, or Taijo's advisors, perhaps? If we went there we'd stand a good chance of being jailed or assassinated."

"This Camarilla evidence has a short half-life," Sintilla pointed out. "The Camarillans will try to discredit it and they'll act in concert. But what if we go to the news services? I've got press credentials. We go directly to them—"

"You'd better scan this message," Corva said. "They've got

Infotel in their pockets, and Transgal and New Pathé. They can checkmate the others, I think."

"And in the meantime, Langstretch would be all over us," Victoria put in.

"Where does that leave us?" Heart said. "We have to move quickly."

"What about the Solar system?" Alacrity proposed. "What about that original scenario, the Letter of Free Import, and taking *Astraea Imprimatur* to Earth? The Solar authorities couldn't stop us, right?"

"Theoretically, the Solar Forces are obliged to respect the letter and at least give us a chance to land," Victoria ventured slowly. "But what could we do there? The Alpha-Bureaucrats have everything under their control. There's no one to overrule them."

"There's Citizen Ash," Alacrity said.

"The executioner?" Sintilla said. "D'you really think he'd defy the Alphas?"

"I've met him," Alacrity answered. "Nobody controls that guy. And besides, the Solar Defense Agreement covers Terra. The Spicans and Srillans couldn't move against Earth without getting involved in a shooting war. Earth may not have any defense forces anymore, but the Lunies and the other Solarian governments would be tough for anybody to mess with on their own ground."

"I'm afraid that there are already Spicans in the Solar system, a whole flotilla," Corva said.

Alacrity groaned; Corva explained. To forestall any attempts by Floyt to return to Terra, a Spican flotilla commanded by a Camarilla member had been dispatched to the Solar system under the cover of a goodwill tour.

"The boltholes are closing fast," Sintilla said. "Maybe we ought to run for it, get way out where nobody has ever heard of us and nobody'll come looking, until we figure out what to do."

"There isn't time," Victoria said. "We've got to get this information out somehow before they can preempt us with disinformation and psychprop and counteraccusations. Besides, with the Repository gone, they might get into an internal struggle that will cost millions of lives."

"It is too bad, about Earth," Corva said. "It would have been the optimal place to go public. I believe the Spican flotilla is there only to blockade; it's too bad we have no way past it."

"They'll certainly keep ships in position to monitor vessels approaching Terra," Heart said. "The Solarians would try to stop us from landing on Terra too, unless Hobart transmitted his letter of Free Import, which would tip our hand."

"But if we *could* get past the Spicans, get close enough to land on Terra, the Solarians would keep them or anybody else from interfering," Alacrity contended.

"It comes back to the same thing." Corva sighed. "The Spicans will be watching. Even *Astraea Imprimatur* couldn't fight her way through."

"What does that leave?" Floyt asked. "Is there some other document or immunity—like the letter—that the Spicans would have to recognize?"

"Oh, diplomatic credentials or something like that would work, I guess," Victoria said absently. "Nothing we could come up with. Not too many people can tell the Spican Navy *and* the Solar Defense Forces to mind their own business and get out of the way."

"What's the matter, m'love?" Alacrity said as Heart leapt up with a cry. "Lingerie creeping up?"

She raced off, leaving them mystified, returning shortly from *Harpy*, which was nestled in the *Stray*'s boatlock. She'd been digging through the plunder they'd inherited from Sile.

"It's right here. Remember, Alacrity?" She slipped a memory lozenge into an adaptor so the *Astraea Imprimatur*'s system would accept it. It was the tape of Praxis, leader of the Church of the Human Potential.

"Well, so what?" Sintilla said. "I mean, I know he's a right slime, and I'd love to see this splashed everywhere, but even Praxis doesn't have the kind of gees it'd take to keep the Spican Navy off our necks."

"No," Heart agreed, "*but he's in charge of the Regatta for the Purple*. Of who gets to enter and what course it takes."

Alacrity gathered her into his arms and locked his lips to hers.

"The chief justice of the Interstellar Peace Court is participating," Victoria said. "The chairwoman of the Currency Regulation Board. The high arbiter of the Interspecies Cooperative!"

"And the Spican defense coordinator," Sintilla said. "Even the Spican Navy wouldn't dare stop the regatta. Shiva's snatch, the last time anybody even mentioned it the regatta members imposed informal sanctions and brought—what was it?—the Dungaling Coalition to its knees!"

"But—a race," Janusz said dubiously. "Some of the fastest vessels in human space will be in the regatta. I'm not at all certain the *Stray* could even begin to keep up, and we certainly don't have photon-sailing capability for that phase of the race."

"We don't have to run the *whole* race," Heart reminded him. "Just stay up with them long enough to get past the Spicans and close to Earth."

"If anything were to go wrong, we could always run for Hawking again," Corva mused.

Alacrity was looking up at the erotic frescoes, scratching his Adam's apple, and thinking, with great relish, reckless thoughts. "We've got that oversize Hawking back there; we could probably hold our own in translight. But in normal space—we'd have to ask an awful lot out of our conventional engines."

"Then we'll have to ask it," Floyt said with unswerving conviction. "Alacrity, we have to."

"You're right; we'll have to," Corva said. "Don't worry, Hobart; the engines will deliver."

"Ahem!" Sintilla said. "Have any of you stopped to consider how well insulated Praxis is? Well, I have, because I did a feature on him once. We can blackmail him if we can get to him, but how do we get to him? He spends most of his time sequestered in that neon basilica of his, in the Redoubt of the Self."

"If my father has gotten through to Praxis, I can," Heart said, leaning her elbow on Alacrity's shoulder.

"Do we get to wear little captain's hats with rockets on them?" Sintilla asked.

* * *

"There must be *some* way around it!" Alacrity growled.

Praxis' august image stared at him and the others crowded into the *Astraea Imprimatur*'s bridge. "For the last time, young man, there is no way around it. In order to qualify, all captains must attend the Sendoff Wassail and personally tender their entry tokens to the master-at-arms. That is an inflexible tradition and not even I can alter it."

"It's a trick," Janusz said.

Praxis' noble face showed vexation. "Do not be an ass, sir! Do you seriously think that I want to risk creating a scene at this point? You've been admitted to the race—over strong opposition, I assure you!—and the course will be as you wished it. I shall probably be persona non grata at the Great Tables, and perhaps be blackballed from every influencial institution in human space, but I've kept our bargain.

"But if you violate the protocols of the race you'll be barred, it is as simple as that. The choice is yours."

"Don't go away." Alacrity put Praxis on hold. "What d'you think, Ho?"

"Out in the open like this—what could anybody do to us?"

"We don't all have to go," Sintilla said. "It would be just plain foolish for Janusz and Vickie to show their faces; too much chance of Langstretch stringers."

"I rather fear I'm out of the question, too," Corva admitted.

"Well, according to the info from the Repository, nobody's actually put Ho's and my likenesses out in a wanted bulletin to the general public yet. This won't take us a minute. What've we got to wear that's purple?"

"Captain and First and their escorts, Praxis said," Sintilla pointed out. "I think that means Heart and me, and it's just as well you two lugs won't be wandering around out there among the patricians on your own."

"No!" Alacrity resolved. "I don't want you two in the middle of this."

"You don't seem to have many options," Victoria reminded him. "And besides, Heart knows the ropes in places like this. Tilla too."

Alacrity reconnected with Praxis. "All right; we'll be there. Uh, has there been any sign of Dincrist?"

"No. He and his *Celeste Aida* have been scratched from the race. Be at the grand pavilion in one half hour. If I should encounter you, do not speak to me. If you're wise, you'll stay well clear of me henceforth."

"Don't waste your wind threatening us," Floyt replied. "There're too many people ahead of you. But I'll tell you something: there're times when I wish you hadn't given in, because now you get to keep your secrets and your image. I wish we could've pulled you down."

Praxis's white, bushy eyebrows rose. "Oh, but I know that, young man. I saw it in your face, and your friends', from the outset. I knew you weren't bluffing." He signed off.

Janusz clapped Floyt's shoulder. "Everything has its price, Hobart. Some deals are harder to strike than others."

"We have to get moving," Heart said. "Where's that captain's entry token Praxis gave us?"

They ransacked *Astraea Imprimatur* and the adjoining *Harpy*. The two couples emerged with only a little time to spare. Floyt had fastened himself into a uniform of Sile's that was the right hue. It was decided that, since his uniform most resembled that of a real regatta captain, he would be the one to hand in the token. The idea tickled him.

Sintilla was on his arm, wearing matched galligaskins and blouse and a purple cloak, all of them Constance's. Alacrity had on the ice-blue shipsuit with an improvised sash of the race color, and Heart was in a tinselmesh skinsuit, Constance's, in purple. Theatrical, often bizarre makeup was commonly worn by both sexes at the gathering; Alacrity and Floyt were fantastically done up with the contents of Sile's disguise kits and Constance's cosmetic cases. Heart and Sintilla hid their faces behind modesty veils.

The sky of Rialto was a restful sepia, lending the planet an air of aged elegance. Its primary, an amber immensity called Moloch, was lowering toward the placid brown waters of the Orphean Sea, along whose shore the race's starting-point encampment had been pitched. Rialto was an agreeable, languid sort of planet, hypercivilized, its population interbred and rather aloof. *Astraea Imprimatur*, a late arrival, was grounded on the fringe of the noisy camp. The *Stray*'s contingent began making its way to the palatial purple canopy of the great pavilion.

They passed aging captain-owners of both sexes, escorted by friends, crew, and hangers-on. Race entrants had the double draw of the regatta's glamor and their own wealth and power; their coteries included only the most famous or influential, rich or sexually desirable. Crewpeople, dressed in the uniforms of their vessels, enjoyed their high-profile status within reason, the stern Rialto constabulary could be very harsh on disruptive outsiders or commoners.

Alacrity was secretly gratified to get a closeup look at some of the racing craft. They were grounded in casual disorder, starships so beautiful and right for their purpose that it pulled at his middle and wrung a kind of hopeless love out of him. All sorts of designs were present, though they all incorporated aerodynamic principles; racers had to handle well in atmosphere.

He saw a streamlined, delicate craft scarcely bigger than the *Harpy* and wicked-looking vessels longer than the *Stray* but far leaner. Despite his prejudice, he had to admit that the *Stray*, only a converted privateer, was out of her element, simply outclassed and outshone.

There were none of the hawkers and vendors, pickpockets, crowd hustlers, panhandlers and gawkers, celebrity chasers, newspeople, or social climbers Floyt had expected. The Rialto constabulary and various private guards were firm about keeping out the rabble. Being caught on the site without proper documentation would earn the guilty party instant ejection along with a possible broken arm or fractured skull.

Guards and security systems had already verified the identities of the *Astraea Imprimatur*'s complement several times over—once on approach, once upon landing, and twice since in spot checks. But all that had done was match I.D. data with the phony names Praxis had entered into the system.

Many captains and other important personages had provided entertainment. The four passed bagpipers, poets, boxers, philosophers discoursing in tag-teams, tightwire fiddlers, clowns, caricaturists, and such.

Alacrity recognized a few of the people they saw, and Heart quite a number, but Sintilla seemed to know almost everyone by sight. There were ambassadors, overlords, military heavyweights, megastars from all the arts, and titans of commerce and industry, intellectual cynosures, and academic and scientific luminaries.

"What if we run into somebody from the compounds?" Floyt suddenly thought to ask.

"You were masked most of the time and I doubt any of 'em would remember me," Alacrity answered. "I was just another subhuman in a collar. Anyway, I've got a hunch most of them went to ground until things cool off."

"What about you, Heart?" Sintilla said through her veil. "Will any of these people know who you are?"

"Not in this ensemble," Heart said, adjusting her own veil.

"They'll be too busy admiring all that luscious skin," Alacrity reasoned.

They came to the pavilion, with its smorgasbörds and bar, human servants and staff, and where there wasn't a serving robo in sight. People were assembled for the ritual gathering of the tokens. Most of the hangers-on would, after the start of the race, be shipping out for the finishing line, where the partying would continue.

"Well check my pulse," Sintilla breathed. "I've never seen so many high-voltage types in one place in my life, not even at the Spican Commencement. Nietzsche should only see this place; talk about your will to power!"

"Just another bunch of weekend breakabouts," Alacrity snarled.

"Maybe to you," Heart said. "But you see that rotund little fellow over there? That's Secretary-General Van Baader, Union of Non-Aligned Planets. The woman he's talking to is Gaultine Le Claire, finance minister of the Bamboo Confederation."

"Wait!" Floyt burst out in a stage whisper. "Alacrity! Why don't we take them aside and explain everything to them? We don't need to wait until we get to Earth."

"Because while Gaultine isn't mentioned as part of the Camarilla, her brother-in-law, Maximillian, is," Sintilla explained. "And the president of the Cooperative of Species, there—with the vestigial wings and the cute tail?—is supposed to be clean, but his chief-spouse-queen is in it up to her spinnerettes. See the problem, Hobart? There may be some who've got the integrity, but we can't tell who. And anyway, if you were them, who would you listen to, outlaws and nameless flotsam like us, or your family and friends?"

"You're right, of course," Floyt yielded.

"Let's go get this over with," Alacrity said.

"No wonder your father wanted in with this crowd so bad," Sintilla said to Heart. "Anybody who chums with them has one helluva leg up."

A full orchestra was playing. The place was decorated with stasis-locked water sculptures and fountains of rainbow plumage ten meters high. The four passed on the delicacies and treats; it was no time to sample a medicated fruit ice or drugged licorice pastille.

A general announcement was made by a gargantuan drum major, that the gathering of the tokens and the disclosure of the race course would be made shortly. Competitors and their comrades and guests would then be requested to drink a wassail to the race. After that, captains and crews would retire to their ships. The course was to be revealed by a very prestigious member of the race committee, a two-time winner of the Regatta for the Purple.

Looking around, Floyt abruptly felt Sintilla's fingers dig deep into his arm. *"Are you seeing this?"* she whispered fiercely.

Two meters away a very attractive woman of middle age with magnificent decolletage, her blood-red hair done in an intimidating porcupine bouffant, was gushing to her companion, a dignified older gent with plaited sidelocks and a beard divided into five spikes.

"You absolutely *must* read it! It's so marvelously naughty in spots, and so-ooo delightfully common, but audacious!"

She was pressing upon him a copy of *Hobart Floyt and Alacrity Fitzhugh Challenge the Amazon Slave Women of the Supernova.*

Sintilla pretended to swoon. "Somebody catch me. I'm rich. I'm On the Horizon," She announced.

"Celebrate later, will you, Tilla?" Alacrity said. "Royalties won't do you any good if the Cam—if we have any trouble." He made a mental note to start thinking about a new alias. *Penny Dreadfuls!*

Ruffles and flourishes sounded. A healthy round of applause greeted the appearance of the spacegoing sportsman who was to announce the regatta's course.

"Oh, *hell's entropy!*" Alacrity breathed. It was Baron Mason.

The baron made the rounds of the rich and the mighty, exchanging forearm grips and grace kisses, clasping palms or touching his breast, lips, and forehead. "Easy, take it easy," Sintilla chanted quietly. "He's just here to make the announcement; he'll never recognize us. Stay calm."

Alacrity looked into the Nonpareil's eyes. It was plain what she was thinking; she owed Mason and yearned to pay in full. "Some other time we'll open his gaskets for him," Alacrity assured her. She nodded.

Mason was ascending the platform at the far end of the pavilion joining other power-mongers there. A momentary doubt passed through Alacrity, at the thought of who it was he and the others were screwing with, but he steeled himself to think of the reverse side of the coin: who would dare intercept or search these people, even on a close Earth approach?

After some more gladhanding, Mason opened the sealed envelope of finest papyreen, which was marked with seals of office and computerized security codes. How Praxis had managed to get around those, Alacrity couldn't figure out, but lots of things were possible to someone who had as his lever the absolution of the church.

The banter and toasts had stopped. Mason silently read the paper, chuckled, and lifted his eyebrows.

"We have a first here, I see," he said expansively. "I think we may make a little history this time round, my friends; certainly our racers will *see* some history. The course leads to humanity's very roots, to the Solar system. A course that will pass within close visual range of . . . Earth!"

Many people gasped. After a moment Mason nodded to an underling, who passed the word. Out on Myrmydion, a rocky atoll several kilometers away, a dispatch ship rose, climbing faster than an interceptor missile. It would make the trip even faster than the racers could, to present Solar authorities with a request for clearance that carried the weighty names of the Regatta Club membership, so that the race could be run without impediment.

Conversations resumed. Opinions were mixed, Floyt could see, but the club members had a sense of elevation in the choice, of their individual and aggregate status. No other organization in existence could exercise this prerogative.

Somebody yelled *Sol*! and lifted her wineglass high so that it caught the light. In another second most of those under the huge awning were doing the same, and there were cheers and whistles. Captains were holding aloft their tokens.

They like the idea; *they love it*, Alacrity saw.

"Course and maneuver requirement details are in the hand-out cubes," Mason was reminding the captains. "I must say, the lightsailing portion includes some of the more masterly maneuvers we've ever had in the regatta.

"And as some of you may have heard, we have a last-minute scratch who turned out to be a last-last-minute reentry." Mason gestured broadly out across the crowd.

"Oh, *futtering fate*!" Heart said.

Wearing a handsome working-breakabout captain's uniform of regatta purple, Dincrist stood in a group of applauding onlookers. He was waving, acknowledging the reception, exchanging dangerous smiles with Mason. Alacrity wondered exactly what kind of treaty they'd come to and who'd come out of it the better. Dincrist smiled, picture perfect, a noble, urbane exaggeration.

"We can't stay here," Sintilla said.

"Steady; we've got to hand in that token," Alacrity said in a level tone. He drew them into the lee of a lush violet feather-palm.

He looked around, assessing the tactical situation. A lovely young woman had appeared next to Mason. She wore blue and black skinfilm and carried a cut glass bowl. Captains began dropping their tokens into it, taking their course data handout cubes. Pickups in the bowl noted which tokens had been deposited and displayed the qualifying ships' names on large imagers set around the pavilion. Mason left the platform to press flesh with more VIPs, ignoring the collection of the tokens.

"Ho, you make the drop; just be sure you don't look Mason's way and you'll be all right. Heart and I will meet you by the north entrance—that one, *away* from where Dincrist is."

The wassail was starting. Waiters and waitresses were offering cups of the spicy lift-off grog. Floyt and Sintilla made their way to the woman with the bowl as Alacrity wove through the crowd in another direction, leading the Nonpareil by the hand and trying to think up a surefire prayer. They swept past a waitress who held a tray of grog cups, then went out a side exit. Passing behind splendorous, townhouse-size lounges that had been airlifted in, they came to a service area cluttered with waiting piles of food, beverages, catering supplies, and tech-support equipment.

"We can circle around this way," Alacrity said.

They went between two stacks of mineral water barrels; Alacrity, in the fore, came face to face with Dincrist. "*God-dammittohell!* Not ag—" was as far as he got.

Heart's father brought up an actijot unit and let him have it pointblank. Alacrity dropped back against a guywire and hung there, stupefied. Heart rushed to help him to his feet. Her father swung the jot unit at her with a determined look. "I don't know what he's done to you to make you abet him, but I will use this on you if I must. You have only to try me if you disbelieve that."

She had Alacrity leaning on her. "You know about the jots . . ."

"Oh, yes. I thought my reckoning with Fitzhugh would have to wait, but I made it a point to have this with me always, just in case. What can you be thinking of, coming here with him? Are you trying to ruin me?"

Dincrist shifted to a relaxed pose, holding the jot unit casually, in two hands, then directed his captives to a satellite awning where tables and chairs had been set up. Three servitors converged on them at once. Dincrist unhurriedly put his hand and the jot unit into his side jacket pocket. "Remember, I'll kill you if I must, Fitzhugh." He motioned Alacrity, who was still weak-kneed from the jotting, into an airchair. Alacrity obeyed.

Heart interposed herself with the servitors so that there'd be no confrontation or incident. She lowered her veil and accepted three pewter cups of wassail grog, handing one to the shaky Alacrity. Dincrist accepted the other and sat down with the two, sipping satisfiedly.

Alacrity pulled himself together to say, "So the jinx worked after all; it's all going your way, huh?"

Dincrist frowned. "Jinx?"

"The one you laid on Ho and me at Frostpile."

"Did it indeed? How gratifying, even though this probably has more to do with your own bumptiousness."

Alacrity took an unsteady pull from the cup. "Uh-huh, the jinx dogged us, all along. What now?" He was stalling. There was Mason to consider, and the hope that Floyt and Sintilla might come looking for him in time.

"The obvious. I'd like to do it with more finesse, but I'll simply have to leave your body right where it's sitting for the cleanup crew. As you can see, other things demand my attention."

He waved with casual pride to a ship. She wasn't like anything Alacrity had ever seen before, all folded sail booms and magnificent racing lines.

"So, you got *Celeste Aida* here in time after all," Heart said. "And you'll have your regatta too, at long last. But what about me? Or haven't you given that any thought?"

Dincrist looked at her with genuine regret. "It took me a long time to face the fact that you are with him. I've lost you, lost my little *Facetiae*. It was very painful to face, like losing your mother all over again. And it's so plebeian. Lord! It's absolutely melodramatic. 'After all I've done for you, this is the thanks I get!' How could you let him turn you against me?"

"It wasn't Alacrity," she answered, calmly sipping. "And I don't hate you, even though I see why others do. I simply can't tolerate you any more—the things you do and the things you intend to do."

Dincrist nodded, tasting the spicy grog. "I've come to understand that. I know what you've been doing, how you've been intriguing behind my back. I've uncovered a lot of your new connections. Do you think the rest of you, even united, can stand against *me*?"

"We'll see," she replied indifferently. Alacrity was wondering if overturning the table would merely get Heart injured along with hastening his own demise.

"No, you won't see," Dincrist said angrily. "That nonsense is over. You're still my daughter. After the race is over I'm going to set everything to rights."

"You couldn't; you're too committed to what you already are."

Alacrity waited for that to galvanize the man to action, tensing up for a last-hope dodge or pounce. But Dincrist didn't seem to be listening; he was nodding, looking distracted or puzzled.

The wassail cup slipped from his fingers, spilling on the tawny, groomed turf. His hand made a convulsive movement with the jot unit but Heart was there first, grabbing his forearm, prying his hand from it.

"Fill me in; this makes no sense to me," Alacrity said.

Heart turned to him with a smile, slipping the jot unit into his sash, fluttering her fingers at him, reminding him that she still wore the Ouroboros ring. And she was the one who'd accepted the wassail cups and passed them out to her father and Alacrity.

"I love you as only a man with a whole hide can love the woman who saved it for him," he declared fervently. "How long will he be out?"

She looked at two more cruising constables as she set her father's cup on the table, shielding him from their view as she arranged him in a sleeping pose. "I'm not sure, but long enough. The dosage instructions on the blisterpack were a little vague, but I'd think we have an hour or so at the very least."

"Marginal. Let's collect Ho and Tilla."

They crossed Dincrist's knees and propped his head on his arms on the table. At the same time Alacrity patted him down and confiscated the purse he carried in a forearm pouch. The Nonpareil's face clouded.

"Heart, it's *war* from now on. We're going to need every edge we can get."

Sintilla adjusted her veil as she and Floyt neared the platform and the token bowl. They were among the last to hand in their entry discs.

The gracious mixing and mingling had an undercurrent of sensation, even scandal; the words *Terra* and *Praxis* could be heard everywhere. Floyt nervously patted down his pockets for the entry token.

Sintilla nonchalantly took a couple of wassail cups. Floyt got a grip on the small wheel of metal, drew it out, and tossed it into the bowl. "Here, darling," Sintilla said, handing him a cup.

Mason was nowhere near. He raised his cup and sipped as Sintilla lowered her veil to do the same. Then he took her arm to leave. At that moment the lovely young woman overseeing the token collection bowl called out, "Stop! Stop! Esteemed sir, come back!"

His impulse was to put his head down and forge on, but people had looked around and were directing his attention back to the platform. A few constables had noticed the commotion.

He felt Sintilla stiffen and decided that a dash would be a very dubious undertaking. With what aplomb he could muster, Floyt halted and turned to see what would happen next, trying to keep his heavily made-up face angled away from Mason.

The young woman was stepping down off the platform, holding up what he'd given her. "There's been some mistake, sir. This isn't an entry token."

She gave him a bright smile. "It's a Terran coin, sir, see? 'TERRA: FIVE HUNDRED YEARS IN SPACE.'"

She stopped before Floyt, who now had the real token in a sweat-slick hand. "This must be very valuable, sir; you wouldn't want to lose it."

There were suspicious glances and murmuring from those nearby. Floyt said, "A-ha. Ha. Yes," trying to think of a way to explain away the glaring coincidence.

Sintilla put her hands on her hips and flounced a bit. "I give you my most precious good-luck heirloom because it turns out you're going to the Solar system and what's the first thing you do? You give it away! *Men!*"

Onlookers began to laugh then, particularly the women, and Floyt made the exchange. She gave his arm a discreet yank, pulling him under way. They went out a side entrance opposite the one Alacrity and Heart had taken. They hadn't gotten five steps when Baron Mason confronted them.

"Oh, yes, who *else* could it be? A Terran coin, after all."

Floyt tried not to feel the fire of his jottings and the phantom iron of a collar around his neck. "What do you want?"

Mason took a step closer. "Want? I want to know what it is you're doing here. I should have known whatever you're involved in is bigger than just Dincrist or Blackguard. Bigger even than the regatta, perhaps? Above everything else, I hate being kept in the dark."

He inclined his head laconically toward a pair of cruising constables. "I suggest you tell me."

Floyt licked his lips, feeling Sintilla's grip on his upper arm. "No."

Baronial eyebrows went up. "So? Don't press your luck too far, little Citizen Floyt."

Floyt, the Terran functionary with the high compliance quotient, looked Mason square in the eye. "You weren't so tough the last time I saw you, remember? You should; I could've left a hot cavity between your ears, and *I wanted to*! Only . . . only that's not enough reason, for me."

"Baron, it might be embarrassing for you too, if we all start swapping accusations at the interrogation center," Sintilla suggested.

Floyt made a slashing gesture with his hand. "Never mind that! Baron, you can honor your debt by getting out of my way, or you can raise the hue and cry. Like any upstart would. Like any vulgar *arriviste*."

The frieze held for five of the longest seconds Floyt had ever lived. Then Mason stepped to one side with a courtly inclination of the head. "Who are you really, Floyt? And how did you come by such luck?"

"*Luck?*" Floyt laughed, a bit wildly. "Oh, if you only knew!"

Racers were making final preparations for the regatta's start; onlookers were streaming up to hillside vantage points. "Perhaps some day you'll tell me what this was all about," Mason said.

"Look for us in the newscasts," Sintilla recommended as Floyt drew her away. "Right now we've got a racc to run!"

CHAPTER 23

MATERIAL STRENGTHS

"WITH ALL THE EXCITEMENT THERE, I NEVER DID FIND OUT. Where did we stand in the pack when we went into Hawking?" Alacrity asked as he collapsed next to Heart in the *Astraea Imprimatur*'s salon.

"Not too well. It would have been worse, I suspect, except that most of the other racers were saving themselves for the Solar system leg."

"This old scow was built and rebuilt to take it. And Corva really knows his way around an engine room. Janusz's no tyro either. We got the bottle fields sealed and synched again; they'll hold. But I don't think the normal-space engines can stand that kind of punishment again, at least not without a shipyard overhaul. We were pretty close to a serious malfunction, pushing them like that."

"Well, Janusz can scarcely be faulted," Floyt commented from the mold-lounger where he slumped. He'd been as busy as the others before the *Stray*'s transition to Hawking. Now he was sipping iced tea. He hadn't much choice, right?"

Alacrity rubbed his eyes wearily. "Not really, if we're going to have a prayer of pulling this thing off and getting to Earth. We can make the Hawking-Effect leg of the race about as fast as any, I suppose, unless somebody's got something new or experimental under their hull. It's sublight that's liable to yang us up. The thing is, if we fall way behind or even worse, the normal-space engines give out on us, somebody's bound to come after us—maybe board us. If we have to drop out of the race we might as well go back to Hawking and get lost forever; it can't be too long before word gets out about the Repository raid and the Camarilla starts taking extreme action."

Sintilla, sitting cross-legged on the deck, said, "But what if the sublight engines can't take it? We won't be doing anyone any good by blowing ourselves into the afterlife."

"What if we pass up this chance to throw light on the Camarilla?" Alacrity riposted. "There'll never be another."

He reached over and began massaging the Nonpareil's shoulders. "Besides, Janusz doesn't look like he's giving up hope. He's doing a great job." He said that more or less to Victoria, who'd just come aft from the bridge. She did not seem to register it. "Let's see what he's got to say," Alacrity finished.

"Where is Janusz?" Victoria asked.

Alacrity kept massaging. "Arguing with Corva in the power section. Funny how those two get along."

Floyt nodded, grinning. Sintilla snorted. "*You* two should talk!"

"Anyway, I think they've got some kind of idea but I'm not sure what. They had their heads together, but they're not ready for outside opinions yet."

Heart was playing with a memory wafer. Alacrity looked over her shoulder. "What've you got there?"

"It's from my father's purse. Sintilla and I were going to try to crack it, the way we did Sile's. It can wait."

Janusz and Corva appeared. "Ship's complement's assembled," Sintilla said.

Janusz sat; Corva stood by a holoprojector, looking up absently at the frescoes. Janusz said, "We've roughed it out with computer models and calculations, analyzed the tech readouts, material strengths, all of it. There's no way our sublight engines can keep us up with the regatta; the racers are much faster than we foresaw."

"But we can't give up," Victoria said. "This is our one chance."

Corva said, "Oh, but no one was talking about giving up. Janusz has a plan and I feel it's feasible."

"We're listening," Heart said.

"We're listening *hard*," Floyt elaborated.

"Simply put," Janusz began, "it occurred to me that the *Stray* has two booster engine arrays, quite powerful ones. I propose we use those to augment the main engines long enough to make our approach to Terra."

"Two boosters..." Alacrity's face blanked with puzzlement, then his eyes bugged. "That's the craziest damn thing I ever heard! If you two mean what I think you do, the air's probably too thin in here, that's what's doing it!"

"What are we discussing?" Floyt inquired.

"The missiles, the Annie Vs," Victoria said slowly. "That's what you have in mind, isn't it? Yes, yes! It could work!"

"Stop the printout! Scram the reactor!" Sintilla squawked. "You're talking about mounting the engine arrays from the Annies on the *Stray*'s hull? It can't be done; there's not enough time and anyway, we're in Hawking."

"That's true," Janusz admitted. "So we propose to brace the missiles in their tubes—rather like putting engines in a test mount—and to use them where they are. We'll correct course with the *Stray*'s main engines. Our primary problem is that we cannot control speed; we can only buckle in and ride them."

"The alignment of the missiles and balancing of thrust will have to be very precise," Heart said thoughtfully.

"We can install simple engine cutoffs," Corva said, "and shut down to correct course if we have to. We've been going through stores and other available materials. It can be done, although we'll have to cannibalize part of the ship's internal structure to do it. We'll make giant braces and collars."

"Will that kind of jury-rig hold?" Heart pondered.

"That depends on the material strengths involved."

Structural dynamics. Sleeplessness. Load tolerances. Stresspoints.

Floyt almost stumbled over Corva in the main deck midships passageway, grabbing a hatchframe for balance. "Oh! Sorry, I thought you were aft, rerouting the control auxiliaries."

The humanoid got to his feet tiredly. "Yes, yes; just checking the junctions here."

"But I thought all that stuff there was life support and utilities."

Corva toed closed an access panel. "What can I do for you, Hobart?"

"We're going to try to fit the collar again, if you can give us a hand. Otherwise I think Alacrity and Janusz will rupture themselves, even with the power equipment."

"I'll be right along." Corva bent to the panel again and Floyt watched curiously. Corva looked up. "I'll be right along, Hobart."

Floyt shrugged and went off to draft Heart and Sintilla.

Energy limits. An inflexible deadline. Breaking points.

"One down, one to go," Victoria toasted with a squeezepak of mango juice. "Here's hoping we have less trouble with Tweedledum than Tweedledee gave us."

All seven were gathered in the salon again for the first time since Janusz's plan had been put into effect. They'd been working steadily, with only occasional catnaps, for some forty hours.

"That would be swell," Alacrity said sourly. "Then our only headache would be that the ship's opened up like a dissected frog. What are we going to use for the rest of the buttressing?"

"We'll take out some of the forward frame members and some shielding," Corva explained matter-of-factly, yawning. "I had the figures around here somewhere."

"This whole barge could come apart when we light those sparklers," Sintilla said. "And the air's thin on the other side of the skin."

"We'll all be suited up," Corva said. "And we'll have *Harpy* as a lifeboat if that becomes necessary. But before transition, everyone should check themselves in the mediscan unit in the main head so we can adjust the environmental suits and insure we've no medical emergencies coming up that can't be treated in a suit. Get a printout and give it to Alacrity; that will be his job."

Alacrity couldn't keep from laughing. "We are asking one hell of a lot from this old crate."

"She's already given us one hell of a lot," Victoria reminded him. "It's quite a ship you inherited, Citizen Floyt."

Floyt nodded; he realized that more with each hour.

"What's that you've got there?" Alacrity said. Heart had been playing with the memory wafer again. Now she slid it into a reader.

"I cracked it," she said.

The reader threw up a holodisplay of info in bewildering columns and sidebars, menus and lists. A lot of it seemed to have to do with stock holdings and diagrams of dummy corporations, controlling interests, voting shareholders, and buyouts.

One symbol appeared frequently in the material Heart was fast-scanning. To Floyt it looked something like a flowery maltese cross or cross-moline, or perhaps the chemical sign for white lead, in black with a white circle at the center. It was superimposed on an arc, like that of a planet or celestial body in the background. It seemed familiar, but he couldn't place it. Concentration was becoming more and more difficult.

"It's all about the White Ship," Heart said. "My father's trying to take control of the project. But he's not going to; I'm going to see to that. Some day that ship will unlock the Precursors' secrets and that will determine how we evolve and what we become—what the whole purpose of life is."

"I never heard your old man was involved in the White Ship project," Sintilla said.

"The takeover's top secret, and it's not too late to stop it. There's a lot of competition, always has been: governments, cartels, religions, secret societies."

Floyt was absorbing it all. When he looked to check Alacrity's reaction, he saw that his friend was just staring at the displays—and at that odd symbol.

"If you go up against your father now, you're risking your life," Victoria stated. "Blood will only count now in that it will make him hate you more. He's very powerful, Heart."

"I'm not alone," she answered, looking to Alacrity. If she expected him to second that, she was disappointed. "Other family members are with me, and some of my father's business rivals, competitors. I've had time to gather a lot of information and lay detailed plans these last years. The truth is, I'm relieved that I don't have to pretend any more, no matter what."

She took Alacrity's hand. He didn't withdraw it, but he didn't respond either.

Metal fatigue. Human fatigue. Inertia-shedding limits. Breakdowns.

"That's your last word on it?" Alacrity looked not at Heart, but at the work she'd been doing, patching the improvised controls of the Annie Vs through the board and making sure the manuals were all working properly. Altered and bread-boarded as things were, there could be no trusting voice-activated systems.

"You're not leaving me much choice," she countered. "I've made promises and commitments I'm simply not free to ignore. You'll have to accept that."

"I can't." He faced her. "I have my own agenda; I learned the hard way that I can't go along with someone else's. What happened to my parents taught me that."

The two were more disbelieving than angry. "I'm sorry about what happened to them and to you. I'd take away the pain for you if I could. But some things are beyond my control; you can't have your way in this."

"Well, I'm sorry too because I'll be keeping you from having yours. I'm doing what I set out to do."

"I won't let you, Alacrity."

"You don't have any choice."

Heart gave a sad half smile. "We're not leaving ourselves very much maneuvering room here, are we?"

At that point Floyt appeared, rapping on the hatchframe and easing into sight hesitantly. "Pardon me for interrupting, please. Janusz needs you right away, Alacrity. He's in Tweedledum's launch tube."

"I'll be along directly, Ho. Thanks." When Floyt had left, he asked, "Can we talk about this later?"

"Talk, yes. Fight, no."

Hull integrity. Allocation of forces. Failure bias.

There were more than enough suits to go around. Alacrity

picked the strongest and most durable and began to sweat over adjustments. The hardest crewmembers to fit would be Sintilla and Corva.

He made the rounds, collecting mediscan printouts to calibrate reusable mixtures and tailor suit adjustments to each wearer. When he got to Victoria she struck him as distracted, sitting alone in the bridge, staring. He persisted.

She turned on him. "Leave me alone, damn you! I can adjust my own damn suit! *Go away!*"

He backed off. "Correct me if I'm wrong. Didn't you and me strike a truce?" He started to leave; the data would be in the mediscanner's data bank anyway.

"Come back; I didn't mean that, Alacrity. Please come back."

"Forget it. What's the matter?"

She gave him a searching gaze, then handed him the printout. He scanned, stopped suddenly, then stared at her. "Anybody else know?"

She shook her head slowly. "But it doesn't change anything. We still go to Terra."

He sat down in the copilot's poz. "If you're sure that's the way you want it."

"It is. Just keep mum."

He sighed. "This is a helluva way to run an interstellar mission of truth and justice."

Unknowns. Variables not subject to analysis. Insufficient data. Exceeds all safety limits.

Material strengths.

The race committee's advance ship had done its job well; with only a few hours' warning, the course had been cleared of regular traffic. That wasn't unprecedented, or even surprising. The chairman of the Interworld Banking Trust was one of the participants, and his organization was thinking of granting the Solar Development Corporation an enormous venture loan for construction on and around the outer planets. Another racer was the ruler of the One Hundred League, who was considering a Solarian bid to provide new guidance systems for his entire fleet. There was also the chief operating officer of Bascomb Amalgamated; the locals very much wanted her company to choose Solarian sites for several gigantic manufacturing facilities.

The way "up-sun" toward Sol lay clear of interference. The stymied Spican flotilla, now scattered to various locations on its purported goodwill tour, had no choice but to comply with Solarian directions.

Astraea Imprimatur came out of Hawking surprisingly far up in the pack and immediately began falling back. Praxis' course brought the racers into normal space just inside the orbit of Mars; the starships plunged up-sun to begin the photon sailing leg of the race.

"I'm picking up Srillan transmissions," Victoria said. "It looks like they've got a fleet detachment here too, but they're also out of the way."

"Then they make no difference," Janusz decided.

"We won't get any more speed out of the *Stray*'s sublight engines," Alacrity reported from the copilot's poz. "Time to pull the ring."

From the pilot's poz, Janusz agreed, then instructed them all to make a last check of their suits and the safety cocoons that enfolded them. He and Alacrity checked the remotes that lay under their braced hands on the armrests; the most important of these were the cutoffs for the engine arrays of Tweedledee and Tweedledum.

Floyt, immobilized in suit and cocoon in the weather bridge alongside the encapsulated forms of Sintilla and Heart, acknowledged Janusz, then switched his intercom to Sintilla's line. "What I mind is this is my one and only chance to see the rest of the Solar system and we won't even come close to anything until we get to Earth—not even an asteroid, for Finnagle's sake!"

"Why not worry about the simple things?" Sintilla suggested. "Like surviving?"

"Well, if the inertia-shedding field gives out we'll probably never know the difference anyway—isn't that what Alacrity said? Right. So why not be a bit more ambitious in my carping?"

"Corva, are you okay?" Janusz called over the main net.

"Yes, quite, thank you," Corva answered from the nestled *Harpy*. He was in several ways their only safety precaution: if there was time to abandon ship in case of mishap, Corva could have all *Harpy*'s systems ready and could even make a pickup in the unlikely event that the vessel broke up without killing them all instantly. If the ship veered off course and there was the opportunity, the Srillan might do some good by using *Harpy* for steering.

"We're falling farther and farther behind," Victoria said. "We've got to go before we draw attention to ourselves."

"You think we're not about to draw attention to ourselves?" Sintilla marveled.

Janusz checked all around once more, got an all-ready from everyone. He touched a switch under his braced hand.

Nothing happened.

He tried it again two or three more times, searching his board laboriously through his cocoon viewslit, ignoring the heads-up display in his helmet. "It's not working." He moved the switch back to the off position.

"I'm picking up something," Alacrity said. "Ship coming out of Hawking."

"I'll check the hookups," Corva said.

"Stay where you are; there isn't time," Janusz said curtly, shutting down the ship's engines. The *Harpy*'s protective gear was more cumbersome than *Astraea Imprimatur*'s; it would take the Srillan much longer to extricate himself, then resecure.

"I'll go," Janusz said. "Alacrity, you stay ready." Alacrity, Janusz, and Corva were the only ones who really knew how the modifications on the Annies worked; Alacrity didn't argue.

"I think this other ship's a racer," Alacrity said.

"Good, good," Janusz muttered, making his way aft.

"God, she's fast! She'll be on us in a minute!" Alacrity added, feeling that that wasn't so good. He could only bring to mind one possible late starter.

Janusz reported on his progress as he rapidly made his way to the aft control linkages. In the meantime the racer overtook the *Stray*, and a new problem appeared.

"Janusz, I got a big blip, here. I think it's Spican military."

"How far off, Alacrity?"

"We have a few minutes, but she's closing."

"I have the controls disengaged; I think there's time," Janusz said.

"I have that racer on close detectors," Heart said. "Aw, *di buttana!* It's the *Celeste Aida!*"

Alacrity made a face in the stillness of his helmet. "Chances are he'll know it's us."

"Fire control, ready," Victoria reported.

For all the good it'll do us with our engines down, Alacrity thought. Most of the racers were fairly well armed in case of trouble along the way; it might take him some time, but Dincrist could finish them.

That was not what happened. *Celeste Aida* kept meticulously to her most economical course along the regatta's route, passing no closer to the *Astraea Imprimatur* than several thousand kilometers.

"Wha-aat?" Alacrity breathed.

"My father's waited years for the chance to compete in a regatta," Heart's voice said in the resonant closeness of his helmet. "You know how much it took for him to do it, and how much it represents to him. He hates to lose; he simply doesn't give up."

"Well; put my pizzle in the pencil sharpener," Alacrity said.

"Our other problem's still with us," Victoria said. "Spican cruiser, looks like, closing fast on an intercept course. They're asking if we're in distress and requesting permission to board. Janusz, *how much longer?*"

"All done!" he cried. "Alacrity, pull the ring!"

"Get back to your cocoon!"

"There's no more time. I'm well secured, Alacrity. Now pull the ring!"

Alacrity read the displays and saw that in truth there was not more time. He fired the ship's main engines and she leapt up-sunward. Then he pulled the ring.

This time both missiles fired. The Terran Inheritance exploded ahead. There was a pronounced jolt despite the inertia-shedding field, and Alacrity sucked in breath as he read the velocity display. And speed was still increasing. He bit his lip at the thought of the forces being exerted on *Astraea Imprimatur*. He offered The Infinite a concession-filled deal.

Velocity climbed and the ship's patchwork modifications started to reflect it. Indicators began to go dead or report overloads; everyone was getting readings of damage and danger. Alacrity cut the ship's main engines and still the speed increased.

"Don't anybody move; it's going to get worse," he gritted.

Velocity soared; the ship left the Spican cruiser behind, flickering across the Solar system. A bone-deep vibration began, seeming to come from *Astraea Imprimatur*'s marrow. It built as the inertia-shedding field tried to cope with forces it hadn't been designed for. The vibration became a ferocious jarring. The ship was a sound and light show of warnings and alarms.

"We're passing *Celeste Aida*, more or less," Alacrity told the others in a little bit. More or less was right; in spite of all their painful calculations and exacting work the alignment of the Animus Vs was off. While their speed grew every moment, they were also veering off course, more so all the time.

"Can we correct?" Janusz asked in a strained voice. Alacrity supposed he was holding himself down somewhere physically as well as being hooked or tied to something.

"I'm trying to figure that out now," Alacrity replied.

"We might also begin considering just how and when we should stop," Corva recommended.

"I think what we should do is stop-all and see where we stand," Alacrity said.

"*No!*" Janusz shouted. "These missiles are not wall lights, dammit! We might never get started again. Do not stop!"

"I'm picking up more Spicans, spread out along the route of the race," Victoria said. "We'd better let it ride."

Alacrity let it ride. The acceleration built, until the inertia-shedding field began to lose the battle. Acceleration pulled at them, making the ship's nose seem like *up*, and spreading their faces, flattening their flesh, distorting them.

Corva said he suspected it was some part of the missiles' design that they'd missed. "They're supposed to be going much faster than they are, so they keep trying."

The ship began groaning. They were all eyeballs-in, having trouble breathing. Floyt felt himself sinking into a red-out. Then the inertia-shedding field fluxed and they were slammed and pressed mercilessly. Objects somehow overlooked in the frantic last-minute battening-down flew through the air, smashing into instruments, controls, bulkheads, and cocoons.

Floyt and the others heard Janusz grunt and then cry out in pain just as alarms registered an air leak. They were all hollering to the outlaw, asking what was wrong, confusing things. When Victoria ordered them all to silence they could hear only Janusz's labored breathing.

Alacrity made up his mind, waggled his finger, and hit the chicken switch. Tweedledee and Tweedledum fell silent. He cut in all the retro the ship could huff; she was getting farther off course by the second. *Stray* seemed almost normal again.

Victoria was the first out of her cocoon, diving for a medical kit and an emergency patch case. Alarms were shutting down as the automatics sealed the minor leak. Alacrity told Floyt, Corva, and Heart to stay at their pozzes and hurried after Victoria with Sintilla close behind.

They found Janusz with his back braced against an airlock bulkhead near Tweedledee's launch tube, where he could keep an eye on the control hookups, in case they malfunctioned again. He'd been struck by a thermotorch power pack that had worked loose; it had hit his hard-upper-torso unit hard enough to crack it. He was bleeding from mouth and nostrils.

"Check his vital signs, but don't jostle him," Victoria instructed them as she worked to open the suit. Sintilla pulled out a portable imaging resonator.

"Alacrity," Heart said in a tone so neutral he ached with it, "we're picking up another ship—no, two. Moving this way, but not at high boost. They're quite large, perhaps military."

"No broken ribs," Victoria concluded, studying the resonator as Sintilla cleaned up Janusz with an irrigator and a coagulant applicator. "But he's got a broken shoulder, and I can't tell whether he's concussed or not."

"Let's get him inboard and strapped in the best way we can; we can't hang around here." Alacrity started opening the rings with which Janusz had secured the harness he'd used to fasten himself down.

Victoria glared. "Didn't you hear me? He's hurt."

"He'll be a lot more hurt if they catch us out here. Didn't you hear Heart?" *Heart, Heart* . . . "If we get boarded, he gets arrested at the very least, which in his case could be bad for his health."

Sintilla stopped her ministrations as Janusz's head bobbed and he came around a little. "Get out. 'S right; keep going."

Alacrity looked at Victoria skeptically. "Don't you think it's a little late to get careful? We're all gambling plenty on this run."

She gazed at Janusz for a few beats, then said, "We can secure him in the master's cabin mold-lounger and make him fast with cargo netting; I don't think we should try to put him into a cocoon."

Janusz was out the whole time they were getting him inboard and aft, but he moaned in pain several times. Floyt showed up partway along to help. They rushed to make Janusz comfortable, repair and reseal his suit, and lash him down, opening and tilting back their helmets to facilitate their work. Victoria readied a styrette. Then she anesthetized the shoulder and injected the hypnotic. Alacrity helped her close up the suit.

"We have perhaps another eight minutes before we're in their range," Corva alerted them.

"Man your stations," Alacrity said. "Unless somebody objects, I'm correcting this tub for windage and having another run at it. If I can light the sparklers."

No one objected. Victoria reluctantly let Alacrity pull her away from Janusz. "Take Ho's place in the weather bridge. Move!"

When she'd gone, the others finished resecuring loose gear and made sure that Janusz was strapped in. "It's so strange," Floyt mused. "She swears she's going to arrest him if we live through this, and yet she's so worried about him."

"Has to be love," Sintilla diagnosed.

"There's something else," Alacrity said, making sure his helmet commo was off. "She took a mediscan."

"So did everybody," Sintilla said. "So what?"

"So she's pregnant, that's what. Now let's get cooking."

Alacrity assumed Janusz's place and had Floyt take the copilot's poz. It had occurred to him that Victoria should by rights have taken it, but he felt better with her standing by in the weather bridge. Fire control could be handled from a number of different pozzes. He didn't examine too closely his reasons for not wanting Heart in the conuol room with him.

Corva and the Nonpareil had calculated course correction. Alacrity made sure everybody was back in place, then, his pulse going at two hundred per or so, pulled the ring. Again the *Astraea Imprimatur* surged forward, the Animus Vs rattling her, on the voyage Weir had planned for her so long ago.

The *Stray* was far off the race's course and bound for Terra, crossing the night at speeds the Solar system had seldom seen before. Alacrity cut the Annies again when the acceleration neared the danger level, continuing to use the ship's regular engines judiciously, but still *Astraea Imprimatur* creaked and threatened to snap. Alarms went off again and two more leaks registered, then three, as a rush of escaping air whirled debris and scraps around.

The engine telltales began to light up, and the *Stray* thrummed like a mandolin string. Floyt dimly heard a few pops in the thinning atmosphere as racked, pressurized cannisters of one kind and another blew. "Shouldn't we be doing something about all this?" he yelled as jetstreams of leaking air tore through the ship.

"There's nothing we can do right now. Except hold on," Victoria yelled back.

"The reason I'm happy nobody sane is flying this thing," Sintilla proclaimed, "is because I personally feel that that's the kind of situation we have here."

"Don't worry, Tilla; we'll get there," Alacrity said with an odd ring of conviction.

"Oh, easy for you to say! Who's gonna be around to rub your nose in it if we don't?"

"I mean it," he insisted. "You might say I've seen it."

"Now you can tell the future?" Heart said balefully.

"In a way."

Floyt, head encased in the moist, resilient cave of his helmet, hearing that, thought about Alacrity leaning into the star-broth of the causality harp.

Just then, though none of them could feel it, Alacrity flipped the ship, using her main engines to begin decelerating. In celestial terms, they were almost there. *Stray* vibrated and protested.

"I'm getting a signal," Heart said. "It's a Solarian patrol vessel this time. They're warning us off from Terra and citing the no-starships edict."

"Now it gets interesting," Alacrity said. He was climbing out of his cocoon, making sure the computers were abreast of what was going on, trying to provide for the fastest possible conversion to Hawking if it turned out the *Astraea Imprimatur* had to flee.

"Do your stuff, Hobart," Sintilla prompted. "Sweetie, you can do it!"

Floyt licked his lips and cued up the data wafer they'd prepared from his Letter of Free Import and his other documentation. He brought up voice mode and transmitted.

"I am Citizen Hobart Floyt, of Terra." His voice sounded weak and unsure; he looked to Alacrity. Alacrity gave him a solemn wink. Floyt drew a deep breath and went on.

"You are now receiving my certified authorization to import this vessel to Earth. Please note that this Letter of Free Import was duly registered with Solarian authorities and *cannot be rescinded*. I am also transmitting documentation of my ownership of this vessel."

He'd fallen into stride. "I call on you to let me go in peace. I'm going home."

He switched from transmit back to ship's net.

"Well said, Hobart," Heart called softly.

"That's telling 'em, Earther." Sintilla's voice was a bit thick.

Alacrity leaned over to pat his friend's back.

"You started something," Victoria reported. "That Solarian's burning up the vacuum talking to somebody. It's all encrypted, but I think the Spicans are in on it, and Luna."

"They aren't going to buy it," Floyt said. "I didn't convince them."

"I'm not so sure," Corva said. "That Solarian's no longer on an intercept course."

Seconds later the words came over the commo. "*Astraea Imprimatur*, this is the Solarian patrol vessel *Roll and Go*. You have clearance to proceed. Be advised, however, that you have no landing status that we can ascertain. Nevertheless, under the codes, you are allowed to go your way insofar as Solarian Defense and its signatories are concerned."

Alacrity turned on every running and signal light that would still work—except distress—and started calculating his planetfall. The ship's net was noisy with laughter and cheers.

"We're not clear yet," Alacrity said. "When we get in close, we're going to have to tap into the SATNET system, to get in touch with Citizen Ash. We want *him* waiting for us, not a battalion of peaceguardians."

"Working on it," Victoria said crisply. She was prepared with access procedures and codes, a detailed commo-intrusion plan orchestrated with Langstretch and Srillan classified data and techniques, along with Floyt's considerable input.

It took a while, due to speed-of-light lag. Victoria made contact with Earth's SATNET system, gaining access, aided by her own expertise and the ship's very up-to-date signal-warfare gear. She got SATNET to locate Earth's executioner—who was at a Utah urbanplex—and forward to him a voice-only message taped by Floyt:

"Citizen Ash, this is Citizen Hobart Floyt. There's no time to explain, but I must see you. I'm currently approaching Terra in a spacecraft and need your location. I beg you to meet with me. I know what I'm doing violates statutes and official protocol, but I appeal to you on the basis of a purer and more fundamental duty we both have to Earth."

They sat out the lag and the wait in various states of suspense and agitation, except Janusz. The seconds strung together unendurably. As Floyt's faith began to flag again, the well-remembered voice came.

"Very well, Citizen Floyt. I will meet you on the roof of this urbanplex. But I urge you to make haste, and advise you that you will have to answer for—"

The voice turned to static. "Cut off," Heart said. "They rejiggered the SATNET."

"I have a fix on him though," Victoria crowed.

"That's it, then," Alacrity decided. "We go in." He flipped the ship once more.

Floyt looked up to find that Earth was now large in the

viewpane. He felt none of the discrete emotional sensations—
by parts longing, fear, homesickness, love—that he'd expected.
Instead there was a great tidal swell in him, something to which
he could put no name.

"Trouble," said Heart in the very self-contained tone she'd
been using since the falling-out with Alacrity. "Picking up a
. . . Spican, I think. Coming up from behind on intercept."

Alacrity got the computers crunching numbers. The answer
was astoundingly close, but inarguable.

"He's got us, unless we go to Hawking. The Solarians aren't
going to step in on this one, it looks like, and we sure can't
outfight him."

Floyt felt a burning in his eyes, looking at Earth. "We can't
let them catch us. There'll be another time. Take us into Hawking, Alacrity. Hurry!"

The others simply kept a despondent silence. Then Corva
cleared his throat human-style, which sounded strange coming
from him. "I believe you're overlooking another factor: this
boat I'm sitting in."

"The *Harpy*! Of course!" Alacrity yelled.

"I don't understand," Victoria said.

"*Harpy* is a stealth ship!" Alacrity exulted. "Don't you see?
We let the Spikes chase the *Stray*—she leads 'em away from
Terra, delays 'em as long as she can before she goes into
Hawking—"

"—and in the meantime, the *Harpy* slips down to Terra,"
Victoria finished. "Yes, of course."

"Only," Sintilla said, "who stays and who goes with *Harpy*?"

"I think the gamble in *Harpy* is for me and Ho," Alacrity
said. "We're the ones who're obliged."

"I am obliged no less by my vows," Corva posited quietly.

"If I don't get this story I'll open my wrists," Sintilla said.
"Besides, I'm not much use on a starship to begin with."

"It's rather more a question of who will stay with *Astraea
Imprimatur*," Victoria pointed out. "Janusz cannot go in the
Harpy, and I will not leave him. But I need another trained
hand to help me con the ship, damaged and vivisected as she
is."

There was a prickling silence.

"Oh, Fitzhugh," Heart said softly. "Sometimes the jinxes really break your way, don't they? Are you sad, or are you relieved? Don't answer—I don't want to have to start wondering whether I can believe you."

Within minutes they'd transferred the cream of the Repository data and their few possessions, having time for little else.

Astraea Imprimatur was a mess. Pressure containers had violated their warrantees and blown apart; debris and breakage were everywhere, and one of the sanitary holding tanks and part of its line had ruptured, moisture boiling off in the vacuum, leaving disgusting deposits in the midships area. Everywhere were signs of the immense strain the ship had weathered.

"She'll do, though," Victoria declared, standing by *Harpy*'s lock. "We can repressurize part of her, at least. She'll get us by all right." She patted a bulkhead with a gloved hand.

"I know a safe place," Heart said. "We can get help there, and—" She glanced toward the compartment where Janusz was secured. "And you two can settle what you must, I guess."

Victoria's ambivalence and confusion carried over the commo net. "You all have a right to know, after everything we've been through together. I've revised my decision. There were new . . . potential injustices, and relative values to weigh. Janusz won't be arrested."

Alacrity put his suited arms around her shoulders as best he could, their helmets bumping. "Take good care of yourself, gal."

"We have to go now." Corva's voice came to them from *Harpy*'s cockpit.

While the others were making rushed farewells, Alacrity switched off his commo and signed for Heart to do the same, then pressed his facebowl against hers. They searched each other's eyes.

"I'll find you. There's more for us to say."

"I hope you mean that, Alacrity." Her voice sounded faint and far away.

CHAPTER 24

ON EARTH IS NOT HIS EQUAL

HARPY DROPPED AWAY FROM THE *ASTRAEA IMPRIMATUR*, STILL impelled by the starship's momentum, as the bigger vessel swung away on a new course. The Spican, still closing, changed to follow. She would now pass by beyond visual range of the spaceboat, which ran darkened, only her critical systems operating. Earth was huge beyond the canopy.

"Here's where we find out if Spican detectors are better than the ones on Blackguard and Epiphany," Alacrity said.

Helmets off at last, they crowded, drifting in freefall, around Corva, watching the displays. It was Floyt's first experience with zero gravity, but he was too apprehensive to give it much thought beyond the effort not to drift around.

No one spoke as they watched the silent story of the displays lighting the cockpit. The Spican drew nearer and nearer to the *Stray*, faked away from the spaceboat and its Earth-approach course. Alacrity was silently mouthing *Go on, get clear!* Corva brought up the boat's internal field, and they were drawn to the deck.

The Srillan was cautiously activating the engines, entreating the Stealth Gods, correcting his vector for blue-white Terra, when the Spican released two missiles at long range. Interceptors arrowed back from the fleeing *Stray* and the Spican missiles fired their own counterinterceptors and defensive beams, as did the *Stray*'s. Before the fireworks contest had been played out, Victoria and Heart had taken *Astraea Imprimatur* into Hawking.

Alacrity let out a breath he'd been holding for a long time.

"I may have to go back on my word and write about Janusz, and Victoria too." Sintilla sighed. "'Love conquers all.' It always sells big."

"Of course, they had a little help from biology, making Vic decide what she should do and all," Alacrity reminded her.

Floyt broke his preoccupation with the displays and laughed for what seemed like the first time in years. "They had a lot more than biology going for them. Or am I wrong, Corva?"

The Srillan was uncharacteristically remote, still busy with the controls. "I have no idea what you mean, Hobart."

"What I mean is that coincidences do happen, like Victoria's conceiving just at this time. I guess I'd have accepted it too, except—those *weren't* the control auxiliaries you were working on when I almost fell over you. I know; I looked it up. They *were* the utilities, including the hookup for the mediscan computer."

"Corva, I thought you were sworn by your compact not to interfere?" Sintilla said to break the silence.

"I did *not* interfere," Corva contradicted, "as such. But even a contrition-knight can indulge in a little well-intended cheating."

Sintilla kissed him on his furry head. "I wonder what'll happen when they find out she's not pregnant?" Alacrity said.

"One of two things. And I bet I know which," Floyt replied. "Good work, Corva."

"Don't mention it. Now, can someone tell me what 'Utah' is?"

The Spican interception had been last minute indeed. Before long they were entering Earth's upper atmosphere. The *Harpy*'s detectors said the planet's antiquated warning systems were on full alert, but nothing was picking them up.

"What I'm worried about is your Citizen Ash," Sintilla said. "The Conspiracy might've gotten to him by now, put him out of the picture."

"You don't know Citiz̧on Ash," Alacrity commented as he finished stowing the last of the spacesuits. "And besides, all the Alphas know about so far is the *Astraea Imprimatur*, and they think she's been driven away. I doubt they've tried to tangle with Ash."

No detectors could pick up the spaceboat, but eyes could. Corva told them all to fasten in as he cut a screaming trail into the atmosphere.

"What will they throw at us?" Alacrity asked from the co-pilot's poz.

"How should I know?" Floyt answered over the intercom. "Nothing terribly modern, I should think."

"I'm tracking missiles, or something like them," Corva said. "And I think I've got massive energy buildups, particle beam weapons perhaps."

But the missiles and interceptor drones, their guidance systems gulled, couldn't get a lock on the spaceboat; Corva was careful not to ram into one by chance. It was their good luck that Terra didn't throw something even older and slower at them, something guided by remote optical pickups. The computers that were supposed to aim and fire the beam weapons continued to insist that there was nothing there to shoot at.

"I'm registering a big ground-level explosion here," Alacrity said. "I think one of the beam installations just overloaded and went blooey."

No vessel had moved through Terra's sky that fast in two hundred years. They began their approach on the Utah urban-plex a hemisphere away. "How do we find Ash?" Sintilla thought to ask. "I mean how to we pinpoint him?"

"Victoria tricked his accessor index out of the SATNET," Alacrity explained. "The net won't put us through, but Ash is a shrewd guy; he left his accessor keyed, and we'll home on him."

"Double shrewd," Sintilla said. "Now if he's just trusting, credulous, open-minded, and invincible."

"And if we are visited by the Gift of Persuasion," Corva thought to include.

Somehow, Earthservice came up with three big, armed peaceguardian skyvans, which flew at them in an unpracticed attack formation as the *Harpy*, having shed most of her speed, came in toward the urbanplex. Two kilometers below, on the roof of the admin center, according to instruments, was Citizen Ash.

The spaceboat was no match for a Spican patrol craft, but she outclassed anything the Terrans could put up. Corva didn't want to cause any injuries he didn't have to, both from compassion and because the selling job ahead of them would be hard enough. He avoided their volleys—riot-control energy weapons and a few wall-openers—while Alacrity had the *Harpy*'s guns deftly burn up some grilles and trim. Two vans withdrew, damaged, and the third followed, intact but chastened.

"Now look," Alacrity said over the cop control net, "we're landing peaceably, but I'm warning you: we've got a lot of very dangerous weapons and ordnance inboard. If you attack again, anything could happen."

He played around with the signal-warfare suite a little more and found that they were close enough to pick up Ash's accessor directly. Alacrity patched it through to the peaceguardian net.

"This is Citizen Ash speaking. On my authority, all peaceguardian units are to withdraw and maintain their distance. There are to be no further actions against that vessel or its occupants."

The regional peaceguardian commander got on. "I have my orders from Alpha-Bureaucrat Stemp."

"And I'm countermanding them. You are obstructing me in the discharge of my office."

The attacks hadn't done much good anyway and the commander, like most Terrans, had a deep-rooted fear of offworld weapons and a profound uneasiness where Citizen Ash was concerned. He called off the vans but held his units ready.

The *Harpy* came in on the roof, detectors alert, weapons ready. "The admin center." Alacrity groaned. "Did he have to pick the enemy's backyard?" The admin center was only a small part of the urbanplex, but its roof was forty hectares or so of giant outlets, intakes, vents, stacks, and waste heat dissipators.

The boat landed on one of the largest open areas, roughly

square, some 150 meters on a side, near a bank of chuteshafts. Alacrity, peering through the viewpane, noticed lots of surveillance and security equipment.

"What now?" Sintilla asked.

"What do you think, Hobart? Guns or no?" Corva said. "Are those offensive weapons along with the security pickups on the surveillance pylons?"

"They could be. This is a restricted area. But we didn't come here to shoot it out, did we?"

"That doesn't mean it can't happen," Alacrity said, buckling on his gun. Floyt looked at the Webley for a second, then carefully left it in his seat. Corva and Sintilla didn't arm themselves either.

"Look!" Sintilla was pointing through a viewpane at Citizen Ash. He was dressed in his customary black—a loose shirt with ruffled cuffs and high, frilly collar, tapered trousers, and gleaming shoes. He was walking unhurriedly in their direction. He also wore a sleeveless manteau, open at the front, and satiny sash wound around a slim waist, all in his chosen color.

He was medium Earther height, two or three centimeters taller than Floyt, tanned and handsome in the way the Terrans still called "Mediterranean," with a meticulous mustache.

"Shouldn't one of us stay inboard?" Sintilla asked.

"You may if you wish to, of course," Corva answered. "I have been waiting for this too long. And we must win our case here, now. All of us who feel up to it must bear witness."

The four stepped to the lock as Citizen Ash drew near. Floyt went first, wearing his Inheritor's belt, carrying a satchel filled with Camarilla information.

"It seems you've both been busy," Ash said by way of greeting to Floyt and Alacrity as they jumped down. They looked gaunt and exhausted.

Alacrity still had a wan smile left in him. "Sorry to drop in on you like this."

"I'd like to say that we'll only ask a minute of your time," Floyt told Ash, "but that wouldn't be true."

Ash had a rejoinder but forgot it, and paled. Corva had emerged from the lock and turned to help Sintilla down.

"How dare you," Ash said in a dire monotone. "A Srillan.

Whatever happens to you now, you'll have earned. Say whatever you came to say. So, this is what Weir wanted us to have."

"No; this is." Floyt opened the satchel, showing the documents and data. "And this is!" He held out an old holo 2-D of a conference table. There were officials of the vanished Terran Union Armed Forces and the Spican Colonial Fleet—and Srillans. Faces and poses indicated that it had been taken covertly.

"Two hundred years ago it started, when Earth was devastated," Floyt maintained, willing his voice to ring true. "But, Citizen Ash, *it's still going on today*! We have the proof; we know where there's more to be had. Do you understand what I'm saying? Earth wasn't overwhelmed, wasn't beaten; she was sacrificed. She was betrayed. And Terra is not in reduced circumstances by the natural order of things. She is being held there."

He offered another document, an agreement signed by the original Camarillans. Sintilla interwined her fingers with Alacrity's and squeezed. Ash had been gazing at the 2-D. Slowly, unwillingly, he reached out and took the second document from Floyt. And a third. A fourth.

The chuteshaft indicators lit up. A moment later doors slid aside and Alpha-Bureaucrat Stemp rushed out along with Alpha Chin and Supervisor Bear, flanked by senior peaceguardian brass and some of the biggest rankers Floyt had ever seen.

"Stand where you are!" Stemp bawled, charging at them, pushing a couple of peacers out front for cover. "This illegal meeting is terminated. All offworlders and Functionary Third Class Floyt are under arrest!"

Ash watched them come, and when they were near, held up the flat of his palm to halt them in that odd gesture Alacrity had seen him use before. "Come no further; I am conducting an inquiry here."

The peacers in the lead were massive, bull-necked colonels, but they slowed, looking to Stemp for further instructions. Stemp shoved them aside. "There are no grounds for an inquiry by the executioner's office! There has been invasion, unprovoked attack, and con—that is, collusion, with intent to subvert."

"You were about to say 'conspiracy,'" Corva corrected in an undertone, but they all heard it. Bear and the peacers weren't sure what to do at the sight of the Srillan except pop their eyes at him. Stemp went back on the offensive.

"You traitors!" he sneered at Floyt and Alacrity. "You, Fitzhugh! We gave you back your life and this is how you repay us and keep your word. And as for you, Floyt, you're living proof that *offworld* is poison to Earthers. Look how you've stabbed Terra in the back! A Srillan! And you tried to land a *starship*! You're a pack of mad dogs!"

"We brought back the Terran Inheritance," Floyt countered.

"We were just showing it to Citizen Ash, would you like to see?" Alacrity challenged.

Stemp had gone white, but Alpha-Bureaucrat Chin rallied. "That's not the issue here! You and your cohorts are under arrest! Officers!" She prodded one of the peacers.

Ash was frowning a bit now, looking stubborn. He waved a finger at the peacers, metronome fashion, keeping them back. "I think I will hear more about this Camarilla."

"This isn't in your purview—whatever it's about," Stemp argued. "Your official powers don't extend to this. What we have here is a case for the High Bench itself. Yes, this is a matter for the peaceguardian investigators and the Justice Division. You have no authority in it. Even *you* operate under certain constraints, bear in mind."

One of the colonels coughed tentatively. "Alpha-Bureaucrat Stemp is quite right, sir. This case has not been referred to your office." He faced Alacrity with one hand on his gun.

The surveillance pickups and weapons installations—Alacrity could see that was what they were—were all aligned at the confrontation now. The colonel said, "Hand over that weapon and any others you people may have, and surrender. You're under arrest."

Ash said, "This is a suspect proceeding. I petition you, peaceguardians and Alpha-Bureaucrats, to deviate from official procedure. I'd like to resolve my misgivings here and now."

"Petition denied," Stemp rapped, regaining his confidence. "Be advised: you yourself are obstructing justice."

Ash looked about him, at the Alphas, peacers, at Corva and

Sintilla, at the *Harpy*—and at Floyt and Alacrity last of all. An air of melancholy was on him. The powers of the executioner were conferred only in conjunction with deep and powerful behavioral engineering administered by the Office of the Executioner—passed along by Ash's predecessors.

"They—he's right," Ash confessed. "I function within certain limits. My authority doesn't extend to this situation, though I wish it were otherwise. I can't help you."

He made to give the evidence back to Floyt, but Stemp came forward, hand extended. "I'll just take that.

The cop was about to demand Alacrity's gun again. Alacrity eyed the peacers and the pylon installations, calculating his chances in a shootout. He calculated them as just about nil.

Floyt moved suddenly, desperate that Stemp not get the satchel. He found himself shoving away an Alpha-Bureaucrat. Stemp staggered back into the arms of the cop colonel. The peacers advanced on Floyt.

"Wait! Listen!" Floyt shouted at Ash. "There's something else: Alacrity was framed! For that murder at Macchu Pichu! We have proof; I brought a copy of the message here, somewhere . . ."

He riffled frantically, knowing what would happen to himself, his friends, and the evidence once the Alphas had them. The peacers were closing in as he thrust into Ash's hands the excerpt mentioning Project Shepherd's entrapment of Alacrity.

Ash took a quick glance at the excerpt, then pulled Floyt to him and behind him. The cops wavered.

"I will take charge now," the executioner announced. "Citizen Stemp, you are now an interested party—an implicated party, since your agency was involved in the case. You and these other bureaucrats will withdraw at once and hold yourselves ready to give testimony."

Stemp's face colored. "The devil you say!" He motioned to the peaceguardians. "Take them all into custody! Go on, do as I order!"

The cops were working themselves up to obey. Ash lowered his head at them like an angry bull. "I warn you one last time: this situation is concerned with an adjudicated homicide case.

That takes precedence even over charges of sedition and collusion."

Stemp had been speaking into his Alpha-model accessor. "One more chance, Ash. Then I have the installations open fire!"

Ash looked around. The cops moved back, knowing what that would mean. Alacrity tried to decide why they hadn't just been told to shoot. Then he remembered Ash's behavior when Alacrity had first met him. He was pretty sure the executioner was concealing something a lot more dangerous than underwear beneath that sinisterly dapper attire.

He might be safe from Terran handguns, but nothing man-portable's gonna hold up against heavy weapons. Still and all, Ash didn't look worried.

"Stay near me," was all Ash said to the four. They lost no time closing up tightly behind him. Floyt somehow didn't find it odd to have Corva almost on top of him, hands on Floyt's shoulders. In fact, it was reassuring.

Stemp's face was purple-red. Chin and Bear were watching in profound fury, that of people who are afraid their emotions will shift to solid fear very soon. Stemp brought his accessor up.

He uttered a string of syllables and access code ciphers that made no sense whatsoever to Floyt, who'd been dealing with Terra's systems all his adult life. The Alpha ended with "Fire!"

Ash's voice cracked like a nervefire lash as he yelled directly at the audio pickups on the pylons, "Cancel!" He added a string of the same arcane codewords.

The weapons began realigning, and Alacrity understood why Ash had picked that particular spot for the showdown. Stemp looked as if he'd been given a jotting. Chin started edging back for the chuteshafts and Bear seemed about to faint.

Stemp tried more commands, rattling them into his accessor, and, when that had no effect, screaming them at the pickups, thinking to imitate Ash's magic. All to no avail.

"The cops. He's gonna try the cops on us next," Alacrity muttered to Floyt in a low voice. His gun hand was hidden by Ash's body. He pulled the Captain's Sidearm, still hiding it.

The peaceguardians were irresolute. Ash was speaking cryptosounds to the empty air. The surveillance pickups were all operating, recording the scene, despite Stemp's command for a blackout. Stemp lowered his accessor, baring his teeth at Ash. "What are you doing?"

"The pickups are patched through to override," Ash explained evenly. "This incident is being transmitted everywhere."

Cynthia Chin found that the chuteshaft doors wouldn't open for her and began babbling into her own accessor. It did no good.

Stemp had already come to the same conclusion Alacrity had, and began exhorting the peacers to do their duty. They were still used to jumping when an Alpha gave the command. Floyt had a wild moment in which to picture people everywhere watching the face-off. The cops went for their weapons.

It was a hopeless crossfire but Alacrity just felt like he'd been through too much to go down without a fight. He held his gun up, moving Ash a little with his free hand, about to take a bead on Stemp.

Ash beat the arm down with surprising strength, showing a dark wrath. "You fool! Do you want to be the death of us all?" He plucked the pistol away easily and tossed it aside, far. The peaceguardians, momentarily daunted, brought their weapons up.

Ash shouted a sound. The weapons installations volleyed from all sides with impressive accuracy, an abrupt, brilliant crisscross of the kind of neuroparalyzer Alacrity had been shot with at the Earthservice conditioning clinic, so long ago.

The peacers were outlined in bright coronas, some convulsing for a moment, all toppling to lie unmoving on the roof.

It became very quiet, except for a Terran breeze. Stemp began backing away, lost in a mental disarray, with no notion of what he was doing. Bear was still frozen in place. Chin stood by the chuteshaft doors, arms folded across her chest, resigned and waiting.

"How long have you had *that* one up your sleeve?" Alacrity asked in a small voice.

The executioner didn't look aside at him. "Some things one learns from one's predecessors; some things one learns in the course of investigations, or because someone wants to buy their way out of a dilemma, make a deal. Believe it, my office has its impediments, but it also has its resources."

"And some pretty good trump cards," Floyt reflected. The words brought the ever-thinking, ever-observant Ash back to matters at hand.

"Yes. Well. You have a lot to tell me, I hope, Hobart Floyt. I hope you all do." He picked up the satchel and weighed it in his hand.

"Umm," Alacrity said, nodding his head toward Stemp, Bear, and Chin.

"Oh, yes," Ash said as though he'd completely forgotten them. "You men give them a hand, if you'd be so kind? We don't want them hurting themselves."

CHAPTER 25

OFF KEY ON CAUSALITY'S HARP

"THIS ONE'S IT, I BET," ALACRITY SAID, SHADING HIS EYES, watching the approaching aircar. "Looks new and shiny; it better be ours."

"Ours'll probably be disguised as a hazardous waste transporter," Floyt disagreed. "Half the population of Earth thinks we ought to be drawn and quartered for starting all this trouble."

"Drawn and quartered?"

"Capital punishment as practiced by people without access to airlocks."

"Oh." The car didn't seem to be headed toward them, though. Floyt wore the tuxedo he'd carried all the way to the stars and, somehow, back—white tie and black tails—along with his Inheritor's belt. Alacrity's suit was the trusty ice-blue one, and he had on his venerable pathfinders.

"I've just called; your vehicle will be here shortly," Citizen Ash said, coming up behind them. Floyt hoped he hadn't heard the capital punishment crack but doubted it; Ash missed little. "Can I rely on you both to show up in time for the next deposition taping? Don't fail me; I'm having enough trouble holding things together as it is."

He gestured to dozens of second-level Earth rulers waiting to one side of the landing stage in a gaggle, hoping for a few moments of Ash's time. They were kept back by a squad of peaceguardians who reminded Floyt of Severeemish. With the evidence in hand and virtually all Earthservice media under his usurpation, and all Alphas now under close arrest, Citizen Ash was de facto head of Terra's government. The Solarian, Srillan, and Spican forces canceled one another out and stayed out of the crisis for the time being.

Earth was poised for change. The Alphas were falling over each other trying to make deals with Ash; his position was secure for the moment. To the relief of Floyt and Alacrity, among others, Ash, too, recognized the need for a new shape of things and showed no inclination to become dictator.

"We won't," Floyt promised. "And tell Corva and Sintilla, if you will, that we'll be back by the time their tapings are over."

"I'll do that."

Another aircar arced into view, a soberly rakish unmarked peaceguardian craft. Citizen Ash bade them good-bye and strode from the landing area.

The car landed with two beefy senior plainclothesmen in it. The driver stayed at the controls and the passenger, the senior officer, climbed out, glowering at all the commotion. "You two Citizen Floyt and Fitzhugh?" Floyt nodded. "Okay; get in." He jerked his thumb at a rear door.

"*'Get in?'*" Alacrity stepped forward; he was taller than the cop, lean and dangerous-looking. He yanked open the driver's door after a moment's fumbling with the unfamiliar lock. The driver looked up, frozen, knowing that he couldn't simply start clubbing people.

Alacrity grabbed him by his cheap Earthservice suit. "Move to the rear, Wide Load! Cap'n Floyt does all the piloting when he flies!"

The peacer started to stutter an objection. Alacrity hauled him out onto the landing stage. The senior officer's hand went toward his gun by reflex but stopped. Citizen Ash was looking on from the sidelines, and nowadays everyone on Earth knew just how much could happen when *he* got angry.

"You boys formerly working Alpha-bodyguard detail, were you? Well, don't push your luck." Alacrity jabbed a thumb at the passenger door. With looks of unspeakable resentment, the two plainclothesmen climbed into the rear.

Alacrity, holding the driver's door open, kowtowed briskly to Floyt. "Ready, Cap'n." The watching bureaucrats were transfixed.

"Um, Alacrity, do you think this is really such a good—"

"Dual controls," Alacrity growled under his breath. "Let's go."

Floyt carefully swept his tux tails apart, to avoid sitting on them, and slid into the driver's poz; Alacrity trotted around and belted in behind the copilot's duals. "See? It's a baby pram," Alacrity assured Floyt out of the side of his mouth. Alacrity pressed a button and the doors closed with a solid *chack*!

It wasn't so different from the airsedan on Blackguard, but Floyt's lift-off was a little rocky. Alacrity restrained himself from grabbing for the duals. Floyt headed them away over the urbanplex.

Psychprop holosigns and info flashers had either been blanked or reprogrammed to something neutral and nonxenophobic. The odd riot or demonstration had been quelled, but people were assembling to talk and argue almost everywhere, and so far Ash was letting them.

The dashboard had a simple satnav display, easy to follow. Floyt quickly got the feeling of the controls, and they sailed along, in no particular hurry, high over the Earth, drinking in the colors and the feeling.

Floyt located the control that raised a tinted panel between the front seat and the passenger compartment. "Did Citizen Ash say anything more about when you might get to leave, Alacrity?"

"Huh-uh." Alacrity was still studying the landscape. "He moves slowly and deliberately. He still hasn't released all the evidence we brought him to the offworlders." He chuckled. "Will you listen to me? *'Offworlders!'* I'd give anything to know what's going on in the Srillan and Spican naval contingents.

"But no, he's been dodging talking about when any of us can leave. At least Tilla and Corva are happy."

"They are that," Floyt concurred, trying the aircar in a sharp bank. The peacers, belted in, made no objection.

Corva had righted a wrong for the entire Srillan race—or at least begun the process. The feat promised to be the new definition of a contrition-knight. He was standing by to put himself at the service of the Srillan envoy who would arrive soon to witness and take part in the Earthservice hearings being mounted by Citizen Ash.

And Sintilla had calmly recorded the entire scene on the Utah urbanplex rooftop. She'd somehow gotten Ash to agree that she would be the sole offworld press representative during the hearings. She was also working on two books about the whole episode, in addition to *Hobart Floyt and Alacrity Fitzhugh Face the Menace of the Galactic Illuminati*.

"I'd give anything to know what happened to the *Stray*," Alacrity said, "but the devil of it is, it would put the others in danger even to ask." Floyt watched the terrain roll by, helpless to say anything of comfort.

The role-playing commune where Floyt's wife, Balensa, was currently living with her lover, a Hemingway revivicist named Arlo Mote, was situated on the roof of one of the outer, lower exclaves of the urbanplex. The commune revolved around various artistic and literary figures of the period between Earth's first two world wars; it was a big, rambling garret with broad skylights, and miniaturized Parisian rooftops and skyline around it.

Floyt made a rather good approach and landing; the instrument displays and landing stage navlights made it almost foolproof. Balensa was waiting in the fore of the reception committee of Terran preterists, along with Floyt's daughter, Reesa, and Arlo Mote.

Balensa had been brought up in an extended-family/academic-group concentrating on the Italian Renaissance, but she was now dressed as an Apache dancer. Reesa, who'd been immersed in romantic reenactments of Pleistocene life when he'd left, was now turned out as a flapper. Mote wore faded safari clothes.

Behind them were such other members of the commune as

had managed to get away or happened to be off when word had come that Floyt would be visiting. There was the odd hoplite or cowboy in the throng, but most were dressed in the right period.

Floyt, the lowly functionary third class, booted off Terra by a bullying Earthservice, emerged not from the passenger compartment of the Alpha-perk aircar but from behind its controls. The mass indrawing of breath by the crowd was clearly audible. Alacrity fell in just behind Floyt's right shoulder. His shipsuit was cut to allow the silver-in-gray hair to hang free; the big, oblique, lamp-yellow eyes were uncovered. It wasn't so long ago that they'd gotten him attacked, in Macchu Pichu, as a freak. Now several female members of the crowd began making strong eye contact.

Balensa stepped over to them uncertainly. A few months hadn't changed her, but that somehow surprised Floyt. She had long brown hair and the slender figure of a teenager. Reesa came too, eyes shining. Balensa stopped a meter or so from Floyt.

"What's wrong? Why are you staring?"

"You're so different," she said.

"Well, no. Or only a little. We missed a few meals."

"No, Hobart, it's not just that. Did you really fly that thing?"

"You don't think he trusts *me* to fly, do you?" Alacrity asked. Reesa giggled. The other Terrans took up the laugh and Alacrity grinned lopsidedly.

In a way that changed nothing, but assuaged a lot, Balensa said to Floyt, "I'm glad you came back safe, Hobart. Welcome home." She closed the distance and kissed him soundly, and then it was Reesa's turn.

Reesa went on to hug Alacrity. When Floyt lifted an eyebrow, Alacrity mouthed, *Oh, don't worry!*

Reesa slipped one arm through towering Alacrity's and one through Floyt's, saying, "Please come in, both of you."

Alacrity whistled to get the cops' attention and waved them to come along. They looked at each other, then did.

Floyt was trying not to stare at Balensa. She'd returned to Mote, taking his hand. Floyt allowed his daughter to conduct him into the commune. He was reliving the vast tidal feeling he'd experience when he saw Earth through *Harpy*'s viewpane and wondering if he would ever fit in anywhere again.

The role-playing commune showed them an old-fashioned Terran good time, complete with jazz, French cooking, wine, and reenactments. Alacrity didn't understand it all, but he had terrific fun. Floyt did too, but was preoccupied much of the time.

The Terrans pleaded for stories. Interest in anything off-world, vulgar if not downright illegal only a few days before, was now universal. Alacrity began with the story of the disastrous funeral on Way 'Long. Carbon Dioxide College had reestablished its terrestrial campus.

"Did you really captain a pirate ship?" people asked Floyt. "Did you truly come home through an *exploding star*?"

They did the Lindy, broke excellent bread, and all toasted one another; even the plainclothesmen had a reservedly good time. At last Floyt had to remind Alacrity that their brief furlough was almost over; the peacers were so distracted that they'd forgotten. The commune and its guests trooped back out to the landing stage. Floyt and Alacrity had various souvenirs. The peacers each carried a loaf of French bread.

There was a certain amount of confusion as a number of people jostled to look at the aircar and say good-bye to Alacrity, admonish him to come back, or get a photo or vid taken with him. He ate it up with *noblesse oblige*.

Floyt took the opportunity to draw Reesa aside. "They're starting to talk about letting Terrans offworld again, at least as a pilot program. Don't ask me why right now, dear, but I don't see how they'll be able to avoid it. The rules are about to change, like it or not."

Her face fell. "You mean you and Alacrity are leaving again so soon?"

"No! No, Ash and the others are planning to keep us busy right here for some time to come."

He took both her hands. "What I mean is, do *you* want to go? I think I can fix it. There are people of influence—*beings* of influence—who can arrange it, who would do it for me, I think."

"I don't know what to say! I'd like to go some day, I suppose; everybody's talking about it now, since you got back. But— just on the spur of the moment like this—I can't really think about it too clearly."

"I know; I should've realized. They made it easy for me; kicked me off Earth. *'Bring us your Inheritance!'* "

They both laughed, and sniffed, near tears. Alacrity was warming up the aircar. Floyt turned over one of his daughter's hands and pressed something into it.

"Keep this for yourself, do you hear me? Don't tell anybody. It's my little piece of the Terran Inheritance, to give to you."

It was a small purse fat with the novaseed gems Floyt had earned on Way 'Long and most of the money he'd won at the Grapple with Amarok. "It's yours. Use it as you see fit." He closed her fingers around it.

They hugged, then he turned and made for the aircar. The other Earthers were listening to Alacrity, who was leaning on the aircar, holding court and providing a diversion. Balensa and Arlo Mote were waiting to talk to Floyt.

Mote was a little uneasy, though he and Floyt had made peace. He had one thumb hooked through his imitation leather belt with its ersatz Nazi buckle carrying the words GOTT MIT UNS.

"If we can help you, let us know," Balensa said.

"And you're welcome to stay here whenever you want, to get away from it all," Mote added. "To stay or go as you please."

Floyt knew for certain then that there was no reconciliation with Balensa coming; he could see it in her face and hear it. He wondered if it was because he'd gone from being too much a known quantity to too much an unknown. The oceanic gathering in him, from *Harpy*, stirred again.

"That's very nice of you. No one else on Earth has been that generous to me since I came back." He was about to go, but something occurred to him.

"See here, I have reason to believe Terra will be opened up, a little, anyway, to outsiders, in the not-too-distant future. Now, that's classified, and I don't know how you could best profit from it, but I have a modest suggestion."

They both leaned toward him.

"Lourdes," Floyt said. Balensa frowned and Mote was nonplussed.

"Lourdes," Floyt repeated. "Or better yet, that place, Vichy, where the healing waters were. That sort of thing; especially the ones in Japan. A lot of offworlders still believe in Earth's healing powers, on a mystical level. It's not a sure thing, but you might give it some thought."

"We shall," Balensa promised. She hugged him. Floyt thought, *What the hell*, and shook hands with Mote. Alacrity was calling for him; Mote held onto his hand a moment longer.

"Look here, old man. What's it *really* like out there?"

Floyt had heard the question more times than he could count since returning. At first he'd been confused, giving conflicting answers that didn't begin to do justice to the truth. With Mote and Balensa looking so intently at his face, he gave for the first time the answer that he was to use from then on.

"You'll have to find that out for yourself."

Nazca spaceport was a busier place than it had been the last time they'd been through, but they still ended up in the same terminal gate area, waiting for the selfsame lunar shuttle in which they'd left Terra initially, a whole different lifetime ago.

Most of the bustle was devoted to refurbishing landing, service, and terminal facilities. "What's going on over there?" Alacrity was pointing across the field to where a stupendous building was being renovated. "That's a starship hangar, isn't it? Don't tell me . . ."

"Our shuttle traffic has already quintupled, and that's just for the advance and liaison units of the Solarian and Spican investigative delegations," Ash told him. "No one's voiced it in public yet, but I don't see any avoiding it—starships will be coming again." He thought for a moment. "Like most people, I'm of very mixed minds on that one. The psychprop people have a generation's work cut out for them."

"What surprises me even more," Floyt put in, "is *them*." He meant the Terran bureaucrats and officials who jammed the waiting area, talking politics and jockeying for position, waiting to make inroads with the offworlders who were due in another minute or two. "It was only—not even—two weeks ago that offworlders were anathema." He was adjusting his tuxedo, and resettling the Inheritor's belt.

"Well, yeah, but you're forgetting one thing," Alacrity said. "They're all politicians, and the writing's on the wall. The name of the new graffito is Open Earth. And speaking of XTs . . ."

Sintilla was charging in their direction with Corva in tow, recording her impressions on her proteus while pointing an audvid pickup around with her free hand. The Terran dignitaries stared frankly and curiously at the Srillan, and a few of the women even seemed to be studying him rather . . . appraisingly. He'd become a familiar figure on Terran screens and already Earthly children were imitating his stooping shamble, his droopy-eyed look, and his acerbic, nasal singsong, which scandalized their elders, which made it all that much more fun.

As she reached them, Sintilla rattled breathlessly, "The new rumor is that Stemp and Chin and the others are actually XTs from some superadvanced civilization in the Galactic Core area, all rigged out in human disguises, who for some unfathomable reason or other bothered to come all the damn way out here just to give Earth a hard time."

"That's interesting," Floyt said. "*I* heard that *we* were the aliens."

Ash didn't quite smile. "'We'? You mean me as well?"

"*Especially* you, or so the rumor goes."

Ash's expression clouded for a moment. Then he said, "*I* heard reports that we're all clones controlled by the Illuminati, whoever they are."

Alacrity and Floyt looked off in different directions. Corva coughed behind his hand. Sintilla was the picture of innocence.

"Lunar shuttle arriving in sixty seconds," the PA said. The jostling became more intense, but peaceguardians kept the crowd back. The four from *Harpy*, standing with Citizen Ash, were immune to the indignities of crowd control.

"We must get a shuttle of our own operating soon," Ash mulled, hands clasped behind his back. "Do you think the *Harpy* would serve, Alacrity? A matter of planetary pride, you might say."

Alacrity hummed. "She'd do fine, for now. Especially for the V.I.P. treatment. You'd better start picking some of your best and brightest kids and getting some advice about offworld flight schools."

"*Tch*, oh, yes, yes." Sintilla shunted the subject aside. "What *I* want to know, Citizen Ash, sir, is when you're going to sit still for that interview you keep promising me. I don't think you fully appreciate what a celebrity I'm going to make out of you, you wonderful man!"

Ash looked both charmed and pained. "Very soon, I give you my word. There'll be time; after all, you've got weeks and months of testimony ahead."

"Months?" Alacrity echoed. "Now it's *months*? Months of saying the same stuff over and over? The stuff you've already gone over and recorded five times?"

"I'm afraid it looks that way," Ash said. "I know it's not a just reward, but this situation has taken on a life of its own."

"But you've got Corva and Tilla and Ho for that! And the evidence we brought, and the Alphas' testimony! Can't you just let me go my way, Citizen? It's really important; there're other things I should be doing."

Ash let a little irritation show. "Don't you think I wish you could go? You knew what you were getting into when you came back. Do not lay it all at my door!"

Alacrity chewed that over for a moment. "Yes, all right; fair enough."

Ash subsided. "I'll make it as easy on you as I can, Alacrity. On all four of you. And I didn't mean to snap, because when it comes right down to it I'm very grateful to you and the others who were in on this thing. So is everybody who's managed to start thinking clearly."

"We understand," Corva answered for them all. "And we're very, very glad we could help Earth touch the stars again." When they heard it put that way, the other three agreed at once.

"Shuttle arriving now," the PA said.

"Do you think they're ready for this?" Floyt asked as Terran notables straightened their sashes and primped their hairdos, cleared their throats and wiped sweat from their palms.

"They'll have to be," Ash replied. "As Alacrity said, the

writing's on the walls. Connections to offworlders and non-humans is the key to their place in the new order of things."

"They're politicians," Sintilla said. "Wait till you see *how* fast they adapt."

The Lunar shuttle *Mindframe* descended on rumbling engines, finishing the last few dozen meters on tame tractor beams. She hadn't changed a bit, Alacrity saw; down-at-the-heels as ever. The peaceguardians spread their arms, holding back the eager crowd.

The first two debarking passengers, a Spican military attaché and a Solarian secretary of foreign affairs, courteously stepped to either side to make way for the ranking member of the delegation, the special high commissioner from the Srillan Comity. He shuffled into the reception area, acknowledging the polite applause of the Terrans. He waved and nodded graciously as more passengers came forth and the first handshakes and greetings began. He glanced over and noticed Alacrity and Floyt.

"*Ning-ning-a-ning!* All hail the Strange Attractors! (If only, for once, they'd attract something besides trouble!) *A-ning!*"

"I think everything's going to be all right around here," Floyt said happily.

Lord Admiral Maska came to them first, and no one was inclined to advise him differently. He and Alacrity exchanged the odd pattycake handslap Floyt had seen them trade at Frost-pile, then the Srillan took Floyt's hand in the peculiar greeting of his species, a sort of top and bottom chafing motion.

"Good stories lighten the burdens of life," Maska said. "I hope you children will take some of the weight off my poor old back by telling me yours while I'm here."

"Sure, if you'll tell us what Cazpahr Weir told you about Strange Attractors," Alacrity offered.

"I think that sounds grand." Maska turned to bow low, human-style, before Sintilla, bringing her fingertips to his lips. For the first time that Floyt and Alacrity knew of, she blushed and had nothing to say. "And it is divine to see you again, young lady."

Maska somehow resisted what must have been a powerful temptation to go into a singsong jape dance with his nephew.

Alacrity had a feeling they'd get to it later. The two aliens did a finger-twining double handclasp.

"Nice of you to take up the family business," Maska told his nephew, "of nosiness, intrigue, and cabalistic machinations."

"I lay it all at the door of my genetic inheritance," Corva jibed modestly. "And Director Weir, of course."

"Yes. Why don't we talk about that later?"

Corva bowed and backed aside. Lord Admiral Maska went to Citizen Ash. They shook hands Terran fashion. "I greet you and thank you for your kindness to my kinsman," Maska said. "That message is from myself. From the Srillan Comity I bring you our wish and our word, *tsaalff!* which means healing and building and making new once more."

They were all watching Ash closely. Alacrity couldn't recall ever seeing the executioner so rigidly controlled, and feared the worst; or the tepid, at best.

Ash fooled him. "I've consulted the archives, partly with Hobart Floyt's help. There was once a great accord between Earth and Srilla. It would be beneficial for that to come again, under a new Terran government. Ts—ts—*tsaalff!*" He bowed. So did Maska.

"Excuse me, but just what kind of government are you going to put into place?" Alacrity asked Ash.

Ash evinced shock. "Me?"

"Who else?"

That hit home, wringing a smile out of Ash. "Hobart's been accessing about that too."

The pressure from the massed politicians was about to become a riot; Ash led Maska to take up his duties, Corva taking his uncle's other arm. Sintilla dogged their track, recording and chivying.

"Things aren't going badly, considering how much got jinxed along the way," Floyt remarked.

"That's not far wrong, I guess," Alacrity said, looking down at his pathfinders. "The problem is, for Ash and the others, it's a beginning. They can't see that, for some of us on a different time cycle, it's the wrapup."

Floyt nodded slowly, watching humanity mix with aliens.

"But still, overall, I think it will amount to something good, don't you, Alacrity? Alacrity? Wh—Alacrity?"

Then Floyt saw him, sauntering along casually, well behind the crowd-control peaceguardians and the customs officers who were working furiously to expedite the envoys' documents and luggage. He seemed to stop at the boarding tube entrance by chance; no one beside Floyt noticed him in the confusion of the reception area.

He chatted up the Lunie shuttle crewchief. Floyt realized it was the same man from their first trip. Somebody was starting a speech. The Lunie was yawning and looking around, noting the situation. Alacrity exchanged a rather drawn-out handshake with him. The crewchief looked down at his palm and deigned to raise one eyebrow. He nodded slowly.

Alacrity looked Floyt in the eye across the room. He didn't have to gesture; he merely stepped to the tube entrance, grinning wickedly, and mouthed, *You coming*?

Floyt was on the move before he could be assailed by second thoughts; he knew now what that tidal current was, and it carried him along. Alacrity had reached behind some peacer equipment trunks and drawn out his warbag, complete with brolly. "We're almost out of time," he warned Floyt, when the Earther got there.

"We're *always* almost out of time." Floyt frowned.

"Yeah; that's why people are always mistaking our guile for good luck, Ho. But this time I mean *really*, see?" He indicated the crewchief, who was headed for the shuttle's lock.

"Alacrity, they're never going to let us go."

"We'll know in a second. Look."

Citizen Ash, with the Solarian defense minister nattering in his ear, was glaring directly at them. Alacrity backed a step into the boarding tube. Floyt thought about living on only one planet for the rest of his life, then joined him.

Ash's volcanic look held them, then his lips shaped a single syllable, *go*! He gave them the hint of a smile, then turned to hear more about the joint commercial project being offered Terra by the rest of the Solar system.

Sintilla, who was more or less clinging to Citizen Ash's arm, had caught the exchange. She would've yelled in surprise except that Floyt held a finger to his lips. She shook her head with an exasperated grin, the brown curls bobbing. A tear had started from one eye.

You bums! she yelled at them silently. Alacrity blew her a quick kiss.

Maska and Corva were watching too, Floyt saw, but were doing everything they could, in a decorous way, to draw attention to themselves. Floyt wasn't absolutely sure he saw Maska silently pronounce the words *Strange Attractors!*, but that's what he thought he saw.

Shoulder to shoulder, Floyt and Alacrity backpedaled nonchalantly for five steps, back out of the lights and sounds and pickups and hubbub. Then they turned and doubletimed for the hatch. Floyt vividly remembered having been shoved headlong down that same tube by Supervisor Bear and her assistants.

"Ah-*ah!*" said the crewchief, stopping them with a pointed finger. They skidded to a halt.

"Oh; sorry. Forgot," Alacrity apologized. Digging in his warbag, he handed over the Captain's Sidearm and the Webley. He'd also thought to fetch Floyt's prized all-purpose survival tool, which he also surrendered. The Lunie checked Floyt's Inheritor's belt suspiciously, but let him keep it.

"Awright, gents, take the first seats you come to. *Mindframe's* going right now."

They sweated every second of the time until then. At last the fires flared; the Nazca Lines fell away to take on totemic shape beneath them once again.

Alacrity produced a deck of cards. "Want to learn how to deal seconds and win at blackjack?"

"Yes," Floyt said. "If you'll tell me what that's got to do with somehow getting control of the White Ship."

Alacrity froze in midshuffle. "How d'you figure that?"

"The symbol in that file you took from Dincrist, for one thing—the file that started the row between you and Heart. It took me a second, but I placed the White Ship symbol. It's the same as the crests on the grips of the Captain's Sidearm, isn't it?"

"The very same, Ho."

"And that's why you two fought?"

"That ship isn't Dincrist's and it isn't her group's either. It's *mine*! That ship's gonna be used to do what she was conceived to do, before everything went wrong. Three generations now, my family's been trying to make sure of that. I'm the one who's going to."

Floyt watched the stars. "What happened?"

"Happened? Bad luck; human entropy; behavioral dynamics. What goes up; how the mighty... My grandfather was letting things fall apart even while he was putting everything he had into laying the keel of that tub. My father—that's just a downhill story and at the bottom is dying of undertow addiction. Listen, that's not the important part, not anymore."

"I know, Alacrity."

"It's *not*! The White Ship; sweet Freya! If anything can open up the secrets of the Precursors, it's that bloody ship. And she'll be mine, Ho. No more losing; that's over. Now I know how to get her back, and more important, I know I *will* get her back."

Floyt became circumspect, fearing what was to come. "Know? You can't know for sure, Alacrity."

"Oh, yes I can. Remember the causality harp?"

"Of course. Are you and Heart enemies now?"

"Competitors. She has her plans for the White Ship, I have mine and I can't change that."

He held up a copy of the memory wafer he'd taken from Dincrist on Rialto. "I copied it back in the *Stray*. It came right into my hands. Doesn't that prove something? The harp was right."

Floyt examined it. "What about the harp?"

"That was what I was asking it, Ho! About me and the White Ship; my affinity for it—my destiny, if you want to get dramatic. You saw what the answer was yourself. You're in for a share, if you want it."

"That's awfully generous, Alacrity. Thank you."

"Forget it. Stick with me. You hungry? I'll see if I can get us something to eat." He looked around for a summoning signaller.

Floyt gazed into limitlessness with no appetite, thinking

about the causality harp. He wondered if he owed Alacrity brutal honesty, because after Alacrity had fed in his query, Floyt, bringing up the rear all unawares, had changed things. He'd passed the screen that read WORKING and stopped at the one displaying NEXT TEST RUN SUBJECT:. From that angle, Floyt couldn't see what Alacrity was up to on the gantry; accessor that he was, the Earther quickly figured out how to ask the system about *Astraea Imprimatur*. The harp had acknowledged that they were linked to it—that Alacrity was in particular—with that overwhelming sound and light display.

Moments later, helping Alacrity to the lift, Floyt noticed that the indicator over the original screen, the one Alacrity had programmed with his White Ship query, was red again, that *that* screen was displaying WORKING. Looking back, Floyt realized that Redlock must have made the change, to find out what Alacrity had been doing.

More to the point, the White Ship query had to be the one that made the harp go dim and quiet at the end. *That* was the answer to Alacrity's question, and his hope of taking back the White Ship: a negative.

"What made your father turn to undertow?" Floyt asked suddenly, still watching the stars.

"Hmm?" Alacrity was shuffling the cards again, having summoned the crewchief. He suddenly looked very young, and mournful. "People just give up hope, you know? And after that, what difference does anything make? I tell you, there's nothing worse than that."

Floyt sat back, compelling himself to relax muscle by muscle. "It's too bad your father didn't live to see you there at the causality harp."

"Well, yeah; that's—thanks, Ho. But no more looking back. Um, listen, how much money do you have left? It cost me just about all I had to bribe the Lunies."

"Are you serious? You gave them all your novaseeds?"

"No, no no! Only the two I had left. Most of them I gave to Victoria. I knew Heart wouldn't take them, and I knew they were going to need them."

He still felt a disbelief that he'd lost her; the delphianisms of the causality harp had given no forewarning of love or, much more importantly, the loss of love. *But when I've got the White Ship, I'll find her. Somehow, I'll make her love me again....*

"Alacrity, I gave my daughter just about everything I had, except for what's left of the Daimyo's blood money, which is back in our quarters. I didn't know I was going to be travelling again so soon."

A penurious silence settled over them. "There're Inheritors who owe me a favor, supposedly," Floyt said at last. "And I *do* own a starship that's out there somewhere, after all."

"Well, maybe we're still liquid in a galactic sense, Ho, but we've got a little short-term cash problem, here."

"So?"

Alacrity showed him the mechanic's grip. "So: you hold the cards *this* way, see, and you..."

ABOUT THE AUTHOR

Brian Daley is the author of eight previous novels of science fiction and fantasy, the most recent being *Requiem for a Ruler of Worlds*. He also scripted the National Public Radio serial adaptations of *Star Wars* and *The Empire Strikes Back*. His whereabouts are subject to change without notice, but he favors Manhattan.